Mixed
Blood

THE SENSE OF BELONGING SERIES
BOOK 3

BRENDA BENNING

Writers' Branding
(877) 608-6550
www.writersbranding.com
media@writersbranding.com

To all of you struggling with anything in your life…

"It does not matter how slowly you go
as long as you do not stop"
—Confucius

Disclaimer

Contents

Chapter 1

The happy giggle made Trish smile. *Her* giggle. It would never get old, and she would cherish it forever. The little girl bounced around without a care in the world, jumping in and out of the waves of the Atlantic. Trish watched her beautiful Anyah from her beach chair. She was a smart girl, and even at six, she knew how far from shore she could safely wander alone. She turned many times to show off something or just make sure her mom was watching.

The day was perfect. The sun was shining brightly with only a few wispy clouds around. The sea beyond them sparkled in the sunshine like a million dots of glitter. The beach wasn't packed like most days, but they always waited until the tourists left in late August. The lack of extra people and gentler sun made this time of year Trish's favorite to be on the beach. Even with her dark skin, Trish took care not to let Anyah's skin burn. She always used sunscreen and had a floppy hat that her mother-in-law had given her daughter to keep her face more protected. Thankfully Anyah loved the hat and wore it without a fuss to the beach every time.

A loud male voice boomed from behind Trish, and her smile subconsciously widened. Her husband came running from behind and scooped Anyah up, swinging her high above his head. Maybe Anyah's squeal was the best

1

sound, she thought. Trish was glad he wasn't late. It was already getting later into the afternoon, and she wanted to get home in time to make a good dinner after all the sunshine and water play.

Clayton brought Anyah back to his broad chest and hugged her tightly, the little girl clinging to him just as much. Their relationship was a special one. Trish always felt a little twinge of jealousy for it, but she quickly dismissed it. They were lucky to all have each other and she had just as close a relationship with Anyah as her husband did. But Anyah was definitely a daddy's girl. It always made Trish wonder if she'd had a boy if he would have been a mommy's boy like they say.

Unfortunately for them, they could only have one. Trish suffered a miscarriage early in her second pregnancy that required surgery and then they found out she would need a hysterectomy due to the damage caused by the medical procedure. She grieved the loss of that unknown child for a long time, and it made both her and Clayton cherish the little girl they had even more.

There was never a thought beyond today. This was the best time and place for them to be, just together.

A loud whirring sound followed by a flapping noise, made Trish jump up.

"No, no, no," she shouted, running to the old VCR. She quickly turned the power off and stared at the wretched machine that was threatening to destroy the last video she had of her precious daughter. Her emotions were caught up in her movie again and she took a breath trying to reground herself to the present. Her hands were firmly planted on her hips as she stared, trying to figure out how to take this apart without damaging the tape once again.

Chastising herself for the millionth time for not digitizing the videos, Trish slowly picked up the heavy rectangular device and glared at it.

"You are pushing me, devil," she muttered. After turning it in several different directions, she set it down with a thud and turned to pick up her screwdriver. It happened often enough that she kept the tools nearby.

The small cassette was a reminder of the simpler times in her life. That old Camcorder was a gift from her parents after she graduated college. It was supposed to be a new fun thing to use to capture all her most treasured times. She rarely used it until her daughter was born, and then she seemed to use it all the time. The many tapes she had of her little girl growing up were going to someday be her daughter's memories to share with her children. But that future was robbed from her before her seventh birthday. Now they were all that Trish had left.

As carefully as if she were doing a major surgery, she twisted the screws out of the sides of the player. Once they were all removed, she carefully lifted the cover off and set it aside. Grabbing her tiny flashlight, she lit up the insides of the machine to see where the tape was stuck. Trish grinned when she found the tape still intact but twisted. Hopefully it could still be restored.

It probably took her longer than necessary to unravel the small tape from the wheels and pegs inside the VHS player, but she knew if anything went wrong she would lose the last remnant of her little girl. Her happy laughter and carefree disposition would be gone forever.

Finally free from its unintended prison, Trish lifted the small cassette and slowly turned the dials to pull the tape back inside the safety of its plastic encasement. She stared at the now wrinkled line of tape from one wheel to the other.

With a sigh, Trish examined the tape and scowled at it. "You better not have ruined this you ungrateful dinosaur," she grumbled under her breath.

Her phone sang out the tune from "Jaws" and Trish smiled in spite of herself. She hated cell phones, but knew they were necessary in today's world. And a phone call usually meant something was up and she probably wouldn't like it. Once she was able to choose her own number, she canceled her land line and made her cell number her old home phone number. She knew it was futile, but it was a connection to Anyah. It was the phone number her little girl memorized when she started kindergarten.

"Yeah?" she demanded into the phone.

"Oh Trish, you sound so angry when you answer your phone," her good friend said on the other end.

Trish snorted. "Yeah, 'cuz I usually don't want to talk to whoever is calling."

Sharon chuckled at her friend. "Now come on honey. You always want to talk to me."

"No, I really don't Sharon," Trish argued. "Whenever you call, it involves something semi-illegal." She paused for a second and then continued, "On second thought, I *don't* mind so much when you call." She couldn't help the grin that played on her lips. They had more leniency in some things simply because of her friend's connections.

Sharon used to be an agent in one of the alphabet soups of the government. Trish didn't pay much attention to any of that. But she does owe Sharon for teaching her everything that she has so far. It hasn't led to many of her own answers, but she has helped her friend solve some strange happenings around their small world. Trish had become really good at hacking systems all over the place, including supposedly "secure" or "hack-proof" ones, none of which she would openly admit to. It wasn't where she started out her learning, but she had to admit it had been a fun ride so far. Plus, the pay was better than any other job she'd ever had.

Sharon's friendship came at a low point in Trish's life and ever since that first chance meeting, they have been close. Despite the significant age difference, she always appreciated Sharon's treatment of her. Sharon never talked down to Trish or acted as if she were better or smarter in any way. Trish found herself wishing she'd had a sister like Sharon instead of the one she got.

They had met about thirteen years ago when their paths crossed coincidentally. Trish was looking into a person of interest connected to her situation, but apparently only to her as the police didn't seem to think it was important enough to investigate. Sharon was tracking someone who had escaped custody in a prison transport. They happened to meet at the same coffee shop asking about the same person. When Sharon asked the barista about the person in the photo, Trish snuck a look at the man and let out a gasp.

That brought Sharon's attention to her and suspicion then landed on Trish. They got to talking and Sharon understood the situation better once Trish explained why she was interested in the same man. She had just hoped that her sister hadn't been dragged into whatever this escaped convict did. She wouldn't be able to help Patsy any more than she already had, and a big national case would definitely be out of her price range for a decent lawyer. But Trish kept her sister's name out of that first meeting and focused on why she was after the same man Sharon was.

The only thing Trish enjoyed more than hacking into people's seemingly private systems to discover their secrets is hunting with her granddad's old rifle. He left it to her in his will when she was just fifteen. But they had never used this old gun. This one hung on the wall in his single car garage in a fabric case. But he would point to it and say when she was big enough, he would teach her how to shoot it. She wasn't even sure if the old gun still fired when she'd received it because it looked like a relic from the first World War and probably was. But she cleaned it and kept it close to her heart ever since. Once she was eighteen, she took shooting lessons and perfected her skills, not realizing at the time that she would need those skills later in her adult life.

She had hunted with her granddad many times as a young girl on their old chicken farm that was surrounded by acres and acres of forestry. She learned at an early age how to skin a deer and anything else they happened to come across. This time with her grandfather was when she truly felt like her own person. It was also when she developed a love for the woods and the solace they offered.

She has had many people over the years tell her to get rid of the old clunky thing and get a real gun for self-defense or protection, but she just shook her head and continued to use the old thing. She had gotten remarkably accurate with her targets, even when chasing someone off her property. She also had an older shotgun of her grandfather's. Between the two old relics, she always had a trusty friend with her ready to protect herself.

Trish decided a long time ago that she would make sure she was never in a situation where the wrong gun was in her hands again. This was the main reason she continued to hone her skills with each weapon. Maybe someday she would get a cute and shiny new handgun like Sharon had, but until she felt the need, her big guns suited her just fine. Besides the look of surprise on the men who thought she was some vulnerable old lady was priceless.

"What are we doing today, Sharon?" Trish asked, feigning boredom.

"Oh, I thought we could go see Raelynn at the coffee shop," Sharon said softly.

Trish wasn't sure what her friend was playing at, but she was sure she was up to something. Sharon didn't go to the coffee shop ever or just drop in and visit folks, another similarity making her and her friend connect right away.

Trish clicked her tongue. "Yeah, no thanks. You're up to something and I'm not gonna bite." She was about to press the red button to disconnect the call when Sharon dropped the one trump card she had.

"It's about Anyah," Sharon rushed out.

Trish's breath caught in her throat. It's been so long and so many failed leads. What could she possibly have found now?

"How do you know?" Trish whispered. She tried so hard each and every time there was a new lead not to get her hopes up, but every time she failed to keep it in check. Hope sprung that tiny green sprout, peeking through the darkness of her soul like a new plant just pushing out of the dirt, barely visible, but still there. That was the hope that refused to die inside Trish's heart.

"Please just come meet me, Trish," Sharon said, almost pleading with her friend. "I promise this time we might actually have something."

"Why can't we meet at your place?" She didn't suggest her own because she rarely had visitors and liked her personal space. Besides Sharon had a huge house, bathed in brightness and cheer. Not really Trish's cup of tea, but it was better than having anyone at her house. The last time they had a big group over was when an old colleague of Sharon's needed some help with a family situation. It seemed to take weeks before she felt like her house was her own again.

Sharon sighed dramatically. "Gary is here and so is my granddaughter. Somewhere else is better."

Trish let out a frustrated breath and scowled at her phone. She glanced around her darkened space and knew she was going to give in and leave her sanctuary. "Fine. I could use a decent cup of coffee anyway." She swiftly hung up before Sharon could let out her squeal of excitement. She didn't need to hear it to know it occurred. She shook her head as she thought of her friend. She had this endless positivity and child-like excitement when she solved some crime or found someone who was missing. Even though she was now retired, she still helped out many people privately when they came to her. Trish speculated that Sharon was bored in retirement but didn't really want to go back to working all the time either. This arrangement was a win-win for her friend.

She also knew that if anyone could find out what happened, Sharon would be the one to do it. Letting out a sigh, Trish set the old video tape down on the table and grabbed her bag. She picked up her remote and turned off the screen on the wall. The curtains could stay closed while she was gone. She set the alarms around the property with one button and then watched as her phone lit up with the confirmations. She grinned to herself. It was pretty difficult to sneak up on her with the number of cameras she had spread about her property.

The house was an old farmhouse that she had purchased under her mom's maiden name after the divorce. She wanted to be untraceable, and this offered her that privacy. Sharon had helped her set up the surveillance and then they used the place as a safe house of sorts when it was warranted. She also used it as a command center last summer when Sharon's old friends came to town.

There were three bedrooms on the upper level with an old bathroom. The main floor had a bedroom and bathroom as well as a kitchen and living room. The living space was also big enough for a small dining room, but she used it more for a desk and conference type space than dining. It was just her after all and there was no need for a formal dining table. There was a long moveable table with six folding chairs around it instead. She also had two easy chairs and a small end table between them. The old hardwood floors creaked and groaned with every step, but everything inside was in good condition.

Trish looked at the house one more time as she headed to her car. The outside looked as if it were abandoned, with the missing shutters and worn siding. The screens were dirty, and some were even torn. The windows looked filthy, caked with dirt and grime from lack of care and cleaning. But that was by design, and it kept people from knocking on her door to sell her something useless. She chuckled darkly as she remembered what people said as they approached her home. After all, many of her cameras and devices had sound recording capability as well as visual.

The old wine bottles in the branches of the old willow tree gave off a whistling sound that made people do a double take. They clanked together creating an eerie sound in the otherwise silent environment. But her most prized possessions were the multitudes of creatures she had spread around the yard. Statues and critters of all different kinds were scattered haphazardly around, well, to the unknowing anyway. She had a very precise location for each and every one of them since they provided her eyes on the entire property.

Her favorite was the collection of old dolls she had inherited from her grandmom. They had always creeped her out. But she found that they creeped others out as well. So, she poked out their eyes and replaced them with tiny cameras, offering a three hundred sixty view of anyone who came onto her porch. Sharon had laughed as they worked on the DIY project together, shaking her head on her friend's crazy ideas. But it was very effective.

She even had a statue of the Virgin Mary. It was a relic left over from her grandparents' yard, so there was some sentimental value to it. She kept it as is and didn't make any changes. It didn't feel right to mess with it, and she had enough "eyes" in her yard. The statue was just there as a reminder of those who she had lost looking down at her until they could meet again.

With a deep sigh, Trish unlocked the garage door on the rickety old shed behind the house. She was still old school on some things and hadn't put on a remote garage door opener. It was inconvenient in the colder months, but she preferred to be able to lock it and know that it was secure while she was gone. The small building didn't have much in it that she was worried about someone stealing, but she liked to know that she had control over who went in and out. She also had the old service door boarded over right after she moved in so the only way in and out was through the single stall door.

The old door groaned as she slid it up on the rails. "I know old girl, I feel it too," she muttered to herself.

Her newer model black Equinox sat in the darkened space untouched. It wasn't brand new, but it was new enough that she didn't have to worry about constant car repairs. She would be the first to admit she had trust issues and was careful about who was allowed in her life, let alone have access to her home or vehicle. Trish had gone as far as disabling the navigation system and whatever other systems that were factory installed "safety" features in case of an emergency.

Not paranoid, she insisted to herself, *just very careful*. And given who was in her past, she knew she was doing the right things.

Once inside her vehicle, after closing and relocking the garage door, Trish headed to the place Sharon mentioned. She wasn't sure what to expect, but she would listen to her friend. Sharon was the only one who knew the whole story about Anyah and after everything they had been through together, she trusted Sharon with her own life.

The short drive was filled with the memories of her sweet little girl's smiling face and sparkling dark brown eyes, identical to her father's. Anyah didn't get many of Trish's features, but she was ok with that. The little girl had inherited Trish's love for knowledge and curiosity about the world around her. Trish would have gone to school forever if she had the time and money.

She remembered Anyah's first day of preschool. While other children were crying and hanging onto their mothers' legs, Anyah gave Trish a bear hug, as much as her tiny arms could reach at three and a half, and a kiss on the cheek and skipped off to meet her teacher. The same was true for her second preschool year, kindergarten, and first grade. Trish was worried at first about her ease of separation, but after talking with the teachers, she decided it was just that her daughter's excitement for learning and her ability to understand things beyond her years made the transitions easy for Anyah.

Trish pulled up to the small café near the college campus. She rarely came here because she honestly wasn't a fan of college students. Plus, she hated spending unnecessary money on something you can make at home, although that really only applied to coffee. She parked next to Sharon's Mini Cooper and didn't hide the snort that came out. The woman was crazy in Trish's mind. That car was the smallest thing she had ever seen and she wouldn't ride in it unless forced, and even then she protested like a moody and hormonal teenager.

Sharon wasn't in the car, so Trish parked and turned off her engine. Her college student phobia was overshadowed by a potential new lead in her daughter's case. She wasn't sure what to expect because everything always led back to "a tragic accident." She would never accept this, and she would be forever grateful to Sharon who agreed with her without a doubt or question.

She spotted Sharon right away as she walked inside the small cafe. Raelynn greeted her with a wide smile and handed her a mug of steaming black coffee.

"On me, Trish," the girl said in a hushed tone, looking around as if checking to see if her boss was there. Trish knew it was just for show anyway. The owner of the café loved her barista.

"Thanks," Trish mumbled and turned to sit with Sharon. "Girl knows me too well, I guess," she said as hung her bag over the back of the chair.

Sharon laughed. "You're not that hard to figure out, old friend." She patted her hand as Trish sat across from her.

"You are older than I am by about two decades, so why do you insist on calling me old?" Trish asked with a scowl painting her face.

Sharon waved her hand dismissively. "Oh posh. You know it is just a saying. Why do you insist on making something out of nothing? Besides it seems you like others to think you are older anyway."

Trish laughed darkly. "Yeah whatever. Why did you call me here, to the hell of college perfume showers and stressed out, 'barely out of teen' hormones?" As if to make her point, she nodded her head to a group of four or five students who were dressed in pajama pants and ratty hoodies, looking as if they just rolled out of bed, huddled around laptop screens. "I mean it's what noon? And they look like they just woke up and instead of showering, ran to get a coffee." She clicked her tongue and shook her head with disapproval.

"You are so judgy, Trish dear," Sharon said with a grin. "Let the kids be. College life is hard."

A snort slipped past her lips as Trish just shook her head. She knew her friend was being a little facetious. "So back to why I am here…" she said with raised eyebrows.

Sharon cleared her throat nervously and lowered her eyes. She reached into her bag next to her and pulled out a folder.

Trish almost laughed out loud. *These agents and their damn file folders*, she thought with a shake of her head. She had given Sharon more than one razzing about them and every time, her friend would defend herself with the necessity of keeping things private and this was the easiest way to ensure that.

"I think we might have a new direction to go," Sharon said quietly, pushing the folder toward Trish.

Raising her eyebrows, Trish tipped her head to the side. "What makes you think we have any direction to go, Sharon? I mean we have been over this stuff for over a decade. It's been sixteen years and seven weeks, and I am not about to tell you how many days."

She had been counting every day, as if it were a prison sentence since the day her little girl was stolen from her. She would not rest until the person responsible paid for it—in whatever way she saw fit. Trish wasn't necessarily a violent person, but she did have limited patience when it came to offenders. And the person responsible for her very personal attack will pay dearly. She just had to find them first.

Sharon sighed. "I know. We have been at this for so many years, and you were even before you let me in. I can't imagine the pain every one of these new leads causes you." She put her hands over her friend's and gently squeezed. "I am not willing to cause you undue pain. But Trish, I believe in this one. I know the guy who sent me this personally and he would not mess around."

This caught Trish's attention. She sat back in her chair and studied the woman in front of her. Sharon had never before used her resources to help in the search since she didn't want to raise undue suspicions or something. She had a feeling Sharon had more suspicions than she let on, but then again maybe that's why she was such a good agent and had never really retired like she says.

"I thought you weren't contacting anyone else. This was supposed to be just you and me, Sharon," Trish said, with a bite in her voice. She didn't know who she could or couldn't trust with this situation. She had a few collaborations with different police officers who then circled back after a time and said there was no evidence of anything other than "a tragic accident."

Sharon sighed. "I know. And I'm sorry. But when we were working on Raelynn's father's case, I found out some more information that might help us. In order to get that, I needed help. I promise none of this will get back to you or me. My guy is top notch at what he does and finding people is his superpower." Her eyes pleaded with her friend to accept the new situation as it is.

Trish sighed. "It doesn't really matter what I think at this point does it? I mean it's already done." Her eyes dropped to the closed folder in front of her. After what felt like a long time, she finally looked up at Sharon. "What does 'your guy' want in return?" She made a production of her air quotes, making Sharon snicker.

"He is fine with getting this trash off the street," she said quietly.

Trish smiled, a genuine smile. Her friend didn't like to speak badly of anyone, and she knew it was hard for Sharon to call a person "trash", but she also knew what it meant. If her friend could stoop to calling another human being trash, it was likely a real winner under the cover of that folder.

She reached out her hand and covered Sharon's with hers. "I know that took a lot out of you, insulting a fellow human like that. But it amazes me that with the amount of these losers you have come into contact with and put away in your career that you still have difficulty treating them as the *trash* they are." She was genuinely curious about this "always looking on the bright side of things" characteristic of her friend.

Sharon bit her lip and looked away briefly. When she turned back, Trish was shocked at the look in her eye. It was almost sadness, maybe pity, she wasn't sure. But weren't they talking about the scum of the earth? Killers, traffickers, drug dealers?

Taking a deep breath, Sharon dropped her eyes. "Look, everyone, no matter how bad they are, started out as a good person and their circumstances have brought them to where they are now. Sometimes those things are out of their control and sometimes they are choices the person makes. But they weren't always *bad*."

Trish studied her friend. "You are one amazing person, you know that? I mean I don't think I could find it in my heart to forgive anyone after this ordeal." She waved her hand over the folder and scowled. "And this person will be no exception."

"Well, hold that thought, because you might just change your mind when you see this." She tapped the manila paper in between them.

Furrowing her brow, Trish's eyes drifted to the folder. She hesitated as she stared at it. Did she want to know what was in it now? Her lead, her hope, now scared the daylights out of her. Was it someone she knew this whole time, the same someone she had suspected all along?

She tried to steady her hand as she pulled it closer to her and picked at the edge. She raised her eyes to look at Sharon, who had an unreadable expression on her face. She gave Trish a slight nod.

Deciding to just rip the band aid off, Trish flung the file open and stared at the images in front of her. Two faces stared back. She looked at Sharon, shocked. Even though she knew in her heart, having the face staring back at her made this all too real. Was she ready for what was coming next?

Chapter 2

Trish stared at the photos in front of her. She didn't spend any more time with Sharon after opening the folder. She took it home and laid out the papers with the photos on her table. She was in disbelief as she stared at the photo of the woman. The eyes, the facial structure, and even the hair was all nearly identical to hers. She knew who this was and yet she couldn't admit to herself that the theory she'd had years ago was true. Faced with more evidence than she cared to acknowledge, she still couldn't admit her defeat.

Her eyes were glued to the reality that a part of her still hoped was not true. But the evidence was right in front of her, staring at her with the pale brown eyes that used to hold so much joy. She was so full of life but now nothing was left except the vacant faraway expression that clouded all her features. That girl from so long ago was clearly gone and wouldn't likely come back from the abyss she was lost in.

Patsy. She never left like Trish had believed for the last decade. Patsy ruined Trish's life in so many ways and then just skated through life without a care in the world. Trish's eyes drifted to the now black TV screen on the wall where she had watched her little girl play on the beach not so long ago. The images of her husband, the perfect dad, who had been Trish's whole world played on repeat even without the video showing. What a fool she had been. And the proof in front of her affirming the long-held suspicions did nothing to quell that pain shooting through her body as if it were just yesterday.

She knew Sharon was hoping she would forgive her sister, but Trish knew this was beyond repair. The little speech she gave about how everyone used to be a good person and just got caught up in situations or made bad choices was directed at Patsy. But the trash comment was meant for the man in the other photo. That was for another day. Today was about one photo bringing up all the hurt and betrayal of years ago. As much as she wanted to put this whole thing behind her, she never really thought about what it would be like when she came face-to-face with her again. Seeing the photo brought up things she didn't expect.

Trish wanted to scream, throw everything in her modest home at the wall not caring what broke. Her life had been destroyed so many years ago and no matter what she did, she couldn't find peace. Not until the person or people responsible were brought to their knees. Not even justice would be good enough for her. The bitterness in her soul wouldn't let even her own sister off for what she had done.

The face of a virtual stranger stared back at her. The years of drugs and living on the streets showed in her features. She was only sixteen months younger than Trish but looked more like ten years older. It was eerie how Trish felt she could see her older self in her sister's face. They were raised almost like twins and were always close. Until Patsy decided she wanted more excitement in her life and headed across the bridge to find it.

A teenage girl with nothing to lose but the youthful sparkle in her eye, left without a note or goodbye. Trish's parents were heartbroken. Trish was left to pick up the pieces. She had plans to start college and thankfully was going to school not far away. But she had to forgo plans to live on campus and stayed home to save the money. She gave up the freedom of college life and focused on trying to help her parents at the same time.

Her sister was her world when they were young. They were inseparable and even their friend group was the same. There was only one grade separating them, keeping them close even at school. The year before Patsy went to middle school with Trish was a very difficult one for both of them. But other than that year, they leaned on each other for everything. Their parents knew they would be together and even through high school, when they started to drift to different friends and interests, no one was worried about anything. They were just simply "maturing into each one's own person," everyone said.

But Trish knew it wasn't just that. She knew something was wrong. Patsy stopped engaging with their friends right before Trish's senior year. Nothing she tried could get her sister out of the house with them. Patsy started hanging out with a new group of friends and Trish knew it wasn't a good one. She kept her concerns to herself and hoped for the best though, something she used to feel guilty about.

When she figured out that her sister had run away, she knew it was because of this new group of kids. They had a reputation for drug and alcohol use. Trish stayed away from them as much as she could, but when Patsy went missing right before Trish's high school graduation, she knew she would have to find out more.

Patsy stayed away for close to five years. By then Trish had graduated from college and had started her job as a low-level technology professional at one of the local chicken businesses near her parents' home. She didn't love it, but it paid her well and she was able to stay with her parents, who couldn't seem to get over her sister's disappearance.

Neither of her parents could hold on to their jobs as they were constantly trying to find new leads to Patsy's whereabouts. They didn't sleep and when they did, it usually ended up being on the job causing termination. It wasn't that they didn't try though. Her mom just couldn't find a way out of her self-blame and guilt, and her father couldn't stand to leave her alone in her grief and depression. Trish was trapped in the middle, trying to keep the family afloat while struggling with her own guilt.

And then one day, Patsy just reappeared. It was like the Prodigal Son coming home. Her parents were ecstatic and determined not to let her go again. They hovered and catered to her every whim and want, believing that she left before because she was unhappy. Trish was happy to have her sister home finally, but there was a stark difference in her. Trish was sure her sister's life had taken a drastic turn from her somewhat sheltered childhood with her family when she left, but Patsy never wanted to talk about it.

They had a huge celebration, just like the old bible story. Her parents didn't have a lot of money to spend and did what they could take make a gumbo that was shared with all their closeknit neighbors. Some brought additional items such as bread or sides. It was a feast like they had never seen before for sure.

And then things started to change again. Patsy started to sneak out at night. Trish was still living at home and had grown to be a very light sleeper. She heard every time her sister would sneak out. She ignored it for a long time because she had to get up early for work. Their parents were completely oblivious to the behavior and were blinded by the joy of having their little girl home.

One night, Trish had enough and followed her sister out of the house. Staying out of sight, she watched Patsy duck between the shadows and walked along their street until she got to the main road in and out of Salisbury. She wrinkled her forehead wondering where her sister was going. Eventually, she saw her get into a car and disappear from sight.

Trish laid awake that whole night waiting for her sister to return. When she finally did, it was right before Trish's alarm was set to go off signally her start to the day. She was tired and admittedly angry at her sister. When she confronted her, Patsy played the victim and lashed out at Trish as if she were the one wronged. Trish remembered being especially bitter because she had spent the night awake and worrying while her sister would go to bed and not get up until Trish was home from work.

Her sister's selfishness only got worse. Pretty soon there were things that went missing. Nothing of value at first, but then it escalated. Trish tried talking to her parents, but they refused to see it. They only saw their sweet little girl who was just struggling to get a job. She needed them and they wouldn't let her down this time, they said. Trish made the decision then that it was time for her to move out on her own. She was struggling emotionally. She was supporting her parents and at the same time dealing with the toxicity of her sister's behavior. It became overwhelming.

It was around this time that she met Clayton. He was working in a gas station kitchen near the house and Trish found herself hanging out there more often than at home when she wasn't working. She just couldn't handle the lack of trust her parents had in her and the added stress of feeling responsible once again for her sister. The extra financial demands didn't help her mental health either. This place offered an escape for her, and she was never bothered while she was there.

One day, Clayton had taken a break at about the same time she had picked up her food order. He came and sat across from her with his own meal. Trish had raised her eyebrows at him as if asking what he was doing.

He simply laughed and shrugged, saying, "You are taking up the only free table and I don't have time to wait for the others to finish. You have a habit of getting your food, eating, and then moving on within a short amount of time." He shrugged again and smiled. His eyes were so dark and mesmerizing, she couldn't help but stare. He was frank in his reasons for sitting with her and she could actually appreciate the quick and clear honesty.

Trish had laughed, because she knew she was predictable. It was what made her reliable, especially for her parents and now her sister again. Although truth be told, she felt like it was more manipulation by her sister than anything. She couldn't shake the feeling of warmth that someone had paid attention to her though, even a stranger. Her parents didn't seem to notice all she did for them, and her sister definitely didn't care.

She and Clayton had talked for all of his break, and he asked if she would be back the next day. Trish knew she would be. She felt seen for the first time in a long time and she knew she wanted to be with this person again, even if it was a little selfish.

Over the next few weeks, they met almost every evening and spent Clayton's lunch break together, his lunch being her dinner. She grew fond of him faster than she thought she ever would with someone. She hadn't dated much in high school or college, always seeming to have the next responsibility deal with. But she felt comfortable with him and soon they were dating.

Being with Clayton had offered Trish an alternative to living in the toxic environment her home had become. The first time she brought him to meet her parents was when she had finally secured her own apartment and he offered to help her move. Her parents weren't thrilled with her moving out, but she explained that she was twenty-four and it was time for her to be independent. She had secretly hoped it would also jump start them on her sister, or Patsy herself would step up. Trish tried to dismiss the reason her parents didn't want her to move was because they would miss her, but she also knew that they depended on her income so they could dote on Patsy and work less. She loved her family, but she was starting to lose who she was in the darkness of her family home.

She would never forget the first time Patsy had met Clayton. She acted like a lovestruck teenager. Trish was annoyed, but trusted Clayton and ignored her sister's behavior. Patsy started hanging around the apartment more and tried to cuddle next to Clayton. He would move away just as quickly and told her over and over again he was not interested in her at all. But she never gave up. Looking back, Trish kicked herself for ignoring all the signs that were right in front of her and instead only saw what she wanted to. She knew she just wanted something for herself and wasn't willing to admit the relationship between the two was a bit worrisome.

By the time they got married, Patsy had disappeared again. Trish couldn't help but compare that disappearance with the last one. It was the night before her wedding, just like it was the night before her graduation. Trish went ahead with the day and her plans as if nothing had changed. Even though Patsy was part of the wedding, and her parents begged her to wait for her sister, Trish didn't listen. She had refused to let Patsy control her life anymore.

It only took three years for her sister to destroy Trish's entire life once she reappeared again. But Trish wasn't going to dwell on that anymore. She had moved on, and she wouldn't give her sister that time again. She was grateful for the bitterness that lingered though. It kept her head in the right place and focused on bringing Anyah justice.

Snapping her thoughts back to the present, Trish scowled again at the photo in front of her. "What do you want now, Patsy?" she nearly growled at it. Like she hadn't taken enough, she somehow managed to reappear and now Trish would have to tell Sharon everything in order to get her friend to let the forgiveness thing go. Her sister didn't deserve that from Trish.

Trish's eyes drifted to the second photo. It was the man she was looking for after she and Sharon crossed paths. He was a high-level associate of the drug dealer they had managed to catch. Trish didn't get much out of Johnny, but Sharon was more than happy to take the low life in. They had gotten the name of the face staring back at her now, but he was a ghost and nowhere to be found. *Until now apparently*, she mused silently.

Sitting back in her chair, Trish rubbed her eyes with the heel of her hand. She wasn't sure where to go with the new information. Sharon had mentioned the two of them may be together, but her guy wasn't positive about where. He was working on it, but Sharon felt Trish should know sooner rather than later about the connection to her sister.

"I know it's a lot, but we need to consider Patsy is either stuck in this unwillingly or is at least partially responsible for Anyah's death," Sharon had said quietly.

Trish had just grunted at her friend. She *knew* Patsy was involved. She knew her sister was a terrible shot and didn't pull the trigger herself. But hiring someone to get what she wanted was not out of the question. There was no doubt that her self-absorbed and narcissistic sister would do whatever she felt she had to do to get her way. The only reason Trish was still alive was because the coward didn't expect her to have her rifle ready to fire back. If only she'd had a little more warning, she could have hit him first, saving Anyah. And with any luck would have killed the bastard. To this day she doesn't know if her shot hit its mark, but nothing was found in the woods. If she hadn't been mourning, she would have gone back and tried to track the idiot. It would be a shock if she didn't hit anything. Her shooting skills have always been unmatched, but since this happened, they have gotten deadly.

Slamming the folder closed, Trish stood and walked to one of the few windows not covered by dark curtains. She liked it dark and rarely opened them, but she had opened this one earlier to look at her tape to make sure it wasn't broken. Someone else might turn the lights on, but Trish didn't keep many working lights. There were recessed lights, but they were only used when there was a situation for it.

Every day use was not such an occasion. They were just too bright for Trish. Brightness was something she didn't indulge in unless absolutely necessary.

Her phone let out a high-pitched screeching sound telling Trish she had a text. Sharon hated that sound, but Trish couldn't deny it matched her mood most days. She would intentionally turn it up a little louder than normal when she was with Sharon just to annoy her if she got any notifications. She picked up the phone and scowled at it. She really despised them.

Her scowl deepened as she read the text out loud. "Please Trish baby, can we talk? I need to see you."

Dropping her phone without responding, she chuckled darkly. "Oh, what impeccable timing you have Clayton dearest," she muttered, her voice dripping with venom for the husband she once thought was her everything.

"Not. A. Chance," she said as she aggressively tapped at her screen. It didn't even take a year after Anyah was taken for the divorce to be finalized. Trish knew in her heart what had happened. She had hoped she was wrong or that there was a tiny shred of misunderstanding, but the new evidence in front of her solidified her belief about everything.

Over the past two or three years, Clayton had tried to get her to meet with him occasionally, but she always refused. She was done being manipulated. The first year after the divorce was the worst. He refused to grant her the divorce, no matter how hard she pushed. When she finally threatened him, he gave in, but never gave up that they would reunite again, at least that's what he told her nonstop when he texted her. She was glad when he gave up calling. She never answered, but his pleading and pathetic voicemails were nauseating and jammed up her inbox, which she needed open for leads.

She thought about changing her number, but that little voice in the back of her mind said not to. Without that link, she might lose every last connection to her little girl. But even she knew that it was a ridiculous reason. Maybe there was still a part of her, the tiniest speck of doubt, that hoped she was wrong. But she knew she was right. The motive was right in front of her face and now she had a pretty good idea who might have pulled the trigger.

Trish tossed her phone toward the table, but it missed and fell to the floor. She scoffed at it as if it had fallen on purpose to annoy her. She pulled the shade back down and turned back to the almost completely darkened space. Letting out a sigh, she picked up the dreadful device and made her way upstairs. As if protesting, the phone let out another horrifying screech.

"Good lord, you piece of junk," she muttered. Turning it over in her hand, she saw the newest alert was from Sharon. "Oh great, now what?" she let out a groan and unlocked it, settling herself on a step halfway up.

Call me was all it read.

"Woman, you are trying my patience today," she said shaking the device in her hand. Trish let out a sigh and stared at the ceiling above her. It was low at this point, and she could probably reach it easily even while sitting.

The stairs led to the second floor, but it had dormers out the front and back to allow for bedrooms, and it was a very low roofline. Even Trish's mere five-foot three-inch stature could reach all but the highest peak with little effort. The space above the steps was roomy enough to easily walk up and down, but this part had a small area that jetted out to allow for the bathroom plumbing, making it just a little bit more cumbersome for tall people. It was also awkward enough that you wouldn't want to go up the stairs in the pitch-black darkness or drunk.

Her phone let out another screech making even Trish slightly annoyed.

Before she could look at it though, it rang, and Sharon's face showed on the screen. With a groan, Trish swiped on her screen. She didn't get a word out before Sharon's frantic voice came over the line.

"Trish, you need to come over right now," Sharon said and then the line immediately disconnected.

Chapter 3

"You drag me over here and then you don't say anything," Trish complained. "What is so urgent?"

Sharon dragged out her breath and held her coffee cup with both hands, her eyes staring at the dark liquid inside. "I am just trying to figure out how to say this, Trish," she said quietly. "Give me a second."

Trish scoffed. "Yeah. Just say it. I hate dramatics and you know that. Just spit it out." She pushed her own cup to the center of the table and folded her hands in front of her. There wasn't anything her friend could say that would shock her at this point. She just wanted to get back to her own house and wallow in self-pity.

Thankfully Clayton hadn't responded after her response to his latest plea to meet. She didn't owe him anything anymore. He could run off with whomever he chose, she didn't care. Except that she knew she still did, the little voice in the depths of her soul chided. But that hurt and loss almost parallelled the loss of her little girl. She had to stay strong.

Sharon sighed again and raised her eyes to study Trish. A new look crossed her face and Trish furrowed her brow.

"Now what?" she almost whined at Sharon.

"Can you tell me what happened to your parents Trish?" Sharon suddenly asked.

Trish's patience was wearing thin. She hadn't told Sharon about her parents because it never seemed relevant. Why would she bring it up now anyway?

Narrowing her eyes, Trish said simply, "Car accident. Ten years and change ago. What does this have to do with any of that?" She waved her hands around as if to emphasize her point.

Sharon slowly nodded her head. "Do you remember when we were helping Raelynn out and we found a lot of dirt on some of the side jobs of the Del Rios?"

Trish nodded, leaning back in her chair. She crossed her arms over her chest, still not sure where this was going. "Yeah, but so?"

The Del Rios were a local drug and trafficking gang who had taken over one of the chicken factories in town for over a decade. Not too long ago, Sharon and Trish and some inside help, managed to produce enough information from years of gathering to secure most of the gang a comfy cell for a very long time. The charges were extensive and the evidence irrefutable.

"I think one, maybe two got away before we could grab them," Sharon said, as if it explained everything in her head.

She suddenly stood and disappeared into her back hallway that Trish knew led to her office. She stayed where she was, not really wanting to go back there but also irritated with her friend. Her stubborn streak prevented her from following Sharon.

In less than a minute, Sharon came back into the room carrying her laptop. She set it down, seated herself back in her chair and started to type away. Trish tried to be annoyed, but her curiosity was now piqued.

"Remember Johnny Rodney?" Sharon asked, not looking away from her screen.

Trish chuckled. "How could I forget? He's in prison I thought," she said, trying to think if she had heard any new updates about him recently.

Sharon finally looked up and grinned. "Oh, he's not going anywhere. But this guy is who we are worried about now." She turned her computer to face Trish. "This is Reece St. Claire."

The man looked cocky and had a smirk on his face. His eyes were bright blue, and his blondish hair was cut neatly around his face. He looked like a prep schoolboy who was expecting everyone to fall at his feet. Trish knew his type. And she had to admit her favorite thing in the world was bringing these kinds of men to their knees, usually at the end of her rifle. It was a very different mug shot than the one sitting on her table at her house. She knew this would be a fun one to make cry—just a little bit, she thought with a smirk.

"Ok, spill it. What's going on," she said impatiently, turning the screen back to face Sharon.

The photo wasn't one she recognized but she knew there was a special reason why Sharon would draw her into this without something they discovered together.

The smile that spread across Sharon's face was the one Trish knew would lead to that before mentioned "semi-illegal" activities. But she could use a distraction so she would take the bait. And being as good of a friend as Sharon was, she knew Trish would be in.

Sharon clapped her hands together, knowing without Trish saying anything more, that she was in. "Ok, so Johnny boy had a known righthand guy." She pressed another key and then turned the computer screen so they could both see it. "Meet Simon Cain."

Recognition spread on Trish's face. The photo was the same one she had in the file at home, the same one Sharon had given her just hours ago. The scowl that crossed her face at the memory was a natural reaction at this point. The guy looked like he lived in the gutter. His face was gaunt and his hair was shiny with grease. His eyes had the same vacant look Patsy's had, but his held something else, something sinister and dangerous. She definitely wouldn't want to run into him alone somewhere. At least not without her shotgun, she thought darkly.

"So, you think these two lowlifes have some connection to the Rios and Johnny?" Trish asked, staring at the face in front of her. *And how is he connected to Patsy?* she wondered silently.

Sharon let out a small chuckle. "Nope. Trish, I *know* they are connected and now we get to track them and find out where they are hiding to flush them out."

Trish almost laughed when she saw the look of excitement on her friend's face. She shot her a grin and then shook her head. "I don't know why you ever retired. This stuff is in your blood."

A grunt from the doorway drew both of their faces toward it. "You and I think alike, Miss Trish," Gary, Sharon's husband, said with a shake of his own head.

Both women laughed and turned back to the computer. Sharon waved her hands at her husband and shooed him from the room. He obliged, but not without a hearty laugh and a lift of his mug.

"So why are we looking for these two idiots?" Trish asked. Looking back at the screen, her scowl returned. She couldn't help but wonder if that meant her sister was also connected the Del Rios, not that she would be surprised by anything concerning that woman anymore.

Sharon cleared her throat to get Trish's attention. "Trish, I need to know what happened to your parents."

"Uh, why?" Trish asked, narrowing her eyes. It was a story that she didn't really want to talk about or revisit. But her curiosity was being poked. Why would Sharon be asking about that? They had never really talked about her parents, or either of their extended families actually. Trish knew Sharon had a granddaughter and a couple of adult kids, but the rest was just not important.

"Well, I'm not positive yet, but I think these two might be connected somehow." Sharon's voice was quiet as her intense look made Trish feel uncomfortable.

After a few minutes, Trish shook her head. "No, they aren't. My parents had an accident, and *no one* was at fault." She could taste the bitterness of the words as she said it out loud but hoped it didn't come through in her tone.

It was a long-practiced explanation of her parents' car accident that was spiked by Trish's final warning to her sister and the anger that was directed at not only her sister but Trish's parents as well. They couldn't give Patsy a large sum of money to clear a debt and made Trish feel like the worst person on the planet when she refused to support her sister financially anymore. Everyone seemed to have forgotten that not only was Trish supporting her parents, but she had also been providing a lot of money monthly to her sister because she was struggling to find work. Well, that was her excuse anyway. Really, she was doing everything *except* looking for a job.

Patsy had shown up for about a week, and Trish had avoided her and her parents the entire time she was in town. It had angered her parents, but Trish didn't budge. She wasn't going to forgive her sister anymore and she wasn't going to give her another penny. Not after what her sister took from her. It may have been years since her little girl was stolen from her, but Trish wasn't resting until her sister paid her own debts.

About two weeks after that, her parents were in a terrible crash that killed both of them almost immediately. The brakes on their car had gone out and the police couldn't find any evidence of tampering, just poor maintenance or something. Trish hadn't cared back then. She was too angry with the direction her own life had taken and knew that her parents' anger towards her had everything to do with her "baby sister" who seemed as helpless as a baby. She still didn't blame herself, although she thought maybe the blame was shared between her and her sister. Patsy didn't even show up for their parents' funerals.

The last time Trish had seen her sister was at the hospital when Trish was sitting beside her little girl who lay in a coma. Patsy had been swiftly kicked out of the room and the hospital without so much as an explanation from Trish. She knew what had happened and who was responsible, and Trish had written her sister off at that point. Patsy had disappeared again shortly after that incident and didn't return, or so Trish thought. Every contact was through the phone, email, or texts. Every kind of interaction between Patsy and Trish was done through her parents since Trish refused any phone calls or direct contact.

But did Trish ever believe her parents' death was somehow not an accident? Sure. But up until recently she didn't have the tools at her disposal to find out for sure. Now she had those tools, but there was no way to find out since any evidence from years ago wouldn't be available anymore. Her suspicions were only suspicions, but based on her little girl's death, she had a pretty good idea of what happened to her parents. Trish also knew that if she hadn't thought a little bit ahead and brought her gun on their hike, she could easily have been next. She just should have been more prepared than she was, and he never would have gotten away.

There was never enough evidence for Trish to prove her sister's guilt, but she knew she was responsible, and she also knew Patsy was simply acting out of her desperation for money. Unfortunately for Patsy, their parents didn't have life insurance anymore. Trish knew her sister didn't know they had canceled their policy because they couldn't afford it anymore.

"Trish?" Sharon's soft voice cut into her thoughts.

"Hm?" Trish asked, making eye contact with her friend.

Sharon's hand covered Trish's and she gave her a sympathetic look. "I think we both know that isn't true. When you are ready to tell me we can talk more. But I think these two may be able to give us more answers—to a lot more than just why my friend wants them." She wiggled her eyebrows.

Once again Trish was reminded of the child-like love this woman had for finding bad guys. In spite of herself she smiled back. If she was completely honest, she was looking forward to it as well. It was fun to watch this older woman transform into some crazy agent who could extract information from the most hardened criminals. Maybe it was because she looked so sweet and innocent that they were caught off guard. Either way it was a fascinating experience.

"Ok, Sharon, let's get to work then," she said, ignoring the comment about her parents. She knew her best bet in finding out more about her parents' accident would be with Sharon, but right now wasn't the time to worry about it. It wouldn't change anything about the past anyway.

Today she would jump in and help her friend find the two men who were eluding authorities and see what happened next. She couldn't help the slight shiver that went down her spine as she thought about possibly having to see her sister-not sister again. Maybe she should coin a new term, like the late musical legend Prince had. Make her sister a symbol instead of a name or something.

Shaking her head to clear it, she focused on Sharon, who was talking again, no doubt making plans for their next "job." Trish had to admit it was a nice paycheck when they did these little things for Sharon's old friends. It had helped her not have to work much lately. That and the fact that her house and property were paid for a long time ago. She ignored the pang at the realization that without her daughter and parents, her monthly bills were minimal. The dreadful cell phone, electric bill, and food were about it. This was also a way to pay Sharon back for all of her teaching and training over the years that has made it possible for Trish to be able to do this work.

Trish had a suspicion that Sharon gave her a bigger part of the paycheck, but she kept it to herself. She didn't want to cause any issues, and she also knew that Sharon didn't need any of it. She had a house a couple times the size of Trish's, not that Trish wanted anything bigger, but Sharon and Gary both had high paying jobs before they retired. She would just take the amount Sharon gave her and continue to be grateful for her friend's consideration.

Sharon clapped her hands together once again pulling Trish from her thoughts. "Ok, so we are all set then, right?"

"Yep, sure thing, boss," Trish said sarcastically, knowing Sharon was well aware that she hadn't been listening.

Sharon crossed her arms over her chest and raised her eyebrows. "Ok then, what's the plan?"

Trish snorted. "Sharon *honey*, we have been doing this for a long time. You didn't drop some major life-changing plans. You noticed I was off somewhere in my dark thoughts and took advantage of my distractibility and—" she waved her hand in front of Sharon and smirked. "Here we are. So, let's start over and actually come up with a plan, k?"

"Ugh, I hate it when you do that. Now I understand why my kids hated it," Sharon muttered. "Fine. Here is what we have to start with. I'll need you to access some not-so-public CCTV footage and see if we can find a footprint of one or both of them. I am going to try to access some other information and see if I can get anything more than what is public record."

Trish just grinned. She loved being behind the computer screen and hacking into whatever database or video storage facility she could. After she got her degree in computer science, she worked for a while in the chicken company but found it boring. She and Clayton decided after Anyah was born that she would go part-time, and he would pick up more overtime—or at least she thought he was working overtime. She never really had a chance to verify that piece of info before she left him.

She shook her head and tried to focus again on her friend. Sharon's animated posture and the waving of her hands told Trish she was in a zone, and it would be best to just sit back and watch her mind work. It always surprised her that they had only known each other for a few years. They hit it off right away and it seemed as if they had known each other for decades. There were few people that Trish trusted as much as she did Sharon. She wasn't sure if it was because they bonded over bad guys or if they just had personalities that fit well and complimented each other. Either way, she was thankful they had met.

When Sharon had finished her grand scheme, she folded her hands on the table and met Trish's eyes. Sharon seemed satisfied with her plan and Trish just nodded.

"I am good with all that. I just need a starting point. This will be a good distraction from the obvious issue you dropped in my lap a few hours ago." Trish stood from her chair and stretched, her body cracking in the usual places. They must have been sitting longer than she thought.

Sharon stood as well and moved to her side. She put her hand on Trish's shoulder and gave her a small smile.

"I mean it, Trish. When you are ready to share more details and will let me help, please tell me. I'm here for you, my friend." She gave Trish a side hug and then quickly let go. Trish wasn't a touchy person, having been betrayed too many times, but she welcomed the small contact. She was also grateful that her friend understood her well enough to know what she could and could not handle as far as physical contact.

Trish just nodded and then made her way outside. She didn't hurry but she didn't take her sweet time either. She welcomed the unusually warm air outside for a change. The summer was by far her least favorite time of year. Not because of the heat and humidity but because it reminded her of what she had been missing all these years. Her best memories of Anyah were from summer trips to the beach or park. Sometimes by the river, skipping rocks or just sitting by the amphitheater on the Salisbury Riverwalk.

The current warm weather caused the conflict in her heart to intensify. It was November, but the warmth felt like late September. It was supposed to be getting colder, and she should need a coat. But the last week or so it had been warm enough for summer clothes again. Fall was one of her favorite times mostly because she had survived another summer without her daughter and was glad it was finally over. She felt like she could breathe again. But today reminded her again of the summer months and she couldn't hold in the sigh.

The sadness always overshadowed any positive energy she felt during the summer months. She had a summer wedding; graduation was always late spring, almost summer. These were also the times when Patsy would disappear. Besides the memories of her many losses during the summer, she was also reminded of the intense grief of her parents every time Patsy disappeared.

Trish didn't support them because they refused to work. No, her parents *couldn't* work because of their debilitating sense of loss and grief. Self-blame and failure were also recurring themes in their grief. Trish couldn't do anything else but step up and take care of them as the only one left. On some level she felt like she could help them see that she was an example of their success as parents, but they never really got past Patsy's example.

She had hoped that having a granddaughter would help with their grief, and it did for a little while. And then Patsy would reappear and cause issues with Trish and then disappear again. They started to pull back from even Anyah, much to Trish's frustration. She began to grow angry with her sister's selfishness and that made the relationship with her parents even more strained.

Shaking her head, she looked around her. The corn fields were tall and swayed in the gentle breeze. She welcomed the privacy they provided for her home. The neighbor who farmed the land, cutting down the tall stalks as he moved through the vast fields, had waved when she drove by, but they had never talked or officially met. She wasn't even sure if he knew they were neighbors. Quickly deciding she didn't care, Trish turned into her driveway, mostly blocked by the now towering corn stalks.

It didn't take her but a few feet to realize something was off. She hit her brakes at the end of her long driveway and put the car in park. She pulled out her phone to check the cameras, glancing up frequently to make sure no one could sneak up on her. She scrolled through the footage but didn't see anything strange. Every inch of her property leading to the house was covered by eyes somewhere. But the dilapidated building at the edge of the lot wasn't.

Furrowing her brow, she looked to her left at the old chicken house that was ready to collapse. Trish bit her cheek trying to decide if she should take a look or ignore it and just go inside her house so she could monitor things better from there.

Deciding to take her chances, she slowly drove up the driveway to her old garage. As soon as she stopped in front of it, she sent a text to Sharon. No one came here unless they were up to something. The unsettling feeling didn't go away as she waited a fraction of a second. She glanced around and noticed what was off. Her statue of Mary was turned slightly more toward the road instead of the house. Not a huge change, but enough to let her know something or someone was or had been there.

Trish left the vehicle outside and made her way to the back of the house. She had different things hidden there for defense if needed. She didn't trust anything as much as her old guns, but she was skilled enough that she could use just about anything if necessary. She locked the car and headed toward her back door.

Trying not to look hurried or concerned, she moved quickly and once she was inside her house, she locked the door behind her and glanced around the small laundry room. Nothing seemed out of the ordinary and she slowly moved from room to room as she made sure she was alone. By the time she made it to the kitchen, making sure the door was still locked and all the windows were still intact, she breathed out in relief.

It seemed nothing inside had been bothered. She stood in the middle of the living room and put her hands on her hips, trying to figure out what could have happened outside and why. A deer couldn't have moved it, although it would be strong enough. But it would likely have broken, not just nudged out of place. Trish decided to take a better look at the cameras instead of wondering.

She pulled the desk out and pressed the button that hid the other screens. Three more screens slowly rose from the back of the desk. As she waited for them to get into place, she moved to the window closest to her. She looked out the window from the side of the shade, trying not to disturb it too much. Something moved quickly across her line of sight, and she squinted, looking side-to-side to see what it was.

Again, she didn't see anything. Letting out a frustrated sigh, she dropped the shade and turned to her now fully set up desk. Sitting down, she pressed the power button, lighting up all the screens at once. Her laptop sat in the middle of the desk with the three screens above it. Trish pressed a few buttons on the keyboard and each screen lit up with a different view of the property. She studied the images and still didn't see anything unusual.

Then something caught her eye. Off to the side of the Mary statue one of her garden gnomes was facing down. That could only mean one of two things. Either something or someone tripped on it, or someone intentionally turned it around so it wouldn't see anything. Most were reinforced into the ground and not easily moved. If someone tripped over it, they would likely be hurting, she thought with a smile.

Trish bit her lip and pressed a few more keys. She pulled up video from the time she left, focusing on the area where her Virgin Mary statue stood. A blur pulled her eyes from her recorded video to a current view. She narrowed her eyes and watched as the figure slowly approached the front door. Trish resisted the snort. The person thought they were being sneaky but obviously didn't know how much she could actually see.

She crossed her arms over her chest and watched with amusement as the shadowy person dressed in all black, in broad daylight, stalked around to her porch.

"This should be fun," she muttered, not moving.

She watched as the person approached the door, but then something made them turn and disappear from view. Trish sat up straight and pressed her keyboard trying to figure out where they went. It was like the person disappeared into thin air.

Chapter 4

"What did you find out," Sharon asked as the two sat at the table.

Trish sighed. "Nothing. The person just disappeared."

She had forgotten she had texted Sharon as she made her way into the driveway. The sound that distracted the person was likely Sharon's car turning into the driveway. Trish couldn't worry about that at the moment though. She needed to figure out how they got on her property without being noticed or setting off any of her alarms. The person wasn't limping so that could only mean they intentionally moved her gnome. That was the most irritating part of it all.

Sharon was sitting next to her at the desk, glasses on her face, staring at the replaying feed from earlier. "I think that's a man, or a very large woman," she said thoughtfully.

"The bigger question is why would they come here? I have absolutely nothing to offer anyone, or for them to take," Trish mused. Maybe they would be interested in her tech gear, but that was largely hidden and not visible through windows so who would know it was even there?

She was frustrated that there were more questions than answers at this point.

"Look at this," Sharon said suddenly.

Trish focused on the screen and watched as a different person was seen in her yard. This one did in fact stumble over the little gnome, making her laugh out loud as she watched the person limp away. But then it dawned on her that there were two people in her yard, and she didn't get a single alert.

"I guess I need to upgrade," she mumbled. She watched as the second person, or actually the first given the time stamp on the video stumbled again and fell into her Mary statue. "Well, that explains how Mary was moved."

Sharon turned to look at her friend. "It moved a fraction of an inch. How did you know it moved?" she asked curiously.

Trish snorted. "Seriously? Like you don't have every inch of your property memorized to know when something has been moved or gone missing."

"Ok, good point. But when did you notice it? When you first turned into the driveway? Because that is top notch awareness, Trish." Sharon gave her shoulder a bump and added, "You'd make a pretty good investigator with that much sensitivity."

"I'm good, thanks," Trish said, pushing Sharon back. "But I still can't figure out if they are connected or not. If they aren't then I have a bigger problem on my hands."

She had chosen this property because it was hard to find and not visible from the road. So, who were the two people wandering around it and what could they possibly want. It was too far away from anything to be a couple of squatters looking for a cheap place to crash. Given the time of year, it could be someone looking for a place for the winter, but that was still a stretch.

"Well, your safety is the most important thing to me, so this is my priority. We can work on the other stuff later." Sharon started to tap away at the computer while Trish sat by and watched. Normally she didn't like anyone messing with her equipment, but Sharon wasn't just anyone.

The duo watched in silence as episode after episode replayed from the short time Trish was gone from her house. Nothing new appeared and the feeling Trish had when she first pulled into her driveway didn't lessen. Something wasn't right. She wasn't the type of person who dwelled on a feeling either. She had faced many *thugs*, as she liked to call her sister's acquaintances over the span of her adult life, and she had developed a strong armor around any part of her that appeared weak. Someone lurking around her property wouldn't spook her. But she did appreciate her friend's concern.

Finally, Sharon pushed away from the desk and sighed. "There just isn't anything here, Trish. The only photo I got was the one you have already seen. What should we do about it?"

"Nothing," Trish said with a shrug. "Some low life with nothing better to do than mess with my cameras and try to spook me isn't worth my time." She stood and stretched, moving toward the door to the kitchen.

She poured herself a cup of black coffee and stared out her dirty window. She wasn't afraid, but she was definitely annoyed. She drank the entire cup and poured another, grabbing a second mug for Sharon. Trish set up a small tray with the two mugs and the dreadful things she knew her friend liked to put in her coffee. She only kept that stuff around for Sharon.

Sharon raised her eyes as Trish came back into the room. She picked up her cup and added her creamer and stirred it. Trish wrinkled her nose as she watched.

"So, what do you want to do now, Trish?" Sharon asked, after taking a long sip of her drink.

Trish just shrugged. "Get started on your new case," she stated matter of factly. "This isn't an issue." She waved her hand at the screens in front of them for emphasis. "It's probably nothing and no one scares me. I have my guns and cameras. So, let's get going with this." She picked up the folder Sharon had set on the table when she first got there.

Letting out a sigh, Sharon nodded. "Are you sure? I mean this is pretty unusual. No one ever comes out here. I always thought you were a little paranoid when we set it all up because nothing ever happened."

"That's not true. It saved your friend's niece if I remember correctly." Trish pointed her finger at Sharon and gave it a wiggle.

Sharon chuckled. "Ok, you're right. But when has it helped before that?" She crossed her arms as if in challenge.

Trish just waved her hand. "It doesn't matter. I don't like being surprised. Let's focus on this." She dropped the file on the table and moved to sit. "Why are we looking for these guys instead of your bigwig friends?"

"I'm not sure but I am going to guess it has something to do with the limitations of the agency," Sharon said with a wink.

Trish knew what that meant. They were going to be working outside the box on this, which she was just fine with. Since Sharon had taught her everything she knew about tech and computers, Trish had enhanced the skills with some online classes at the local community college and a few other institutions. She had never realized just how much she loved sitting behind a computer screen. It wasn't always videos that she hacked into either. Sometimes they had to get financial information for embezzlement cases or as backup information. Whatever the reason, Trish was able to break into almost anything digitally. She'd be lying if she didn't admit she loved the power she felt from it.

Not being particularly religious, Trish always thanked whatever higher power was around for the chance meeting of her and Sharon. She was grateful for the change in occupation and wished she had discovered this path sooner in her life. Maybe it would have prevented a lot of heartache and pain if she had known how to do some of this back then.

Brushing that aside, she turned to open the file on the table. She settled into her seat and studied the photos of the two men. Neither looked like fine upstanding men, even though Reece was clearly wealthy. The sneer on his face just made him look sleazier than Simon. She couldn't help but wonder what led them to the life they lived. She didn't ever consider people as inherently good as Sharon did. Trish relied on what she saw and heard herself, which was probably why religion never felt right to her. Blindly believing in something that you couldn't see or touch just didn't seem right to her. Then again, she did learn that lesson the hard way when it came to blindly trusting her ex-husband and ex-sister. She attempted to hide the sneer that threatened to escape as her memories tried to push through her walls again.

"Give me more info, Sharon," Trish said, shaking the other thoughts from her mind. "What are we looking for and where do we start?"

Sharon picked up the laptop from the desk and came to sit next to Trish. "Well, they want us to find out anything we can from their movements over the past two or three months and then try to figure out what they might be up to now. My guy thinks they might be trying to find a way to break Johnny out of prison."

Trish raised her eyebrows at the new information. "Seriously? I thought prison breaks were a Hollywood thing."

"That's because they are typically caught pretty quickly especially where he is being held. The place is like a fortress and makes your surveillance system look like child's play."

"Well now I don't know if I should be offended or impressed," Trish said with a grin. "Maybe we should do an upgrade here. I should know what I missed that both of those idiots made it onto my property without an alert."

Sharon snickered. "Sounds like a great idea. Do you have more creepy dolls? Or maybe some psycho clowns?"

"Oh, now that would be fun!" Trish said with a laugh. "If only grandmom collected horror paraphernalia too. We could do a thrift store run."

Shaking her head Sharon laughed with her. "Alright, let's get you set up first. I worry about you all alone out here in the middle of nowhere."

Trish felt like a little kid at Christmas. She grabbed her tool belt with all the tools she would need and a box of old parts. "I think I have a couple of miniature devices I can hang under the gutter runs and a few more gnomes somewhere.

The two of them gathered any more supplies Trish could find and made their way outside. Trish tackled the turned over gnome first and noticed the camera was missing.

"Hm, that's odd," she mumbled, turning it over to see if it just got pushed inside the ceramic statue. But it wasn't there.

Sharon glanced over. "What's wrong?"

Trish looked up and showed her the gnome. "The camera is gone. Who would have known that it had a camera in it?"

They had taken great care making sure the cameras were not visible, even if someone picked them up and studied the statues carefully. They just looked like shiny eyeballs and would have been hard to see as a camera, especially for someone not trained. The thought that someone who may be well trained had been in her yard made Trish a little more nervous than she liked to admit. The camera was removed without ever triggering her alarms as well, which didn't sit well with Trish.

Seeming to think that same thing, Sharon's brow furrowed. "Trish, this is not good." She bit her lip, a sign that she was lost in her thoughts.

Most likely plotting something, Trish thought with a grin. She moved to her friend's side. "What are you thinking?"

"I am not sure, but I think we might have to up our game a little bit, just in case this person, or people, is actually smart," she said, glancing around. "We should do a broad sweep of everything and see if anything else is off."

Trish just nodded and started to walk off toward her whistling willow.

"Wait. When was the last time you checked everything, Trish?" Sharon suddenly asked.

Crinkling her brow, Trish turned. "I checked it all on my alerts before I left for your place. Why? What are you thinking?"

"I'm not sure but look around for some type of device that would interfere with your connections, maybe disable them somehow. That would explain why you didn't get anything when the gnome was moved." Sharon then turned and walked in the opposite direction as Trish inspected things.

Trish shook off the irritation that someone outsmarted her and started to look at her glass bottles. She loved these things and was always brought back to the movie *Because of Winn Dixie*, her daughter's favorite. The old lady in the movie had the same glass bottles in her tree branches and Trish always thought it was funny. She knew Anyah would call her that crazy old lady now, if only…

She inspected every bottle carefully, making sure the few that had motion sensors still did. Her phone sent her a quiet ding with each one she moved. Satisfied that they all were still working, she made her way over to the collections of gnomes and other random statues. She had picked them up at different yard sales around town. She had specific details she looked for. They had to be hollow inside and have big enough faces so that she could tap out the eyes without breaking the entire thing.

Trish figured she had about twenty or thirty statues scattered around. Her dolls on the porch comprised at least another thirty. She started at the edge of the property, taking care to cover every inch of the yard to make sure she didn't miss anything. As she stared at the overgrown corn field, she wondered if it was worth it to put a couple in the rows. She knew Sharon would have ways to keep them hidden and still not get damaged by the farm equipment that would eventually cut the stalks down.

As she turned to ask her friend just that, she caught sight of a shadow near the old chicken house. Trish squinted her eyes but couldn't make anything out. She hated that old thing and had plans to take it down but had never gotten around to it. Although it wasn't the best place to hide for long given the disrepair, it was still easy for someone to stay just out of sight. And as she said over and over again, she hated surprises.

Glancing quickly to the side, she saw Sharon looking at a small statue of a dog. It was pretty battered by the weather and age, but it worked well for her surveillance. She gave a quiet whistle to Sharon, turning back to the building in front of her. She knew her friend would get the message since they had some crazy kind of nonverbal connection. She sometimes wondered if they were soul sisters from another time, since they were close to thirty years apart and different ethnicities.

Trish slowly made her way toward the chicken house and looked out of the corner of her eye to see Sharon calmly walking toward her, as if looking for something. Trish wished for the second time today she had her gun on her. Maybe getting a little toy thing like Sharon had wasn't a bad idea after all. She tried to tell herself she wasn't a violent person, but she did love her guns and wouldn't hesitate to use them for protection if necessary.

As she closed in on where the door used to hang, she narrowed her eyes. The building was in such bad shape that if anyone tried to jump out of one of the openings that used to be a boarded-up wall, they would definitely be seen. Their only real option was to slink deeper into the chicken house, but with the doors all decayed off and the walls barely hanging on, it would be nearly impossible to hide in there for long. And if this was one of the idiots who messed with her cameras, she had given them way too much credit.

Sharon caught her eye as she motioned to the side. Nodding, Trish let her go and she continued to the opening. A sudden rustling from behind caught her attention and she turned to see what it was. She was greeted by a rather large rabbit who had jumped out of the overgrowth of brush. Trish shook her head and turned back to the building only to be pushed aside as someone rushed out and took off into the fields.

Sharon was at her side in an instant. "Trish! Are you ok?" Sharon rushed out.

Trish held her head. She was lucky she didn't fall into anything with the force she was pushed with. "I think so. What was that?" She looked off in the direction where the person went.

"I don't know. But whatever or whoever that was, we need to get this place more secure right away." She looked around the property with her hands on her hips. "This just will not do."

Trish stood and brushed herself off before mimicking her friend's stance. "We won't find him now," she said quietly, annoyed that he or she had alluded them.

Sharon nodded glumly. Trish was well aware that her friend hated being outsmarted just as much as she did. She smiled thinking about what must be going through her friend's head as she looked around the property.

Finally, she sighed. "I guess we just have to upgrade and hope it is good enough," Sharon conceded, tossing her hands in the air.

Sharon made her way to her car and Trish watched as she opened her trunk and took out a brown box. Her curiosity was piqued as she watched her friend set it down and begin rummaging through it. Sharon held up a few different devices and examined them in the sunlight. Then she turned and showed Trish. She wasn't sure what Sharon had but knew that the older woman knew her stuff so she would just give her whatever permission she was looking for and move on. Sharon would tell her later what she had and what she was doing with it.

Trish just gave her a nod, and they got to work checking and rechecking all the existing cameras. Sharon had joined her at some point and showed her the new and upgraded devices. They worked to get those set up as well. It didn't even strike Trish as odd that her friend had security cameras and other surveillance equipment just conveniently sitting in her car. She knew Sharon had things no one would expect an older person to carry around with them.

As they continued to work, Trish's thoughts drifted to her friend. Sharon was the first real friend she had since her divorce. Even before Clayton, there were few friends after high school. Trish had spent so much time and energy getting her sister back, and then sober, that she just didn't have much social availability. She worked her full-time job and then worked overtime on her family. Her difficult young adult life had aged her in more ways than one.

Although she liked to give Sharon grief about being older, she felt a kindred spirit in the other. Trish never revealed even to Sharon how much she admired her friend and wanted to be equal to her. Insecurity wasn't something she showed, it was a weakness and could easily be taken advantage of. But even when they were alone, she never let on that Sharon was more of a role model and mentor for Trish than she knew.

Her appearance changed dramatically in the last ten years. Part of it was her own doing. After her sister disappeared the last time, she decided to change completely. She no longer wanted to look like the person who she believed destroyed her perfect family. They had always worn their hair similarly and with the physical features they shared, almost always looked like twins.

Trish had let her hair grow and began to twist it in locks that she took a lot of time and care with to make sure they stayed tight and neat. When they were long enough, she began to twist in gray strands to give her hair a naturally older look. One thing Clayton had always said he liked about her was her free-flowing hair. It wasn't ever nappy like a lot of her friends' hair and had a gentle curl and softness to it. Trish had always liked it down and free.

Maybe it was a rebellion of sorts, but everything Clayton had liked about her appearance made her want to change it even more. The line she drew was with her eyes. Anyah had inherited her deep brown eyes, and she wanted to keep that connection. Contacts weren't really in her budget anyway, she had thought.

Sharon's hands clapping together drew Trish out of her thoughts. She straightened and pushed a stray lock away from her face.

"I think we got it covered, my friend," Sharon said with a stretch.

Trish secretly hoped she was as nimble as Sharon when she reached her seventies. She gave her friend a smile and nodded.

"I can't think of anything we missed, but I'm sure we will find any blind spots soon enough." She glanced toward the cornfield where the stranger had disappeared a couple of hours ago.

"Unfortunately, I think you may be right," Sharon agreed with a sigh, looking in the same direction as Trish.

"I'm hungry. Let's get some food," Trish said suddenly, pulling both of their attention from the unspoken threat.

Sharon clapped her hands together. "Sounds good. Where to?"

Trish shrugged. "Let's clean up and double check everything inside and then we can decide."

After agreeing, they moved around gathering all the tools and leftovers from the devices they set up. It didn't take long before they were back inside with Trish turning on the screens. They checked every view and picked a few of the previous trouble spots and the new ones they added, then Sharon went back outside to trip them. Trish made sure everything was sent to her phone as it was supposed to. She furrowed her brow, still wondering how the alerts weren't triggered before.

They hadn't found anything in the yard to suggest anything external was used to alter the connections, which was more frustrating than anything. After they agreed it was all working properly, they made their way outside. Sharon had her little Mini Cooper parked behind Trish's vehicle, making her snort.

"You make fun of my little baby, but let me tell you, I sure get a lot of compliments on it," Sharon said with an air of defiance and pride.

Trish just shook her head. "Not ever in my lifetime. That is one of those times that I make a friend agree to shoot me if I ever buy one." She laughed as she thought about it and continued to her own car. "Meet you there," she said with a wave.

She watched Sharon turn around and pull out of the driveway. Before she did the same, she looked around the property. The new cameras they had set up were completely invisible, even to her, and she helped hang them. Sharon had suggested using the bottles in the trees. They used a less sensitive one, so it didn't send an alert every time the wind blew. But she also picked a heavier bottle that didn't move as much. That one would likely stay on most of the time, and they hooked it up to record as well. Not all of her cameras recorded everything in the yard, only after it was activated by something. That one would record constantly and not just when it was tripped.

They had also put one in the barely visible hole in the bird bath at the edge of the cornfield. You really had to get down and look under the basin to even see it. That one would be the most helpful she thought. Sharon was brilliant when it came to surveillance, and she was grateful again for whatever higher power brought the two of them together.

Trish slowly turned around in her yard, careful to avoid all the statues, and watched as her phone lit up with various alerts as she drove down the driveway. She smiled as she watched the screen. Everything showed up just as it was supposed to. She felt a deep sense of pride in their work and breathed a sigh of relief as she made her way out to the main road.

Her eyes wandered to the old chicken house as she passed it. A weird feeling came over her as she looked into the darkened space. Only she knew what was hidden deep in that building and hopefully she never had to use it. But with the recent events, she couldn't shake the slight chill that came over her skin as she recalled the shadow that came out of there earlier. Did someone already know her secret?

Chapter 5

Trish sat across from Sharon at a local Chinese place. The space wasn't crowded even though it was a relatively small area. She liked this place the best because it was a darker restaurant, and she preferred a dimly lit room to a bright one every day of the week. The lighting was always kept low, even during the lunch hour.

The restaurant was divided into two spaces. The entrance led into the first area. It consisted of a bar area stretching almost the length of the space. There were a few booths set for four along a wall. A doorway led to a larger dining room with more tables and some set for larger groups. The wooden paneling stretched halfway up each wall from the floor with ethnic murals painted above.

Since she always knew what she wanted here, Trish set her menu at the edge of the table and waited for Sharon to decide. She glanced around and noticed only two other tables with patrons in various stages of their meals. She watched each table exchange conversations in between bites of food. It didn't escape her that the tables were also occupied by couples.

Resisting a sigh, she looked away. Trish liked to tell herself she didn't miss being married or even missed her ex. But she would be lying. She never gave in and actually admitted it though, and she firmly believed that these were mutually exclusive. Maybe it wasn't the person she missed, but the idea. Having someone to come home to or share something exciting, or even the mundane details of her day.

Sure, she had Sharon, but it wasn't the same. And even Sharon had her husband. If Trish was completely honest with herself, she knew she alone was responsible for her isolation. She wasn't going to open herself up to that kind of hurt ever again. Sharon was the only one she trusted enough to let in, and she was even guarded with her at times. If they hadn't met under the circumstances they had, she knows they wouldn't have become friends.

"I guess ginger chicken it is," Sharon stated, placing her menu on top of Trish's.

Trish smirked. "You always get that here. Why bother with the menu at all?" she asked.

Her friend just shrugged and grinned back. Sharon folded her hands on the table. "So, what do you think about all this going on?"

Letting out a sigh, Trish closed her eyes. How did she feel about everything? She hadn't given it too much thought, but she knew that later she would be thinking more than she liked. It was barely supper time, and a lot had happened since she met Sharon earlier in the day.

"I guess I haven't really yet," Trish admitted. "I am still processing how someone got onto my property without my knowledge—twice today!" In all honesty, she knew that was what irritated her the most.

"Hmm," Sharon said in response. "Maybe I should take a look at my system too. It has been a while I guess." She looked up and met Trish's eyes. "You should come over tomorrow and help me do that. Then we can see if there is anything new on this situation." She waved her hand around as if the job was in the restaurant where they were seated.

Trish just shrugged. "Sure, I got nothing else on my agenda at this point. I can do 'research' from your place just as easily as I can from mine." She made air quotes with a smirk. They both knew their research would likely involve some questionable and potential illegal activities.

Their waitress came back at that moment, and they placed their orders. Besides the ambiance, Trish loved this place because it was rarely busy, and their food always came quickly.

Just as the waitress left, Trish received an alert on her phone. With a frown, she opened the app to see what had tripped her camera. She scowled as she saw a dark cloaked figure pass in front of one of her new cameras. The green tint of the bottle clouded the clarity, but she knew she would get a clearer picture of the intruder with one of the other cameras at her house. With a deep sigh, she watched as the person seemed to almost float through her property. The figure turned one of her gnomes over again and Trish scowled. He knew where her system was tracking and knew where to move to avoid and then disable them. She glanced up and turned her screen to show Sharon.

Surprise lit her friend's face. "Wow they didn't waste much time, did they?" she asked with her own scowl. "Good thing we put that other stuff to use. It clearly hasn't been discovered yet."

Trish met her friend's concerned eyes. She knew Sharon would be more worried than Trish was. She simply shrugged it off.

"They haven't tried to get inside the house, though, which is weird," she mused more to herself than Sharon. "It's almost like they are just playing a game to see if I will catch on."

Sharon nodded. "Or they could be preparing for something bigger."

Trish looked up. "What do you mean?"

"I'm not sure yet. But I want you to be very careful. I am not dumb enough to think you will allow any extra protection, but you will need to be careful," Sharon said with a stern "mom" look.

Trish grinned. She always found it funny when Sharon tried to play her mother and tell her what to do without actually saying it. It was one of the few times that their age difference showed. Plus, Sharon had parented kids into adulthood and probably had her ways to get them to do what she wanted without outright telling them.

Trish knew what she was doing though, and she had been on her own for long enough to know she could handle whatever storm was coming her way. Even when she wasn't physically on her own, she was alone, providing for her parents and sister as if she were the parent and adult in the situation. The only time she didn't feel completely alone was the short time she was married and had her little girl by her side. Unfortunately, that time was only a small portion of her life to date.

This wasn't anything she couldn't deal with. She knew she would always have her friend's support if things went sideways, but until then, she was going to be just fine. Her and her two besties would be just fine, the two most reliable things in her life. Spring and Winnie would cover her just fine, she thought with a grin.

Something was lurking in the back of her mind though. Why would anyone be targeting her at this time and what did they want? She didn't have anything of value so she knew it couldn't be some kind of robbery. She didn't have high value files, or a secret safe in her wall behind some nondescript painting. The only thing she had of any kind of value was her computer system and various monitors. But none of that would be visible from outside and definitely not worth the kind of surveillance this person or people were scouting for. Their training spoke volumes about what kind of person this was, which had her slightly concerned.

The only thing she could come up with was it had something to do with her sister and the latest case Sharon had given her. The video she had of the idiot who tripped over her gnome earlier in the day made her chuckle. He sure looked like someone associated with her sister. But the one who disappeared into the corn while they were outside was much stealthier and was the one she should probably be careful of.

Trish looked at the screen again. Was it the same person or could this be someone else? And if it was the same person, did they just hide out in the fields until she left? She realized that they hadn't tried to disable the new ones they had placed, so if they were hiding out, they didn't know what she and Sharon had done.

A throat clearing brought her eyes back to Sharon. She was surprised to see their food already on the table. *Had I zoned out that much that I missed the waitress completely?* she asked herself. Trish shook her head and picked up her utensils and started to cut into her lemon chicken.

"I think I should head back with you and make sure our new devices are still safely where they should be," Sharon suggested, digging into her own food.

Trish just nodded. "But you do know I can also check everything from inside, right? I don't want to give away their positions if this person is still hanging around."

"I guess that makes sense," Sharon conceded. "But I would still feel better if I came over as well when you go home."

Trish knew she wouldn't win this argument and just gave her friend a slight nod. She wasn't afraid of anything and certainly not some stalker idiot who was creeping around her property. She lived in the middle of nowhere and had long ago armed herself with enough skill and ammunition to keep herself and house safe. She also had an escape plan if it ever got so bad that she had to flee. But that was a fleeting thought in her head because she knew she would never run in fear. She would always stand her ground. Never again would she let someone drive her away.

They finished their supper in silence, both women lost in their own thoughts. After they paid their bills, Trish focused on driving back to her place. She glanced behind her now and then to see Sharon still behind her. She couldn't resist the grin that graced her features. It didn't bother her that Sharon was being overprotective. If she was ever in a bind, she wouldn't want anyone else beside her. Sharon's skills were unmatched and even with her age, she was still more nimble than anyone Trish knew. Between her fighting ability and her interrogation skills, she must have been quite a force to be reckoned with as a younger woman.

Trish pulled up to her garage and unbuckled her seatbelt. She preferred to have her vehicle tucked away in the small shelter overnight given the strange activity around her property the last twelve or so hours. She glanced around as she got out and watched Sharon pull in behind her. She looked around the yard and didn't notice anything obviously altered or moved. Satisfied, she moved to unlock and open the garage door.

After she had secured her car, she pulled the door down and locked it. Sharon was standing next to her car looking around the yard. Her arms were crossed over her chest as she squinted her eyes. Trish chuckled to herself. Sharon looked like she had x-ray glasses on, scouring the area for any signs of danger.

"Come on, woman. Let's go inside," she called to Sharon, waving her toward the back door. By force of habit, she looked around the back of the house. There was less surveillance there, but for good reason. This area was easily covered by one camera hidden high in the eaves of the roof line. It was invisible to the naked eye, and you would have to know exactly where it was to see it. Because of how high it was, it covered the entire space behind the house and even into the woods a little behind the house. The only blind spot was behind the garage. It was Trish's favorite camera because it caught everything back there. It has saved her life more times than she could count.

Now with the shortening days, the security flood light was triggered by the motion in the area and would then light up the yard making everything visible in the camera. Trish and Sharon had rigged it up to be more sensitive to movement and light up even during the bright and sunny days. The camera would only record while the light was on, so the motion sensitivity was imperative to the camera working properly.

Trish glanced toward the front of the house where the camera showed the earlier intruder. Nothing looked disturbed this time but she wouldn't know for sure until she got inside. She was now grateful for Sharon's idea to plant more than one camera solely for continuous recording purposes.

They moved into the house and Sharon locked the door behind her. Trish couldn't help the grin that passed over her face. Even as good as Sharon was, she still locked the door like it would stop anyone from coming in if they were determined enough.

Sharon settled at the table while Trish double checked the shades. They were still closed from the morning, but she wanted to make sure nothing inside had been disturbed either. Satisfied, she peaked through the doorway into the kitchen and didn't see anything remarkable. The space still looked as cluttered as ever and nothing appeared to have been moved. She kept it like that intentionally to look like a pack rat and hoarder. Trish smiled as she remembered the looks on people's faces when they first walked into her kitchen off the front porch. She had kept the old swinging doors that separated the kitchen from the rest of the house to prevent anyone from seeing past her staged facade up front.

Turning back to Sharon, who was already looking through the security footage on the computer, she asked, "Coffee?"

Sharon hummed a response, distracted by the screen in front of her.

Trish nodded and moved fully into her kitchen to start a pot. She noticed the darkening skies outside as she slowly moved about the space gathering her supplies. The only thing she seemed to use in the kitchen was the coffee maker. She rarely ate at home and wasn't sure if the oven actually still worked. The refrigerator was stocked with basics like soda and a few fruits, maybe a loaf of bread and a few supplies for sandwiches.

She leaned against the counter as she listened to the machine gurgle and eventually spit out the darkened liquid. Trish reached above her and took two mugs from the shelf. It was the only one that she removed the doors from after she moved in. The small shelf was perfect for her mugs, and it saved her countless hours opening and closing a useless door since her coffee was a mandatory thing multiple times a day.

The smell of the freshly brewed coffee brought Trish out of her thoughts, and she sighed contentedly. The smell was reenergizing, making her feel alive as if the caffeine was in the air. She poured the dark brown heaven into the cups and added the sugar and cream that Sharon needed. Trish never understood the need for all the fluff. Just drink the black stuff and suck it up, she thought with a grimace.

She carefully carried the mugs into the other room and set them on the table. Sharon didn't look up from her screen but picked up the mug and took a sip. She nodded her approval, still not lifting her eyes.

Trish sighed and sat down across from her friend. "So? Find anything yet?" She knew that Sharon's eye was better than hers and she would find something in the fraction of a second it took Trish. She figured that had to do with her training and years of experience that Trish just didn't have. She knew she was good, but Sharon was far better.

A few minutes of silence went by before Sharon sighed and pushed the screen away. "Well, the good news is all the cameras are still where they are supposed to be, and everything looks as it should." She bit the side of her lip and Trish felt a sense of foreboding from her friend.

"But..." she asked, waving her hand to get Sharon to continue.

"This is so frustrating, Trish," Sharon said slowly. Her gaze shifted away from Trish and back to the now darkened screen in front of her. "There is definitely something or someone lurking around." She grabbed the laptop and woke up the screen to show Trish something. After pressing a few keys, she turned it to face Trish.

"There is a shadow...here," she began as she froze the screen.

Trish narrowed her eyes, not seeing anything. It looked like a darkened part of her property, shaded by trees. Sharon must have seen the confusion on her face, because she sighed and turned the device back to face her and then played with the keys some more.

When she finally turned it back to Trish, she was shocked. An outline of a person was shown on the screen. It wasn't a clear figure though, but more like a shadow of someone. It was strange.

"Now you see it?" Sharon asked. "That is what I am worried about. This is a trick used by some organizations to disguise people and allow them to go almost invisible around security cameras. The new ones we just put in will pick up these slight changes in the environment."

Trish snickered. "So, like if a ghost walks through my yard, it will pick it up even though the ghost is essentially see-through." She leaned back in her chair and watched Sharon's face darken. "I wonder what Casper is up to these days."

"Trish, this isn't funny," Sharon scolded. "This means someone is possibly stalking you."

Not worried, Trish just waved her hand. "I am not worried, Sharon. If there is a ghost out there, they could literally just sail through my walls. No gun you or I have will stop that. I will just keep watching things and see what happens." She shrugged and put her hands behind her head.

Sharon shook her head. "I don't think you understand the importance here, hon. Someone is clearly keeping tabs on you, and it worries me. Especially with the new info we just got." She raised her eyebrows, and Trish knew what she was talking about.

But Trish was not going to show fear to anyone. That was a weakness she would not ever let anyone see, even if she were worried. She was confident in her marksman skills, and she hadn't been surprised yet. Whoever this ghost was, she wasn't about to bow to them. Besides they had plenty of opportunities to break in already. They seem to just lurk around the property. Weird, yes. But not something she would worry too much about. And there was nothing she could offer anyone, aside from a bullet, if they were out to get her for some odd reason. So, she shrugged it off.

"But we need to do something about this Trish," Sharon insisted. "You could be in danger."

Trish waved her hand again. "No, we don't. Look if they wanted to get in, they would have already. My vehicle is in the garage; the shades are closed as they have been all day. Nothing is different now than it was two hours ago or even ten hours ago. They are just probably some vagrants looking for an easy entrance into some place to hunker down until the next place. I am not worried."

Sharon let out a frustrated breath. "I don't think you understand, Trish," she started.

"No, really, Sharon," Trish interrupted her. "I am not worried about someone lurking around. If it is someone that we are looking for, all the better. I know what to look for on the cameras now and if anyone shows up again, I will take a shot at them. If nothing else, it will scare them away. If it is someone we want to ask a few questions to, then even better." She stood to refill her empty mug, not even noticing she had already finished it.

Sharon leaned back in her chair and crossed her arms. "Why are you so stubborn?" she asked, with a scowl on her face.

Trish resisted a laugh at her friend's face. "I have faced so much in my life, some vagrant wandering around is not going to stress me out. Want some more?" She lifted her cup as she asked.

Shaking her head, Sharon groaned. "Fine. You do whatever. But I am not far away if I need to come rescue you. I better head out though. Everything here is working the way it should, so I feel better about that at least. I put in a device that should prevent anyone from scrambling or disabling your cameras too. That will prevent something like this morning."

She stood and followed Trish into the cramped kitchen. She chuckled as she looked around. "You should really fix this up, Trish."

"No way!" Trish said with a grin. "I love the vibe in here. Plus, it messes with people. They never know what is going to jump out from behind something." She chuckled as she thought about it.

Sharon laughed and just shook her head. "Whatever makes you happy I guess." She took one more look around the space and gave her head another shake.

She opened the door to the porch and Sharon stopped and turned to look at her friend. Her mouth opened but nothing came out. Finally, she just closed it and shook her head lightly. "Be careful, my friend," Sharon said and then walked to her car.

Trish walked her to the door and relocked it behind her. She turned and put her hands on her hips, admiring the work in this room. When she first moved in a lot of the things on the counters were already there. She just left them. It made her laugh, and she didn't use it much anyway. As long as she had room for her coffee maker and mugs, she was good. Maybe a better diet would be an idea, but she always had something else to think about. The meetings that seemed to come up with Sharon managed to take care of most of her meals anyway.

She looked through the foggy front window and saw the blurred taillights of Sharon's vehicle turn onto the main road. With a sigh, she moved back to the living space and fired up her computer and screens. She wanted to look more closely at what Sharon was talking about. She hadn't noticed it before and joked about it. But she needed to be aware of what she was looking for—or what Sharon saw—so she wasn't caught off guard. That was something she hated.

Whatever Sharon was trying to say as she was leaving didn't escape Trish. But what was she going to do about it if Sharon wouldn't tell her? *Nothing*, she thought. But she knew something was eating at her friend. Hopefully she will share it with Trish soon.

After almost half an hour of studying the films, she finally saw what Sharon was referring to. It was a very subtle movement and disappeared quickly from view. She furrowed her brow, staring at the screen. She rewound it again and again watching the picture change slightly and then return to normal. This was a game changer in her eyes. This person was good, and she was starting to think this wasn't some vagrant or homeless person wandering around. This was something completely different. The person on the screen was a professional and knew very clearly what they were doing. They had managed to avoid all the cameras except the one that Sharon insisted they put in the tree.

Sitting back, Trish stared at the screen that was frozen on a slightly blurry outline of a person. This couldn't be good, she thought. But who would be after her enough to want or need to hide so much from her cameras? And who even knew about them? She literally had close to fifty cameras scattered throughout her property. This person had managed to avoid all but one. And in some kind of stealth mode on top of everything.

This was going to take a bit more concentration than she thought. How could she make sure that this person didn't get the surprise jump on her and find herself in a position where she couldn't escape or call for help if she needed to?

Trish took a photo of the stilled picture with her phone and then moved to turn off the lights. She needed to figure this out, but it wouldn't be down there. She made sure her computer was locked, and she set her house alarm. She rarely used it since she had all the cameras set to alert her of any movements outside but today she felt the extra security would be helpful since she wasn't sure what she was dealing with.

She grabbed the folder Sharon had given her earlier in the day and then headed upstairs. She left one lamp turned on downstairs. This was a habit she had started a few years ago to make it look like she was still there and awake, but also because if she needed to see due to an intruder, she wouldn't be shuffling around trying to find a light switch. She had a timer set to turn the lamp off and a different light on in her kitchen to simulate movement.

Settling on her bed, the only room upstairs with any furniture, Trish set up her small desk lamp beside her. She didn't use any big lights ever, but upstairs she wanted even less light alerting anyone to where she was located in the house. Her room-darkening shade provided her with privacy inside and out. No one would be able to tell where she was in the house with them closed.

She opened the folder. "Alright sexy thing," she said as picked up the photo of the homeless-looking man and flicked his forehead. "What are we going to do about you?"

Chapter 6

Trish didn't sleep well thinking about who might be watching her property and thoughts swirling about her sister being around again. Suddenly she was reminded of Clayton's recent message. Was her sister back and that's why he was reaching out again? This one had felt different, almost desperate.

Over the years he had sent her messages denying the affair with Patsy, but Trish never believed him. It only made sense to her. She knew in her heart that she was right, and she would not be made a fool of by believing in some new story or lie they cooked up together. But if Patsy was the reason for him reaching out again, she wasn't sure what to do. She knew they had never run off together, since Patsy disappeared again right after the accident.

If he knew she was back, would he know where she was? Maybe he was hoping Trish would believe him this time or think she had forgiven them by now. Then they could all get along like family again. Trish snorted at the thought. She would never consider Patsy her sister or Clayton her husband again. The level of betrayal and heartache wasn't something she would ever be able to overlook.

Trish sat up in her bed and stretched. The papers fell to the floor, and she chuckled. She must have fallen asleep studying them, which would make sense why she woke up thinking about it all. She flung the covers aside and leaned over to pick up the file and documents. Ironically the photo of her sister's sunken and pathetic face was staring back at her.

"I feel nothing for you, Patsy," she grumbled to the photo. "You destroyed everything for me, and I just don't have it in me to care about whatever it is that you are caught up in." A new thought popped into her mind. Was Clayton trying to get Trish to help her sister out of whatever new mess she was in? Another snort escaped her lips as she thought about how stupid that would be of him. If he knew her at all, he should know she wouldn't help the killer of her child.

Throwing the blankets back over her bed, Trish stretched again, the familiar pops in her spine making her chuckle. She picked up the file and dropped it on the bed. She moved to the tiny bathroom and stared at her reflection in the mirror. Her face was clear of wrinkles, but the grays in her twists gave her the older look she was going for. She rarely wore any makeup, especially since losing her family, but she still didn't look like the forty-something she was. The grays gave her a few extra years, but if someone really looked closely, they would see her clear and dark skin still showed some youth. Satisfied, she moved about the small space doing her morning routine.

She thought for a second about her sister who looked like she was well into her forties, maybe even early fifties. The choices she had made since high school showed clearly on her weathered face and empty eyes. Even with all the stress Trish had been through the last few years didn't come close to what Patsy's face showed.

Feeling better and more awake, Trish made her way to the main floor for her morning caffeine addiction. She glanced around the space as she moved down the stairs. Pausing on the last step, she narrowed her eyes. Something felt off. She looked around but didn't see anything out of place so she just brushed it aside.

An alert sounded from her phone, reminding her she forgot it upstairs. With a sigh, she quickly moved back upstairs to get it. As she turned to return to the main floor of the home, she heard the door to the back of the house slam shut.

Trish stopped and opened the camera app on her phone. Selecting the camera at the back of the house, she squinted at the screen. Nothing looked strange and it didn't appear that anyone was around. That camera picked up everything in an almost panoramic view, so if someone was out there, it would show it. But there was nothing. She told herself to look closer at the video, after she had her coffee in her hand.

She let out a frustrated groan and continued down the steps. "Coffee first," she muttered as she glanced through the small laundry room at the door as she walked by to make sure it was in fact locked. The intruder didn't get into the house, so there was that she figured. Maybe she was imagining something that wasn't really there. Maybe the wind caught the screen door and that's what she heard.

Shrugging her shoulders, she moved into the kitchen. Trish flipped the switch to turn on the coffee maker and then filled a small pitcher of water to dump into it. The familiar and calming gurgle made her smile as she leaned against the counter looking out her foggy windows. The temperature from what she could feel in her house suggested her windows were probably as much fogged up by her intentional means as the contrast in outside and inside temperatures. *It must be more like November air out there today*, she thought.

She scooped two spoonsful of grounds from her container and dropped them in the top of the maker. It wouldn't take long, and she could almost taste the dark goodness. Arguably her favorite part of the day. It reminded her of an old commercial her parents used to sing every morning, an old Folger's coffee ad she remembered with a smile. Something about "the best part of waking up."

Trish picked up her phone from the counter where she dropped it on the way in. The screeching sound reserved for texts, the psycho sound from the old movie, interrupted her coffee memories and she saw Sharon's face pop up.

An unexpected flash drew her attention outside. Out of the corner of her eye, Trish thought she saw something move quickly past the window. She didn't see anything when she leaned forward to look out though. Thinking it was likely a deer or something, she picked up the partially filled pot and poured a mug of steaming coffee into it. She took it with her phone to the other room and sat at her desk, firing up the screens and computer. But she wasn't going to waste any more time wondering. She needed to see if it was the wind this morning and if that was just a frightened deer running off just a moment ago.

"Maybe I am losing my mind," she mused out loud. *Or someone is trying to make me think that*, she said in her head.

Trish chuckled darkly. If someone thought they could get to her they really were stupid and didn't know anything about her. She had spent years building the hardness around her. That armor was strong and solid, and nothing could penetrate it.

Once she was settled, she opened the text from Sharon. Her brow furrowed as she read her friend's words. Sharon wanted to meet again, and Trish really didn't want to leave. Not that she was afraid to leave, she just really liked staying in her house and avoiding people. She wondered for a half a second if she lived in town if the neighborhood kids would think she was a scary old witch who would trap and eat them.

Trish let out a laugh. *That would be fun*, she thought. She could just hear Sharon's disapproving sigh at her imaginary antics, feeding into the mystery of "the crazy old witch at the end of the block." A snort escaped as she tried to focus again on the task at hand. She would never live in a neighborhood again after everything that happened.

"How about later?" she said out loud as she typed back to Sharon. A quick glance at the time showed eight sixteen. She wanted to dive back into whatever she needed to take her mind off her sister and their history. Maybe she could start looking around for the mystery man in the second photo. She suddenly realized that the second file Sharon had shown her the day before was missing.

Looking around the living room area, she focused on the table. "Didn't she leave it yesterday?" she asked no one in particular.

Trish bit her cheek. It wasn't like her to forget things. Did Sharon bring it with her when they worked on the cameras, or did she just show Trish while they were together? Shrugging it off, she moved to her desk and woke up her screens. She wanted to get a better look at the cameras and make sure she didn't have someone trying to get inside her place while she slept.

She wasn't a particularly heavy sleeper and due to the years of having to look out for her junkie sister, she had somehow learned which noises needed her attention and which didn't. Someone breaking in is definitely a noise that would be coded as "need to wake up immediately" in her brain. Shaking her head, she opened up the apps for her various camera views and started to sort through videos captured and stored since last night.

It didn't take long for her to again focus on the strangest one. She stared at the stilled image. It looked like part of the lens was looking through the bottom of a clear bottle, a slightly distorted and wavy image of a shadow. There was little definition in the image and when she skipped ahead just a few more stilled images, the distortion was completely gone. There wasn't anything she could think of to explain what she was seeing. Somehow the person made themselves essentially invisible. But that wasn't possible—*was it?*

Trish pushed away from her desk and picked up her mug. Finding it empty, she groaned. She looked at her computer to see that it was already ten and she had agreed to meet Sharon for lunch at eleven.

"Ugh," she complained as she moved back to the kitchen to fill her cup. She was surprised to see the pot was nearly empty and she didn't remember refilling her mug at all while she had been sitting there sifting through the videos.

"Maybe I really am starting to lose it," she said with a sigh. She leaned toward her window and looked out at the yard. The fogginess of the window prevented a good view of the landscape, but she knew it well enough to know if something was amiss outside.

She noticed the sun was shining brightly, which was a stark contrast to her darkened living room. The cloudless sky and green grass made her subconsciously take in a breath. Trish closed her eyes and envisioned what her little girl would be doing if she had lived here with Trish. Even at six she was a breath of fresh air.

Anyah was a lover of everything bright and shiny, pink and fluffy. The complete opposite of what Trish was—now and back then. But Anyah had managed to bring out some playfulness that Trish had thought she lost when her sister first disappeared, leaving Trish to care for herself and her grieving parents. She didn't get to wallow in self-pity or worry. She had a family to take care of and that required maturity and many hours of work.

But Anyah somehow turned time backwards for Trish. She found herself enjoying the silly games and playing outside. They would walk on the beach for hours and build in the sand. The little girl's excitement of seeing a crab for the first time dig its way out of the sand and scurry sideways back to the sea made Trish smile. Anyah had followed the creature back to the edge of the water, squealing and clapping, jumping up and down as it disappeared beneath the surface. It was like Anyah had cheered the small animal on until it made its way back home.

That kind of excitement and high on life attitude disappeared the day that gun shot was heard. The day that instantly turned from bright sunshine to darkness as if the sun was mourning right along with Trish. The day that Trish lost one of the two most important things in her life.

The second would follow in a few short months. The pain of those losses never faded from Trish's memories either.

A sudden and sharp noise brought her attention back to the present and Trish moved quickly to the living room. She scanned the area and didn't see anything unusual, so she moved back to her desk to pull up her cameras. Her phone sat silent next to her computer, and she scowled at it. Why wasn't it alerting her to anything? she wondered.

Trish tapped the keyboard, and the different screens lit up with various camera views. Nothing stood out as unusual, but now that she knew what to look for, she zoomed in on them and scoured each view for a glimpse of the shadowy figure from yesterday. She found herself wondering about the validity of ghosts and if this was an apparition watching her or if it was just a figment of her imagination. Either way, she would get to the bottom of it because she built her life on what she could prove. Nothing ever pointed to the existence of ghosts, so she shoved that idea away. She needed something more to prove this was a ghost.

She paused one of her views on an image. Zooming in she could see the slight variation in the picture and a tiny sliver of darkness along the edge of the frame showing the potential figure moving quickly through her view. Trish backed up the video to see if she could capture a better view. Even with the blurred image and almost see-through quality of the figure, she could make out outlines.

"Gotcha!" she said with a smile. She printed out the image and then grabbed her phone. She hoped this would help in her conversation with Sharon, suddenly glad they were already planning to meet. The fact that the person was back again after just being there the previous day irritated her. What were they up to, she wondered.

She tried to see where the figure went after it passed by her camera, but it seemed to just disappear again. It looked to be heading toward the old chicken house, but she couldn't be sure. It occurred to her that just yesterday a figure had come out of the same building when they were working on the cameras. Could it be the same person? And more importantly are they squatting in the building that was barely standing? Trish would have to investigate later, not until she had one of her trusted besties in her hand though.

It didn't take long for her to be out her door and heading to the small garage. She stopped and looked around the yard, wondering if the mysteriously invisible guy was hanging around watching her. She felt a slight chill as she squinted at the woods behind the garage.

"Not gonna get caught up in that," she muttered to herself. She moved quickly to the door, unlocked, and lifted it.

Grateful for the small space, she moved sideways along her car to get in the driver's seat. Once inside, she started it and quickly moved out of the small structure. As she got back out to close the door, she caught a glimpse of something from her periphery. She turned, but instead of a person standing there, she saw a truck speed by.

Trish shook her head. "I'm getting spooked by nothing." She was irritated with herself as she pulled down the garage door and relocked it.

She took one last look around the property as she moved down the drive to the road. Nothing was moving besides the corn stalks gently waving in the breeze, as if serenading her departure.

Brushing off the events of the morning as best she could, Trish drove quickly to the nearby deli that Sharon had chosen. It was a small place but had great food. The tables were set in rows like a cafeteria and most held more than four people. The counter as you walked inside was for take-out orders and just past that was for eat-in ordering. Everyone seemed to know each other, as was the case in a small town anyway. But this place had regulars too.

As soon as she walked in, Trish noticed Sharon standing off to the side of the counter talking to someone had looked to be a work colleague. But her friend seemed to know everyone in this town, and even beyond Salisbury. Being born and raised on the Eastern Shore, coupled with her outgoing personality, it shouldn't surprise anyone.

Trish was the opposite. She wasn't a complete hermit that hated people, but she wouldn't go up and talk to a stranger ever. If they spoke to her first, she would respond politely, but Trish didn't have the same desire to talk to everyone she meets. So, she decided to leave her friend to chat and found a table for them a short distance away. She laid the file folder she brought in front of her and folded her hands over the top of it. She nearly laughed out loud when she put her printed image into the folder because she gave Sharon so much grief about it before.

Sharon gave her a slight nod and Trish took the hint that it was likely a conversation she wasn't supposed, or didn't want, to be a part of. She could see the menu from where she was seated on the board above the cashier, so she studied that while Sharon finished her meeting. Trish knew what she was getting already. She was a creature of habit and chose her meals based on where she was. At this deli she always ordered the same thing. But she didn't want to look suspicious, like she was waiting for someone, so she pretended to look for something to order.

By the time Sharon had finished and the man had left, Trish nearly jumped up to order. She was hungry and thinking about what she wanted for so long, made her stomach protest more than she liked. She stood as Sharon sat, but Sharon grabbed her hand making Trish stop.

Trish gave her a questioning look. "What's wrong?"

Her friend sighed. "We have a new problem."

Chapter 7

"So, Luke says that the guy we are looking for is also wanted for some higher up things that are out of our, well *his*, jurisdiction," Sharon said with a smirk as they sat down with their food.

Trish raised her eyebrow. "And since when did that stop you from doing something about some bad guy running around?"

Sharon laughed. "That's what I told Luke. But he's worried. This guy is a special kind of scum, and he wants to make sure I don't get too deep in something, *given my age and all*," she scoffed, making air quotes with her fingers.

Not being able to contain her own laugh, Trish shook her head. "I don't think he needs to worry, Sharon. And I'm sure you have been in plenty of sticky situations over the course of your career." She leaned forward and picked up her sandwich, anxious to mute her complaining stomach.

"Yes, but I am older now and slowing down a bit," Sharon stated stoically.

Trish couldn't hold back her chuckle as she said, trying to be serious, "I am sure he has concerns, and we should take them seriously, Sharon. I mean, you are really getting up there in age."

The pair laughed together as they dug into their lunch. Trish couldn't help but acknowledge that if the higher up was worried about this guy, they would have to be very careful as well. She didn't have Sharon's training and if something happened that required her to be active "in the field", she wouldn't know what to do and would have to depend on Sharon. That could present a whole different set of issues for them if Sharon then had to be concerned about her own safety as well as Trish's.

She decided she couldn't worry about that at the moment. There were more pressing things to work on. Trish suddenly remembered the photo she printed that morning. She pulled the folder out from under her plate and opened it to show Sharon the paper.

"What's this?" Sharon asked, looking at Trish's outstretched hand. Trish was able to enhance the photo so they could see some features though it was still heavily shadowed.

"Well, I think it's the same person as yesterday. I caught this on my system this morning," Trish explained, keeping out the other details about the person possibly trying to break into her house. No need to worry her friend over something that could have happened but didn't, she thought.

Sharon stared at the photo for a long time. Her brow furrowed as she studied it. When she finally set it down, she had a frown on her face.

"Trish, this is an amazing photo," Sharon said as she pointed to it. "We can definitely see a likeness here, even though it is blurry. It is clearly not a Caucasian person based on the facial features we can make out. I think we can agree based on build it is likely a male as well. Given the darkness of the face, it could be an African American or it could just be that the face is shadowed." She picked it up again and traced something with her finger.

Trish agreed, she thought it was a black male as well, but the idea of a shadowed face made her pause in her assumption now that Sharon mentioned it.

"So, what do we do about it? How do we get a clearer image of whoever this idiot is creeping around my property?" Trish asked, clenching her teeth. She hated that someone was on her property without her knowledge.

Sharon looked up and grinned. "Well, your work is amazing. I think we can turn up the sensitivity on the camera that captured this view, and we might actually get something even clearer."

Trish nodded. That was something she was looking forward to. What would make her even happier would be to catch the person, preferably with her rifle in hand, or shotgun, either way would work for her, she thought with a smile. Maybe she did have a dark streak after all.

Sharon shared some new information regarding their "target" as Sharon called the people they were looking for. Trish just shook her head. The terms didn't matter much to her. The guy just needed to be caught.

Trish looked at the photo Sharon showed her the day before. The man looked like some rich and spoiled trust fund kid, which was odd around this area. They were more likely to be up close to DC, but then she figured he could be more prominent up that way too. Most folks around here were farmers or blue-collar workers, although Trish hated that term. He could have a rich family on the ocean shore, but that was still more vacationers than permanent residents.

The smirk on his face told everyone everything there was to know. A cocky kid who thought the laws and rules didn't apply to him. The kind of individual who skated through life as if nothing touched them. The parents who raised this kid gave him everything he wanted as well as everything he didn't. He got in trouble, and they made it go away with money. He likely never had to be accountable for his behavior his entire life. This would be someone Trish was happy to bring down.

"Ok, let's head over to your place and see if we can mess with those cameras a little bit and make this image clearer, shall we?" Sharon asked, brushing off the crumbs from her hands.

Trish stood and grinned. "Absolutely. We got some bad guys to catch."

They dumped the trash from their lunch trays and returned them to the designated place by the counter and headed outside. Trish had parked close to Sharon when she arrived, so they made their way to the vehicles together, not that the parking lot was very big anyway.

As she drove back to her house, Trish's thoughts drifted to her two mysteries. One being where the lowlife, rich kid was hiding and the second the ghost lurking around her property. The thought of it being a ghost made her snicker. She didn't waste time on things she couldn't prove. And since she could see it better now, she was even more convinced it was a crazy person that she would be able to catch sooner or later. Hopefully with the help of Sharon's cameras, she would be able to get an even sharper image so facial recognition could identify them.

The thought of catching someone who thought they were smarter than she was had Trish all kinds of excited.

She wondered again if she didn't have that violent streak Sharon did and it had just been hidden for so long. Now that there was a threat against her it was becoming more visible. Her thoughts drifted to her ammo supplies. She kept her things easily accessible since there was a lesser chance of an accident happening without kids around, reminding her of the loss of her little girl again.

Brushing that aside, she mentally calculated her supply. She hadn't been out hunting in a while, which reminded her she should go soon. It helped with her restlessness to be out in the woods and engrossed in a hunt. It had to be close to deer season, she remembered. But on her property, she had more leeway and was less likely to get caught out of season.

Trish made a mental note to double-check her toys after Sharon left. She chuckled lightly at her friend's reaction every time she brought out the big old guns. They were clumsy and too big, she would complain to Trish. But Trish loved those guns, and they had special meaning to her. She also knew if tested, she could outshoot even Sharon with her favorite rifle. If she challenged her friend to a shotgun competition, Sharon would say she was "just showing off."

Driving past the familiar corn field, Trish wondered how long she would have the cover of the long stalks. She thought about trying to purchase a small part of the land from the neighbor and plant large evergreens that would give her privacy all year, but somehow always resisted. She had planted some at the border of the two properties to try to give some cover, but they were still small and would take years to be big enough to be helpful. Maybe next spring she will plant more, and some already big ones.

The farmer was once again out cutting his fields down. She intentionally looked the opposite way to avoid having to wave or acknowledge him. Some might say she was antisocial, and maybe she was, but she just didn't like to draw attention to herself. She liked being anonymous, but mostly she simply valued her privacy.

Glancing in her rearview mirror, Trish noticed that Sharon wasn't behind her. She didn't really think too much of it and just pulled up to her garage. As she exited the vehicle, she looked around. Nothing seemed out of place, and she didn't have that strange feeling like the day before.

"Maybe the ghost figured out its unfinished business and crossed over," she muttered to herself with a snort.

After securing her car in the garage, she relocked the door just as Sharon pulled into the driveway. Trish waved and then waited for her friend to meet her. Sharon grinned as she pulled out a small box from her passenger seat. She pressed her key fob twice, forcing out a pitiful beep from the tiny car. Trish resisted her laugh, but Sharon knew what she thought of the thing anyway.

"Sorry, I had to stop at home quick," Sharon explained. "I have a few things we can try out. Luke gave them to me about a week ago to hopefully help us track the sweethearts in our file. But we can spare one for here." She tipped her head to the side and smirked.

Trish raised her eyebrows. "What kind of toys?" She was intrigued. Whenever Sharon got new gadgets, they always tried them out first. They were typically some new spy tech that Trish had no real use for, but Sharon knew what to do with all of it. Trish would learn how to hack it quickly, but how it worked she didn't waste her time or energy on.

Sharon just shrugged her shoulders. "We need tools though. So, let's head inside and see what we can use."

Trish just nodded and led them into the back entry. Checking once again that everything was as it should be, she moved through the house to the kitchen. Coffee was always the first thing on her mind when she got home.

Walking back into the room a few minutes later, Trish was surprised by the amount of tech that was spread out on her table.

"Uh, Sharon, what is all this?" She asked as she set down the two steaming mugs.

Sharon glanced up and gave her friend a small smile of thanks and picked up her cup. She stood tall and stretched her back. "I just took everything out so I could look it all over. I am not sure yet what we can use to spruce up the cameras, so I wanted to see it all before I decided."

Trish picked up a tiny metal object that looked like an electrical connector with wires hanging out of both ends. "What is this stuff?" she asked as she examined the tiny piece.

"A little bit of this and a little bit of that," Sharon said with a grin.

Resisting a scowl, Trish set it back down and pulled out a chair to sit. "Ok, then what are we doing with it all?"

Sharon sat across from her and shook her head. "Most of this, nothing. I am looking for one piece to put inside one or two of the cameras we have already installed outside to make our images clearer and speed up the video. The goal would be to capture a clearer image. Some of this new stuff can combat the tech the bad guys have now and unscramble their scrambling of our feeds."

Trish waved her hand dismissively in the air. "Too much mumbo jumbo for me. Just tell me what to do with it and how to access it." She studied the contents of her table again. Most of the do-dads looked like cheap things from an old gumball machine. She knew they were probably metal but looked so small and cheap. There were colored ones and black ones, as well as silver and copper. She wasn't sure what to make of it all and was glad that wasn't her concern. She would leave all the techy terms for Sharon.

Her friend was studying the table as well, still standing with both hands holding her mug. Trish's phone sounded with the familiar screech, making Sharon cringe.

"Oh, I hate that sound," she complained.

Trish shrugged, smirking at the expected response from her friend. "I hate these devices, so it's fitting."

She picked up the phone and opened her alerts. Trish dropped her phone just as quickly and turned back to Sharon. "Ok, so what are we doing?" she asked. For some reason the man wouldn't leave her alone. He hadn't been this persistent since right after the separation. She was not going to help him locate her ex-sister no matter how much he begged. Maybe years ago, when she wasn't so damaged by betrayal. But today? That was just not who Trish was anymore.

"Trish, who was that?" Sharon asked, concern evident in her voice.

"No one," Trish said, dismissing the topic. She picked up her mug and took a long drink from it.

Sharon sat down across from Trish and folded her hands in front of her. "I'm a good listener," she said softly.

"Nothing to listen to, Sharon," Trish said through clenched teeth. "I'm not talking about it. Let's get to work on this." She waved her hand again, avoiding Sharon's eyes.

After a few minutes of not getting a response, Sharon sighed loudly. "Fine, but you can't just ignore your demons, Trish dear. You need to face them."

Trish looked up and scowled. "I don't have demons. I have unimportant fleas that won't die and leave me alone."

"Fleas?" Sharon asked, her face a mixture of confusion and humor.

"Yes. Now moving on…" Trish resisted pounding on the table, although she wanted to. She could tell Sharon just about anything, but this wasn't something she would waste her breath or time on. Clayton could try all he wanted but she wasn't giving in. She gave up on him a long time ago. It was high time he did the same and disappeared from her life, much like her sister.

Sharon finally gave in and sighed again. "Ok, when you're ready then."

Trish shot her a scowl. The woman never relented. But she wasn't going to get this one out of her.

She kept two big secrets from Sharon. One was her husband and sister's affair; the other was out in that damned chicken house. Sharon knew Trish suspected her sister was involved in her daughter's death, but she didn't know *how* connected Patsy was. That part Trish kept close to her stone-cold heart. Somehow Trish knew that if she ever revealed that part of the secret, Sharon would somehow get her to soften her heart and buy into some stupid and ridiculous theory that her sister was coerced or manipulated or not even involved. But Trish wasn't gullible or naïve.

Focusing back on Sharon, Trish picked up her now cooled mug of coffee. She took a sip and grimaced. "I'm going to nuke this quick. Be right back."

Trish walked into the kitchen, grateful for a break from her friend's concerned face. She stood at the sink, looking outside thinking again about that day. As if sensing her sadness, a cloud crossed in front of the bright sun, causing slight darkness outside. Trish just smiled and gave the universe a small and grateful nod.

The beeping of the microwave broke her thoughts. She grabbed her hot mug and moved back to the living room. Hopefully the break will have Sharon back on track. She didn't want to dwell on the past at the moment. She wanted to get moving on the mystery of the two men Sharon wanted to track down. Something to take her mind off her own stuff was most welcome.

Trish settled back at the table and Sharon glanced up when she sat down.

"Ok, I figured out what we can use." She picked up a tiny circular thing with a few wires sticking out of it in different directions.

"Uh, ok, Sharon. That looks like one of those tiny toy tops we used to play with as kids," Trish said, baffled at what the tiny thing could do.

Sharon laughed. "Yeah, I know. This little do-hickey will help us clarify the images on the cameras. It actually acts like a shutter on a regular camera. It speeds up the feed slightly so the tech these guys are using won't be effective and ours will capture any slowing of the devices they use. I think I can attach it to the camera we hung in the tree, since that one seems to be picking up the most. If I can get my hands on another one, I'll attach it to one closer to the house, preferably one that we just put in, since the others are detectable." She pushed around the objects on the table looking for another one.

Trish watched and then thought of something Sharon had said before. "Do you have anything to block the signal or whatever it is the person is using to detect my cameras? Maybe counter their measures so we can un-detect their detection?"

Sharon bit her bottom lip in concentration. "Hm, let me think," she mumbled more to herself than Trish. "This will affect their devices, but I'm not sure we can prevent it all together."

Another alert sounded on Trish's phone, but she chose to ignore it. She knew it was a text and not the cameras and she didn't want to bring anything up again. The only two people who texted her were Clayton and Sharon. She didn't give the number out much.

"You're not gonna check that?" Sharon asked.

Trish just shook her head. "No need."

Sharon just shook her head and continued her search. "Ah-ha! Found it!" she finally exclaimed. She held up another tiny device in triumph with a grin on her face.

"Ok, what does that tiny thing do?" Trish asked, as if she were uninterested. But in reality, she was intrigued by what these tiny devices could do. She didn't do programming or electrical set up, she focused on breaking into them instead. Maybe they went hand in hand in any other instance, but she was "field trained" as Sharon liked to say, so she skipped the technical part. Besides her degree didn't cover the level of this tech.

Sharon held it up to the light. "This little thing will block everything but our own signal. You should probably learn more about this," she suddenly said to Trish. "With all the new advancements being made in surveillance, you are gonna want to figure out how to scramble and unscramble stuff. These little guys are the key."

Trish took it from her friend and studied it. It couldn't be that hard to figure out, she thought. She snapped a photo of it with her phone and then put it back down, ignoring the flashing text alert. She would do some research later. For now, she just wanted to get it set up so she could get to work instead of worrying about this.

Sharon clapped her hands together. "Ok, let's get these little guys set up." She picked up the devices and then her small set of tools and headed for the door.

It always surprised Trish that the smaller the device the more powerful it seemed to be. Sharon was expecting incredible things from these tiny pieces. Then again, the small computer everyone carried around with them as a cell phone was a miraculous invention as well. Kids didn't realize the amount of power held in that single device.

Trish thought about her computer gear inside the house. With so much wireless technology nowadays and easy access to the internet and ability to communicate with other devices, it was like living in a small town with no privacy and yet you are completely alone in your space. It was baffling actually. Maybe that's why she hated her phone so much. It was a reminder of how much she wasn't isolated, even if she thought she was.

Shaking the thoughts, she followed Sharon outside, glancing around again to make sure nothing was amiss. She found her eyes being drawn to the building at the edge of the property. She couldn't help but wonder if that was where the person was hiding out. It wouldn't provide much for shelter, but it would provide a decent hiding place for a short time. She could imagine with the right materials a person could create a small shelter from the wind but not much else.

She tried as best she could to keep extra trash and junk from lying around her property. She prided herself on the organized chaotic look of her yard, she didn't want anything to potentially cause issues with her cameras. The only thing she could imagine would be helpful might be materials from the chicken house itself or things found in the woods behind. Maybe the people who owned the property before her had a hidden tree house out there.

Trish shook her head from her rambling thoughts. She was reminded again about tearing that old building down. But she knew why she kept it up despite her reasons for wanting it torn down. Maybe she could find somewhere else, she thought.

"Ok, Trish, come hold this for me," Sharon called from across the yard, drawing her attention to the opposite end of her property. Sharon was standing next to the bottle where they put the new camera.

Trish made her way over to her friend. "Show me what to do," she said, standing in front of Sharon.

"Just hold this still for me," she instructed.

Trish watched as Sharon effortlessly attached the tiny device to the even smaller camera. She had moved it to be outside of the bottle now so the green tint wouldn't get in the way of their pictures. Sharon had somehow made what looked like a cork top for the bottle and attached the new device and camera to it, making it look completely invisible to the naked eye.

"That's amazing, Sharon," Trish said. "Brilliant, actually."

Sharon grinned. "Yep. I have my moments."

They moved around the yard to a couple of other spots and in less than an hour, they had installed the new tech and were heading inside to test everything out.

"Alright, all done. Let's go double check then I have a date with Gary tonight, so I need to get going," Sharon said, putting her tools back in the tiny case.

Trish rolled her eyes. "Whatever, Sharon."

They sat side by side testing the new devices. Trish was amazed at what she saw. Everything looked like it was enhanced, and she could see things clearer than ever before. She didn't think it was bad before, but these new devices were a game changer.

She sat in front of the screen a long time after Sharon left, in awe of the new views. She was curious how sensitive they would be now and if every living creature would set them off. Sharon assured her that only large things would. Deer and coyotes might, but squirrels and birds wouldn't, unless they landed right on top of the bottle.

Satisfied with everything, Trish finally stepped away to start her research into the file. She would start small and look for any recent CCTV footage. As she began to set up, she wondered if this person was close and if she needed to begin her search in Salisbury. As she picked up her phone to ask Sharon, another text alert came through. This time she couldn't avoid it.

Chapter 8

Trish dug into her work, trying to find any trace of the pretty boy Sharon gave her. His smirk was starting to annoy her. The only photo she had was the one in the file and it was beginning to frustrate her. For two days, Trish scoured the local footage from traffic cameras to the speed trap ones by schools to Ring doorbells—the easiest to hack into. But she found no trace of him yet. Every time she came up empty, she would pick up the photograph and scowl at it.

"What am I missing?" she mumbled, flicking his forehead for the millionth time. It didn't ever take her this long to find someone, and she was becoming more irritated as the hours wore on. The hacking was easy, combing through countless hours of video was another story. Sharon had given her some facial recognition software a while ago but even that wasn't helping much. She still only got a few hits, and those were not who she wanted.

Trish tossed the picture down on her desk and stretched her arms above her head. She heard the familiar cracks in her neck as she stretched that out too. She had been spending too much time sitting at the computer the last few days. She needed to get up and move.

Thankfully there hadn't been much activity around her place with the new devices in place. She knew they were working because the deer were passing through often enough to remind her the cameras were there still. Pushing away from the desk, she stood and put her hands on her hips, trying to decide what to do. She needed a break.

The lovely screech from her phone sounded and she picked up her phone to see a text from Sharon.

"Got something" was all it said.

Trish waited a few minutes for more to come, but nothing did. With a sigh, she sent a message back with a simple "ok". She smirked, pretty confident that would annoy Sharon, but her friend's vagueness annoyed her, so it seemed fair.

When her phone rang a few seconds later, she let out a satisfied chuckle. "I win," she said into the phone.

Sharon's sigh sounded through the speaker, making Trish's grin grow.

"You know sometimes I question your maturity, Trish," Sharon said, slightly annoyed.

Trish's grin didn't falter as she shrugged her shoulders. "Yeah, well it just wouldn't be me if I didn't share my annoyance with you, especially when you are at fault first anyway."

"Whatever are you talking about? I simply told you I found something. You could have been nicer and asked me what I found," Sharon insisted.

Trish snorted. "Yeah, and you could have just told me what you found instead of leaving me hanging."

"That's not how a conversation goes, Trish dear," Sharon said with a hint of that mother coming through.

"Sharon, *dear*, a conversation is not done through text, now is it?" Trish admonished back. She preferred a phone call over text every time and Trish didn't care much for the etiquette of texting, if there was such a thing. "So, what did you find? I'm bored already."

Sharon sighed again. "Oh dear, you need to be patient. What are you doing now? Can you come here, or should I come there? I think it is best if I show you."

Trish glanced at the clock. It was close to lunch time. She figured she could eat on the way or pick something up. She would always choose somewhere else to meet than her place.

"I can pick up some lunch on the way and head there shortly," she said quickly before Sharon got some idea in her head about heading to her.

"Ok, I trust your judgement. Just get me whatever. See you soon!" Sharon sang out and then hung up.

Trish laughed. She knew her friend was just trying to get the jump on her by hanging up first. But she was going to see if she needed to bring anything. She looked around her space and thought she should just bring everything.

She hadn't left the house much since the last time they met, and her sandwiches were getting boring. Maybe she should get some actual groceries, but then she thought better of that. A good Philly cheesesteak sounded wonderful. She began to pack up her things and tucked her laptop into her computer bag. Trish slid the file folders along the side of the computer to keep the photos straight and neat. She eventually found the missing file Sharon had left the other day. It had fallen under the table somehow, but with the camera situation and Sharon's pile of parts, it could have just been pushed aside accidentally.

Trish loaded everything in her bag and then picked up her phone to place the order. It would be ready by the time she arrived at the café. She took her time leaving the property, making sure everything was as it should be. She noticed most of the fields were now cut so her property felt a little more exposed than she liked. She secretly wished those baby pines would hurry up and grow.

The rest of the drive was uneventful as she made her way closer to town. She noticed the brisk air earlier, but the bright sunshine contradicted the cool air. She put her sunglasses on and looked around. It was a weekday and there wasn't a lot of traffic around, not that there was much anyway in Salisbury.

She stopped at a stoplight and waited for the light to change. She glanced around the corner and noticed a person standing at the corner, looking in the opposite direction. Trish squinted as she tried to make out a better view of him. Something was bothering her as she studied the figure. A loud honk from behind her made Trish jump and notice the light had turned green.

Trish glanced to the side and was surprised to find the figure had disappeared in the time it took her to turn around. She scowled at the car behind her in the rearview mirror. Maybe if they hadn't honked, she would have been able to get a better look at the man. She was sure it was a man given the stature. He had a dark colored hoodie on with his head covered and matching dark colored sweatpants. Now he was gone, and she would be annoyed for a while trying to figure out where she had seen that figure before. She made a mental note of the intersection to see if she could find anything later.

She stewed the rest of the drive to the café. If only she had gotten a photo. Trish had been thinking about getting a dash cam for her vehicle for a while and now she was kicking herself for not doing it already. Maybe Sharon had something at her house Trish could rig up so this wouldn't happen again. She hated missing something or feeling like something was there, but she couldn't put her finger on it, especially when she was looking for someone.

The rest of her trip went by in a blur. She barely recognized her stops and only when she pulled into Sharon's driveway did she fully snap out of her fog. Thinking she had to ask Sharon about the camera right away, she hurried from her vehicle and let herself into the large home.

Sharon was standing in the kitchen with her hip resting against the counter and her phone in her hand. She gave Trish a nod as she watched her enter the room. Trish set the food down on the table and moved to pour some coffee from the warm pot. She wondered briefly if her coffee needs were a bit unhealthy, but only for a single fleeting moment. She settled at the table with her warm mug and sandwich.

Sharon continued to stare at her phone and scowl. Trish almost laughed as she stared at her friend, in between bites of her sandwich. Sharon was the epitome of cheerfulness. She rarely had a frown or scowl. It must be work related that made her upset, Trish thought.

She was nearly finished with her lunch when Sharon finally sat at the table across from her. She let out a deep sigh and set her phone down.

"Well, it looks like we might have a bigger problem," Sharon began as she unwrapped her cheesesteak. She took a large bite out of it, almost angry at it.

Trish resisted a laugh, but the smile was not hidden well. It drew another scowl from her friend.

"What? You say something like that and then shove a huge bite of food into your mouth," Trish said with a chuckle. She sat back and wiped her hands on the napkin and waited for Sharon to tell her the news.

After a few minutes, Sharon finally had her mouth empty. She wiped her mouth and hands with a napkin and then picked up her phone again. "It turns out the Executioner is back in play. I have no idea what he is doing here, but it seems there has been some chatter the agency has been tracking." Sharon let out a sigh and set her phone back down again.

Trish furrowed her brows. "What are you talking about?" She had never heard about this 'executioner' character and Sharon wasn't making sense. What does this person have to do with their search and why is it important for Trish to know about him?

Sharon looked up and sighed. "The Executioner is someone who has been beneficial in the past for us but recently has been targeting an agent."

"Sharon, you are not making sense right now. What does this have to do with me?" Trish didn't care what was going on at the agency. She just wanted to get going on her part in their case. The politics of her former workplace didn't matter to Trish at all.

"Ok, let me explain better," Sharon started. "A number of years ago, we had a case that was really complicated. We couldn't find evidence to support our theory and catch the bad guys. We hit a brick wall and were forced to back off. Out of nowhere a file was delivered to Luke. It had all the evidence we couldn't find. It was strange and amazing at the same time. But we could never identify him. He is the idol of everyone at the agency. He can get around every obstacle and has helped us capture and convict more criminals than we can count."

Trish waited for her to continue. But Sharon didn't. She just stared at her hands folded on the table, her lunch pushed to the side. She seemed to be deep in thought about something. Trish wasn't sure what to do or say. She wasn't sure if her friend was upset or star struck as she watched a few different emotions cross Sharon's face.

Finally, Sharon looked up and smiled. "If he is here, we need to be careful not to get in his way. He is a legend and whatever he is looking for in our tiny little town must be important."

Starstruck, Trish decided with a grin. She was impressed. Not many people left a mark on Sharon like this person has. She just hoped it wasn't a trap or something. If she had learned anything since starting to help Sharon out with cases, it was that nothing was as it seemed. There was always a different angle.

"Ok, so where does that leave us, Sharon?" Trish asked carefully. She needed to know what she could or couldn't do, and if she was completely honest with herself, she didn't give two hoots about this executioner character. She would find her man and the evidence to put him away—hopefully right alongside her sister for her sins, related or not.

Sharon let out another sigh. "Trish, dear. We need to be careful. The Executioner has accused one of my good friends of being a spy." Her eyebrows were raised as if she were challenging Trish.

"Oh the irony," Trish said with mock surprise. "One of *your* friends? A *spy*? The shock must be showing on my face, right?"

"Trish this isn't funny," Sharon said, crossing her arms.

Trish couldn't resist the chuckle that escaped her lips. "Sharon, dear, aren't *all* your friends spies? You know, the *agency* and all?"

Sharon didn't find her friend's antics funny at all it seemed. She scowled at Trish and pushed away from the table. She moved back to the counter and refilled her mug.

A little taken aback, Trish stood as well and grabbed her own mug. "Ok, I'll bite. What am I missing?" she asked, pouring the steaming dark liquid into her cup.

For what felt like the millionth time since she had arrived, Sharon sighed. "He has accused a colleague of working both sides, a double agent if you will. No evidence was ever provided that would confirm his accusations and given this is a very close friend of mine, I didn't believe it. I still don't. It is the only thing this man has ever presented that wasn't proven correct."

Trish noticed Sharon was really affected by this accusation. She had never seen her friend so quiet and upset. She moved closer and stood next to Sharon at the counter.

"Maybe this guy isn't as good as he thinks?" Trish suggested.

Sharon looked up and gave her a small smile. "What worries me more is that he has never been wrong before."

Trish nodded. Now she understood. Sharon was worried the double crosser was so good that even this executioner person couldn't find enough evidence to prove him guilty. That would drive Trish crazy too.

"Ok, so how about this? We find the guys we are looking for, while keeping an eye out for this executioner you idolize. I must admit though, idolizing a being that is essentially invisible, or even a made up one, is dangerous, Sharon dear." Trish gave her friend a smirk and bumped her shoulder.

Sharon swatted Trish's shoulder in return. "The Executioner is real, Trish. He is also deadly. A few of the bad guys we have been able to apprehend were handed over pretty badly beaten. He doesn't go to the level of brutal torture that I have seen but he isn't exactly a hands-off kind of interrogator."

Trish shrugged. "Don't really care. As long as we get our guys, it doesn't matter much to me." She moved back to her seat in front of her computer.

"Well, it does matter to me. We don't want to get in his way either. But if you find out anything about him in your searches, please let me know." Sharon finished pouring her mug full and then turned to return to the table across from her friend.

"Maybe if you send me a photo of the mystery man, I can keep an eye out," Trish suggested.

Sharon looked up. "Well, now that would be the million-dollar photo, wouldn't it?"

Trish looked up from her screen. "What are you babbling about? Just pull up a picture and forward it to me." She shook her head at her friend and started working on her keyboard again.

Another sigh came from across the table. "Trish, no one has seen him before. He calls in a nine-one-one tip that someone needed to be apprehended and then leaves the evidence in the location of the suspect."

"Seriously?" Trish asked, her fingers paused in midair. "How do you know it is the same person then?" She leaned back and looked at Sharon with curiosity.

Sharon shrugged. "He leaves a signature of sorts. There is always a folder he leaves with a mark on it. The symbol is an old African one called a sepow. It is the symbol of justice, shaped like an executioner's knife. It really looks like a gnome to me, a triangle with a circle underneath. He is always long gone by the time we get there. We have even tried to have dogs follow his scent, but it never leads us anywhere. He is truly a spirit in the wind."

Trish chuckled at the faraway look in her friend's eye again. "Should I let Gary know you have a secret crush, Sharon?"

"Oh, posh," Sharon said with a wave of her hand. "Let's get to work. Have you found anything so far?"

With another laugh, Trish started tapping away at her keyboard again. "Not yet. Do we have dates of when these losers were in town?"

"Unfortunately, no," Sharon said with a groan. "All we have is the 'last few months' which doesn't give us a lot of specifics or places to start."

Trish's eyes shot to Sharon's. "That's fantastic. So essentially work from today backwards. Terrific." She held in her frustration at the task at hand, but the sarcasm wasn't missed on her friend. This was going to be a lot more work than she had initially thought. She brushed aside the irritation at this executioner situation Sharon was worried about and focused on the task at hand. She didn't really feel like it affected her at all anyway.

Not too much later, Trish's annoying phone alert sounded. *Another text message*, she thought. She wondered when he would give up. It's been way too long for him to still be hanging on to her. Especially after everything else. He should be off doing whatever with Patsy, not bothering her. Maybe she dumped him too after it wasn't any fun to flaunt him in front of her sister, Trish thought. A snort escaped her, and she covered her mouth when she realized it was out loud.

She looked up to see Sharon watching her carefully, a question in her eyes.

Trish shook her head. "Nothing to worry about, Sharon." She looked back at her screen and scowled. She wished Clayton would just leave her alone. It was getting old. But somewhere in her annoyance a curiosity started to creep in. Why was he trying to talk to her the last few days? He had been quiet for a long time, maybe close to six months.

"What are you avoiding, Trish?" Sharon asked, still looking at Trish.

Trish looked up and waved her hand. "You just worry about this case, Sharon, dear," she said with mock sweetness. "This isn't anything. Just an annoying bug flitting around my head that I can't get rid of." She lifted and dropped her phone to emphasize the source of her irritation. "Obviously I need a stronger fly swatter," she muttered to herself.

Sharon hummed and then sighed, something that she had been doing way too much for Trish's liking. She looked up at her friend and folded her hands in front of her lips.

"Is everything ok with you, Sharon?" Trish asked. Sharon wasn't normally upset or down. But today she seemed off. It had to be something more than just this mysterious person appearing, but Trish couldn't figure it out.

Sharon sat up straighter and shook her head, as if clearing her thoughts. "I'm fine. Just trying to find directions. I am a little worried that the Executioner will take over our search and we won't be able to get other things answered." She gave Trish a pointed look, almost startling her.

"What are you talking about? What kinds of questions?" Trish was intrigued. But at the same time, she was a little worried that Sharon knew more than she let on about Trish's situation. There were things she kept to herself for good reason.

"I think you know what I am talking about. I hope we can finally get some answers for you as well, dear friend," Sharon said quietly.

Trish narrowed her eyes. "What are you talking about exactly?" She hadn't told Sharon about everything involving her sister and her ex-husband. There were things that didn't need to be out in the open. Maybe it was shame or embarrassment, but either way it wasn't necessary to divulge those details. All Sharon knew was that her daughter was killed and she and her husband divorced not long after. And she preferred to keep it that way.

Sharon folded her hands on the table and Trish caught the slightest curve of her lips.

"Oh, I know you aren't smirking at me, woman," Trish said with annoyance. "What in the world are you hiding?"

She pushed herself back and mimicked Sharon's stance.

They held each other's eyes in a sort of standoff and finally Sharon caved first.

"Look, I know you don't want to talk about what happened, but you are going to have to at some point, Trish," Sharon said gently.

Trish shook her head defiantly. "Nope. I don't have to share anything. And you need to keep your alphabet soup agency history out of my life. This doesn't concern you and there's nothing you or anyone else can do to change what happened. It is what it is, it happened, and I have moved on. End of story."

"Answer your texts, Trish," Sharon said, nodding her head toward the table where Trish's flipped over phone sat. "Who knows, you might be surprised."

Trish let out a huff of irritation and pushed the phone further to the center of the table. "Not a chance," she grumbled.

As if to further aggravate her, the wretched thing let out another piercing scream.

Sharon covered her ears. "That thing is awful. You should change it or silence it!"

Trish just laughed. It always got the desired effect. She picked up the dreadful device and turned it over. The black screen seemed to be taunting her as much as the terrible tone she programmed for it. For a few moments she just stared at the screen, arguing with herself. She knew if she read his text she would do one of two things—send a snarky reply or toss her phone.

Giving in, and wanting to shut her friend up, Trish woke up her screen. If she was honest with herself, she really just wanted to smack Sharon. She didn't understand and would prefer she just stayed out of it.

Trish punched in her passcode and raised her eyes only to glare at Sharon, who had the nerve to smirk back. Rolling her eyes, she opened her texts. She wasn't gentle about it as she continued to her new texts. Finding the only two conversations she had, she pressed on the one from Clayton, only to be surprised to see four unread texts. She had only heard two of the alerts.

"I need to see you."

"Please, Trish, we need to talk."

"I have something really important to talk to you about."

"Please don't continue to ignore me. I need you right now."

Trish snorted. "Yeah, you need me like I need another shotgun. One does the trick just fine," she mumbled as she angrily tapped out a simple message back. "Nope," she said out loud, popping the "p" to make her point. Satisfied, she put her phone down and returned Sharon's smirk. "Happy?"

Another text came through almost immediately, bringing her attention back to her phone. Trish scowled at it as she read the new message out loud as she raised her eyebrows. "Sweetheart, you are in danger. Please meet with me."

Chapter 9

The hot steam from the coffee kissed Trish's face as she leaned over her mug. Her thoughts were scrambled. She hadn't been near Clayton in years, not face to face anyway. She avoided it for so many reasons, but the biggest and possibly craziest is because she knew she still loved the man. Despite his betrayal and the worst possible person to betray her with, she knew deep down she still loved him. Facing him would bring all that back and she wasn't sure she would be able to ignore it.

She never told Sharon about any of these feelings or about how she discovered their betrayal. There wasn't any chance of a misunderstanding and she knew that. But her heart refused to believe it and continued to hold that little flicker of hope alive, much to Trish's irritation. She wasn't a sentimental person; she wouldn't pine for someone who couldn't be faithful. She definitely wouldn't go back to someone who ultimately caused the death of her little girl. There wasn't any room in her life for that.

Trish lifted the cup to her mouth and took a small sip. The liquid was already cooling, and she scrunched her nose up. If it wasn't steaming hot, it wasn't worth drinking. She pushed it to the middle of the table and closed her eyes. *I can do this. He's just someone I used to know*, she thought. Maybe if she thought of Clayton as an old high school friend that she hadn't talked to in decades then she could get through this.

Her thoughts involuntarily drifted to that night. She had worked a little later than expected trying to get a problem fixed with one of the employees' computers. It was an annoying part of her job, but she wouldn't leave until it was done. When she had finally figured it out and returned it to the IT department ready to be used, she headed home quickly. She hated being late and missing dinner with her little family.

That night was one of the latest nights she had worked in a long time. The problems with the computers had been increasing lately and no one could figure out why. One of her responsibilities was to look for possible solutions and routinely perform upgrades to make sure things ran smoothly. This had been making her workdays longer and time at home shorter.

She knew she had missed dinner but hoped she hadn't missed bedtime for Anyah. It was her favorite time of the day. She would cuddle her little girl, and they would read until Anyah fell asleep. Trish loved to sit there and just watch her sleep. Her little miracle Clayton used to say. Their angel on earth.

She had parked on the driveway and as soon as she opened the front door knew something was up. She could hear voices coming from the kitchen and slowed her pace to see who he was talking to. She then heard her sister's voice, whiny and pleading like it usually was when she wanted something she wasn't getting. Trish rolled her eyes but kept quiet. She moved slowly toward the kitchen entry. She wasn't one to eavesdrop, but she couldn't ignore the feeling in her heart. Something was off.

Lately Patsy had been trying to get closer to Clayton and although it annoyed Trish, her husband seemed to shut her down every time. Maybe that was why she took her time to be quiet and listen that night. Typically, she didn't pay her sister much attention. But that night was different for some reason she didn't know at the time.

"Trisha, baby, no one is coming between us. I love you and only you," he would say. "It took me long enough to find you and there is no way I am letting anything, or anyone, get between us."

She never minded the nickname, and she had to admit it was better than "Trishy" or something annoyingly cutesy like that. Her name actually was a derivative of Patricia, same as her sister's. Trish's mom's grandmother was named Patricia and died when her mom was young. She wanted both girls to carry her own mom's name within theirs as some kind of homage to her. Trish always thought it was a little odd, but it wasn't her choice what her name was anyway. At least they weren't both named Patricia and just had different nicknames.

He would hold her close, sometimes a little too tightly, and insist no one could get between them if he held her as tight as he could.

Trish would laugh at him and give him a smack on his shoulder. It had become so routine that she came to expect it every time she brought up any insecurity. But she never questioned it. Even standing in front of the kitchen entry, hidden behind a wall, she knew what he would do. She leaned against it and crossed her arms waiting for the words he always used with Patsy.

But she never expected the next words that she heard to come from him. It was the beginning of the end of her blind trust. A tiny pin pricked the wall she had built around them. A tiny hole that was virtually invisible but big enough for doubt to drip through, slowly making the hole bigger and bigger until it gave way to cracks, and then ultimately a flood of doubt and suspicion flowed through without anything standing in its way.

"Patsy honey, you are out of line," he said quietly. "This is my home. You cannot come in here talking like this."

A sigh escaped her sister's mouth. "But Clayton, you and I are supposed to be together. This little fake family with Trish is just an illusion. And you know it."

Trish could imagine her sister's hands on her husband's chest as she gave him that annoying child-like pout. It annoyed Trish that her sister thought it would work.

But Clayton's voice lowered and softened as she listened.

"Patsy dear, this is inappropriate, and you know it. Now Trish will be home soon, so you need to leave," he said with a softness Trish hadn't heard from him before, at least not directed toward her sister.

"I don't have to leave. I have just as much right to be here as you do. This is Trish's house not yours," she said indignantly. "And besides, my sister is stupid and will never suspect anything. We're all family anyway."

Trish heard the chair scrape against the vinyl floor as her sister sat down in it.

"Patsy, listen to me. There is nothing between us. And even if there was, I will never leave my baby girl. So you can give up on that thought forever." His voice was firm this time and it sounded like he was on the opposite side of the kitchen, away from Patsy.

Her sister pushed the chair back angrily and it hit the wall, making Trish jump in her hiding place.

"How can you choose anyone over me?" she screamed. "I'm so much better for you."

Something else hit the wall and Trish jumped again. She couldn't process what she was hearing. Was Clayton only staying with her because of Anyah? Was she wrong all this time and Clayton actually did have something with her sister?

Deciding she had heard enough, she went back to the door and slammed it shut, essentially announcing her arrival. She removed her shoes and made her way into the now silent kitchen. Patsy looked at her with a smugness Trish wanted to slap off her face. Clayton smiled, like he normally did, and Trish just pushed by him and opened the fridge.

Something wasn't right and she could feel the tension. She grabbed a drink from the fridge and then moved back to the living room to watch TV. She wanted to be alone, to process everything she heard, but she didn't want to leave them alone either. She had to figure out what she was going to do next. Did she confront him again with her doubts? She was irritated that she allowed the doubts to come in again.

Should she pretend like nothing was wrong and just keep moving forward for Anyah? But she wasn't sure she could do that. She was never very good at hiding her feelings, especially from her husband. *For better or worse my ass*, she thought with a sneer.

Clayton had appeared in the doorway, and she could feel his eyes on her. Eventually he moved to sit next to her, and she felt his hand on her thigh.

"Sweetheart, is everything ok? I can warm up some dinner for you. Anyah and I had some chicken and sweet potatoes. There's plenty left," he said quietly. His gentle tone almost made her angrier. It was the same one she heard him use on her sister not too long ago.

Trish simply shook her head and flipped off the TV. "I think I'll just go to bed. It's been a long day." She pushed off the couch and Clayton grabbed her hand.

"Trish, what's going on?" his eyes were full of worry as she studied them.

Those were the eyes that she fell in love with, so concerned about her. The eyes that could tell when she had a bad day or when things with her family were too hard. The eyes that made her believe that she was the only one he held there. Now she couldn't be sure. She didn't know what to believe or what to ask him. She just knew something wasn't right.

But there wasn't time for her to process any of those thoughts. The seeds of doubt that were planted bloomed in full when three days later Anyah was gone. Trish knew beyond any doubt that this was Clayton's out. Although she hadn't believed he had anything to do with her death, she couldn't be sure. But she was convinced her sister had orchestrated it to get Clayton to her side. Ultimately it didn't matter to Trish. The outcome was the same. Now he could choose her sister and move forward with the life he wanted without a wife and kid he had outgrown or whatever. What she thought was her perfect life had shattered right before her eyes.

A bell broke her from her memories, and she looked up to see someone enter the small café. She let out a breath of relief when it wasn't Clayton. But as she turned back to stare at her mug again, she realized it was not steaming at all anymore, which meant it would be cold and disgusting to drink.

"I can't do this," she mumbled. Trish grabbed her drink, her bag, and stood to move toward the door. She dumped the contents of her cup into the bin on a cart and set the now empty mug down next to it. The door opened just as her hand reached the handle, and she looked up to meet Clayton's eyes.

"Trish—" he started, reaching for her.

Trish stepped aside and put her hand up. "I can't do this." She moved quickly past him and made her way to her car.

"Trisha stop, please," his voice pleaded, just as she opened her car door. She paused and it was just long enough for him to catch up to her. "Please, just give me a minute. I promise, I won't push. I just need to see you. Even if it's just for a moment."

His voice dropped lower and lower the more he talked. Trish was struck by the emotion in his voice, and she wondered if maybe he cared so much for her sister that he could hardly keep it together. She couldn't help the scorn she felt in her heart. Of course he missed her. Patsy likely ghosted him after everything just like she did her own family. She's toxic, which is why Trish cut ties with her sister so long ago.

Maybe that's why he was trying to get back in touch with Trish. He realized she dropped him as soon as he was available and he wanted to get back with Trish. Unfortunately for him, she was no one's second choice or last resort. She had more self-respect than that.

She turned to face him, hardening her heart again. Crossing her arms over her chest, Trish leaned back against her car. "Clayton, I am not helping you find my idiotic sister. She's your problem, not mine. Leave me alone and stop texting me. I am done. I am done with all of this." She waved her hand around for emphasis and then reached for her door again.

Clayton grabbed her hand. "When will you get it through that stubborn head of yours that I have never had anything for or with your sister. Trish, I love you. Only you. You are the only one I will ever love. Please, can we talk?"

Trish snorted. "Right. No, Clayton. I am not falling for your sweet words anymore. Leave me alone."

She opened her door and slid inside, slamming it hard behind her. She started the vehicle, staring at her ex-husband. She would not let him get to her. She wouldn't be made a fool of. She backed out of her spot and out of the parking lot, leaving Clayton standing alone and staring after her. She couldn't find it in herself to even feel bad. It wasn't her fault he was late. If he had come earlier, she might actually have listened to him. But she was left with her memories and pain and couldn't take it anymore. And the best part was, she didn't have to either. She didn't owe him or anyone else anything.

The drive back to her house was silent. Trish didn't even turn the radio on. She was lost in her thoughts and didn't even register the drive. She moved from her garage and into her house still in a daze. As she closed the door and relocked it, she leaned against it and sighed. She was annoyed that he still affected her. She was annoyed that she still felt a little bad about not listening to him. But she had to protect herself from more lies and whatever else he was going to try.

Trish was particularly sensitive to manipulation, having lived with her sister's issues and lies for so long. She wasn't going to let Clayton play her either. He obviously wanted something from her. Patsy used to do the same thing. "Oh, I love you, you're my only sister, please listen to me. Please help me. Blah blah blah." Always the same thing, pulling at her heartstrings.

"Not anymore," she said out loud. Trish slipped off her shoes and moved to her desk. She was going to put this all out of her mind for now and see what she could find for her friend. She opened up her laptop and then turned on all her screens. As was her usual protocol, she fired up her cameras to make sure everything was working properly. The camera views all looked correct, so she moved to her research.

Trish sat back in her chair and interlaced her fingers behind her head. The last group of CCTV cameras she looked at was set for the dates of the last few days. Sharon had mentioned this could go back a few weeks. So, she pulled up her search criteria and typed in the dates for five weeks back. This would take some time for the data to be pulled and sent to her, so she moved into her kitchen to make some hot coffee. She was still a little annoyed that the coffee she paid for had cooled so quickly, at least it seemed like it was fast. She honestly wasn't sure how long she had sat there.

She stared out her window as she waited. The comforting smell quickly filled the small room, and she smiled involuntarily. The tree outside swayed in the breeze, making the bottles clang together lightly. The sound made her sigh, and she turned and watched them silently. *Anyah would have loved those stupid things*, she thought.

A shadow crossed her peripheral, and she turned to see what it was. At the same time, an alert sounded on her computer, and she raced back to look at her cameras. The screen showed movement past her kitchen window, but the figure was covered by a dark hoodie or something. This wasn't a blur, but a clear figure.

Trish knew this meant it was someone other than the weird thing that she and Sharon had isolated on her camera feed. Now she had to track two different idiots on her property as well as try to find these two guys Sharon is looking for. At least it was work she enjoyed, she thought.

"Who is messing with me?" she asked angerly. She typed a few things on her keyboard and watched the person move around her property as different camera views picked them up. She tried to gather as much as she could from the form, but it was difficult since the person wore all black. There wasn't any definition, just baggy black sweatpants and a sweatshirt. The hood remained in place, covering the person's face. They may have actually been wearing a full-face mask as well.

She continued to watch as they eventually moved into the last few rows of corn, which surprisingly hadn't all been cut down yet. *Odd*, she thought, but pushed it aside.

Trish sat in front of the screens waiting for the person to reappear, but they didn't. The alarm on her coffee maker sounded and she quickly moved to grab a cup and then get back so she wouldn't miss if they came back into her yard. She was confused by the situation. The person didn't look like they were even looking at the house and seemed to be on some sort of mission, which appeared to be getting off her property, rather than looking for a way inside.

It was weird because she didn't live in a community, but in an isolated area where houses were spread apart and cutting through her yard wasn't like a short cut to a neighbor's house. She stared at the screen in confusion for a long time. The person never reemerged. Trish sat back in her chair and shook her head. Maybe she was imagining things. She refused to believe it was a ghost of some sort.

The mysterious character Sharon mentioned came to mind as she stared at her unmoving screen. Sharon's Executioner seemed to be a ghost of some kind since no one had ever seen or could identify him. Could this person be a concrete sort of ghost and not some supernatural specter? Trish chuckled at herself. "Absurd," she mumbled.

Glancing at the clock, she realized she had spent a lot longer than she thought staring at the screens. With a sigh, she decided to grab a snack and go back to what she was supposed to be doing. She looked outside as she moved back into her kitchen. It was already close to dusk, and she shook her head. The last few days have seemed like a waste. She was frustrated with herself for not getting more done. She needed to focus and get somewhere on this latest situation and hopefully find a new connection to her sister so she could put this thing to rest. Trish needed to finally feel like her baby girl could rest in peace, even if it was as much for herself as anything or anyone else.

She found herself standing in front of her kitchen window again. This time she looked closely out her window to see if she spotted anything. She kept an ear out for the system to alert her again. But given the last few days, she wasn't holding her breath for that to catch anything. Even with the upgrades from Sharon, she wasn't completely confident.

Trish cut up some cheese and grabbed a roll of crackers. She wasn't particularly hungry, but knew she needed to eat something. She planned on working for a while, so she wanted to be able to distract her stomach enough to keep working. Sharon would scold her for not eating right, but she didn't really care. She had plenty of important things to worry about and food was not one of them.

As if it were a déjà vu moment, her eyes were drawn to the window at the same time her alert sounded from the other room. Trish furrowed her brow as she tried to see anything. *Maybe it was in the front*, she thought and moved toward her doorway. Before she got far though, another alert sounded, and she quickened her steps. Grateful her house wasn't huge, she was quickly back in front of her screens, and she watched as two figures crossed her yard, each in a different direction.

"What in heaven's name is this insanity?" she muttered. Trish's eyes scanned the three screens and almost as fast as they were seen, the figures disappeared. It was like a taunting dance. And Trish wasn't amused or entertained in the least.

She contemplated what she should do--if anything. All of a sudden, her yard seemed to be a popular party destination for the spirits and again, she wasn't amused. Her thoughts drifted to her defenses. She had a gun within reach almost all the time, but she realized she wasn't sure where they were at the moment. If she needed one in a hurry, she might be at a huge disadvantage.

Trish straightened and looked around. Her shotgun was usually her go to favorite at home and she looked in the corner to see it standing tall and proud, just as she had left it. She took great care to make sure that if anyone were to be stupid enough to look through the windows into her home, they would never see her baby. She was suddenly glad she thought of this with the current idiots wandering around her property.

Once the figures disappeared from her view, Trish moved quickly and grabbed her gun, sliding it under her desk so it was easy to grab. Then she picked up her phone and sent Sharon a quick text. Setting her phone back down, she scratched her forehead.

"What are they looking for?" she asked her empty house. She didn't have valuables, and her house wasn't exactly the picture of luxury. Those things told her these people were clearly here for her.

With the sun setting, Trish moved quickly around her home, closing any shades that were open then turned on the single lamp on her desk. She knew she had locked her door when she came in the back, but she needed to make sure the front was still secure. She knew that was only a minor delay for anyone who wanted to get inside, but it was a delay that she needed if she wasn't holding either of her guns.

Settling back in front of her computer, her phone let out an alert. She figured it was Sharon and picked it up, preparing to tell her friend she didn't need to rush over. But instead, Trish read a strange message from an unknown number.

"You can try but you won't be able to hide," she read out loud.

Trish snorted. "Yeah, like that's gonna scare me, you fool," she muttered to the screen. Knowing any response she made could be traced, she just shut down her phone again and looked back at her screens. She turned one to look at her search results, while the other two stayed focused on her security cameras. "Gonna have to work harder than that, Patsy, dear, and whoever is working with you to get me off this case," she mumbled as she adjusted the visuals in front of her.

The search she was waiting for started to pop up and she nodded as more and more footage loaded into the results file she created for this case. Trish had aptly named it "Operation Sisterly Love" knowing this would be her final interaction with her sister. If Patsy didn't end up dead in the crossfire after this, she might consider doing it herself. Then and only then would she be able to rest peacefully. Anyah deserved that.

Trish felt her favorite piece of defense at her feet and smiled darkly. "Come get me if you dare."

Chapter 10

Sleep was difficult to come by for the next few nights as Trish tried to stay ahead of the strange activity on her property. The two figures never got close enough to the house for her to feel threatened, but she didn't like that anyone was even within eyesight of her. At least she was able to catch them on her cameras multiple times.

Sitting at her computer, Trish bit her lip. She was trying to decide if she should be proactive and do something to either scare them off or force an encounter but didn't know if it was the smart thing to do. Waiting and watching seemed like a smarter option even though it was driving her crazy. She didn't like things out of her control.

Her phone lovingly alerted her to a call from Sharon, making her grin. Oh how she loved that ring tone for her friend.

"Good morning, friend," Trish sang into the phone.

Sharon snorted on the other end. "Why do I get the feeling you are only in a good mood because of your awful ringtone?"

Trish could imagine the head shake and "tsk tsk" look on her friend's face, making it even more comical to her.

"Why fix what works?" she asked innocently.

"Yeah, whatever brings you happiness, my friend," Sharon said giving up. "I wanted to check in and see how things are there. I know you don't want me to come out, but I want to make sure you are doing ok and nothing crazy has happened."

Trish knew Sharon was suggesting Trish had done something rash, but as hard as it was to sit and do nothing, Trish had behaved.

"Nothing new here. What do you have on your case? I'm not having a ton of luck on the CCTV footage I've pulled." Trish was trying to give more attention to the case, but with people lurking around, she knew she was probably spending more time on the home front issues.

Sharon sighed. "Well, you didn't tell me how the meeting went with Clayton. What did he have to tell you?"

"Nothing to tell. I left before he got there. He was late and I was bored," Trish said, keeping her emotions in check and not giving up anything more than necessary to appease her friend.

Trish spun in her chair, turning her back to her screens. She wasn't sure what to do about these intruders. She knew what she wanted to do, but Trish was smart enough to know that Sharon could only protect her so much. It wasn't worth going to jail over. She had to stay out so she could catch her daughter's killer and then she didn't care what happened. She would gladly go to prison for the rest of her life to bring that low life to his knees. Oh, how she would love him to beg for mercy from her. That picture in her mind made her smile.

"Trish? You still there dear?" Sharon's soft voice cut into her dark thoughts.

"Yeah, just thinking about what is and what isn't worth going to prison for. These idiots roaming my property are not worth it." She snorted when she imagined the look Sharon was giving her.

"Ok, well I wanted to share some new information with you. Do you want me to come over or do you want to come here or meet?"

Trish thought for a moment before answering. She never could figure out why Sharon insisted on meeting all the time. Couldn't she just tell her over the phone?

When she didn't answer right away, Sharon added, "I need to show you, Trish."

"Ugh fine. I will come there." Trish gave in only because she, like Sharon, didn't trust everything digital. It was so easy for her to hack into systems that she knew anyone could get at their shared files if they tried hard enough. It was why Sharon still operated old school with paper files and photos.

She hung up the phone and turned back to her screens. Squinting, she thought she saw something moving near her kitchen window. Trish pressed a few buttons, and the area was enlarged to take up the entire screen. Another shadow moved across her view, cutting into the corner of her screen. Sure enough, the figure had moved closer to her house and, by the looks of it, was standing almost right outside her kitchen window.

Trish reached down and felt her trusty gun between her feet, something she hadn't let out of her sight since these idiots made her yard their playground daily, sometimes more than once a day.

"I guess play time is over, boys and girls," Trish mumbled to the screen. She grabbed her trusty Winchester and pushed away from the desk.

Pointing it away from her, she checked underneath it to see if the chamber was clear and then checked the top as well. Trish was meticulous with her guns and always made sure to empty the chamber for safety. Satisfied that there were no rounds still in it, she slid her chair to the side and pulled out a box hidden in a basket she had filled with yarn. It was a standing joke with her and Sharon. Anyone who knew Trish, knew it was the most out of place thing in her entire house.

She kept her rounds close at all times. This basket was closest to her when she was working. She also had a small bin of fabric pieces upstairs near her bed that also served as a decoy for her ammunition. Since she didn't have any kids around and lived alone, she valued ease and availability over safety of others. She never wanted to be left underprepared again.

Glancing at the screen again, Trish's hand stopped midair. A flash lit up her screen and then she heard the firing of a gun from outside.

"What the hell?" she muttered. She watched as one of the figures ran into the corn and a second one ran into her chicken house. Trish laughed. If only the idiot knew what she had in there. It's that last place anyone should go to hide from her.

She watched as a blur followed the figure into the abandoned building and shortly after, it looked like someone was being carried out of the chicken house on a shoulder and then both figures disappeared.

Trish ran to her front door and then outside to see where the figure had gone. It appeared to just go down her driveway toward the street and then turn as if to just walk down the road. But no one did that around here. The road was too narrow for walkers. She stared at the street as she made her way quickly toward it. No car even drove by, and the road was fairly straight. If she made it to the end of her driveway, she would see them.

Stepping onto the broken-up pavement, Trish looked to her left where she saw the figures going but didn't see anything or anyone. She looked right to make sure she wasn't mistaken. But there was no one on the road at all. She didn't see a vehicle or lingering sound that one had even been there. The road was about a mile long and no turns until you got to the main road. There was no way they could have gotten away that fast, she thought.

Trish picked up a chunk of pavement and threw it across the narrow street with a scream of frustration.

"Where could they have gone so fast?" she nearly yelled out to the emptiness around her. It didn't make any sense.

Standing in the middle of the road now, she put her hands on her hips and scowled. She hated being in this position where she had no power or control. Someone else was pulling the strings and it made her frustrated and angry. The years since her little girl had died, Trish focused on not being unprepared or surprised again. She made her way back to the house, kicking rocks in her path like a pouting child. She actually felt like something had been taken away from her by these people getting away. Justice maybe? Or perhaps a chance for her to get some answers or frustration out on someone else.

Maybe Sharon was right, and she did have a sadistic streak inside. With a shrug, Trish decided she wouldn't spare anyone connected to her daughter or messing with her home. It didn't matter. She would figure out who these people were and then she would deal with them. But first she needed to figure out who this ghostly figure was roaming around. She had lived here for years and hadn't ever had this kind of activity before.

Letting out a groan, Trish dropped into her chair and stared at her screens again. For the first time since the idiots got away, she realized she had left her house completely open and vulnerable. She looked around and didn't see anything out of place, but these days she couldn't be too careful or overly confident.

Trish pulled up the video feeds from the last fifteen minutes. She had two goals: first was to see if she could figure out where the people came from and second to make sure no one got close to her house.

Satisfied that no one was there, she picked up her phone and sent Sharon a text telling her she would be a little later than agreed. Turning back to her computer she tapped at the keyboard a little harder than necessary.

"Where did you come from," she mumbled as she moved from video to video trying to track them backwards. After almost an hour, she could only figure out which directions they came from, which was actually comforting. They had come from the direction of the road, not the woods behind her house, which was a good thing. That means they were likely not camping out in the back wilderness and were hopefully not great in that kind of environment. If she could get them in the woods, she would definitely have an advantage.

Trish sat back in her chair and smiled. "Now all I have to do is get ahead of you morons."

A plan started to form in her head. If she moved or added a camera facing the road, she would be alerted to someone coming from that direction. That short amount of time would be all she needed to scare them to the back and then push them into the woods where she could track them easily with her superb hunting skills.

Satisfied with her plan, Trish set out trying to identify which camera would be best to move. She quickly set about getting that done. Hopefully Sharon would have some new info on their missing guys so she could start to actually focus on something else for a while. The whole time she was working in the yard, she looked around to see if anyone showed up or she spotted anything out of the ordinary. She moved a potted plant, fake of course, to the opposite side of the driveway, as if she were landscaping. Then she moved a few of her statues that didn't have cameras around slightly and moved her favorite little garden gnome with what looked like a shotgun over its shoulder to the edge of the lawn, facing the driveway.

The little guy was equipped with two separate cameras, one facing the front and one in the back. His little rump stuck out and Trish couldn't resist adding a camera there. Juvenile? Maybe, but she thought it was funny anyway. The way he faced, his cameras would catch anything on the street in either direction. Trish hoped that would help catch whoever was walking or driving near her house. She wasn't particularly worried about false alarms because very few people ever appeared on her street.

She stood and stretched out her back, looking toward the field of corn. It was odd that the farmer still hadn't cut it all down. *What could he possibly be waiting for?* she wondered. As she looked closer, she saw that he had cut down all but maybe fifteen feet of corn. It felt intentional somehow because it wouldn't be more than one more pass with his equipment.

Shrugging it off, she moved back toward the house. She wasn't a farmer and wouldn't know anyway. As far as she knew he had always lived on that farm, so there must be a reason. At least he had been there since she had. Her curiosity was slightly piqued as she thought about the mystery man who lived next door.

The rest of the street, though long, didn't lead to any other houses besides Trish's and the farmer's. She had never seen any kids or a wife around. He looked like he was around her age, maybe slightly older. They exchanged a friendly wave now and then but that was it for interaction. Trish didn't like people in general since they were a threat to her solitude and privacy. She wondered for a very brief moment when that changed. She used to enjoy hanging out with people and always had a group of friends around her when she was younger. It didn't take long for her to know exactly what changed. It's funny what manipulation and betrayal does to your general outlook on people.

Satisfied with her work, Trish pulled up her security cameras on her phone to make sure her little buddy was placed correctly. She confirmed it was perfectly placed and then moved to lock up her house and head over to Sharon's. She had been so focused on her own space she had forgotten about what Sharon might have to share.

Trish focused her mind back on the case Sharon shared and what her ex-sister might have to do with it. The man didn't look familiar to Trish, but Patsy ran with so many strange people at any given time, there was no way to know them all. Plus, Trish really didn't care to know any of them.

As she unlocked the garage door, she noticed something on the ground near the door. She hadn't seen anyone near the door in her videos making her scrunch her nose. Trish bent down and picked it up. Flipping the small piece of plastic in her hand, she shook her head.

The piece looked like it broke off a toy or something. It was smooth and black. One side was shiny while the other was rougher and dull. She wasn't sure if it was anything, but she tucked it in her pocket anyway. Maybe it was just trash blown in from somewhere or maybe it was something that was dropped by one of the weirdos who kept trespassing. Sharon was a wiz at finding out about stuff that seemed miniscule or unimportant. *Another weird talent of the woman*, she thought with a chuckle.

Trish's thoughts drifted as she drove to her friend's. She seemed to have three different things going on suddenly in her life. Patsy's involvement in some case that Sharon had dragged her into, Clayton's annoying insistence that they talk again, and the trespassers who appeared to think they were sneaky.

"One thing at a time," she said out loud, watching the mostly empty fields give way to houses.

The drive wasn't more than ten minutes, but the scenery change was drastic. Sharon lived in an upper-class development in Salisbury while Trish lived in an old farmhouse in the country. Both still lived within Salisbury limits, just very different parts of town. The turn into the neighborhood where Sharon lived reminded Trish of one of those picture-perfect family streets.

Sharon's house was a large three-story home with a lush green lawn surrounding it. Most of the homes in this area were large and had lawns that were sculpted to perfection. Few fences were dividing the properties and people were always out and about either walking, talking to neighbors, or leading a dog around. A few kids rode bikes, but it was a fairly mature neighborhood and there weren't many kids.

A bit of nostalgia struck Trish as she watched a family riding bikes down the wide street. She remembered her family doing something similar when she and her sister were young. The street they lived on when she was little was much like this one. Not in economic similarity but rather population. There were families and no fences dividing folks. That changed as she grew older, and people started to fence yards and create distance from each other.

Trish's mind wandered as she watched the family in her rearview mirror. Things could have turned out so differently for her and her family if she hadn't had such a manipulative and sick sister. Her parents would have been able to stay healthy and working. She could have focused on her own college and career instead of always worrying about what drama or danger her sister would bring home. Or even what Patsy would demand when she showed up again. Maybe Patsy could have even held a job and been stable.

She shook her head to clear the "what if's." There was no reason to wonder what could have been. It won't change anything, and she needs to just move forward. Somehow.

Trish pulled up to Sharon's house and laughed at the older woman out watering her flowers. Only she and Sharon's husband knew what those flower boxes actually held. She used to make fun of Sharon just like Sharon did in return for Trish's statues. But it made her look like a normal older person out watering her plants and flowers. Trish wondered if her neighbors were ever curious about the perfectly healthy flowers Sharon had year-round. Even in the winter months, Sharon found a replacement for the brightly colored summer flowers to keep up her ruse. Her watering can was always empty, and Trish had even seen Sharon carry it if it were heavy and full of water.

She parked and stepped out of her car. She leaned against it, crossing her arms over her body and just watched Sharon methodically put her empty watering can away and move toward her.

"I can't believe you still keep up this act, Sharon," Trish said with a wide grin.

Sharon grinned back and shrugged. "I need to keep up appearances. I mean who would believe that I have tiny hidden cameras everywhere? Besides, I have to keep them clean and functioning properly, don't I?"

Trish just smiled back. "I suppose. But why flowerpots? You could hide them anywhere in this yard. It just seems like a lot of work to me," Trish said with a shrug.

"You just don't like flowers," Sharon scoffed. "Flowers, even fake ones, are pretty and cheerful. Your house is the opposite of a happy place."

Trish laughed. "Yeah, and it still doesn't keep the crazies out."

Sharon raised her eyebrows. "More spirits walking your property, dear?"

"I honestly don't know what they want. I mean we haven't even barely scratched the surface of these guys you are looking for and I haven't had any other things going on. It's weird." Trish pushed off her car and met Sharon on the sidewalk. She hadn't told her friend about the threatening text and honestly wasn't too worried about it, so she kept it to herself.

They moved into the house and Sharon went right to the fridge to grab the pitcher of sweet tea she always kept around. Coffee was Trish's go-to, but she would occasionally drink the tea to keep Sharon from acting like her mother and telling her she needs to drink something other than coffee.

"Well, we may have a new lead. Johnny apparently had a few visitors recently." Sharon set down the pitcher and glasses and pulled out a chair opposite Trish.

"Ok, so who else are we looking for?" Trish asked, eyeing the folder on the table.

Sharon sighed. "You may not like this, but it's pretty important to consider everything." She slowly flipped open the folder and pushed it toward Trish.

Looking at the photo paper clipped to the cardstock, Trish scowled. *It always seems to come back to her somehow.* She really just wanted her sister to disappear so she could leave that all in the past.

"So, she has a relationship with Johnny? As what? A girlfriend or call girl? Because I can't imagine she would be a loyal companion. It probably has as much to do with dealing his product as it does any kind of sexual thing," she mused.

Sharon cleared her throat. "We think they have a relationship, but it's complicated. What we have uncovered so far has to do with Johnny and his cousin Billy Cain. You have his photo in the other file I gave you."

Trish furrowed her brow. "I don't understand. Like a threesome type thing or the new age throuple?"

"No, not exactly. Patsy has visited Johnny in prison every Tuesday since we put him there. She never misses a day." Sharon paused and looked at her friend.

"What?" Trish asked, trying to prompt her friend. She knew there was something coming and wished her friend would stop with the theatrics and just say it. Just as she was about to say as much, Sharon continued.

"We need to know what they are talking about. So, we are going to set up the visitation room with recording equipment to try to figure out what they are saying. Tomorrow is Tuesday, Trish," Sharon said with raised eyebrows.

Trish leaned back in her chair. Different thoughts ran through her head as she stared at Sharon. What did this mean? Was Sharon asking her to go? Or something else?

When she didn't say anything, Sharon spoke again. "No, you won't be expected to go there. I just want to know if you are going to be able to monitor the recording devices for us."

Letting out a small breath, Trish nodded. "I can do that. But don't ask me to make contact with her. That I will not do under any circumstances." Her firm voice was misleading. She felt stronger on the outside than inside. Her stomach was churning as she thought about having to face her sister after so long. She meant what she said about not wanting to see her ever again, except behind bars.

Sharon lightly touched Trish's hand, drawing her eyes to her friend's sympathetic ones. "I know where you stand,

Trish. I don't necessarily agree, but I get it. For now. I'll get things set up and send you the links."

Trish nodded numbly. She wasn't sure what she thought about all this. Patsy's appearance is more than an annoyance. And now she had a contact if Clayton still continues to annoy her for information.

"Ok, so what else do you have for me?" Trish asked, trying to change the subject. "That can't be the only thing you had to have me here for."

Sharon shook her head. "Nope. I also had something sent to me about this Reece character." She pulled out a new folder and flipped it open to reveal the clean-cut young man who looked like he came out of an underwear ad. He had short, light brown hair gelled and styled perfectly. His skin had a healthy tan, maybe a mix of Hispanic heritage. His clothes looked like a prep boy kid would wear with no flaws at all in his appearance.

"Ah, my trust fund baby," Trish said with a smirk. She picked up the photo and studied it. It was similar to the one she had at home.

"He's a lesser-known associate of our friend as well. We are trying to solidify his connection. He seems to keep his hands very clean of any of the drugs somehow, but we can't figure out how." Sharon opened another folder and sighed. "It's just not adding up. How can someone be so clean but still known as an associate? We are just starting to connect the dots to who is connected to who. What we need to figure out *how* they are all connected and where they are hiding."

Trish thought for a minute. Maybe he has help on the outside? These trust fund babies have ways to keep others quiet. Money is a big motivator."

Sharon nodded. "I suppose so. But then there would be a paper trail, right? Something you could track maybe?" she asked, leaning forward.

"Possibly," Trish said slowly. "But if they have money, they have the means to hide it too. If there's any connection to law enforcement or other agencies, that will make it even harder to find."

"True, true," Sharon mused absently. "How about this? I'll give you the info I have on Reece, and you can dig wherever you need to. If we can track and connect him to Johnny, we could take another bad guy off the streets. And maybe get your sister out of another bad spot." Her words trailed off and Trish barely heard the ending.

Shaking her head, she chose to ignore her friend's words. Maybe one day she would divulge everything, but for now, Sharon could argue all she wanted that everyone deserves a second chance. Only she wasn't aware that Patsy has had more second chances than Trish was willing to admit. She wouldn't be doing anything to "clear" her sister of anything. In fact, her goal was the exact opposite. That goal would not be shared with her friend unless absolutely necessary.

Chapter 11

"Ok, Patsy what are you up to now?" Trish muttered at her screen, trying not to break the keyboard as she aggressively hacked into the monitoring devices. The room they were using was the same one the prison had been using for all of the visits up to this point.

Trish was surprised at how accommodating the prison staff had been. But she figured it had to do with Sharon's boss's clearance. She was also grateful for the consistency so neither knew nor suspected anything was different in this visit from the others. Trish chuckled darkly to herself, pleased that she would be able to catch her sister red-handed in something nefarious.

Patsy always seemed to get away with everything she did, the death of Anyah was probably the most egregious of all though. She had been able to convince their parents time and time again that she was clean or that she was working when she was actually meeting a dealer or someone willing to pay for whatever she could offer in return for drug money.

Shaking her head of all the injustices her sister had delivered to her, Trish scowled at her screen. The white-gray walls of the small room reminded her of the stereotypical interrogation rooms in her favorite "Law and Order" show. The long fluorescent light reflected on a silver loop in the center of the table innocently waited to be connected to the handcuffs on Johnny's wrists.

The door in the corner of Trish's screen brought her attention away from the table. She waited for emotion to cloud her thoughts, but none came. Should she feel bad that she no longer felt anything for the woman who now faced the table? She decided she wasn't going to dwell on it. This woman didn't deserve anything from her anymore. Patsy forfeited that right when Anyah took her last breath.

Trish watched as Patsy slowly walked around the room. Her hair was braided tightly against her scalp in cornrows, showing more grays than black in her short braids. She looked showered and clean, Trish thought, but not a drug-free kind of clean. The bags under her dark eyes were unmistakable. A clear sign to Trish that she was still actively using. Her eyelids were a little droopy and the tiredness in her body could be felt through the screen.

Patsy moved with nervous anticipation. She was wringing her hands together and then wiping the palms on her baggy jean-clad legs. She looked thin, but then again, she always had since junior year of high school when she started using heavily.

It didn't take long for the door to open again and a man clad in a dull orange jumpsuit walked in with cuffs around his wrists and ankles, a guard on each side leading him into the room. Trish watched as they clipped his wrist cuffs to the table and then both guards stepped out of the room. Trish heard the click of the lock through the feed.

It was interesting to her that they allowed these visits in private. Aside from her surveillance gear, there were no other devices in the room. It wasn't like the ones on her shows where there was a two-way mirror with a team sitting on the other side. The guards were close, likely standing right outside the door, but other than that, no other supervision was present.

"These people are idiots," she muttered out loud. She typed on her keyboard to start her recording and then looked over to make sure Sharon was also watching the interaction. Trish was surprised to see Sharon looking at her instead of the screen. She had an unreadable expression on her face. Pity maybe? She shook it off and turned back to the screen.

Patsy had settled across the table from Johnny, and they held hands. Trish narrowed her eyes, zoning in on the audio.

"Just a little bit longer, babe," Johnny said in a quiet voice.

Patsy shook her head. "I don't even know what that means anymore, Johnny. I mean this wasn't supposed to happen like this. You promised me."

Johnny sighed. "I know. I just need you to do this one last thing and then everything will be what it is supposed to be," he said with a gentleness that surprised Trish.

This guy was one of the front runners of a gang that had taken over a local chicken processing plant for years before they were finally stopped. Most of the gang were imprisoned as a result of a major operation that Sharon and Trish helped facilitate not too long ago. Johnny seemed to be one of the lead guys who called the shots, ordering many tortures and killings of people over the almost two-decade long reign they had at that location.

Through their research, many more locations were found and had been taken over by these dangerous gang members, wreaking havoc on local workers and their families. Mercy was not in their vocabulary. The authorities had so much information on the Del Rios that there was no way any of them would get out of prison any time soon.

Which led to Trish's next question—what was this guy planning with her sister?

"Does he really think he's getting out of there?" Sharon asked the question on Trish's mind.

Trish shrugged, not taking her eyes off the screen. "No clue what goes on inside that crazy head."

Their voices were quiet, as if the people in front of them could hear what they were saying. If only they could ask leading questions, but they knew there was no way Patsy would ever wear a wire for them. It wasn't in her nature to be a helper. She was a fire starter, a patroness of chaos. Trish wondered if Sharon was thinking the same thing. The difference is that Sharon would hold out hope for Patsy while Trish knew better.

"But how much longer?" Patsy whined, making Trish smirk. *That* was the girl she remembered.

Johnny patted her hands folded under his. "Not much longer. I promise. But I don't want to say too much. I just need you to finish the job Oscar couldn't, disgusting rat trash. I trust you more, baby. Billy's just as bad as the rat and deserves whatever is coming." He pounded his fist on the table, as much as he could with the restraints. The links were so short he couldn't even lean back in his chair and Trish could see the frustration in his body language.

Patsy nodded. "I got it. What about the baby, Johnny?" Her voice became quiet with her question as if she were afraid of the answer.

A snort came from the man across from her. "I don't care about the kid, Patsy. You should know that. I gotta get back and rally the troops here. Be a good girl for me, ok? I'll see you soon."

"But Billy..." Patsy said so quietly Trish almost missed it.

Johnny looked at her sharply. "Don't ever say that name to me again. Baby, I trust you."

The couple leaned in and kissed and then Johnny yelled to the guard. He slipped something into Patsy's hand before the guard opened the door. The two double-teamed him again and led him from the room. He glanced back and winked at Patsy as he was led through the door.

Trish and Sharon watched Patsy pace the room a couple of times before she was led out of the room as well. Her hand dropping to her stomach didn't miss Trish's watchful eyes and she wanted to vomit. So now Patsy is pregnant, still using drugs, and Trish's little girl didn't get a chance at life past kindergarten. *How is that fair?* she mused silently.

"Well, there is definitely a relationship there," Sharon said, breaking the silence in the room.

Trish let out a frustrated laugh, which probably sounded more like she was choking. "Yeah, sure seems that way." She needed to draw Sharon's attention away from the screen in front of them. She was not going to talk about the pregnancy that was alluded to. She needed to focus on something else before she spilled everything to Sharon.

"Ok, so what did we find out?" Trish asked, turning in her chair. "Besides the obvious that is." Trish was referring to the pregnancy, but she knew there was also a clear relationship between the two.

Sharon sighed. "I understand how hard this must be for you, Trish, dear," she said gently.

Trish waved her hand. "Honey, you have no idea. Let's move on. Any kid that comes out of her will be in serious danger of staying alive and will likely be taken at birth given the drug use she is clearly still engaged in. Moving on…" She waved her hand as if to emphasize her words.

Sharon was quiet for a moment and then clapped her hands together. "Ok. We know now that they are clearly in a relationship. So, I am not sure what that means for any of the others. We are going to have to see if we can find out anything about the others and potential meetings between them and Patsy."

"Did you see what he slipped to her on the way out?" Trish asked her friend.

Sharon shook her head. "No, I couldn't tell what it was."

Trish sighed. "Probably drugs," she muttered quietly.

"Maybe, but why would he give her drugs from inside? You would think it would be easier for her to get it out on the streets," Sharon asked, thinking the same thing Trish was.

"Unless, maybe he was using it to control her," Trish said. "I mean we all know you can get some pretty high-quality stuff in prison. If what he is giving her is higher potency than what she can get herself, it will keep her coming back for more. Plus, it will feed the addiction."

Sharon tapped her chin. "True, but that's pretty risky."

The pair was silent for a minute, processing the short interaction they watched. Suddenly they both turned at the same time and grinned.

"The guards must know something," Trish said to a nodding Sharon.

"Just what I was thinking, Trish," she confirmed. "We need to find out who else he has been dealing with in prison, and which guards he has on his side."

Trish looked back at her now blank screen. "He could be planning something big at the prison to cause a distraction and escape."

Sharon started tapping away at her computer and let out a frustrated sigh. "Johnny is supposed to be transported to a federal facility within the month. I have a feeling this is the opportunity he is waiting for."

"Ugh," Trish groaned. "I hate prison transport breakouts, especially with these kinds of scum. They do make good movies though."

Sharon turned in her chair to face Trish. "Psh. I couldn't agree more. If only they could stay in the movies. Let's get this info to Luke and see what he wants us to do from here."

Trish went back to her setup and made sure the audio and video recorded correctly while Sharon was on the phone. Then she pushed in a thumb drive and made two different copies. She had a habit of making multiple copies of whatever she recorded. One copy always went to the one who requested the service, and she always kept a copy for herself in case the original got damaged. Since she had started to work more with Sharon, she had never needed her copy, but it was always better to be safe than sorry.

"Well, that was odd," Sharon said as she stared at her phone.

Trish looked over. "What's up?"

Sharon sighed and dropped onto her chair. "Luke doesn't want me to do anything with this yet."

"Hm, that's weird. Why do you think he wants to sit on it?" Trish asked, pulling the drive out of her laptop.

"I'm not sure. It doesn't make sense. Especially if there is some sort of escape plan in the works. I would want to get ahead of it, not wait and see," Sharon said, her voice sounded distant as if she was trying to figure out what her boss was thinking.

The pair sat in thoughtful silence for a minute before Sharon's phone rang. Trish slipped into the kitchen to refill her mug and when she reentered the larger room again, she heard Sharon's frustrated voice rising as she continued her call.

"What do you mean? How is that possible?" Sharon's voice was rising as she talked, making Trish smirk at her.

She rarely got to see her friend angry or flustered. So, the opportunities she does make her smile. *She is human after all*, she thought. Trish settled at her desk in front of her screens and prepared to rewatch the video they recorded. Something wasn't sitting well about her sister, and it was bothering Trish. Her mannerisms seemed off somehow. Maybe she just hadn't seen her in so long and that's all it was, she considered.

"How can you be sure, Luke? I mean we haven't even been able to get him on any of our surveillance equipment yet," Sharon said, clearly not believing whatever Luke was telling her.

Trish tried not to listen but couldn't help it. She stared at her blank laptop screen, fingers hovering above the keyboard waiting for Sharon to do something other than sigh at her boss. Or maybe they were colleagues. Trish honestly wasn't sure.

Sharon's voice dropped to a very low volume as she muttered back to her phone. "Fine. Give me ten. I have to finish up the video we did at the prison then we'll head that way."

About a half second later, Sharon's eyes shot to Trish who had now turned to watch Sharon. "Why alone, Luke? Trish has been...ok, fine...yes, I understand...got it Luke, bye."

Trish snickered as she watched Sharon aggressively disconnect the call and drop the device.

"Your inner teenager is coming out, Sharon dear," Trish said in a mildly mocking tone, making Sharon scowl at her.

"Something is not right here Trish. Luke said Billy just showed up by the river, badly beaten, barely alive." She let out a deep sigh before continuing. "He suspects Johnny orchestrated it behind bars, with the help of your sister."

Trish furrowed her brow. "But how is that possible? I mean we just got the footage today, not even an hour ago. How could he possibly think they could work that fast?" Trish shook her head. Strategy and efficiency were not her sister's strong suits. And there wasn't even enough time for that to have happened already.

Sharon sat back down next to Trish and shook her head. "I'm not sure what he is getting at, but he thinks the prison somehow manipulated the visit and had some high-tech system setup to make the visit look live, but it was actually recorded, and we rerecorded the video."

Trish turned back to her black screen. "Is that possible?"

"I'm not sure, but I suppose. I mean we didn't set up the equipment. All we did was set up the recording," Sharon said thoughtfully.

"Ok, but who set up the equipment?" Trish asked.

Sharon was quiet for a moment and then looked at Trish. "Luke did with one of the other guys. But he said he waited outside the room while his partner went in with the warden. I wonder what happened in that room." She thoughtfully tapped her chin.

Trish nodded, but for the first time she didn't think she and Sharon were thinking the same thing. She decided to pull up the video again and see if she could find signs of re-recording. That would help them confirm if the interaction they watched was live or not.

"I am a little confused about all this," Trish started. "I mean how would they even be able to make this recorded visit thing happen? It sounds a little weird."

Sharon shook her head. "No, it's actually pretty easy. It would have required significant cooperation with the prison staff though. They had to have known and were bribed or something to keep it quiet. Someone had to just feed the recording into our camera lines so it appeared live."

"But what would be the purpose?" Trish asked. "None of this makes sense honestly. What would they gain by doing that?"

Sharon was quiet. Trish turned to face her friend with a question in her eyes. Before she could get another question out, Sharon sighed.

"I'm afraid we might have a mole in our ranks, Trish," Sharon said with resignation.

The comment surprised Trish. She thought these people had been working together for many years. How could there be a mole now? That seemed a little extreme.

"What does Luke think?" Trish asked.

Sharon shrugged. "He didn't say. But I am sure he has his questions just like I do. I better go find out what's going on and see if Billy is conscious yet. Do you want to come along?"

Trish shook her head. She hated hospitals and wasn't a huge fan of meeting new people. Plus, if Patsy is behind the beating and near killing of this man, even if he was one of the bad guys, she didn't want to get caught up in any additional drama. She swallowed her disgust for the former relative and turned back to her screen.

"No thanks. I'll see if I can get anything from this video and audio, maybe I can tell if it is actually a copy or live."

"Do you still think it might be live, Trish?" Sharon asked. She seemed genuinely curious about what her friend was thinking.

But Trish didn't have much to add yet. She wanted to check something out first. She would let Sharon do what she did best, and Trish would do what she could to help out her friend. Something didn't feel right with this situation, but she would wait for some evidence first. Sharon had enough to worry about and Trish wouldn't add to the stress until she knew for sure.

"Let me worry about that and you go do what you do, ok? Be careful Sharon. We don't know for sure what is going on here," Trish warned, and then added quietly, "Or who to trust."

It was a little comical warning her friend who was a long-time agent. Trish was sure Sharon had to deal with all kinds of issues over the course of her career. This was a fairly new experience for Trish though. One thing Trish was confident about was that she wouldn't be blinded by her sister. One way or the other, she knew she and Sharon would be able to figure this out.

"You don't need to tell me to be careful. But I know my people and I trust them completely. This has to be something within the prison system and nothing else." Sharon's conviction was strong, and Trish decided to just trust Sharon to know her people. Trish was also aware of her acute distrust of almost everyone, so her suspicions would always spiral more than Sharon's. It was pretty clear who the calm and clear-headed one was in the current situation.

"I know. I'll review this and see what I can come up with. Do we know where Patsy is right now?" Trish asked, thinking if this was her sister's doing, she could be anywhere by now.

Sharon sighed. "No one knows. She has kind of disappeared in the wind again."

"Yeah well, I'll find her. Now that I have a better picture of her current look, I will find her. There's no worry there." Trish snorted as she thought about her skills. Patsy wouldn't be able to escape her now. She resisted the evil laugh she wanted to yell from the rooftops, not that there were many tall buildings in Salisbury. She finally felt like justice was close, so close she could taste it, as the saying goes. Patsy wouldn't get away this time.

Her thoughts drifted to what that moment would feel like, watching the handcuffs slap on her sister's wrists and finally having closure from so many years of grief and pain. The effects of the ultimate betrayal could finally be put away and hopefully Trish could feel like she was living again. She wasn't sure what that would even look like right now, but she had to admit she was looking forward to finally getting this proverbial monkey off her back.

"Trish dear, you're in your head again," Sharon's voice full of humor broke into her thoughts.

"Yeah, well, when you are so close to finally finding peace, you get lost in your thoughts," Trish said simply.

Sharon just nodded sympathetically. "Ok well, I better get going. Luke is meeting me at the hospital to see what we can get from Billy, if anything." She stood and brushed her hands over her black dress pants.

Trish watched as her friend packed up her supplies. Sharon was carefully wrapping cords and gently packing up her computer bag. She was always methodical in her process, but Trish noticed her friend seemed hesitant. She sensed something was on Sharon's mind.

"Sharon, is something wrong?" Trish asked, turning again to face the older woman.

With a sigh, Sharon put down her bag and sat in the chair again. "I'm not sure Trish. Something feels off. I agree with you. But I can't put my finger on it. What do you think?"

"I honestly don't know. Let's just get more information and keep it close to us," Trish suggested. She held back from telling Sharon she thought something was up with her coworkers. Sharon was the best judge of character she knew, so she didn't need to tell her who to trust or be weary of.

Sharon just nodded. "Ok I will go while you do what you do, then we will go from there. I'll check back with you in about an hour or two."

She stood again and slung her bag over her shoulder. Just as she got to the door, she turned back to face Trish, who was still seated at her computer. "Be careful, Trish. I am not sure what your sister may be up to yet."

"I'm not worried about her, Sharon. You don't need to worry about her either," Trish said with a wave of her hand. If Sharon thought Trish would try to connect with her sister or warn her or something, she was dead wrong. The only time she wanted to see Patsy again would be with a wall of bars between them.

"Ok. I'll touch base in a little while. Let me know what you find," Sharon said and then moved quickly out the door.

Trish listened as her friend's vehicle started and then faded as she exited the driveway. She turned back to her equipment. Her face contorted into a scowl as she stared at the first image on her screen. Patsy sitting across from the notorious Johnny, holding hands with the convicted criminal.

"So fitting," she muttered at the pair. So why did she have to blow up Trish's marriage and life when she had this fine specimen in her life. Trish snorted as she thought about the words in her head. Johnny was no catch, and the sarcasm loaded in those words made her laugh. "Ok, back to work," she mumbled.

The video in front of her was paused. Trish stared at it and creased her brows. The frame was frozen but there was something off about it. Maybe it was a recording after all. She dragged the tiny dot on the bottom of the screen and clicked it at the beginning of the video. Slowly, frame by frame, Trish moved through the video, trying to find any evidence that it wasn't a live feed.

After almost thirty minutes of slowly rewatching it, she zoomed in on her sister's wrist and sighed.

Chapter 12

"So, what are you saying, Trish?" Sharon asked as she stared at the stilled photo on Trish's screen.

Trish stayed silent, knowing her friend just needed to verbally process what was in front of her. Trish wasn't even sure what the new information meant so she needed Sharon to have a clear head so they could tackle the next problem.

"So, what you are showing me is that the time on the video matches the time on Patsy's watch?" Sharon rubbed her forehead. "Then why did Luke tell me it was prerecorded? Why did he think it wasn't live?"

Trish sighed. "Well, we don't know exactly what he knows yet. He just said they picked up Billy badly beaten and they assumed it was Patsy because of the order from Johnny. Is it possible that his information was wrong?"

Sharon looked over and shrugged. "Maybe, I guess. He wasn't watching the visit like we were though. He was supposed to call me in after we were done, but he wouldn't likely know when it was over until I called. I'm so confused right now." She slumped back in her chair and stared at the screen, which was zoomed in on Patsy's watch, the time matching the timestamp on her laptop screen.

The pair was silent, each lost in their own thoughts. Trish wasn't sure if she trusted Luke like Sharon did and figured he could be dirty. But he could also have been misled. He seemed pretty sure that the video was fabricated. But it didn't take her long to figure out it was in fact live when they watched it. Which led to the next questions she had, what happened to Billy and who was responsible?

"Sharon, how did it go with Billy? Did you get anything useful while you were there?" Trish asked suddenly.

Her friend looked over and shook her head. "He's still unconscious. Took a pretty bad beating and the doctors aren't sure he'll even wake up." She let out another sigh, this one a little more frustrated than the last. "I don't know what to make of this. If Patsy was still in the visit when this happened, then who went after Billy and already knew that Johnny was going to order Patsy to do something?"

Trish knew Sharon trusted her team completely, but right now they had no other leads on who would have done this. She knew she had to ask the obvious, even if it upset the other woman.

"Sharon, who knew about the meeting? Could someone have already known about what Johnny would ask Patsy?" she asked carefully.

Of course there were other possibilities. Johnny could have given the order from within the walls of the prison, and had it carried out in case Patsy didn't or refused. It may not be anyone within Sharon's organization at all. But the questions had to start somewhere because someone was lying.

"I know what you are thinking Trish. But there is no way anyone on my team would be working on the other side. So, let's try to find out who else had known about Johnny and Patsy's visitation schedule." She paused and then looked at the screen again. "Do you think Patsy could do something like this?"

Trish shook her head. "I couldn't even begin to answer that. I guess if she were desperate enough and the drugs were the payoff, she could do anything. The drugs really did drive all of her behavior." As much as Trish hated to admit it, she did believe Patsy could do just about anything. After all, she believed her to be responsible for her own daughter's death. But could she do it with her own two hands? That she couldn't answer confidently.

Sharon clapped her hands together. "Ok, then we need to treat this like any other case we are trying to solve. Start with what we know. We now know the video is authentic and not a copy." She stopped and bit her lip before continuing. "Maybe I will ask what Luke has that made them believe it was a prerecorded video. Then we can figure out if he knew something or not. But let me be clear, I trust him with my life." Sharon shot Trish a look as if to tell her not to challenge her.

Trish just shrugged. "I'm good with that. We have just learned over the years to expect the unexpected. I want to trust who you trust but you know I am not good with blind trust. Or really any kind of trust," Trish added with a smirk.

"Oh, I know, dear, I know," Sharon said with a gentle tap on her friend's arm. "Now let's see what we can find here."

The two women got to work on the laptops in front of them. They had moved things around to have a work space side by side. A steady beeping pulled their attention from their screens, and both focused their eyes on the monitors above Trish's computer. Her screens were set up to shift from whatever she was working on to her cameras outside when they were tripped. Trish scowled at it as she watched someone walk through her yard yet again, as if they had no care in the world.

"What is this, Trish?" Sharon asked in a low tone. "I thought this ended."

"Nope," Trish said simply. "This hasn't stopped just had a few lulls in the actions now and then. This guy looks like a new one though." She tapped a few things on her keyboard and watched as the angle changed and they could see the person on two different screens, looking toward the street. Much like the others who had been trespassing through her property, this one had on dark colored clothing with a hoodie over his head. Trish knew she was making assumptions, but the build strongly suggested a man's physique. If any were females, they were oddly large women, she thought.

Sharon wrinkled her forehead. "What in the world is he looking at?" she mumbled, not tearing her eyes from the figure.

Trish snorted. "So, these idiots have come from all directions. I am not sure why he is looking toward the street, but it would seem he came from the field. I can't wait for Farmer Joe to cut that corn, which is something I never thought I'd say," she complained as she watched the figure move toward the house but focused solely on the street.

"Is that his name? I didn't know you knew him," Sharon asked, moving her attention to Trish.

Trish snorted. "I don't know his real name, he's just a 'Farmer Joe' to me," she explained with a shrug.

Sharon chuckled. "Only you, Trish dear. So, what do you think they are looking for?"

"I have no idea. It's odd. They rarely get close to the house and haven't tried to get inside," Trish said carefully. She kept the one incident that she heard her screen door slam to herself. She had no evidence to suggest there was actually anyone trying to get in or if it was the wind.

The pair watched as the person's head turned in every direction except toward the house. He managed to avoid every angle that would have given them a clear look at his face. Trish resisted a groan and was tempted to take her rifle outside and scare the intruder off. But the person stopped walking and suddenly turned toward one of the cameras.

Sharon let out a small gasp as Trish thought they would finally get a clear photo of his face. She stared at two of her views and had her fingers ready to freeze any frame she could that would give them a good photo. Her eyes squinted, willing him to turn just slightly to his left. Just as he did what she silently asked, her fingers froze.

"What the hell?" Trish muttered. She couldn't believe what she saw. Was there something wrong with her camera?

Another gasp was heard from behind her. "Impressive," Sharon whispered.

Trish turned to stare at her friend. "What? Impressive? Sharon, this is crazy." She turned back to her screens and started to press keys and shift her cameras to see if she could find something else.

Sharon slowly dropped into a chair next to Trish and when Trish looked over, Sharon had a goofy grin on her face like she was fan-girling.

"What is with you?" Trish asked, annoyed. "This is ridiculous. I can't get a clear picture. It's like his face is just a huge blind spot, blank, nothing there."

While Trish continued to press buttons on her keyboard, Sharon sat still, watching the man turn back toward the street and then disappear again into the corn field.

Trish slammed her hands on her desk in frustration.

Sharon let out a sigh. "Trish dear, there's nothing you can do with that."

"What are you talking about?" Trish demanded. She turned to face Sharon, no doubt a scowl deeply seated on her face.

"It's a new technology I've only heard about. It's like a clear mask, but it actually distorts a camera image, so it looks like the person has no face. I've never actually seen it in action before." Sharon was still staring at the screen in awe.

Trish turned back to her screen and pulled up one of her recorded videos. She pressed a few more keys and then paused the image when he had turned to look almost directly into one of her cameras.

"You mean he is wearing something that will literally remove his face from our camera? That can't be possible," she muttered as she stared at the blank face in front of her. "What kind of voodoo whack a doo is this?"

Minutes passed while both women stared at the photo in front of them. Trish didn't know what to make of this new technology she was seeing. This could be a game changer in the spy world, she thought. But even more irritating was the idiot testing it out on her property with her gear. That part was rubbing her the wrong way, and she really wanted to go after him now. She would admit that her pride may have been hurt a little bit.

"Well, let's get back to work, shall we?" Sharon said, as if nothing just happened.

Trish turned to look at her again. "Are you kidding me?"

"What?" Sharon asked. "There's nothing we can do about that. If he has that kind of tech, he is working for someone pretty high up in this business. And he wasn't even looking at the house. Is it weird, sure. But there's nothing there. Not much different than a wild animal walking through your yard."

Trish stared at Sharon. She had never heard her friend so flippant about anything before. Normally she would be all worried whenever someone walked through or even got close to Trish's home. This behavior baffled her. She watched as Sharon turned her attention to a file in front of her and grew more frustrated as she watched. Trish moved from her chair and stood. She walked toward the shade-covered window and crossed her arms, staring at her friend.

It wasn't that Trish was worried about the person outside; she wasn't at all, that was nothing new. This was about the weird behavior of her partner in crime fighting. Sharon was always the worried grandmotherly type when it came to Trish and her safety. She should have been trying to figure out how to bypass the new technology, not just giving up without a fight.

"You're really going to just dismiss this? Just like that?" Trish finally asked.

Sharon finally looked at her. She lifted her shoulder slightly. "I mean what should we do, Trish dear? That tech is top of the line even cutting edge. There isn't anything around that we can counter it with." She matched Trish's position, crossing her own arms across her body. "Luke has been trying to get his hands on that for years."

Trish just stared at her friend. This was so out of character. "So why aren't you trying to figure out how some random person got a hold of this when your guy can't even do that?"

She watched the wheels start to turn in Sharon's head. She bit her lip, like she always did when she was thinking, making Trish smile. This person she could read. But she didn't know what to do with the fangirl.

"You know that's a good question, Trish," Sharon started slowly. She looked like she was moving in slow motion as she reached for the laptop and started to tap away at it. Sharon's fingers sped up as she dug deeper into whatever it was she was looking for.

Trish felt better the longer she watched. It wasn't sitting right with her that Sharon, who had all the latest tech, didn't have access to something. Who was this person stalking around her property and what did they want? They had to be someone important if they had this kind of equipment.

Suddenly Sharon pushed back from the desk and clapped her hands. "Ok, so what I can find out from Luke is that it's not readily available yet. So, if this person has the tech, it's because it is some sort of trial thing. Which means all the bugs are probably not out of it yet. You should be able to hack into it, Trish. We just have to be creative here and if you are successful, he said it would completely negate the tech and the guy's face would almost be magnified with the reversal."

"That's an interesting detail," Trish said thoughtfully. She wondered if the information was reliable. But if it was, then hacking into this was a priority. She would be able to get to the bottom of whatever was going on around her house.

Sharon turned back to the screen in front of her and hummed to herself.

"Where do we start, Sharon?" Trish asked, anxious to get started.

"I'm not sure. I guess let's see if we can bypass it on your video." Trish noticed she didn't sound too sure of herself, which again was odd.

Trish settled next to Sharon and moved the mouse to wake up her own laptop. She looked at the faceless figure in front of her and scowled. "I am going to figure this out. I'm tired of these idiots thinking they can walk around my private property as if they had a right to be here," she grumbled.

She felt a hand on her arm, and she turned to meet Sharon's concerned eyes. "Trish, we need to be careful. We have no idea who this is or why they are here."

"Exactly why we need to figure this out as soon as possible. All this is doing is keeping us from working on your case. The sooner we figure this out the better, Sharon." She wasn't sure what her friend's issue was, but she wasn't going to worry too much about it. This was her property, and she wouldn't let anything prevent her from protecting it.

Sharon let out a sigh next to her. "I understand your concern, Trish, I really do. But this person has access to tech we don't. We have no idea where they're coming from or what their intentions are. Saying we need to be careful is an understatement."

Trish caught Sharon's eyes as her groan slipped out. She couldn't ignore her irritation.

"I'm sorry Sharon. I am not going to just sit back and ignore this. It's my property we are talking about. If someone thinks they can go sneaking around they are going to have to think again. I will not be pushed around. You know me, Sharon. You know I won't stand for it." She paused and then looked at the now black screen in front of her. "You can choose to help or not, it doesn't matter to me," she added with a shrug.

"You know I would never ask you to stand down, Trish hon," Sharon said quietly. "I am only asking for caution."

Trish was quiet as she contemplated her next steps. How was she going to get around some new and cutting-edge tech? Sure, she had amazing hacking skills, but would it be good enough for this? The only thing she could do was try. It wasn't like she had anything to lose anyway. But the questions continued to nag at her. Why were people lurking around her house and what did they want?

After a few minutes of silence, Sharon cleared her throat. "Can we look at this to see what we can find in the video?" she asked hesitantly. "I know you want to get going on this other thing too, but I need to report back to Luke about this whole other Billy and Johnny situation."

Trish was lost in her thoughts, but Sharon pulled her back to the task at hand, which she was grateful for. The other conversation would likely lead to a disagreement between her and her friend. Trish knew it was the kind of mother-daughter disagreement she didn't want to get into. As much as she hated the idea of Sharon having any "elder" control over her, she knew that Sharon was a seasoned mother and would be able to make even Trish cave if she pressed hard enough.

"Yes, ok," Trish said, sitting straighter in her seat. "So how do you want to proceed with this? It is clear from our video that with Patsy's watch and our own clock that our feed was live." She wasn't sure how to make it any clearer for her friend.

Sharon nodded. "Ok, so then what was Johnny planning if not to have Billy beaten almost to death?"

"I think we need to figure out who Oscar is, Sharon," Trish said slowly. "Johnny mentioned him as a "rat" in the video to Patsy. Do you think he is an undercover informant?"

"Hm, I hadn't thought of that angle. I figured he was arrested and then sang like a canary on the rest of the group to get leniency or immunity." Sharon sat back in her chair and stared at the still image on the screen in front of her. "I can ask Luke if he know anything about an Oscar."

Something still didn't sit well with Trish about Luke. She couldn't shake the feeling that he was hiding something from them. Well, from Sharon anyway since Trish had no contact with the man. She knew it would be hard to convince Sharon though. From what Trish understood they had been in too many to count life or death situations for Trish's gut to sway her friend.

Who am I to judge anyway? she thought.

"Before you do that, let's go over our files and see if we can get a visual on the guy. Then I can start looking around for him," Trish suggested, trying to delay Sharon reaching out to Luke.

Sharon shrugged. "Ok, let's do that first. Maybe I can do a workaround and find out if he's undercover without involving anyone else. That will actually help everyone involved if we could keep it under wraps for now."

"And I hate to point out that we don't know for sure if Billy was the target of the 'order' given to Patsy," Trish said hesitantly.

Trish could guess Sharon was complying a little to ease Trish's concerns. They had a strange way of understanding each other and many times it felt as if they could read each other's minds. It was a crazy thing they'd discovered shortly after they became friends. Maybe it was the shared intensity of their work or maybe they were just meant to connect. Their friendship was a strong one for only being a few years old. But she had felt an instant connection when they met, and their friendship felt as if it had been lifelong.

The pair spent the next few hours going through their evidence in the case against the Del Rios gang, from their grunt workers and thugs to leadership. Since they hadn't figured they would need it after the trial, Trish never sorted through it to make things easier to find.

"You have got to be kidding me," Trish groaned.

Sharon glanced up from her laptop, her eyes visible just above her reading glasses. "What's wrong?"

Trish turned her screen to face Sharon, earning a similar groan from the older woman.

"I don't understand. Everyone was photographed when they were taken in. How do we not have a picture of him?" Sharon asked.

"No clue," Trish admitted, "but if he *is* an agent, it would make sense not to have his photo in this pile of evidence wouldn't it?"

The suggestion made Sharon visibly deflate. "Then our job just got more difficult. If Oscar is an agent, we will have to do whatever we can to protect him. That means--"

"We have to find him before Patsy does," Trish finished for her.

The two women's eyes met, and they shared a sad smile. "I guess we have more to uncover than we thought," Sharon mused.

Just then, Sharon's phone rang. Trish almost laughed at how soft and quiet it was, much like her friend's personality when she wasn't in agent mode. Their personalities were so opposite it was strange they got along as well as they did.

As if reading her mind somehow, her own phone let out its telltale screech. She rolled her eyes at Sharon who was getting up from the table with her phone to her ear. The annoyed look Sharon gave her made Trish laugh out loud.

Trish flipped over her phone to look at the screen. "Of course," she mumbled. There was literally nothing the man could say that would change her mind. Why did he keep trying.

Out of curiosity, she opened her texting app. She picked up her cup and made her way into the kitchen to fill it. Trish set her mug on the counter and scowled at the empty coffee decanter. She set her phone down to make a new pot. As she dumped in more than enough grounds, she liked it strong after all, her phone reminded her to check her texts again. She filled the water and then picked up her phone again.

"Might as well see what he wants this time, since he feels it necessary to annoy me multiple times in five minutes," Trish complained to the universe. She switched on the coffee maker and then picked up her phone again.

Swiping to read the new messages, she saw three texts and the little bubbles saying he was sending another. Trish was tempted to just shut her phone off, but since Sharon was on a call, she had to wait anyway.

Trish honey we need to meet soon.

I know you don't want to see me, but I have to see you as soon as possible

Please, Trish. I think you might be in danger.

I'm sorry I was late. Please give me one more chance to talk. Patsy's back and I think she might be up to something.

The last one was what made her pause. *Trish it's about Anyah. Please*

Chapter 13

Trish stared at the steam drifting above her piping hot mug. The warmth from the cup kept her hands firmly wrapped around the porcelain. She found herself sitting in the same small café waiting for Clayton to show up again. She sat again questioning why she would do this twice in a matter of days.

"Anyah," she whispered. Her one weakness. No matter who or what happened, Anyah's name would keep Trish coming back. *Damn him,* she thought. She wanted to pound her fists and scream like a preschooler who didn't want to take a nap. How did everyone know what her single weakness was?

She didn't notice when he sat down across from her, but she jumped when she felt his coarse palms cover her hands. Instinctively, Trish pulled her hands away, nearly knocking the mug over. She looked up to see Clayton with his hands up.

"Sorry, Trish, I didn't mean to startle you," he said quietly. His voice was rough, as if he was emotional or just woke up.

Trish would believe only one of those scenarios. She leaned back in her chair and pulled the cup closer to the edge of the table and lifted it to take a long drink.

"I'm here. What do you want?" she asked coldly, not wanting to stay any longer than necessary.

Clayton sighed and hung his head. He was quiet for a few minutes before he finally spoke. If she was completely honest, she was close to leaving again. She didn't have the stomach to sit here in his presence as some sort of trick to get information out of her.

"Trish. It's good to finally see you. Thank you for coming. Again," he said slowly, his eyes never leaving hers.

She resisted a sigh. Those eyes were the ones that she fell so hard for years ago. She used to see such honesty and love in them. Now she wasn't sure what it was she saw. The look might be the same, but it was clearly misunderstood all those years ago. It wasn't love, that's for sure. But she didn't really want to think about it too much. She wasn't going to go all "teenager falling for the crush."

Get the info and get out, Trish reminded herself. She would be able to do some of her own research if Clayton had any information that she didn't—which, for the record, she highly doubted.

Trish avoided making eye contact with him. It was self-protection. She knew her body may betray her if she stayed too long in that fantasy; the one where her sister stayed gone and her little girl didn't die. The perfect family that their photos showed in the early years of Anyah's short life.

Clayton sighed across from her. "Ok, I understand. I'll get to the point. I have reason to believe that someone is after you. I am not sure what for yet, but I trust my, um, resource." He cleared his throat and looked away.

Trish narrowed her eyes. "What resource, Clay?" She tried to keep the sarcasm out of her voice, but she would be lying if it were completely true. *How dare he think he knows more about my wellbeing than me,* she sneered to herself. She crossed her arms over her chest and glared back at him.

"I…I can't tell you that. But it…is…reliable," he stammered.

Trish snorted. "Ok, so you are warning me about some phantom threat, and I am supposed to trust you, just like that?" She shook her head. "Clay dear, that time of blind trust has long passed. If you want me to believe anything you say, you better have something better than a 'reliable' source." She didn't even try to hide the scorn in her voice. Who did he think he was, telling her she was in danger when she had already been watching people crossing her property over the last few weeks. And he thinks he's got a head start on her?

Pfft, whatever, she thought.

"I know it sounds crazy, but please trust me," he begged.

Clayton leaned forward and grabbed her hand. Trish pulled it away and pushed from the table. He looked hurt as he watched her carefully. Trish thought she might have seen sadness cross his face, but she brushed it off. He had his chance, and he threw it away without even thinking twice.

"While I appreciate the very weak warning, Clay, I am fine. And I am done here." She stood and was about to leave when he used those dreaded words against her again.

"I think it's the same person who took our baby away, Trish," he said, barely above a whisper.

Trish froze. Could the people who have been crossing her property really be the ones behind Anyah's death? She shook her head. How would they have found her and how would they ever connect her place to Anyah or Patsy.

"No way," she said, straightening her back. "You will not use her against me, Clayton. Leave me alone. I am not worried about anyone or anything. I hope they are connected to Anyah, and I hope they do try to come after me. I welcome the chance to finally avenge her."

She turned and hurried out of the café to her car. She didn't turn back; she didn't want to lose her nerve. It jarred her, how much she still felt for him, even though he betrayed her in the worst possible way. Her heart betrayed her too it seemed. She would never understand the ways of the heart. But she knew her brain would win this fight. She wouldn't let him see that he was and always would be a weakness for her, just like her daughter.

As Trish turned into her driveway, she finally let her mind relax. With it came a flood of tears she swore she wouldn't ever shed again for this man. How was he still able to penetrate her walls, the massive concrete walls that kept everyone at bay? How did he do it?

She parked in the driveway by the garage and just sat there, not fighting the tears anymore. Maybe some kind of closure would come from the release, she thought, trying to convince herself that's what she was doing. This wasn't sadness or grief. It was simply a release of frustration. That's all.

Trish wiped her cheeks and took a deep breath. *No use crying over any of this*, she scolded herself. Release or not, it was weak. She couldn't afford any weakness right now. Straightening herself, she moved out of her car to put it away. She glanced around the yard and didn't notice anything amiss. She would look at everything again once she went inside.

By the time she was firing up her system, her thoughts had drifted to what Clayton had said. Is it possible that the people lurking around had something to do with her daughter's death? And if so, what did that mean for Patsy's remarkable timing as well? She suddenly wondered if everything going on in her life was somehow connected.

The Jaws' theme song interrupted her thoughts, and she looked over to see Sharon calling. She didn't waste any time calling to see how the meeting went, did she? *That woman's annoying romantic soul*, Trish thought with irritation. She almost declined the call, but she knew that would lead to even more annoyance from Sharon. Best to just answer and get it over with.

"Yes, Sharon," she said after pressing the green answer button. Before she could get another word in, Sharon interrupted.

"Trish, we have a new problem. I need to come over again. I'll be there in about ten minutes." The line cut out immediately after Sharon's words, leaving Trish staring at her phone.

"What has gotten into her?" she asked the black screen.

Shrugging it off, she turned back to her screens. She had a little bit of time before Sharon got there to review anything from the last few hours. Everything looked like it was in its place outside, so she wasn't too worried. Trish did grab her trusty shotgun on her way to her desk, and she felt it with her foot as she sorted through the footage. She had decided that it wasn't worth the risk being unprepared and until she knew what these hoodlums were doing, she would protect herself and her property. She had trained to be a dead-on shot with either of her toys and as long as she could use the self-protection law, she was covered.

The review of her videos left her feeling somewhat satisfied. Nothing new was on the feeds and she settled in to start looking for the faces of Sharon's case. She decided to try a new tactic. If she could find Billy in the footage, she could possibly retrace his steps. Maybe she could catch a break and see who beat him or who dumped him by the river. That would give her a new focus and hopefully make some progress on this mystery.

By the time Sharon arrived and let herself into the house, Trish had spread out all the files and papers from various folders on the desk. There wasn't much space left.

"What are you up to Trish, dear?" Sharon asked as she looked over Trish's shoulder.

Trish glanced up and then looked back at her computer. "I was looking for a track of Billy's movements over the past few weeks. He has been out and about quite a bit." She turned, pressed a few buttons, and a timeline lit up showing multiple dates.

Sharon pulled a chair over and read the screen. "Ok, so he's been busy and very visible."

"Yes, he has. He was definitely not hiding out somewhere. I wonder if Johnny knew this. I am also curious if someone else ordered the hit on him before Johnny could." Trish pushed back in her chair and spun slightly to face Sharon.

"But who?" Sharon asked.

Trish bit her cheek. She really wanted her sister to be good for this, as bad as she knew it sounded. But if someone other than Trish was after Patsy then it would be that much easier to put her away. Trish wouldn't have those lingering guilty feelings whether she was doing the right thing or not. She knew her sister had to be held accountable for her part in Anyah's death, but she didn't know if it would be enough to keep her in prison very long.

Did that make her a terrible person? Maybe, she admitted. But she wouldn't let her get off just because she shared blood.

"I can backtrack and see if I can find anything interesting or anyone paying attention to Billy as he wandered around," Trish suggested. "That might give us a starting point."

Sharon nodded. "Maybe we can see the same face in the different places Billy went and go from there. Good idea, Trish. First though I have to let you know what Luke told me."

Trish looked up and turned slightly. "You did say we have a new problem on the phone. What's going on?"

"Billy regained consciousness, but doesn't remember anything," Sharon said with a sigh.

Trish nodded. "Ok, but that could be normal getting beat like he did. Do the doctors think he'll remember in time?" It might be a long shot, but having a witness would help everyone's case—especially Trish if Patsy was involved.

Sharon shrugged. "They don't know at this point. But he lost consciousness again shortly after we started asking questions. Point is we may not be able to get anything from him even if he does wake up again."

"Ok, so we go back to the videos and see if we can find anything," Trish said. She didn't like dwelling on things she couldn't control. The surveillance videos were something she could do so her focus had to be there.

She pulled up her folder with Billy's videos. There were a lot of him, which was interesting because the other two guys they were looking for seemed to be ghosts.

Suddenly Trish stopped on one of the videos. "Sharon, is this..."

Sharon looked over and Trish watched as recognition crossed her friend's face. "What is Luke doing with Billy?"

"Maybe they are working together?" Trish suggested. "Maybe Johnny was right, and Billy's an informant for the police. Or could Luke be on the wrong side of this?" Trish asked her question gently, knowing that her friend trusted this man completely.

"No way," Sharon said sternly. "But I need to talk to Luke and find out what he knows. Because he is clearly withholding information."

She picked up her phone and Trish put her hand on Sharon's arm.

"Wait," Trish started. "If he thinks you suspect him of anything, he won't tell you. And it could put you in danger, Sharon. Let's see what we can find out for ourselves first, ok?"

Sharon paused and looked at Trish. "I guess you are right. I just can't imagine being wrong about Luke."

The pair was quiet for a few minutes then Trish turned back to her laptop. "I wonder if there are other connections with Billy," she muttered more to herself than anyone.

"Have you been able to find anything on the other two? Reece or Simon?" Sharon asked suddenly.

Trish shook her head. "Nope. It's strange. I can't find anything on either of them, but there is so much on Billy. Don't you find that odd, Sharon?"

Sharon had a thoughtful look on her face as she nodded. "I think I am going to go back over my notes on the case with the Rios and see what evidence we have on their involvement. Maybe that will help us track them."

"That makes sense. I can't find either of the other two anywhere. But maybe we aren't looking in the right place," Trish said. "You know, Reece looks like a rich kid. Do we know where he is from? Not too many trust fund babies down here on the shore."

"Hm. Good point. Let me see if I can get a 'last known' address for Reece. Maybe that will give us a better location idea," Sharon said as she typed at her keyboard.

Trish watched over her friend's shoulder and when the screen popped up with a photo and address, Sharon sat back with a satisfied look on her face.

Crossing her arms, she grinned. "Got it."

"Perfect." Trish typed a few things on her own keyboard and turned with a grin in less time than it took Sharon to find an address.

Sharon chuckled. "We are a good team, huh?"

"OK, now to hack into some CCTV footage…" Trish said, typing away. "And…got it."

A large white manor appeared on the screen. It had a wrap-around porch covering the entire front elevation. There were two turrets on each end and a series of windows that showed off a third floor. The lawn was meticulously cared for with the brightest green Trish had ever seen. It was perfectly landscaped with just enough color spread out in front of the house. It looked like an old manor from "Gone with the Wind." The windows were massive and were likely floor to ceiling inside. *Yep, trust fund kid,* she mused.

Trish shook her head slightly and continued to type, trying to gain access to different cameras around the new geographical area. It didn't take long as she watched a barrage of stilled videos pop up on her screen. She continued to move things around and then they started to pop up on the other monitors above her desk.

Finally satisfied, she sat back in her chair. "What do we want to search first?" she asked Sharon.

Her previous searches had been around the Salisbury and Ocean City areas. The new location would hopefully give her a better view of what Reece had been up to.

"Well, just try to do some facial recognition on public devices first and then we can move to more of the private sector stuff," Sharon suggested.

"Aye, aye Captain," Trish said with a mock salute and grin. She wiggled her fingers over her keyboard. This was her favorite part of any job she got from Sharon.

She didn't pay attention to anything else, as she loaded and examined video after video. Each feed was live until she had to scroll back and change dates. When she had finished with the dates, she sent the facial recognition software to each and almost immediately, she had hits. She leaned back, pausing her hands as she watched each of her screens light up with photo after photo of Reece with the signature red square highlighting his face.

"What do you make of this, Sharon?" She watched, not taking her eyes off the flashing screens in front of her. It was like one of those spam nightmares where random advertisements were sent out, layering one on top of another, covering the screen. But these were all sightings of Reece in the local area around his last known residence—which given his age had to be his parents' home.

Sharon snorted, "I'd say young Reece thinks he's invincible."

"Or maybe making sure he has an alibi," Trish said thoughtfully.

Sharon caught Trish's eyes as she turned. "Explain, Trish, dear."

Trish took a deep breath. "Well, what if he *does* have something to do with all of these things and *creates* an alibi after the fact so he can't be pinned with anything? If he is visible on cameras throughout the town, it 'proves' he was there, right?"

Sharon tapped her lips. "Interesting thought, Trish. I wonder if we can try to make that theory stick. Go back a few days ago and see what his exposure is."

Trish typed at her keyboard again and then waited for the screens to fill again, but they were blank. "That's odd," she said.

"So, the day of the attack on Billy, Reece is nowhere on camera around his last known residence," Sharon said slowly. "Ok, when does he reappear?"

Trish forwarded the videos hour by hour to see when he would pop up again. Reece's face did not appear on any cameras until four hours prior to Billy being found by the river. Trish caught him exiting his vehicle at a gas station not far from his address.

"Ok, is it only me who thinks it is weird that he isn't anywhere near his residence, assuming he lives there, until hours before Billy is found?" Trish asked, turning to face Sharon.

"Nope. Let's go back to the views around Salisbury. Actually, see if you can get into the Bay Bridge cameras. If we can see him cross the bridge, we may be able to track him backwards from there. I'll do a search on the tags from the car you caught him exiting." Sharon set her glasses on her nose and focused on her own screen and paper tablet in front of her.

Trish didn't waste a minute getting into the bridge cameras. It didn't take long for her to find out exactly what time he crossed the bridge into Annapolis. Focusing solely on the time stamps, Trish moved to a different camera over another bridge and found what time he crossed that one. She continued backwards until he wasn't picked up on a bridge for longer than what it would take to get there, even with a bathroom or food stop.

She sat back and scratched her forehead. Sharon glanced over and put her glasses on her head.

"What's the matter, Trish?" she asked.

Trish looked away from her screen. "I'm not sure. Where would he go from Easton? He doesn't make it to Cambridge, at least not the bridge or pier cameras there. If he's not there, he would have taken a different way to Salisbury," she explained.

Sharon furrowed her brow and had a pensive look on her face. "What if they didn't pick Billy up in Salisbury. Maybe he cut across before he got to Easton and went into Delaware. Have you tracked Billy's movements up until he was discovered?"

"Hm, good thought," Trish said thoughtfully. "If Reece cut across into Delaware here," she pointed to a map where highways fifty and four oh four cross, "he would have gone through Wye Mills and on to Denton. That gives me a different direction."

"Smart. There are so many bridges down fifty that he bypassed a lot of cameras," Sharon mumbled.

Trish grinned. She knew her partner wasn't praising him, she knew he would slip up. But she would give kudos to the ones who would use their head and try not to get caught.

"Are you having any luck with the tags, Sharon?" Trish asked.

Sharon nodded. "A little. But everything comes back in a different name. This kid was pretty slick for a spoiled rich kid."

"Or had resources to keep law enforcement a step behind," Trish pointed out. There was no doubt a spoiled rich white kid would have the means and resources to evade the law and also get out of a lot of sticky situations their minority counterparts couldn't.

With a groan, she nodded, understanding what her friend was suggesting. Trish hoped he slipped up somewhere along the way so they could catch him, as she was sure Sharon did as well.

They worked side by side in silence for a long time before either had anything new to share. Trish continued to watch and track videos, switching from public cameras to private ones, through people's Ring doorbells or property surveillance systems. She was able to track him back and forth through Maryland and Delaware to a small town and what looked like an abandoned property near Federalsburg Maryland. It was situated at the edge of the protected forest. It could be the perfect hideout, she thought.

Turning her screen to show Sharon what she had found, Trish sat back and waited for Sharon to finish what she was writing down. As she waited, Trish zoomed in on the property. There were several buildings but even Google Maps couldn't show everything. She noticed what looked like a camouflaged roof hidden in some trees. There had to be something there, she thought. Something worth hiding.

When Sharon had finally finished her notes, she looked over at Trish's screen. "What did you find?"

"Not sure, but we might have a hideout of sorts. Wanna go for a road trip?" Trish asked with a grin.

"I do, but we need to make sure we are careful. This is getting strange, and I am not sure who I can trust at the moment."

Trish knew Sharon was referring to her old boss, and she wasn't going to argue with her. Trish had her reservations about Luke as well. She wasn't worried though. She and Sharon had always made a good team.

Chapter 14

An alarm went off next to Trish's head, startling her from her sleep. She wiped her eyes and looked around trying to figure out the sound in her sleep. She turned off the alarm, which was just loud enough to wake her and not alert anyone else. Sudden awareness made Trish jump from her bed and grab her shotgun.

She stood at her slightly ajar door and listened for any noise on the lower level of her home. She rarely closed her doors all the way so she wouldn't be surprised by anyone or anything in the middle of the night. The alarm indicated someone was inside the house, not outside, which bothered Trish as she tried to figure out why she wasn't alerted by an outside camera again, but didn't have time to dwell on it.

The house was still dark and that meant it was still dark outside. She glanced at the small window across from her bed. Even with the room darkening shade she had, it was still easy to tell what time of day it was. She turned to look at the clock on her small night table and saw that it was only three in the morning. It was going to be a long day if she would be going off of just a couple hours of sleep, she thought.

She hadn't been sleeping for long because Sharon had left around one. They had gone over more information they had found while tracking Reece's movements from two days ago. Sharon had discovered that Reece didn't have a single vehicle in his name. There were a couple in his parents' names, who she found were both diplomats in D.C. They were also making their plans for the day, which included a short trip to the abandoned property Trish had followed him to via camera.

A creak brought Trish out of her thoughts, and she refocused on her bedroom door. Listening, she tried to figure out if the sound was from her stairs or the spot on the floor by her laundry room. She had learned all the creaks and croaks of the house over the time she had lived there. It wasn't difficult to distinguish between them. Only two sounded almost exactly the same, and it just so happened to be these two.

Trish focused on the quiet of the house again. *If it was the sound from downstairs, there should be another one right about now*, she thought, just as a lower toned groan was heard. She smiled in spite of the potential danger in her home.

Ok, I know it is coming from downstairs, and moving toward the kitchen, she mumbled in her head, still trying to shake some of her sleepiness. She gripped the barrel of her favorite weapon and slowly leaned out the door, listening for the next sound from the old floor. Trish moved at a snail's pace as she moved from her bedroom to the landing just outside it. Since she knew all the sounds in her house she also knew which ones to avoid to keep her presence unknown.

She waited a few moments before she made her way down the first step. The dull light from her single lamp lit up the bottom of the steps, but she was shrouded in darkness for the first four or five. This gave her the ability to sneak up on whoever dared to enter her home. *They were obviously stupid if they thought that was a good idea*, she laughed to herself silently.

Waiting on the third step from the top, she listened for the creak of the swinging door to the kitchen. Only one made noise, and that was by design. If someone moved one and it was silent, they wouldn't hesitate to move the other. Another ingenious idea from the depths of her mind, Sharon told her.

Trish made it to the fifth step before she stopped. She hadn't heard anything more and was slightly concerned. The only thing she had in the main part of the living space was her computer gear, most of it being hidden from view. You would have to know what you were looking for to know there was more than a laptop and tv screen on the desk. Even if they tried to steal anything there, Trish had it so complicatedly encrypted no one would get any information from it.

Learning how to hack almost any kind of encryption had taught Trish how to protect her own gear, making it nearly impossible to crack. She'd risk saying it was impossible to hack, but she knew there was always someone out there better than she was. So, it wasn't because she was worried about the idiot stealing from her. It was more the intrusion and lack of movement that had her frozen in place.

"What are they up to?" she mumbled. Trish carefully sat on the step. She leaned forward slightly to try to see past the partial wall blocking her from being seen down below. Her gun was resting in her lap with her finger firmly pressed on the trigger. She kept one shot in the chamber when she went to bed every night, just in case she needed it for a situation like this. She usually grabbed a few and stuck them in her pockets but she had forgotten. Hopefully there was only one fool in the house, she thought briefly.

A very quiet click brought her attention back to the issue at hand. Leaning forward a little bit more, she could see a figure all in black leaning over her computer. She inwardly sneered. Such an easy shot, she thought.

Positioning her baby against her shoulder, she gently pulled the safety back. Trish cringed when she heard the tiny snap of the release. She kept her focus on the figure and almost immediately after the click from her gun, the person bolted through the kitchen and out the front door. The sound was very small and only the most sensitive ears would have even caught it.

Frustrated, Trish dropped the gun off her shoulder and moved the rest of the way downstairs. She checked all around to make sure she was alone and then through the kitchen to relock the front door. There was no movement she could see outside her windows, but she knew she would have to scour her videos to see which direction the intruder had gone.

Trish leaned against the counter in her kitchen facing the doorway to the living space. What could the person have wanted inside her home? This changed the game. Now it was clear someone was after her or what she had. Trish had no clue what that was, but she would find out. That wasn't even negotiable. No one broke into her home without consequence. And this idiot just signed his or her death wish.

Moving back into the other room, Trish looked at her desk. Nothing was amiss and she noticed her laptop was still shut down. Did she interrupt things before they got anything?

She fired up her computer and lifted her screens from behind the desk. She wouldn't be sleeping anytime soon, she thought. Now she had to figure out who was in her house and why. Maybe even more important was *how* they even got inside. The alarm woke her up, but it had to have been the one right by her door and nothing before that. Did that mean the person actually came from the woods this time? There was no way the cameras in the front would have missed someone lurking around, even in the dark of night.

Starting with the camera in the back of her house, Trish focused on working backwards from the moment she saw the figure rush out. She watched in reverse as the person snuck in through her back door and laundry room area. She only had one camera inside her house, and it was positioned at the door looking inside. This one caught them coming in the door and closing the screen door silently. Trish had to admit she was a little impressed. That door wasn't exactly an easy door to use quietly. Like everything else, she kept the noisy stuff on purpose, but that proved to be pointless tonight.

She switched cameras to the outside one, her favorite. It could catch things a few yards into the woods behind her house. It was the best way to get info about things happening in the backyard. Trish was surprised when she couldn't find where the person came from. There were only two blind spots on her property; behind the garage and up front by the chicken house. But both were pretty well covered in trees behind the structures. Anyone lurking around back there would be visible once they stepped out in the open.

This person seemed to almost appear from nowhere. "Not this again," she groaned, rewinding and replaying everything over and over again. "It appears the ghost is back."

Trish leaned back in her chair and locked her fingers behind her head. What was she going to do now? This person managed to get inside her home without alerting her until it was too late. Luckily they didn't get anything and didn't come after her for some reason.

"Maybe some booby traps would be fun," she said out loud as she watched again how the figure seemed to appear before her door without a trace anywhere else. She chuckled and shook her head.

No, she needed to figure out what they wanted and take care of it so she could focus on her ex-sister and her latest boy toy. Her priority had to stay focused on vengeance for Anyah. She would just have to increase the sensitivity on the camera outside her door and maybe add another one inside. A quick call to Sharon would be easy enough to add a camera similar to the one Sharon put in the front. Hopefully it will be undetectable as well.

With no way of knowing where the person came from or what they were looking for, Trish pushed away from her desk and stood to stretch. The sun was starting to peek through her shaded windows, and she glanced at her phone to see that it was already seven. With a groan, she shut down her gear and headed back upstairs to get ready for the day.

"Nothing a pot of hot and strong coffee won't cure," she mumbled as she moved.

As she passed the door to the laundry, Trish looked into the room and stopped. It wasn't a huge room, just big enough for her stackable washer/dryer and a small coat tree. Trish rarely left anything there except maybe a single light weight jacket and a pair of shoes; easy to grab, comfortable, and multifunctional.

Walking slowly into the room, Trish glanced to each side and then focused solely on the door. There wasn't a window on this door, only a tiny peep hole. She reached the door quickly, since the room was small. She gently opened it and checked the hinges to make sure nothing was stuck in them.

Next she turned her attention to the screen door. Why didn't she hear it, she wondered. Even asleep, she seemed to be hyper attuned to the noises in her house. She slowly pressed the latch and pushed the door until it was completely open. Then she pulled it closed. She crossed her arms and stared at it.

"How the hell did that happen?" she asked, as she glared at the now silent screen door. Then she wondered *when* it happened. Trish found herself questioning if she heard the signature squeak of the door the day before but couldn't remember. The squeak she depended on to alert her to someone coming inside her home was gone.

This morning can't get much weirder, she thought. Then again, she knew that wasn't true either. If there's anything that working with Sharon taught her it's that things can always get worse. Shaking her head of the thoughts, she closed both doors and locked the inside one. She knew she had to shower and didn't want any more surprises.

Before she started to get ready for the day, Trish sent a message to Sharon. They needed to alter their plans for the day. She wasn't going to leave her house completely unprotected for the entire day. If this person was brazen enough to come in while she slept, they would see the house being empty as a great opportunity to finish whatever they started earlier.

Trish moved through her morning ritual quickly, not that it took much time anyway. Standing in front of the mirror, she studied her reflection. Her locks were getting a little outgrown and she may need to get a retwist soon. Her hair wasn't something she spent a lot of time or money on, but she did like it to look taken care of. It was the one luxury she did indulge in once a month though. Having her hair tightly twisted definitely did help her self-esteem and confidence.

Growing up her parents didn't have a lot of extra money, so her mom had learned to braid and tie up both Trish and Patsy's hair neatly. The tighter she was able to do it the longer it stayed, and Trish learned early on that it was worth it in the long run to have "brain pain" for a few days. It meant fewer times having it done. Trish's childhood favorite was tight corn rows, while her sister loved the beads and making noise shaking her head. Maybe it should have been a clue to the attention Patsy needed that maybe she didn't get as a youngster.

A quiet "ding" drew Trish's attention to her phone. She picked it up to see Sharon had just arrived. She quickly wiped off her vanity, rehung the towel on the ring, and made her way downstairs.

She glanced at her door to make sure the lock was still turned. She met Sharon in her kitchen. Her friend was the only person who she trusted to have a second key to her house for an emergency. Trish would never hide one on the property. She couldn't count the places she would look when they were working on some case to find a spare key. Breaking doors wasn't her thing, but she could pick just about any lock. Trish chuckled as she thought about her skills. One would think she was raised with a group of criminals and thieves with how quickly she learned and honed the skills she had.

"Trish, dear, is everything ok?" Sharon asked, grabbing her friend's arms. "Your text had me so frightened, I thought something had happened." She looked around as if she was missing something.

"I'm fine, Sharon," Trish assured her. "No one is here, and they had a few brain cells because they left as soon as they knew I was here and awake." Trish rolled her eyes as she remembered her irritation at the tiniest sound scaring them off. Most people wouldn't even notice it, but this person did. It made her wonder if this person had some sort of special training. It also surprised her that the person never turned around to look at her, they just bolted out of the house. It was odd.

Sharon was quiet, seeming to be lost in her thoughts.

"I wonder if this is the same person who has been messing with my cameras," Trish said suddenly.

This caught Sharon's attention. "I was just thinking the same thing," she admitted. "It would make sense. This person has managed to bypass your cameras and seems to come and go as they please. We could be dealing with someone who is well-trained, Trish."

Trish almost laughed at her friend's raised eyebrows. The concern she had for Trish was sweet, but unnecessary, she thought. "Eh, I'm still not worried."

She wasn't trying to put a show on for Sharon either. She really wasn't too worried. Sure this guy managed to escape some of her cameras, but they had managed to catch him on the new ones. And yes he (assumption, she knew) did get into her home and somehow bypass her camera without her knowledge, but she was able to be awake and watch before he got spooked and took off. *Chicken*, she thought. She was prepared for a confrontation, even after only two hours of sleep, but the coward ran.

Sharon sighed loudly. When Trish looked up to meet her eyes, Sharon tried to give her friend her best "mom" voice.

"Now Trish honey, we need to figure out how to keep you safe. I do not like that someone made it into your home, with as much security as you have here," Sharon insisted. Her arms were crossed over her chest, and she was leaning her hip against the counter studying Trish.

Trish just shrugged and waited for her coffee to fill. "Still not worried," she simply stated. Trish could see her nonchalance visibly irritated Sharon. She may be able to intimidate her kids, but Sharon couldn't do the same to Trish.

After a few minutes, Sharon gave up and moved through the doors of the kitchen to the living room. It made Trish grin when she knew she got under her friend's skin. It wasn't like she enjoyed the frustration she caused, she just wanted Sharon to know she could handle things. She wasn't scared and Sharon needed to just trust her.

As soon as the decanter was full, she filled two mugs and moved out of the kitchen. She didn't need to walk into the room to know what Sharon would be doing. She grinned when she looked toward her computer to see she was correct. Sharon sat huddled over the keyboard and was watching the screens. The images jumped from frozen photo to photo. Trish knew what she was looking for, it was the same thing she had been trying to figure out. Even in the shower, she couldn't get the confusion out of her head.

"How…?" Sharon stopped and stared at the still image of the hooded intruder standing at Trish's door.

Trish set down her mug and then chuckled. "Don't know, Sharon. It doesn't make sense. I am thinking we need to add a camera or two behind the garage and maybe one inside. I would hope they couldn't mess with the one inside, right? It should alert me as soon as the door opens, like the now fixed squeak for the screen door." Her discovery this morning still rubbed her the wrong way.

Sharon stared at the screen. "I think you're right, Trish. If we have one to alert you when the door opens but is virtually silent so only you hear it. That would give you a head start." She nodded as if the ghost-like figure was staring back.

Trish let out a snort. "I don't need too much of a head start, though," she said with pride. She was ready and the only way she would have lost the upper hand was if the intruder had gone upstairs instead of staying on the main level. But he didn't seem interested in her, just her computer, which she suddenly realized.

"Maybe we could put one on the side of the stairs that would be unseen but would alert me if they went upstairs." She moved to the stairs and walked a few steps up and turned around. There was a ledge there where the ceiling was lower and provided a small lip. "Here," Trish said, pointing to the flush side facing her bedroom door.

Sharon moved to get a closer look and agreed. "Good idea. It will be completely invisible unless you are already upstairs." She moved back to her bag that had been dropped on the table. "I have another tiny one we can rig up. If we set it in the corner there, you won't even be able to see it from downstairs, and it would get a little more of the steps." She lifted a tiny thing from her bag and held it up.

The pair got to work setting up the small device and within minutes Trish was checking it on her phone and computer system. She hid a program in her computer connected only to that device to record and save to an encrypted folder marked "puppies." She had no intention of getting a dog, but it would be a good folder for anyone to ignore if they were looking for something secret. But that way if someone did get a hold of her camera before she did, the recordings would still be on her computer until it was disconnected.

Once that was complete, they moved to the garage outside. Sharon hid two more cameras on opposite corners of the roofline. They went through the same checking process and once satisfied, they stood in the yard with matching poses, hands on hips and staring out toward the road.

"I sure hope we catch this moron soon," Trish said. "I really want to get this case solved and move on." She motioned toward the files on the table, but in her head knew it was to move on from Anyah's murder.

Sharon put her arm around her friend's shoulder. "I know, me too."

They went back inside to double-check the computer feeds and make sure all the settings were correct.

"Maybe I should get one of those fancy watches you wear, Sharon," Trish said suddenly. She hated having a lot of techy stuff, mostly because she knew how easy it was to hack. But a watch might make this surveillance stuff easier when she wasn't at home. Her phone worked fine, but a watch might give her an alert as well so if one failed, the other would pick it up. Then again, maybe she was just trying to figure out anything that would work to get her attention the quickest way possible.

Sharon shrugged. "Maybe but with your hate-hate relationship with your phone, the watch is just an extension of that. You might find it more annoying than anything." She smiled at her friend and raised her eyebrow as if challenging her words.

Trish just grinned back. "Truth, my dear friend. Ok, no watch. At least no smart watch. I'll keep my analog one for now." She tapped the face of the small watch on her arm. It was something she had always worn since she was young.

Moving back to the table where her bag was, Sharon pulled out a file. She opened it and handed it to Trish.

"I think we have the route mapped out and where to park the car, so it's undetected. Shall we move on and see what we can find out about Reece's whereabouts last week?" Sharon asked with a mischievous smile.

Trish nodded. "Absolutely. I need a different focus than here and this morning." She glanced through the papers in Sharon's file and nodded.

It was all what they had stayed up most of the previous night deciding. It would take a couple hours of driving and maneuvering to make sure they were undetected. Trish had drawn up a route to make it look like they were driving and had gotten lost, just in case anyone checked their location. Since neither was sure who they couldn't trust, they were being very careful.

"Alrighty, let's go then," Sharon said with a snap of the file. "Your car or mine?"

Trish snorted and shook her head. "I am not riding in that microwave death trap for hours. Mine."

She grabbed her keys, and they headed out. The plan was to secure Sharon's car in the garage, so it appeared as if no one was home. The cameras were all working properly so if anything was amiss, they would be alerted.

Chapter 15

"Do you have any idea who might be trying to get to you, Trish?" Sharon asked as they drove in a zig zag pattern across the Delaware and Maryland state lines.

Trish shook her head, looking to her left to check for traffic. "No idea," she admitted. She wasn't about to overthink it though. She had priorities. "I will figure it out though, don't you worry." Then she chuckled darkly adding, "Hopefully before he ends up bleeding out on my floors. Imagine the damage that would do to the hardwood." She gave her friend a smirk and an exaggerated shiver.

Sharon just shook her head. "You have a dark streak in there, dear. You better keep it in check or someday it might come out and cause you some problems."

"Ah, that motherly warning," Trish said laughing. "You know I wouldn't go too far. I don't have the stomach for it like you do."

The wink she shot Sharon's way was met with a scowl.

"Hey! I will have you know I do not *enjoy* hurting people as you suggest. I just know the soft spots for getting information," she said with a shrug.

Trish snorted. "Yeah you say that like torture is just a 'soft spot for information,' Sharon." She used air quotes and everything, making Sharon grin and wave her hand in dismissal.

"Well, I just want to make sure you are safe, my friend. You know that, right?" the older woman asked.

Reaching out her hand, Trish patted Sharon's arm. "I know. But again, I am not worried. Besides, I'll do my best to get the idiot out of the house first, so the blood doesn't soak into the wood. Bleach on the wood might be bad, huh?"

Sharon just shook her head and turned back to the road ahead. "How far out are we?" She pulled out a map of the area.

Neither of the women would use their GPS for this trip. No evidence or ability to track their route was ideal, making paper and pencil the only way to go. Sharon traced her finger along the route they had drawn in red pen before they started their journey. Trish glanced over. Having been raised on the Eastern Shore, she knew the peninsula pretty well. She didn't need a map to know where she was or where she was going, from the William Preston Lane Jr. Bay Bridge crossing from the Shore to Annapolis down to the Chesapeake Bay Bridge Tunnel crossing into Virginia Beach. She had drawn up the route without thinking much about it, with Sharon just nodding along the way.

Both women, though very different backgrounds, knew the area very well. Sharon spent a good amount of time throughout the world, while Trish didn't travel much. Their socioeconomic backgrounds and upbringing provided different things when it came to vacations or family time. Then add in their adult lives and the experiences outside of their hometowns weren't even comparable. Trish again thought it was such a strange coincidence that they ever met at all, let alone become friends.

"One more turn up here then about five miles or so. We can park along the street about a quarter mile from the structure," Trish said, looking again for traffic. Since it was a workday and midday, there wasn't much traffic or movement on the streets. Trish had tried to get a better picture of the structure they were looking for, but it was perfectly concealed by the forestry from above and the street.

Sharon admitted she was slightly uneasy about what they might be walking into, but they figured they could use their "old lady" looks to talk their way into or out of anything. That was the plan anyway, unless someone surprised them.

Trish admitted to herself she wasn't feeling as secure as she would if Sharon had let her bring her rifle along. Yes, it might be a little big and obvious, potentially blowing their cover story of two senile old women. But she felt unprepared going in. Sharon told her not to worry, she had her covered, but nothing made Trish feel as secure as her trusty old friend, and not the human one.

The rest of the drive was quiet as they were lost in their own thoughts. Trish didn't need to guess what was on Sharon's mind. She knew it was her friend shifting from civilian to agent. The transition only took a few minutes to happen, but it was unmistakable when it did. Sharon was amazing at playing whatever part was needed. Trish marveled at that talent. Or maybe it was training. But Trish couldn't do it. What she felt her face showed, and there was no way to hide it.

They drove a mile or two outside of the quaint downtown area of Federalsburg, named for the Federalists who used to conduct meetings in town in the 1700's. It was located on the Marshyhope Creek, part of the Nanticoke watershed. The forest nearby allowed for an abundant supply for shipbuilding. The other main commodity was farming, which was common on the Eastern Shore. The old buildings stood proud as a tribute to the rich history of the area.

Trish slowed the car along a wooded part of the road. There were a few houses scattered along the street, but they were set back into the trees. It would provide the two women cover as they walked the rest of the way to their target. Trish exited the vehicle first and moved to the trunk. She had a few things she wanted to have on hand, one being a tiny camera that Sharon had given her. They had rigged it up the night before to record whatever they saw as they made their way around the property. It would act like an officer's body cam. She also took out a small thumb drive and tucked it into her pocket. If they came across any computer equipment she would want to make sure she could copy whatever they found.

Sharon met her and reached into a bag she'd put back there. She tucked a small handgun into her waistband and pulled the band of her "Best Grandma Ever" sweatshirt down to cover it. She also tucked something that looked like a Smith and Wesson M & P at her back as well. Then she turned to Trish and handed her a Glock 43.

Trish raised her eyebrows at her friend.

"I told you I got your back, Trish," Sharon said simply.

Trish scowled. She hated these prissy little things, she told Sharon constantly. But she would have to suck up her pride and take it for her own safety. Once again, she cursed her friend for not letting her bring her own pieces.

Sharon chucked at her friend. "It's just for today, Trish dear. I can't have you going into this with no protection. And mine are police and military grade. I can't give you that, you understand right?"

"They're all too small if you ask me," Trish mumbled, earning her a pat on the back.

"I know, I know," Sharon said softly. "Better this than nothing." She shrugged as Trish tucked the weapon into her waistband like Sharon had.

Sharon then took out a small case that held two small earpieces. She put one in her ear and handed the other to Trish. Once they confirmed they could hear each other, just in case they were separated, Trish closed the trunk and pressed the lock on her key fob twice to make sure the vehicle was locked. Both women hoped this wouldn't take long and they would come back with some answers. The stack of unanswered questions was only growing.

They had decided to keep their "investigation" between them, not bringing in Luke or anyone from Sharon's team. In her years active in the field, she had dealt with many different types of betrayal. She wasn't about to jeopardize anything by telling the wrong person. Since she didn't know who that was currently, she would keep quiet for now. It took some doing by Trish to convince her to finally say the words, but Trish knew it would be for the best. They rarely had backup on their little adventures, so they weren't risking anything by keeping it to themselves anyway.

Sharon jumped into character, and the pair walked down the street looking this way and that. Trish had told her the night before that an actress she was not, but that her natural temperament would be just fine. Sharon had laughed but didn't argue.

As they walked, Trish considered where she was at in life. She hadn't always been so cynical and ornery. She knew life had handed her a deck of cards that was stacked against her. But she would survive this and once her little girl was avenged, she hoped she could be a little more like she used to be. Maybe she could embrace her forties instead of jumping right into her fifties. Maybe cutting out the gray extensions and leaving it naturally black would be a start.

She was distracted by her thoughts when Sharon put a hand on her arm and let out a frustrated breath. Trish startled and stared at her friend, completely forgetting that they were walking into an unknown situation.

Trish glanced up and saw a man with an AK-47 standing in their path. Sharon was babbling about being lost and needing directions. The man remained unmoved and just stared.

"What's your problem, young man?" Trish demanded, folding her arms over her chest, careful not to lift the waistband too much. "Never seen an old woman with dementia before? Sheesh, maybe call your grandma or something." She turned to Sharon and grabbed her forearms. "Dear, it's ok. This nice man was just going to tell us where to go."

Trish turned back to the giant in front of her. This man wasn't just tall, he was huge. She barely came up to his shoulder and was probably half of his girth. But nothing intimidated her, and she moved closer to him, almost standing toe to toe.

"Are you gonna help us or not?" she asked him.

"Oh honey, let's just go a different way," Sharon begged in her weak old lady voice. It almost made Trish laugh. Sharon was anything but weak.

She patted Sharon's arm comfortingly. "We will get lost even more. No, we will ask this nice gentleman, who needs to call his mommom apparently," she said as she glared at the man in front of her.

"Look ladies, I don't know what you are looking for, but you need to get off this property," he said gruffly.

Trish waved her hand dismissing him. "Oh, come on. Just tell us how to get to the memory care facility in town and we will be gone. This old coot needs to take her meds." She grinned inwardly. She knew she would pay for that later.

The man shook his head. "Don't know what you are talking about." He continued to stare straight ahead like he was a royal soldier or something.

"Well maybe someone up at the house can tell us," Trish suggested, looking past him to finally see the structure in front of them. It was not a house, she noted and wondered what they were hiding and protecting up that small hill.

When he remained silent, Sharon leaned forward and gripped his hand, making it fall from the gun. She jumped back as he swung his hand at her.

"Don't touch me, woman!" he yelled. He was about to push her away when Sharon side stepped him and then as he stumbled she tripped him. The huge man fell flat on his face and when he realized she had bested him, he got up angrily.

He pointed a finger in her face but before he could say anything, Sharon grabbed a hold of the finger and bent it back until a sickening crack sounded in the silent air.

The man screamed in pain and as he fell forward, Sharon pulled her weapon from behind and hit him with the butt of the gun knocking him unconscious.

Trish just stood on the side and grinned. She didn't have to do anything but get the guy to move. Sharon was so much fun to watch.

"Stop standing there like a crazy person and help me move him," Sharon told her.

Together they moved him just inside the cover of the trees. He would be invisible to anyone driving by so it would buy them some time and not bring unexpected police activity. They stood and looked at the structure in front of them and Trish sighed.

"Well, if there were cameras around here, there would be more coming. I don't see any movement, but I'm not sure what that means exactly," Sharon said with her hands on her hips. "Let's just move slowly from the sides."

Trish nodded. She moved into the trees and grinned. This was her comfort zone. She had great instincts in the woods from all the hunting she had done. Her first order of business was to track any trail cameras or trip wires. These were things she had learned with Sharon years ago. She didn't go much out into the field, but she knew some of the basics.

She had almost made it to the structure when she heard Sharon over the coms. She was talking to someone, giving Trish hints as to where she was as she talked. The old lady was back, and "dementia" was in full force. Trish crouched down and tried to see through the trees. She saw Sharon talking to someone about eighty yards from where she was. There was a single man standing in front of her trying to see around her, likely looking for his comrade. Sharon kept pulling on his sleeve, asking for directions to the Salisbury Zoo, making Trish almost chuckle out loud.

Glancing around, Trish noticed another man was walking toward the pair. She had always been told by Sharon not to engage unless she heard the code word, which was "Bahamas." She was fine just watching her friend work anyway. But she stayed vigilant, making sure her friend was safe.

"Look, lady, you are in the wrong town. Go back where you came from. Go to the gas station on the corner. They'll get you back to wherever," Trish heard in her ear.

At least this guy was a little nicer than the last one, she thought. She watched as Sharon continued to beg for them to take her.

"Maybe I should just call the police. Do you have a phone I could use?" Sharon asked.

Trish watched as both men froze. They wouldn't let her call the police, that much Trish knew. Smart move on Sharon's part. It could also be a fatal move if they are desperately trying to hide something.

The other man stepped in. "No, no. Here, I'll walk you to the corner and show you where to go, ok?" he asked, attempting to lead her toward the street.

"Oh, thank you, young man. Your mother should be so proud of the way she raised you," Sharon gushed to him. "It seems like it would be easier to just call the police though, I don't want to trouble you."

"It's just fine. I have a friend coming and he doesn't like people, so I need to get you somewhere safe," the man said as he continued to walk with Sharon down the driveway.

Trish watched as the other man made his way back into the building. She slowly moved in that same direction, watching continually for any surprises. She was almost at the building, a steel-covered structure that didn't appear to have any windows. But it had a chimney on the roof blowing out smoke. It wasn't cold enough for a fireplace to be running, she didn't think. And with no windows, she couldn't begin to imagine what was going on inside. Maybe it was a metal shop of some sort.

She stopped in her tracks when she heard Sharon ask the man his name.

"Oscar, ma'am. You be safe now."

Trish could no longer see them so she couldn't get a look at the mystery man who had no face in their files. She waited for a few minutes and then heard Sharon in her ear.

"Did you get that, Trish?" she asked. "Let's go back. I should have his face on my camera."

Trish grinned. A lead. "On my way," she said as she backtracked through the woods.

There was a part of her that didn't want to go. She wanted to find out what was happening inside that metal shack, but there would be another time to find that out she was sure.

They met back at the car, just as the man Sharon knocked out when they first arrived stumbled out of the woods. They were safely inside the vehicle before he could see them. But they were also far enough away that he wouldn't recognize them from this distance anyway.

The drive back to Trish's was a much easier and faster trip. Sharon had brought her laptop along and she loaded their camera footage while Trish drove.

"Did you recognize Oscar, Sharon?" Trish asked. "I didn't get a good look at his face from where I was."

Sharon let out a sigh. "No, but our facial recognition software will help with that. Now that we have a face, we can see what else we can find out about the mystery man."

"I can't wait," Trish said with a grin.

Sharon's phone rang when they were just entering the Salisbury city limits. Trish ignored the conversation, thinking instead about the strange place they had just left. What could they be doing inside that metal building? She figured it could be a meth lab or other drug lab of some sort. It was pretty well protected given the large men with guns, although two old ladies had easily wormed their way in.

A deep sigh from Sharon drew Trish's attention back to the passenger seat.

"What's up?" she asked, glancing to her side.

"Luke wants me to put this whole thing on hold. Something about the higher ups have something going and don't want interference," Sharon said with an eye roll.

Trish snorted. "Does he even know you? Like that seems to be the perfect way to push you to keep digging," she pointed out.

Sharon shrugged. "Maybe but he had the signature tone that meant no messing around. I just don't know who would want these guys more than Luke," she mused, staring out her window.

A few thoughts occurred to Trish, but she had to be careful how she brought her suspicions up to her friend. Trish couldn't help wondering if Luke was up to no good. Before she could formulate a response, her own phone let out its familiar screech.

"Oh my lord, honey. Change that tone," Sharon groaned.

"Never," Trish said with a grin.

Sharon picked up Trish's phone and asked, "Do you want me to check it for you?"

"Nope," she responded simply, popping the "p" for emphasis. "Whoever it is, I don't care."

But Trish already knew who it was. She didn't want her friend to see the history of messages between her and Clayton. She looked in her rearview mirror and noticed a black vehicle following them closely. She furrowed her brows and glanced over at Sharon.

"I think we have a tail. I'm going to see if I can lose them." She pressed the gas pedal a little harder, keeping a close eye on the car.

All of the windows including the front windshield were tinted so dark she couldn't imagine it was legal. There was no way to see inside to know who was driving or how many were inside.

"I wonder if this is what Luke was warning me about," Sharon wondered quietly.

Trish looked over. "You think we're in some kind of danger here? Seems a little far-fetched given who you are and how insignificant I am to everything."

"Don't disregard yourself, Trish dear," Sharon said calmly. "With your sister in the middle of this, you have no idea what role you may unknowingly be playing."

She hadn't thought of that. If someone was on to her sister and her contact with Johnny, she may actually have some people after her as well, but Trish tried not to worry about her sister's safety. She wouldn't allow that concern into her hardened and fortified heart. She knew if her parents were still alive they would be pressuring her to forgive her sister and make amends. But since they aren't, there's nothing forcing her to do anything of the kind.

Her phone screeched again, and Trish rolled her eyes with a sigh. "Relentless," she muttered under her breath. But Sharon heard and turned to look at her.

Trish just shook her head and waved her hand, focusing back on the vehicle behind them, which seemed to catch up easily and was again following very close to her bumper. She bit her lip and glanced to the side. There was a second car that appeared there, and Trish's mind was spinning with how to outmaneuver them.

As if reading her mind, Sharon sat up straighter and focused her eyes on her own side mirror. "Take a right up here, Trish," she said. "There's a spot we can hide but will take some good driving skills." She smirked at her friend, and Trish knew what that meant.

Trish made the quick turn off highway thirteen and then another quick left. She was on a small two-lane road that barely fit two cars side by side. She knew if they weren't careful they could easily be overtaken by the other two vehicles. But she and Sharon were pretty experienced and skilled in the ways of the back roads, and she hoped the two following her weren't as familiar to giving them an advantage.

She made a right turn and then a second and third quickly. Then she made a left turn that went into a large mobile home development. They would be able to hide in there if the others caught up. Trish made multiple turns and was quickly well hidden in the development. She pulled up to a heavily wooded area at the back of the complex. There was a small, overgrown opening that she pulled into.

Sharon jumped out of the vehicle and Trish put it in park when she got a little further into the woods. She got out and helped Sharon to pull the long branches out and covered the back of her car. The black color helped them out significantly in this situation. By the time they were done, it was completely blocked from view.

They stood outside the line of trees with their hands on their hips and grins on their faces. Even if the cars managed to follow them here, they wouldn't find the car.

"Ok, follow me," Sharon said with a wave of her hand.

Trish obediently followed. They had been here one other time, but Trish didn't know the way. She just nodded and stayed close to Sharon as the older woman ducked between homes along the tree line.

They finally came to a mobile home at the very back of the development. It was an old, dilapidated building that didn't look remotely inhabitable. Trish smiled as she remembered the place from a few years back. When Sharon knocked on the door three times and then two short ones, it slowly opened to reveal a very large African American man. Trish grinned when she remembered that the scowl this man sported reminded her of her own.

Chapter 16

"So, Miss Sharon, what did you get yourself into today?" the man asked with a grin on his face.

He had set a tray with sweet tea and three mismatched mugs on the table between them. His face had a wide grin, and his large frame barely fit on the chair.

Trish looked around. The place looked like an abandoned structure from the outside, but much like her own home, it was very well kept inside. It looked like a time capsule from the nineteen seventies though, with old orange shag carpet, the kind you actually have to rake, lining every floor's surface except the small kitchen area. The kitchen had old olive-green appliances and looked like a vintage photograph. She wondered if they even still worked.

But the biggest surprise walking into this home was the pristine, though dated, inside. George kept his home looking perfect inside, creating a direct contrast to the outside. Where the outside showed broken windows and ripped screens, the inside had clear glass covering the openings, completely invisible from the outside. The shutters on the outside were broken or missing, some hanging desperately by one nail. But the inside had neat and clean curtains on either side of the windows with blinds to block out the light.

Sharon laughed. "Oh, you know. Bad guys following me, blah, blah, blah."

George nodded. "That sounds about right for you, sweetheart," he said with a grin. "So, you just need a bit to hide out or are you staying for a while?" He leaned back in his chair and crossed his large arms over his broad chest.

Trish chuckled as she thought of how big this man was. He barely fit through the opening of the door. He looked like a former body builder who had retired a long time ago but failed to keep up with his workouts. She had no doubt he would still win any fight he was in though. Even with his large frame, he was remarkably quick on his feet.

"Well, I am hoping Trish here lost our friends, but I want to make sure. So, we can chat for a while, maybe play a little pinochle? I know you used to beat the pants off the rest of us back in the day, George," Sharon said with a grin.

George smiled back, revealing a wide gap between his front teeth. He waved his hand at her. "No, no. I don't want to hurt anyone's ego, Miss Sharon."

As if he had just realized Trish was there, he turned and gave her a strange look. He quickly shook it off again and then moved into his kitchen to grab a bucket of Fisher's popcorn, a staple in most Eastern Shore homes. He set the container on the table and then grabbed some napkins for them to use.

"Miss Trish, what are you up to these days?" he asked her, settling into his chair across from Sharon.

Trish shrugged. "Not much. Trying to keep this one out of trouble it appears." She gave Sharon a smirk, earning her a glare.

"Right, right," George said nodding. "Our Miss Sharon is surely a troublemaker." He winked at Sharon who just huffed in response.

"If I got into half the trouble the two of you do, I would be in jail or something by now," she said, crossing her arms and scowling, mostly at Trish though she noticed.

But Trish just laughed. "Oh whatever. You love us and you know it. I mean we keep you young, right George?"

George let out a deep and hearty laugh. The trio sat around the table for over an hour just talking. Trish noticed him glancing in her direction a few times, but he didn't say anything. She wasn't sure what was on his mind, but she didn't care so much to ask. She didn't know him as well as Sharon did, so she tried not to think much about it.

Eventually Sharon stood and stretched her neck. "I think we should be good by now. Thanks for the hospitality George, my friend."

Trish and George stood as well and the three exchanged hugs. As George gave Trish a tight squeeze, he whispered in her ear, "Be careful beautiful girl." He slid something in her hand as she pulled away. "Keep this between us until necessary."

Trish looked down at the black plastic in her hand. She looked up to see that Sharon had disappeared, maybe to use the restroom. Turning her attention back to the man in front of her. "What is this and what are you talking about, George?"

He folded her fingers around it. "Keep it. Don't tell anyone about it just yet." His eyes drifted to the hallway where Trish guessed her friend had disappeared. He gave Trish a nod and then stepped away just as Sharon reentered the room.

"Ready, Trish?" she asked, smoothing the front of her shirt as if it were wrinkled.

"Yep, I think so," Trish said, sliding the item George had given her into her front pocket. She glanced at George and gave him a nod. She wasn't sure what he was giving her or what it was for, but she would wait to look closer at it until she was at her house alone. Her curiosity was piqued though. Why would he slip her something and not want Sharon to know?

The pair waved to George and then headed back the way they came. Trish drove slowly to make sure there were no more surprises along the way. They were quiet for much of the forty-minute drive. Trish was lost in her thoughts as the small piece burned a hole in her jeans and occupied all of the thoughts in her head.

"Everything ok, hon?" Sharon asked as they were nearing Salisbury. "You've been pretty quiet."

Trish glanced over and smiled. "No, just thinking. Wanna grab dinner before heading back to my place?" She shook off the worry her friend expressed and focused on something else.

She hadn't noticed any more trailers or really too much traffic at all since they got back on the road. She surprised herself at how nonchalant she was about the people following them before. This wasn't her lifestyle or job, never was. But she must just be used to it from Sharon. Trish tried to think of the last time she was followed by anyone but couldn't remember a single time. Maybe she just knew that with Sharon around, there was always a way out or something. It suddenly occurred to her that between searching for the drug dealers her sister was tied up with in high school to now looking for the people responsible for killing her daughter, she was never worried about being followed.

"Huh," she blurted out, drawing Sharon's attention to her.

"What are you thinking about?" Sharon asked.

Trish looked over, surprised it was said out loud. She shook her head and shrugged. "Just thinking this is the first time I have been followed. And I really didn't get all freaked out or anything. Weird, right?"

Sharon chuckled lightly beside her. "Well, this may be the first time you have been physically followed, but you have helped out on numerous occasions behind the computer where others were in danger. You have had a lot more practice than you think, Trish dear."

Trish just nodded. "I guess so." She had never thought about her work with Sharon and various other parties as being the same as what Sharon did, but she supposed it was similar enough that it had prepared her.

"How about some Italian for dinner? I could go for some shrimp pasta and crab cakes," Sharon suggested.

"That works for me," Trish agreed. She detoured slightly and made a turn off the highway to get to a side road. She didn't need to ask where because they tended to have their favorites.

As she parked in the lot, Sharon turned toward her. Her voice was soft as Trish felt her gaze. "Hon, I know George gave you something, but I am not going to pry. I want you to know when or if you need any help with it, please ask. I am not sure what he is up to, but I respect his reasons for only giving it to you."

Then Sharon patted Trish's arm and got out of the car as Trish turned off the engine.

What was that about? Trish wondered, again amazed by her friend's uncanny ability to sense things happening around her. Shaking her head she got out of the car as well, to meet Sharon. They walked to the entrance side by side; no words being spoken as they both knew and understood none were needed.

The restaurant was pretty quiet, and they were seated quickly. Trish had requested, as she always did here, a booth at the far corner. There were few people in the restaurant anyway, but she knew they would be talking about things no one else needed to be a part of. She wasn't sure if they were still being watched and didn't want to take any chances.

A waiter came to take their drink orders, but neither even needed to look at the menu to order. After he disappeared to start their food, Trish's cell phone made its presence known in its most annoying way.

"Trish, who keeps messaging you? Clayton?" Sharon asked as she lifted her glass of tea.

Trish let out a groan when she looked at her screen to see it was in fact her ex. "The guy needs to just give up," she said dismissively.

Sharon put her glass down and studied her friend.

"Don't stare, Sharon it's rude," Trish sneered at her friend.

"Oh posh," Sharon said dismissing her attitude. "I just think you might need to get some things straightened out before it gets worse, or beyond repair."

Trish resisted a stare back and just waved her hand. "I am not going there, Sharon. And you should know better than to pry." She pointed her finger at her friend for emphasis. "I am not interested, and he needs to get the hint." *How does she always know it's him?* she wondered. Then she remembered that no one else sends her messages.

Sharon was quiet for a minute and then quietly said, "Not everything is always what it seems, my friend."

She wanted to refute her friend's words, but Trish was doing the same with Sharon's colleagues in a way, so she swallowed her retort. She did not have to justify why she felt the way she did to anyone. He knew what was said and done.

With a sigh, Trish focused on the waiter walking over to deliver their dinner. She was a bit relieved by the distraction. She dove into her shrimp scampi, a favorite of hers since childhood. It was one of the dishes her mom had learned while she worked at a nearby restaurant. Trish rarely splurged on food and seafood was expensive, at least for the good stuff. After the day she'd had she felt she deserved it.

"So, who do you think was following us, Sharon?" she asked after a few forkfuls of linguini were eaten.

Sharon shrugged, pausing her own fork filled with crabcake in the air. "I'm not positive, but I would guess it was the nice gentlemen we encountered at the shelter, or whatever that building was." She put the food in her mouth and stared over Trish's shoulder as if she were contemplating something.

"I thought that too, but I'm not sure. Those guys weren't moving fast enough to catch up to us or know which direction we were heading," Trish said thoughtfully. "I am wondering if we were being watched or followed before that."

Sharon bit her cheek. "I guess that's possible. I wonder why though."

Trish wanted to laugh. Wasn't it obvious why someone would follow them? With everything all kinds of confusion at the moment, and Sharon's boss telling her to lie low, it didn't surprise Trish, so why would it surprise her friend?

She decided not to push any further on the topic. She would get to the bottom of it herself. Maybe Sharon was just too close to Luke and couldn't see past their history. Trish wasn't close to him, and he actually didn't seem thrilled with Sharon working with her. But thankfully Trish didn't care too much about others' opinions. She knew her skills and she knew Sharon trusted her.

They finished their meal with a lot more silence between them than was typical. Trish was lost in her thoughts about getting home to dig into her video and getting her own answers.

Sharon left her part of the bill on top of Trish's on the table, and they made their way outside. After Trish had buckled her seat belt and started the vehicle, she looked over at Sharon. "Are you ok, Sharon? You haven't said much since we left George's."

Her friend sighed. "I guess so. It has just been a long time since I have been this frustrated and confused by a case. I feel like I am letting you down, Trish dear."

"Ha. I don't think you are letting me down at all. But I do find it quite funny that you are stumped on this," Trish said with a smirk. "I know you think there is some sort of redemption in this case with Patsy, but you can just let that go. I am not looking for anything more from her." Trish silently added *except prison* in her head.

She definitely didn't want her friend to stress out about somehow helping the two make up and be family again because she knew that wasn't part of this case in Trish's mind. This was finally bringing her sister, *ex*-sister, to justice.

Sharon sighed again and looked out her window. "Have you gotten anymore trespassers, Trish?" Sharon asked suddenly. "I'm curious if our improvements have worked."

"I forgot about it actually with everything else going on. But the only alert I remember is the one at the table. And I have no interest in answering that one," she scoffed. But Sharon's reminder gave her pause. She wondered now too if what they had done worked or not.

Thankfully they were going back to her place together so they could check the footage before Sharon left for her own house. The drive to her house was quiet again. Normally it would bother Trish that her friend was this quiet, but she had a number of things on her own mind as well, so it was a welcome silence.

As Trish approached her driveway, she noticed that more of the cornfield had been plowed, but the part closest to her place was still standing tall and brown. *Weird*, she thought. There wasn't much left to be cut down, so why did he leave some there? Maybe she would be pleased any other time, but now that she had people trespassing on her property through the field she didn't feel as grateful.

"That's strange," Sharon muttered next to her.

"I was just thinking the same thing," Trish agreed. she chuckled to herself, reading her friend's mind reading her own.

"Why would he do that, Trish?" Sharon asked. "Is that how he normally cuts down the field?"

"You know the answer to that already Sharon," Trish said pointedly. "I have no idea what he is up to but with everything else going on around here, I am not second guessing anything."

She pulled into her driveway slowly and looked around checking her statues. Everything looked to be untouched, so she moved to the garage, parking slightly off to the side. She hopped out to help Sharon remove her vehicle and then she could put hers away.

As they entered the house after all the vehicle rearranging, Trish paused in the doorway from her laundry room. She had left a light on, and the setting sun cast a strange glow on the space. The lamp was in the corner by her desk so she could see right away if anything was amiss. She felt a slight chill over her skin as she looked around. She wasn't sure why, but it felt different, and she couldn't explain it.

"Trish, dear, was someone here?" Sharon asked quietly.

So, she felt it too, Trish thought. They really were connected on a different level.

"I can't tell. But I feel it too. Almost like there are eyes somewhere watching," Trish replied in a whisper.

Sharon moved past her and looked high, while Trish bent at her waist to look low. They knew what they were looking for—recording devices. Something that would blend in and not be seen or detected.

After combing the entire room twice, switching positions so they both had a chance to look for anything, Trish sighed. She dropped in her chair at the table and looked around.

"What do you think is so amazing in here that they want?" she asked Sharon.

"I don't think it is *what*, Trish," Sharon said slowly. "I think it is *who*."

Trish just laughed. "Sorry, Sharon dear. No one wants me for anything. I mean come on." She waved her hand

and shook her head. "Nope. There is nothing I can offer anyone," she added.

Her mind wasn't as sure as her voice was though. Could it be that Patsy had some other unfinished business with her? Maybe she didn't get what she wanted by taking Anyah away. Maybe she had a darker plan. Trish shrugged it off and moved into the kitchen to make her necessary black drink.

"Do you want some coffee, Sharon?" she asked over her shoulder as she moved through the swinging doors to her kitchen.

She heard Sharon sigh and then follow her into the small space. "You really need to take some of this stuff more seriously Trish," Sharon said with a tiny bit of frustration, which was uncharacteristic of her.

Trish filled her mug and offered Sharon an empty one to fill if she wanted. She took it with a sigh and filled her cup, adding in her extras. They met again in the living room where Trish was already seated at her desk. The screens were lit up and she was waiting for her laptop to connect.

"Let's see if we can get some facial rec on this Oscar guy, shall we?" Trish asked as her equipment finally connected.

Sharon seemed to finally snap out of her melancholy mood and came to life again. "Yes, let's do this, Trish. I need a distraction and maybe he will give us some answers."

Trish nodded. "If I'm honest I didn't think he would be at that place. I figured he would be a higher up character, but then again we don't know what is going on there either."

With a hum of agreement, Sharon fired up her own laptop and was laser focused on the screen. Trish almost let out a sigh of relief. Her friend rarely got down or upset about things, so Trish was admittedly a little worried about her. Sharon always seemed to know which direction to look and next steps to take. It was unnerving that Trish was leading the way on this.

She focused back on her screen and started to share her laptop screen with Sharon's so they could work together. Sharon did the same and they were watching things unfold at the same time. They were both surprised to learn that Sharon's camera that they depended on for getting a photo of Oscar didn't work as well as they had hoped. But with Sharon's training, she was confident she would be able to get a close second to having a photo with her own memory of his features.

Sharon had put so many details in the description, Trish was amazed. She was pretty observant, but she knew the specifics Sharon added were even better than what she would remember from just interacting with someone just once. The color of his eyes and the slight wrinkle at the edges when he smiled were very specific.

Sharon's description of Oscar came together to reveal an attractive man probably in his mid-forties. He had lighter skin so he could be a biracial African American/Caucasian or a Latino male. His eyes were a soft brown color that seemed to have specks of green or something in them. His hair was trimmed perfectly, and his hands were clean with no dirt or callouses, Sharon had told Trish. His smile was warm, and he didn't give off a threatening vibe to Sharon.

"Wow," Trish breathed out. "You are amazing. I never would have been able to remember this much about someone in just a few minutes of interacting. No wonder you get the big bucks," she joked with Sharon.

Her friend just shrugged. "Habits of the trade I guess. Do you want to plug that into your system and see if we get any hits?"

"Already on it," Trish said with a grin.

It didn't take long for hits to pop up on Trish's screen. Since they were sharing, Sharon was able to see the results as well. Trish mentally did a quick inventory of the short list popping up. She could see some of the photos as they popped up and could tell where some of them were. Trish knew Sharon could as well. They had both spent a lot of time honing their skills to be able to process things quickly.

Trish looked at Sharon the exact time that Sharon looked at her, eyes wide. They had both stopped on a photo of Oscar exiting the Salisbury police barracks where they knew the processing of the Del Rios was being handled.

"What is he doing there, and with a smug look on his face?" Trish asked.

Sharon shook her head. "I don't know but I intend to find out." She cleared her screen and started to type frantically on her keyboard. Pretty soon a file popped up on her screen and she shared it to Trish's. In front of them both was a list of the Del Rios they had caught and tried for various roles in the terror reign the gang has in town for years.

"He's not here, Sharon," Trish said as she looked through the photos twice.

"No, he's not, which could only mean one of two things," Sharon said solemnly. "Either he is an agent, or he pled out for immunity."

Trish shook her head. "There is no way they would have pled out someone in the gang for total immunity, Sharon. He has to be an agent."

"But then why can't we find him anywhere else? And how do I not know anything about this guy, Trish? I am starting to wonder if there is something more going on here than just this case with Billy and Reece."

"Well, then I think we found a new focus, Sharon," Trish said with an evil grin.

She hated being told what to do and how to do it. So, if Sharon was just as annoyed about this whole thing, then she would have an ally in it. And even if Sharon didn't want to dig in any further because her boss said not to, Trish knew she wouldn't sit idly by and let someone who wasn't her superior tell her what to do. She would dig until she found what she was looking for—starting with Oscar dearest.

Chapter 17

Sharon and Trish worked at their stations for almost six hours before Sharon decided she should head home before her husband worried. Trish knew he wouldn't because they had been texting through the entire evening. But it was late, and she wanted to get to bed herself. It had been a long day, and she was looking forward to some uninterrupted sleep.

As she settled into bed an hour after Sharon left, she stared at her ceiling wide awake. Groaning, she rolled over and wondered if she should get up and take something.

Just as she was about to move, the red light connected to her phone started to blink. It was the new camera they had put in behind the garage.

Trish sat up and opened the link on her phone. Someone was definitely coming from the woods. It made sense now why she could never see anyone coming onto the property. She squinted at the small screen and tried to take note of the person. The area was dark because she didn't want to draw attention to that spot, so that camera wasn't connected to a motion light. Instead, all she could go by was the light of the moon, which was surprisingly bright.

The person was shrouded in black, or dark clothing. A hood covered their head and even shaded their face so Trish couldn't use any kind of identifying information. She could guess that the person had dark skin because even in a shadow a pale face would show some dimension.

Reaching for her basket of ammo, Trish also grabbed her trusty old shotgun. Her poppop would be so proud of her right now. *Level head, focus on the target, never lose your grip on your weapon.* She grinned. She could still hear his voice in her head, singing her praises and correcting something minor.

She picked up her phone and watched as the person once again moved to the back door of her house.

"Idiot," she mumbled. "Two days in a row? You must think I'm stupid." She straightened her back and turned off the small lamp on her nightstand. She could maneuver in total darkness in her own house easily. She crept to the door and slowly opened it wide. She sat down on the first step and watched on her phone as the person again opened the screen door in complete silence. She couldn't help but give a little fist bump. That was amazing work, even if it was someone breaking into her home.

The heavier door had the lock picked silently while Trish watched on the camera, now switched to the one outside her door. This time she did get an alert, but she had silenced her phone. She crouched on the steps and slowly moved down a couple more. She would have about a second and a half between the door being unlocked and the intruder entering the laundry room and then another second before they were in her sights from her perch.

She moved down one more step, now about eight from the main floor, perfect placement for her shot to hit the person center mass. She wasn't out for a kill shot, although that would be easy. She needed information and injuring enough to give her the upper hand was all she needed.

Trish lifted the weapon and set it against her shoulder, watching and listening. The dim light from the single lamp lit up the space perfectly. The intruder, however, wouldn't have any indication she was there. No shadows would alert them, and she was as still as a statue, just like her grandfather had taught her. She was completely in control of how this moved forward. They would only see her when it was too late, and she had already gotten her first shot off.

The final click of the door lock giving way alerted Trish to her countdown. She raised the shotgun and held it steady as she waited for the intruder's entrance. The one creak in the floor by the main door was her first count. Next was the door to the laundry room moving. It didn't make noise except for the miniscule brush against the rug she kept there, nothing anyone else would even notice.

The first glimpse of the idiot breaking into her home was a shadow when they opened the door enough for light to shine in. It wasn't a lot, but for Trish it was enough to see exactly where she needed to aim and how much further she needed them to move into the room.

Another half step and then you're mine, she said in her head. She closed one eye and waited. It seemed to be taking the person a lot longer than it should. Trish briefly wondered if they were taking a long time because they knew she was there, but just as quickly dismissed it because there was no way that was possible.

Finally, a hand moved into her line of sight. She put her finger on the safety release but waited to make sure she had the right visual before she alerted the intruder to her presence. This way there would be less chance of escape, like last night.

As soon as Trish saw almost the entire back of the person, she pressed the release and then immediately after fired the weapon. She jumped up as she heard the grunt. Her shot hit its target, but she couldn't tell how much damage was done. Judging from the tone of the curse, she guessed it was a man. He was fairly tall and had a broad back, making her shot easier. But she didn't hear the thud of him falling, which concerned her.

She moved quickly and made it to her door just as the screen door slammed shut. Trish didn't waste any time though. She now knew where he'd come from, and he wouldn't get away this time. She moved quickly to the opposite side of her garage, further from the house, hoping to cut him off. She wouldn't fire again unless he didn't cooperate, but she kept her finger on the trigger, keeping the gun pointed down. It wouldn't take much for her to flip and shoot it quickly—a technique she had perfected with a lot of practice.

Rounding the garage, she heard a few curse words and a soft thud against the garage building. He hadn't tried to run and was likely thinking she was scared and wouldn't follow. She snorted in her head at the stupidity.

Trish moved slowly as if she were approaching a wounded and scared animal. Silently, she moved from the end of her garage to the corner, ducking under a low tree branch. She squatted down, moving slowly. She reached the edge and was relieved that the intruder was still leaning on her garage. He wasn't in a hurry, which bode well for her.

Jumping out from the shadow, she lifted the weapon back to her shoulder and stared at the face staring back at her. The shock that ran through her prevented her from saying anything. He looked just as shocked as she was.

"What the hell is wrong with you?" she yelled at him.

He laughed. "Me? What is wrong with *me*? What are you doing here? And why are you shooting that thing at people?"

Trish chuckled darkly. "Well, when idiots like you break into my house, what am I supposed to do? Squeal like a little girl and cry? Come on. If you knew me at all, you should know that is not me."

She dropped the gun to the ground, resetting the safety. "What are you doing here, Clayton?"

He sighed and looked at her. "I didn't know you lived here Trish. I swear. I actually didn't know *anyone* lived here. I was trying to get information and was told this place, well, your place I guess, had what I needed."

Trish narrowed her eyes. "Now where would you hear something like that?"

"Can't tell you," he said simply.

"Well, now that's just not going to do. Again, do you even know me, Clay? I mean it has been a while and deceit and betrayal does something to you, but even you should know that I wouldn't just accept something like that." She picked up her shotgun again and pointed it at her ex. "Try again."

Clayton stood taller and put his hands in front of him. "Trish, I can't tell you, seriously. But if this is really your place, then we may have some things to talk about. Please, let's go inside and talk."

Trish studied his face for any clue as to what he was doing or what his game was. But she couldn't find any reason to refuse him, aside from the obvious anyway. She noticed his arm was bleeding pretty badly and she felt a tiny bit of remorse, but only a little bit.

With a sigh, she nodded and dropped the weapon. "Fine, but don't get too comfortable. I'll get you patched up and you can tell me what you want and then leave."

Clayton nodded and pushed off the garage, holding his bicep. He had somehow had the time to rip part of his shirt to make a torniquet of some sort to keep pressure on his wound. Trish had to admit she was a little pleased with herself. She never really wanted to get even but there was a tiny bit of satisfaction watching him bleed.

Hmm, maybe I am a little more into causing pain than I thought, she considered.

A chuckle came from Clayton who was walking ahead of her back toward the house. Trish resisted the urge to poke him in the back, like he was some sort of prisoner.

"What?" she growled out. She was already irritated by him being there, even with her curiosity piqued. But to have him think this was a funny little joke was almost more than she was willing to tolerate. Although she did admit whatever information he had regarding her house would be good for her to know. Sharon might also have some ideas for what they can do about it.

"You just look like the old lady in the old 'Tweety bird' cartoons with that gun in your hands." Clayton shrugged and smiled back at her.

Trish scowled. "Granny had an umbrella moron, not a gun."

"Ok then, Elmer Fudd with long dreads," he laughed.

"Ha Ha," Trish said sarcastically. "And black skin because we all know Elmer was whiter than an albino's butt."

Clayton laughed loudly this time. They had made it back to the screen door and Clayton stopped at it. When Trish stopped behind him,

"What's your problem? You can break in but can't open it when it's unlocked?" Trish asked, not hiding her snide tone. "Too complicated for you, Clay?"

Clayton shrugged. "I kinda have to keep pressure on my arm 'cuz someone shot me."

Trish chuckled. "Yeah, that was fun. Poor baby. Let's get a band-aid for you." She reached around him and opened the door and then held it so he could duck inside.

When she had left the house, she hadn't closed the main door, so they made their way into the living room area and Trish motioned for him to sit at the table. She went into the kitchen and grabbed her first aid kit. When she reentered the room, Clayton had started to remove clothing to get a better view of the damage Trish had done.

She stood in the doorway and watched with a little bit of pride. She hadn't killed him and had caused damage like she had planned, even though she was hoping for a little more than just a flesh wound. But she couldn't help but notice how it seemed like he had been in a similar situation before. As far as she knew he was never in the armed services, so where would he get that kind of training? What had he been up to since the divorce?

She moved from her spot and settled next to him to help clean and dress his arm. She furrowed her brow as she stared at a single cut that was now clean and free of all cloth. She leaned back and looked at Clayton.

"How did I miss that badly?" she asked, studying the wound disappointedly.

Clayton chuckled. "Well, anyone else you might have taken off their arm. That was a good shot. But I'm a bit better than most." His voice was loaded with pride and Trish just stared at him.

She narrowed her eyes again at him and crossed her arms over her chest. "Spill. What are you talking about? This is hardly a cut. It's almost stopped bleeding already. I had a clear shot. So how did you escape major damage?"

"I have a lot of training, Trish. I heard you click the safety and with my increased sensitivity and reflexes, I just couldn't get completely out of the way." He glanced down and scowled at his arm.

Trish didn't move, just stared at him. Then she just shook her head and pulled out a large band-aid and stuck it over the cut.

"So, is this your way of making me listen? Break into my home and make me feel guilty almost shooting your arm off?" Trish asked as she picked up the wrappings.

Clayton sighed and pulled the sleeve of his shirt over the bandage. "No, Trish. I honestly didn't know this was your house. Heck if I did, I would have been here a long time ago."

"Well, who did you think was here that had you trying to break in?" Trish asked, ignoring his comment. It was a little unnerving having him inside her home, but the tiny seed of guilt gnawing at her conscious made it hard to just throw him out after shooting, well barely grazing, him.

Clayton shook his head. "Not who, but what." He looked around the room and his brow furrowed. "This really doesn't make sense though."

Trish followed his eyes with her own and creased her brow. "What doesn't make sense? It's just me so I don't need a lot of furniture," she said defensively, defending the sparce furnishings.

"No, that's not what I mean," he said hesitating. Clayton rubbed his hands together and then shrugged. "Somewhere along the way we got some bad information I guess. But with all the security…" His voice trailed off as he looked around again and then let out a chuckle.

Trish sat back and crossed her arms. "What are you babbling about, Clay? Spill it."

Clayton leaned back in his chair and stared back at her. "You've gotten bossy, Trish." He smiled and then leaned forward and tried to take her hand in his.

She pulled it away and shook her head. Trish was worried about her reaction to him, even after all these years and the betrayal he'd handed her. But her body betrayed her being this close. It wanted to forget all about the past. It was going to take a strong and steeled heart to resist falling under his spell again.

Closing her eyes tightly, Trish took a breath and hardened herself to his touch. She tucked her hands under her legs and opened her eyes again, giving him a cold stare.

"Clay, we're not in this situation because we are reuniting. You broke into my home. What's going on?" She used her no-nonsense voice, channeling Sharon's agent tone. She didn't know if it worked, but Clayton at least leaned back and didn't try to touch her again.

Clayton studied her face and then dropped his eyes. "Ok. I guess you deserve some sort of explanation." He paused again, looking up at her. He leaned forward again but didn't reach out. He just studied her face. "My partner is looking for information that she assumed was here." His arm swung around the room and then he shook his head. "What was she thinking?" he mumbled.

Trish listened to his words, not understanding what he was talking about. *Why would someone assume there was information here?* she asked herself, looking around as well. And what kind of information were they looking for? She tried to ignore the "she" he might be referring to.

"Look around, Trish," Clayton said gently.

She looked at him and then around the room. She brought her eyes back to him and lifted her hands.

"I don't know what you think is here or why you think something is, but there's nothing of value here." She stood to go into the kitchen. She needed coffee. Maybe something stronger, but coffee would have to do for now.

Clayton got up and followed her. She tried to ignore his presence behind her but could feel it. *Annoying*, she thought. He still managed to affect her.

Trish stood in front of her favorite appliance and fed it all the things to make the magic potion to calm her nerves and give her strength. She knew her ex was behind her, but she did everything she could to ignore him. She leaned forward with her hands resting on the cold counter and closed her eyes. She reminded herself of all the hurt and pain from the past to harden her heart to this man. His betrayal took everything from her, and she would not allow him back in, no matter how much her heart wanted it.

The gurgle from the coffee maker brought Trish's attention back to the present. She pulled two mugs from the shelf and filled hers. She turned and found Clayton leaning against the opposite wall watching her. She lifted the cup in his direction, and he simply nodded. She made his cup—two spoonsful of sugar--out of habit and handed it to him, with the spoon placed inside.

Clayton took the mug and smiled. Trish waved it off and then walked back into her living room. Instead of going to the table, she moved to her desk. She hesitated to start up the laptop though. She still wasn't clear on what Clayton was there for. Was he the one stalking around her property for the past weeks?

She turned to face him, now standing behind her. "What are you looking for Clay?" she asked.

"I can't tell you that," he replied stubbornly.

Trish stood from her chair and moved toward him slowly. "Then you can get your ass off my property and don't ever come back. I won't miss next time." She really wanted to have another shot at him for the irritation he was causing her anyway.

She started to move toward her door and when she looked back, Clayton was still standing in the same spot with a conflicted look on his face. She waited and watched as he seemed to struggle internally. She resisted the smirk that was threatening to appear. Trish crossed her arms and glared at him.

When he finally looked up at her, his whole body held an air of defeat.

"Fine what harm could there be anyway," he mumbled under his breath.

Trish had a sudden realization as she watched Clayton struggle with himself and whatever his partner wanted. He didn't think she had anything of value for whatever he needed so she was going to try to get some information from him without him suspecting anything.

Clayton sat at the table again and waved for her to sit as well. As she sat, Trish tried to play dumb. Clayton didn't know her skills and she was well aware that she did have valuable information, heavily encrypted, on her computer. They hadn't had any meaningful contact for a decade at least. So how could he possibly know what she did now with Sharon? She was glad the files they had been working on were currently hidden from sight.

"Ok, so none of this will probably make sense to you, but I have been working with…someone…to get some things…answered. I can't tell you everything. But we are trying to hold people accountable for stuff they did. My… um…partner can't really help right now so I am doing it all," he stumbled around with his words.

Trish held up her hand to stop him. He was rambling and it was giving her a headache. "You are not making any sense." She paused and then narrowed her eyes at him, realizing something. "What exactly have you been up to these last few years?"

Clayton chuckled darkly. "Well, that's a loaded question." He looked around and then smirked at Trish. "Tell you what. I'll tell you if you tell me what *you* have been up to."

So, he did *suspect something after all,* she thought. Trish shrugged. "You first. The truth, if you are capable of that anyway. Not some coded b.s., but the absolute truth."

He sighed with resignation and nodded slowly. "Ok, but you can't tell anyone. At least not until I finish what I started."

"Sure, ok," Trish agreed. Her curiosity was piqued now.

Clayton turned toward the table and folded his hands on top of it. As he moved to put his hoodie back on, covering up his now bandaged arm, something fell from his pocket. Trish's eyes followed it to the floor under his chair. As he looked around for it, she stooped down and picked it up. It was a small black piece of plastic. It had sharp edges, like it was broken. She looked at it and squinted her eyes. It looked familiar.

Suddenly remembering what George had given her, Trish went to her desk. She moved a small box that had a secret compartment on the bottom of it, a perfect place to hide thumb drives or other small things. She pulled out the small black piece that George had given her and lined them up. A perfect match made her look up at Clayton, who had moved to stand right next to her.

"Where did you get this?" Clayton asked, taking both pieces from Trish's hands. He fit them together in his hands and then looked at her. His eyes were curious and yet concerned as he studied her face.

Trish shrugged. "Tell me who you are first and then I will answer your questions. But not before."

She turned away from him and walked back to her table. She sat down and took a long drink from her cup. She would not be the first to speak. She would not let him manipulate her into spilling anything before she got information from him first. Her own curiosity was spinning in her head, but she was trying to keep it in check.

"Fine," Clayton said, moving back to the table. He shook his head and then started to explain. "After Anyah, and then you leaving me, I had a hard time coming to grips with everything. I was angry. I was sad. No, I was downright depressed, almost suicidal. I could barely breathe." His voice was quiet as he admitted his vulnerability to her.

Trish listened while he talked, keeping her own pain in check. Now wasn't the time to be weak, she thought. She didn't know if this was a trick to play on her own emotions or if it was genuine. She had to stay strong.

"I decided I couldn't live like that anymore. I had to find some meaning in life. So, I tried to find a way out. I had a friend step in to help. She saved my life," he continued.

Trish felt her lungs collapse. Of course, a friend "helped;" probably her ex-sister if she had to guess. What she couldn't figure out was why it bothered her to hear it out loud. She knew already, so why was she hurt? But that thought made it harder to connect the dots in her head. What was Patsy doing with Johnny if she was with Clayton? And now she wondered whose baby her sister was carrying. It didn't make sense why he kept calling her to talk or reconnect either. *Another game.* She scolded herself for even thinking about something else. *Why do I care?* she asked herself.

"I started with Anyah. I knew you were sure it wasn't an accident. I didn't believe you. I didn't want to believe someone would intentionally kill our little girl. But the more I looked, the more I realized you were right," he said softly, his voice full of emotion.

Trish looked up when he admitted what she had been saying all along. What would he think when he found out what she already knew—his precious Patsy was responsible? Deciding not to offer anything until she knew what he had found, she bit her lip and listened, taking another large swallow of her quickly cooling drink. Maybe she needed a refill. This wouldn't be an easy conversation.

She stood to fill it, but Clayton's hand stopped her.

"Trish, Anyah was targeted. Someone wanted her dead. I believe you too," he said.

Freezing, Trish stared at him. She had never thought about the possibility that the person wanted her dead too. She always thought it was just to get her daughter, Clayton's daughter out of the way.

"What are you talking about? Anyah was the target," she whispered.

Clayton shook his head. "No Trish, you were also. They wanted you and her gone. I'm just not sure why yet."

Chapter 18

The sun was rising by the time Trish and Clayton had finished their conversation. Trish sat in shock as she stared at the virtual stranger in front of her. She hadn't even gotten to share much about what she had been up to. Her questions and Clayton's patient answers consumed the entire night. Seems he had been busy these past few years, and she was shocked at all he had told her.

"Ok, your turn," Clayton said with a grin.

Trish just shook her head. "There's no way you have been doing all that, Clay," she stated simply.

Clayton lifted his shoulders and nodded. "Yep, all true. I have been doing a lot of training. Actually, that's how I was able to avoid most of the shells from your trusty old shotgun. My hearing and sight have gotten crazy sensitive, and I have been able to avoid getting shot more times than I can count."

"But how? I mean there really wasn't a sound made before I fired," Trish said confused.

"Call it almost a sixth sense, Trish," he said. "I have trained my senses to be hypersensitive. I heard the click of the safety and moved back. Somehow you still managed to hit me though. How, Trish? When did you get so good at shooting that old thing?" he asked. He looked toward the weapon now standing tall and proud against the wall. "I can't believe it still shoots if I'm honest. Your granddad would be so proud." His voice dropped as she smiled, slightly embarrassed.

She would not be flattered, she told herself. He knew things about her past that no one else did. It was just a fact of being married in a former life, that's all, she chastised. But she couldn't ignore the ease in which they fell into conversation, even after so many years had passed.

Outwardly, she shrugged. "Poppop would be thrilled to know this thing is still in great condition. Probably better than when he gave it to me honestly." She looked back at Clayton as another thought crossed her mind. "Was it you the other night too?"

Clayton hung his head. "Yeah. I thought it was some sort of booby trap and this time I would just avoid that spot and pay more attention. I didn't expect someone to actually be living here."

"So, what did you think this was if not a person living here?" she asked, waving her hand around in the air, avoiding answering his bigger questions.

Clayton sighed and looked at his hands. "I guess I have shared so much that a little more won't hurt," he conceded. Taking a deep breath, he started to explain.

"So, about a month ago, maybe six weeks, my partner and I stumbled on some information leading to a former member of a gang that used to run the factories around here. We had found out that a large number of them had been taken down but there was a small cell still trying to gain its footing on the shore, outside of Salisbury this time. I had been able to get my hands on some information that pointed at a member of the CIA who was helping them set up. We have been trying to get our hands on more information to link the two together to bring both down.

"My partner is out of commission currently because she is expecting so I am running around trying to get the information she needs to work her own magic to put them all behind bars. She thought this place was some sort of information station, like a vault of stored intelligence. The amount of surveillance equipment around sort of confirmed that in our minds. But then I find you here and I am all confused. So, Trish, catch me up. What have you been up to and why do you have so much surveillance set up if you just live here?" He tipped his head up to indicate he meant the house as well as her activities.

Trish was still stuck on the information he had shared. She had always believed that he would go after Patsy. Then the fact that Patsy was pregnant as well as his "partner" suddenly made some sense to her. Was it possible that he was actually helping Patsy with whatever Johnny was instructing her to do? All the talk about bringing people to justice suddenly seemed like another long tale of deception. Who did he think he was that he somehow thought she would believe everything he told her? Those days were long gone.

He did confirm a couple of things though. He was in fact one of the trespassers she had seen on her property—at least she could make that assumption. But who were the others?

"Clay? How long have you been stalking around my property?" she asked slowly.

He studied her face for a second and then admitted, "About three or four weeks."

Trish nodded. "So, who were the others wandering around? I have footage of multiple people and even some activity that could result in some jail time if it gets into the wrong hands." She was referring to the time she heard the gun shot and then a man carrying another off the property. She wasn't sure if Clayton could shoot, but she could assume one of two things. He was either responsible for the shot, or he was saving the other person from the shot. Either way, he was up to something that was not good.

Clayton let out a deep sigh. "I don't know for sure, but I think they were after you. Some sort of 'finishing the job' from years ago or something. I am not sure. All I know is that you are in danger and you really shouldn't be out here alone."

Trish snorted. "I think I am just fine. I seemed to beat your superpower senses, didn't I? Plus, I welcome the idiot who killed my daughter to try to take me out. I have waited a long time to have a face to face with him—or *her*," she said, emphasizing "her" because she knew who had a hand in it already. But would her sister have the guts to come after Trish herself? She doubted it.

Narrowing his eyes and leaning forward, Clayton studied her face. "What do you know, Trish? And how can I help?"

"Nope," she said defiantly. "You don't get to walk in here and make yourself out to be some kind of hero. You are a part of this too, whether you admit it or not. I heard everything and I know why our little girl was killed. And if you were even half as good as you say you are, you wouldn't have to go digging very deep to know yourself."

She stood and went back into her kitchen to make more of her favorite black heaven. Hopefully it would help calm her nerves as her mind started to spin.

A thought suddenly occurred to her. If Trish was a target, what would be the purpose of getting her out of the way? The only thing she could come up with was Patsy. She wanted Trish and Anyah completely out of Clayton's life, so she didn't have anything hanging over her head anymore. That made sense. She finally understood. And Clayton playing the good guy was probably to gain her trust to make it easier to take Trish out.

The thought that Clayton and Patsy were still working together and he was lying to her again made her want to yell and scream like a toddler. She couldn't allow herself to fall for his story. He was probably just trying to make himself look good to get into her head, like some sort of savior. The perfect setup, she thought angrily.

She could feel his presence behind her while she refilled the pot and started it up again. She didn't turn around. She didn't want to face him.

"Trish, I don't know what you think I know, but I can almost guarantee I don't. Please tell me. Let me help," he pleaded.

Trish didn't move, just stared through her dirty windows as the light from the rising sun revealed all her tiny protectors. She shook her head. "I can't," she whispered. "I can't do this, Clay. You should go."

She heard him sigh. She couldn't turn. She couldn't face him. Maybe it was the lack of sleep, but she didn't have the energy to fight him. He didn't believe her then, why would he now? It was pointless in her mind.

A hand touched her back and Trish startled. "Trish, please. I don't want to leave. This is the longest you have allowed me to be close to you in years. I need to stay. I need to help. Let's figure this out together. Please."

Trish sidestepped his hand and turned to face him. "If you didn't believe me back then, why would you now?" she demanded.

Clayton took a step back as if she slapped him. "What are you talking about?"

"I don't have time for this. Stay if you want, but I am not doing this with you." She tried to walk past him, but Clayton grabbed her wrist as she walked by.

"No. I won't accept that. Something is going on and I need you to tell me." His voice went from pleading to almost demanding.

She shook off his hand again and glared at him. "Maybe start with your so-called partner, Clay. I bet if she told you the truth or you told me the truth for once in your pathetic life, none of this would have ever happened." She turned to flip off her coffee maker and pushed past him to the steps. She was done with this conversation. She was chastising herself for feeling even a little guilt when he was and apparently still is conspiring with Patsy.

Clayton followed her but didn't try to stop her this time. He sighed. "Ok, I'll go. But I do need one last thing from you, if you are willing."

Trish froze on the third step but didn't turn. "What?" she barely whispered.

"I need you to give this file to your friend. I don't know her name, but I know what she used to do. She will hopefully be able to use the info I have gotten so far.

The agency is ridiculously good at keeping their people's names inaccessible."

She could hear the humor in his chuckle, something she didn't expect. She heard something dropping on the table. She turned because she hadn't seen him come in with a bag or anything. What did he have?

Trish saw a black file folder placed on the table. There was a gold outline of some sort on the cover. She furrowed her brow staring at it. "What is it?" she asked, taking a step down.

Clayton shrugged. "You have my number. If you need anything, and I mean anything, please text me. I'll leave you alone for now." He dropped his eyes and moved toward the door. "I hope you know I would never hurt you, Trish."

Trish snorted in response. "Right. You mean you never will *again*."

* * * * *

"Trish where did you get this?" Sharon demanded as she walked through the door.

Trish had tried to sleep after Clayton finally left. The information he had given her left her a little more confused, but not shocked. After all, she had done some similar types of training hadn't she? She had to admit that she was surprised they had taken similar tracks after their split. He had trained hard, and his body showed the effort he had put in. He had definitely developed a more muscular build and while she tried not to notice, she did, more than she cared to admit. The man still caught her attention and still made her wish they could be together, even after everything.

She knew she could never go back to him though. The betrayal had cut too deep, and the pain was still there. But she was somehow drawn to him, even after everything. She wondered if she would ever get past that. Would she ever stop loving him, even after all that had happened?

"Trish?" Sharon's voice took her from her thoughts again.

"Yes, Sharon?" she mimicked back, earning her a scowl.

Sharon sighed. "I asked where you got this file from." She held up the black folder that Clayton had left.

Trish shrugged. "Why?" She wasn't trying to be difficult, but Sharon was being weird.

"This symbol. This is the sepow, Trish. The one the Executioner leaves on all his evidence," she said, clearly frustrated with her friend.

Trish turned sharply. "What?"

Sharon nodded. "Yes, so where did you get it?"

"You mean the one who has been handing you solved cases and the main suspect on a platter? Cases your people couldn't solve? That guy?" She was shocked. Was what Clayton told her true? Was she wrong all along about him? But then what did that make Patsy? She almost choked as she thought about her sister being a good guy. *Nope, not possible*, she thought.

"Yes, Trish!" Sharon nearly shouted. "How did it get here?"

Trish sat at her table and hung her head. This didn't make sense to her. Could Clayton really be Sharon's idol?

"Clayton was here last night," Trish said, still in a daze.

"Clayton?" Sharon asked. "What does he have to do with any of this?"

All Trish had ever shared with her friend about her ex was that he had betrayed her. She never went into too many details because she didn't think they were important. She suspected Sharon had more information because she was the type of person who wanted to know more—about people, about events, about everything. And if it wasn't given to her she would find it elsewhere.

Trish took a deep breath. "Maybe I should start at the beginning," she said quietly.

Sharon seemed to sense her internal struggle and just pulled out her chair and sat, waiting patiently for her friend to continue.

Trish slowly relayed the events from the previous night into morning with Clayton. She was stunned as she retold everything that she had learned. Did she actually have it wrong? There could be more pregnant women in the world than just Patsy after all, right? But she didn't want to alter her beliefs too much because that could lead her to believe other things and she refused to be manipulated again. Hope made her vulnerable, weak.

"So let me get this straight," Sharon said slowly. "Clayton Trottwood, your ex-husband, is the Executioner we have been looking for? The one who has been solving impossible cases for years?"

Trish just stared at Sharon. Was that true? *Could* that be true?

"Well, what did he tell you?" Sharon asked excitedly.

Trish smirked at the teenage cheerleader coming out. The teen-like crush her friend had on her newly revealed ex-husband's superhero persona was comical. She just shrugged.

Sharon waved her hand, dismissing Trish and opened the file. She gasped when she saw the contents, bringing Trish's focus there as well.

"What are we looking at?" Trish asked. But when she saw the first photo, she knew what was happening. If she trusted that Clayton was this mysterious miracle worker, that would mean that the photo on top of the stack of papers meant Oscar was definitely working both sides. The agency photo Clayton had included wasn't from the same agency Sharon used to work for, which now made sense why she didn't recognize him.

Sharon spread out the papers on the table and started to work through them one at a time. "Trish, this is amazing. The leads we started with, he has already connected the dots to."

"How is that possible?" Trish asked, looking over the papers as Sharon passed them to her.

They sorted through everything and then pulled out their own files. The things they were trying to connect were indeed connected, exactly as she and Sharon had suggested. There was a document included that had a photo of Oscar with a different name, likely his legal name while Oscar is his cover.

"But if he's working undercover, why wouldn't you or Luke know about it?" Trish asked. Something wasn't quite adding up.

Sharon shook her head. "I'm not sure. But you're right. We should have known this before we went in and took down the gang."

Trish thought for a minute. "What if he *was* working undercover but has now turned sides and is working *for* them instead?"

"Maybe. But when we have an agent turn, we typically issue a statement out to other agencies to keep an eye out, so the traitor can't use their agency connections or name to get out of anything," Sharon said, her voice distracted by her thoughts.

Trish just nodded. It made sense, but then why didn't Sharon's agency know? Maybe they were working on something and that's why Sharon had to back off, since she is technically retired.

As if hearing her thoughts, Sharon nodded as well. "I think you are thinking what I'm thinking," she said simply.

None of the files mentioned Patsy though, which Trish found annoying. Of course, Clayton wouldn't include anything about her, protective as ever for her. She felt her anger return. All his nice words from earlier, just a ruse as she had suspected. She was glad she didn't fall for it, but the realization still stung.

"So, what do we do about it?" Trish asked, trying to avoid the feelings in her heart.

Sharon stared at her friend for a moment longer than Trish felt comfortable with. She turned her eyes away and looked at the documents again, avoiding her friend's stare.

Sharon cleared her throat. "Well, I think we might need his help, if I'm completely honest, hon," she said simply, as if it wasn't a big deal.

Trish felt her heart rate increase as she turned to face her friend. "I'm not sure I can do that, Sharon," she said and then pushed away from the table to find her mug. She could get Sharon and Clayton connected but then she would have to step aside. Given how her heart reacted to his presence earlier, she didn't trust herself to be that close again and be used or manipulated.

She felt Sharon's presence behind her and much like with Clayton, she ignored it. She stared out at the now brightly lit yard and listened to the faint clinking of her bottles in a light breeze. The sound brought back thoughts of Anyah again, as they always did.

"I understand this might be hard, Trish dear," Sharon said gently from behind. "But it is the only way we can get answers quickly. He has done a lot of the work already."

The fangirl was gone, and the logical friend was in her place. Trish turned to face Sharon and sighed. "I know but there are things that still don't add up. And things I want to stay in the past," she said, weakly justifying her position.

Sharon nodded. "I know. And I also know that you want to get these answers too. Trish, sometimes those things in the past simply can't stay there. They need to be brought back up so light from a new day can clarify them."

Trish groaned. She didn't want the light of a new day to clarify anything. She didn't need someone to explain why things happened the way they did or what she did to sabotage or damage her own marriage. She didn't want someone to tell her what was her fault and what wasn't. She only wanted to focus on her vengeance and move forward with her life.

She had an idea that Sharon knew this as well but was gently pushing her forward because that was Sharon's way. There was a reason for everything in Sharon's world and sometimes it irritated Trish, because most of time, Sharon was right.

"Fine," she grumbled.

Sharon just patted her arm softly and whispered, "You won't regret anything, Trish honey. Let's get to work."

Trish almost groaned as her always cheerful friend reappeared and nearly skipped out of the room. She turned to fill her coffee and then headed there herself. This was going to be another long day and night, she mumbled in her head. She felt like a mopey teenager, but she didn't care. She had spent so many years protecting herself from just this and now her best friend was inviting the devil into her home. Her anxiety outweighed the irritation at Sharon's excitement to finally meet the mastermind who stumped everyone at her former workplace.

Trish grudgingly moved back into the living room with hot steam floating from her cup. How was she going to handle all this, she wondered. *One thing at a time*, she thought.

She settled back at the desk and turned on her computer and lifted the screens from behind the desk. She didn't have to call Clayton right away did she? She would feel better if she could try to find more footage of these characters before giving up control. As she stared at her home screen, she tried to remember where they were in their search.

"We need him, Trish," Sharon said quietly. "I know it's hard, but I'll be here for you."

Trish sighed. "Fine."

She sat back in her chair, defeated. She wasn't going to win this one and she knew it. Sharon was still in charge, and she wouldn't let Trish avoid Clayton anymore. She could only hope that her reach ended there, and Sharon didn't push her to go into other pieces of her past.

Sharon was right though. In order to put these pieces together, they needed more help. Trish just wasn't sure who to trust—her ex-husband or Sharon's ex-boss. And then there was her sister who was also mixed in this mess, not that she was a risk to trust. Trish would never trust Patsy again and never was too soon to come face to face with her.

Trish picked up her phone and sent Clayton a text. It was simple. *Be here at seven.* She dropped her phone and leaned back, closing her eyes. If he had to ask any questions, she would answer but she was not going to initiate any conversations. This was for Sharon and no one else.

She steeled herself to be in his presence again. At least this time she would have Sharon with her. And hopefully with her friend's little crush, there would be little time for Clayton to play any games with Trish.

"Ok, let's get all of our things in order so we can hit the ground running when he gets here," Sharon said with a clap of her hands. "And dinner. I'm starving."

Trish chuckled. "It's only four, Sharon," she stated, glancing at the time on her phone.

Sharon shrugged. "Well, I came over as soon as you texted me, so I didn't get lunch."

As if that explained everything, Sharon turned on her laptop and started to gather her own documents. Trish ordered food and then joined Sharon in their documentation gathering. After compiling a stack of papers and photos, Sharon volunteered to go pick up their dinner. It was after five when they finally finished printing and organizing everything. Trish admitted she was hungry too, even though the very thought of the impending evening was making her feel slightly queasy.

She tried to focus on the task at hand while she waited for Sharon to return. She looked again at the photos of Patsy, Simon, Billy, and Reece. Her thoughts drifted back to Johnny and Patsy at the prison. Was it possible that Clayton knew how all these people fit together already, and she and Sharon didn't? Trish had her doubts. Trish and her friend were an incredible team. She didn't know how someone could have gotten a jump on this before them. But then again, Clayton knew about Oscar and where he fit in, at least partly. So maybe she needed to just sit back and watch her ex and friend work all this out. With them joining forces, Trish had no doubt this thing would be blown wide open soon. And she would avoid the drama of her past while everyone focused on the present.

Trish tried to ignore the niggling in her brain about how trustworthy Clayton was. But there was a tiny doubt that he was who he said he was. She hoped Sharon would be able to tell if he was being truthful and they could trust him.

Sharon returned quickly with food and as they settled to eat, Trish's screen lit up with an alert to someone on her property. It was too early for Clayton, so she furrowed her brow and moved to the screen. She groaned and watched two figures approach the tree with all her bottles. The new camera they had placed picked them up as soon as they emerged from the last of the cornfield her neighbor had yet to cut down.

Just as quickly as they appeared, Trish watched as a figure all in black, whom she now knew was Clayton, emerged right after them and easily took both out. He tied their hands behind their backs and left them lay on their faces. He looked up at the camera pointed in his direction and gave it a smirk. He hadn't bothered with the technology from his earlier visits to hide his identity. *Damn him*, she thought.

Chapter 19

Clayton stood awkwardly in Trish's living room as if he was meeting her for the first time. She couldn't help but remember the first time he met her parents, among the many boxes she had for moving out. He had looked so out of place that she felt sorry for him. They made the trip quick so he could relax. She had teased him about it afterwards for a long time. She hadn't seen him so nervous since then.

"Sharon, Clayton," she said simply, waving between them.

Sharon moved forward and held out her hand. "It is so nice to meet you, Clayton," she said. Trish could tell she was trying to keep the awe out of her voice, making Trish roll her eyes.

Clayton bowed slightly, taking her hand and giving it a gentle shake. His eyes met Trish's, and he raised her eyebrows in question. "Nice to meet you Miss Sharon. Uh, why am I here exactly?" He looked between the two women and Trish just shrugged and gestured to her friend.

Sharon waved her off. Turning back to Trish, she shot her a scowl. "Come on Trish dear. Let's get him all caught up."

Moving slowly to the table, Trish groaned inwardly. She knew this was going to be uncomfortable. She just hoped Sharon kept it professional and didn't push for more than she was willing to give. Clayton was a wild card on what he would say if Sharon pushed for more information.

"Shall we get started?" Sharon asked, motioning toward the table.

They assembled around the table. Trish snuck a look at Clayton and noticed a little uncertainty as he slowly moved to sit. Sharon had positioned herself on the opposite side, leaving Trish to sit across from her and Clayton in between. It probably looked like some sort of intervention to Clayton, making Trish fight to hold in a chuckle.

Clayton glanced at her and Trish bit her lip. *Could he hear me with his enhanced abilities*, she wondered sarcastically.

Sharon put their files in the middle of the table, still closed, and opened the one Clayton had left with Trish earlier.

"Can I ask a question before we do this?" Trish asked, raising her hand like a third grader.

Both Sharon and Clayton looked her way, and she nervously cleared her throat. "Um, Clay, where are the two people you 'handled' outside? They better not be littering my yard," she said with a scowl at Clayton.

Clayton laughed lightly. "No Trish. They are taken care of, safely off your property."

His simple answer didn't sit well with Trish, and she leaned back folding her arms across her body. "That is not an answer, Clayton *dear*."

"Well, it will have to do for now. At least until I understand why I am here with the two of you." He swung his gaze back to Sharon who just nodded.

Sharon picked up the folder Clayton had left, and he relaxed, nodding his head. "Ok. So, I assume you have questions?"

"Not so much questions, but more information," Sharon clarified. "We have been tracking the same people it appears, and we may be able to help each other out."

Clayton looked at Trish and raised his brow. "What exactly are you two up to?" he asked, not taking his eyes off his ex-wife.

Trish was confused. She thought Clayton knew who Sharon was since he specifically told her to give the file to her. But now it seemed like he didn't know who she was. She looked between her friend and ex and was about to ask that question, when Sharon jumped in first.

"Clayton, didn't you ask Trish to give this to me?" Sharon asked slowly.

With a frown, Clayton studied Sharon. Slowly recognition started to show on his face. "Wait, so you two are working together and you used to work for Luke," he stated, pointing at Sharon.

Sharon nodded and looked at Trish. Both were confused by his reaction.

"Clayton, you told me to give this to my friend," Trish said impatiently. "This is Sharon, said friend. Now what is going on in that head of yours?"

Waving his hands in front of his chest, he started to laugh. "Ok ok. I was confused for a second. I need more information before I elaborate on what's in that file. It was meant for the agency, not you specifically."

"That doesn't even make sense. You knew who she was. Why are you playing dumb now?" Trish asked. She was close to losing her temper. Maybe her attempt to keep him at arms-length was making her more frustrated and impatient.

Clayton turned to Trish. "I'm sorry, baby, I was thinking of someone else. I haven't been keeping close tabs on your place, my partner has, and she told me to look for a, no offense, younger woman who was here often."

Trish pointed her finger at Clayton and almost growled at him. "First off, don't call me *baby*. You lost that right a long time ago. And second—" she paused and glanced at Sharon, who had a worried look on her face, "Who else has been here?"

Sharon stood and moved to stand behind Trish putting her hands on her friend's shoulder. "I'm not sure, but we will figure it out, Trish. This just keeps getting more and more complicated," she mused, lost in her thoughts.

A million thoughts crossed Trish's mind as she tried to figure out who else had been on her property, and again without tripping her security. *What's going on around here?* she wondered.

"Ok, so this younger person," Sharon started as she moved back to her chair. "Give me more details please. Black, white, brown, green, purple? What are we looking for?"

Trish snickered in spite of herself. Leave it to Sharon to be snarky when someone unintentionally calls her old. Sharon knew how to get the answers she wanted, by pretty much any means necessary.

Clayton was silent and then said thoughtfully, "Let me do some digging. There may be something else." He disappeared before either woman could stop him or ask any more questions.

"He's an odd one, isn't he?" Sharon asked with a small laugh.

Trish just shrugged. She moved to her desk and watched Clayton through her cameras as he exited the house and disappeared around the corner. She zoomed in on his hands and phone and grinned as she watched him put in a numerical password. She would go back and figure that out and maybe get a look at his phone when he takes a bathroom break or something. He had told her what he had been up to, but she was curious who his partner was. She found herself hoping it wasn't Patsy.

Damn that tiny seed just won't die, she thought with annoyance.

"What are you up to, Trish?" Sharon asked from behind her.

Trish felt her friend's hand rest on her shoulder. She leaned back and showed her screen to Sharon. "See what I see?" she asked with a smirk.

Sharon chuckled. "Ok, what is going on in your head, my friend?" She moved to the side and leaned against the desk.

Trish shrugged. "Oh, you know, just a tiny bit of snooping. I want to know who Clayton's partner is. Maybe he is somehow connected to all this too. He and Patsy were pretty close after all."

Her eyes didn't move from the screen as she tried, but failed, to read her ex's lips while he was on the phone. Not all of her cameras had sound recording and he must have known which ones didn't, or just got lucky, because he had avoided those. She wished she could hear what he was saying. That would help answer some questions as well.

Sharon's phone rang as Trish concentrated on the screen in front of her. She ignored her friend's conversation until she heard her name.

"No Luke. Trish can help. We need her to help us on this," Sharon had insisted.

Trish turned in her chair and shot her friend a questioning glance. Sharon just shrugged and shook her head back.

Letting out a frustrated sigh, she turned back to her ex. He hung up the phone and she watched him just stand there looking out toward the woods. Trish furrowed her brow. *What is he looking at?* she wondered. She tried to look past him, zooming out her camera view to see. But she couldn't see anything but trees. Finally, he turned, gave her camera a wink, and moved back into the house.

Trish rolled her eyes and pushed away from her desk. *What was he looking for out there and who was he talking to?* She was getting more and more frustrated with his behavior. But she knew she couldn't tell him to leave just yet. Sharon wanted his help. She would just have to figure out how to get her hands on his phone and look some things up.

Sharon hung up her call just as Clayton walked back through the door. The loud thud of the phone made Trish look at her first.

"Everything ok?" Trish asked Sharon, who had dropped into a nearby chair.

"Not really. Luke just keeps shutting us down. Now he wants you off the case completely," she groaned.

Clayton had stopped in the doorway of the room and Trish could feel his stare. She turned and raised her eyebrows at him.

"What?" she asked simply.

"Uh, nothing," he started, sounding like he wanted to say more. But then he moved further into the room and sat in a chair next to Sharon. His eyes shifted from Trish to Sharon and then back to Trish again.

Trish turned her attention back to Sharon. "What is he up to now?" she asked her friend.

Sharon glanced over to Clayton and then said quietly, "I am not sure Trish. But he has something against you on this. I think it might be a conflict-of-interest kind of thing." Her voice had dropped, and she was looking only at Trish.

"Ok, so what? You know I don't care what Luke says. I am not under his jurisdiction, nor are you anymore, Sharon," Trish pointed out. She hated political games and had always liked the freedom she and Sharon were given. She couldn't help but worry even more about Luke now.

Sharon waved her hand. "I technically am, but you are not." Her eyes drifted to Clayton who looked confused by the discussion in front of him. "And he is not."

Trish shook her head. "No way Sharon. If you are suggesting what I think you are, there is no way in hell I will partner with him. Not in this or any future lifetime."

"You don't have a choice, dear," Sharon said gently. She got up and moved back over to where Trish was sitting. "I need your help, and he is the only one who can help us. I have to follow what Luke says, at least in any way that he can see or track. But I agree with you. Something is not right about him and this case. I need your help, both of you."

Clayton's expression continued to show complete confusion and Trish wanted to laugh. She remembered she hadn't told him what she had been doing all these years. She hadn't wanted to if she was completely honest, but here Sharon was forcing her to disclose her own secrets. She would love to be able to read minds because the look on his face was worth almost any sacrifice she would have to make.

She leaned back in her chair and crossed her arms over her chest. She tipped her head back and grinned at her ex.

"So, Clay, what is going through your head right now? 'Cuz I know *something* is," she asked with a slight mocking in her voice.

Shaking his head, he looked at her and then at Sharon again. "I have no idea what you two are up to, but I am going to guess it is out of your league and you should both stand down."

Trish snorted and Sharon laughed, making him scowl slightly.

"You better tell him, Trish, before he gets really upset," Sharon said with a grin.

Trish shook her head and grinned back. "Naw. I think I will keep him in the dark a little longer," she teased, earning her a glare.

"Ok, Ok," she said, waving him off. "Geez, so impatient. But first I am going to tell you don't ever tell me to stand down again. You have no idea what *we* are capable of." Trish pointed her finger between herself and Sharon as she spoke.

Clayton put his hands in front of his chest in surrender and moved to sit. "Fine, I will just sit here and listen, since you owe me that anyway," he said pointedly to Trish.

She scoffed. "I honestly don't owe you anything, Clay. I have been to hell and back and if anything you owe me a lifetime, and a little girl's life back." The venom in her voice was unmistakable and she noticed Clayton swallow nervously.

"Trish, dear, now is not the time," Sharon said quietly, pushing a file toward Trish to refocus her attention on the task at hand.

With a sigh, Trish took the folder aggressively and handed it to her ex. "We have been following these losers for a couple of weeks but haven't been able to get their exact locations."

Clayton opened the file and raised his eyebrows at her. "What have you been up to, Trish? These people are dangerous."

"That's cute, Clay," she said with a dismissive wave. "Anyway, we tracked them to a structure near Federalsburg yesterday and finally figured out who this guy is." She handed him the photo they had computer generated from Sharon's description.

Sharon chuckled as she watched from the sidelines. Trish shot her a glare as she continued.

Clayton was silent, but he looked from the photo to Trish and then to Sharon before he looked back at the photo. He finally shook his head.

"There's no way," he mumbled.

Trish and Sharon smirked at each other and waited for him to say more.

A few minutes passed as he continued to battle with himself. Finally, he looked up and studied Trish.

"Ok, you have to explain this. I have been trying to get solid evidence on this guy for years." He turned back to the photo and shook his head. "I don't get it. How?"

Sharon smiled and glanced at Trish, who stayed quiet. With a sigh, she started to explain.

"We have been following these two," she paused to find the photos of Reece and Simon. She handed those to Clayton, who took them, but seemed to be hesitating. "We finally tracked down Reece's movements and located this place." She handed him the photo Trish had printed from the aerial shot she was able to save.

Clayton moved his eyes from one photo to the next, sifting through the stack twice before he sighed and set them down on the table. He folded his hands and rested them on his lap. When he spoke, his voice was soft and still had a trace of confusion.

"I still don't understand how you found all this." His eyes locked on Trish, and she looked away.

Maybe she should feel flattered that he was amazed at their skills, but she was still afraid that this was all a game and giving away all their information felt risky.

Clayton moved in his seat, drawing her attention back to him. He made a move like he was going to take her hand but quickly thought better of it and just continued to watch her. She hid the smirk that was trying to break free. At least he had some common sense, she thought. She sat with her arms crossed, not giving anything away.

Sharon finally broke the silence and reached for Trish's hand. "You are going to have to let him in to get to the bottom of all this dear. He may have the key to everything we have been trying to figure out, maybe even more than you think."

Her eyes held something Trish couldn't quite figure out. Did she really know something and had been keeping Trish in the dark all this time? The thought irritated her. It wouldn't surprise her; Sharon always seemed to be one step ahead of everyone. But the two of them had been working together for a long time and almost always were on the same page. Was Sharon really that good that she knew so much more than Trish even imagined?

Finally giving up, Trish let out a frustrated groan. She pushed away from the table and grabbed her mug. This would need more than just coffee, she thought. She muttered a frustrated, "Fine," and went into her kitchen for a little more caffeine. The last thing she wanted to do was make herself even more vulnerable in front of her ex, freely giving away the secrets she'd held for a long time.

"Trish, I know this is hard, but please give a little bit. I really think Clayton has some information that will give us, and more importantly you, answers," Sharon quietly tried to convince her.

With a sigh, Trish slowly turned and stared at her friend. She narrowed her eyes as a thought occurred to her. "Did you set this up, Sharon? Did Luke really ask you to step out and leave this alone? Or are you just trying to play matchmaker with me and my ex?" She crossed her arms over her body and stared.

Sharon shook her head and smiled. "Luke has asked me to be careful and maybe let them handle things. But you know as well as I do that I'm not good at sitting around doing nothing." She shrugged and moved to stand next to Trish.

She knew she really didn't have much choice but to move forward as Sharon wished. But she would keep

Sharon involved as much as she could. The last thing she wanted was to be alone with Clayton for too long. Even Trish had to admit though that they would get further together than separately, given what he had been up to these last few years. She hoped she could keep distance between him and her, as well as the involvement of Patsy. That thought made a sick feeling settle in the pit of her stomach. How did Sharon expect her to deal with that part of this investigation?

Clayton entered the kitchen and stayed just inside the room, leaning against the wall. "Shall we get to work?"

Trish narrowed her eyes at him. "I have two questions first."

He looked at her for a long time and then gave her a simple nod.

"First, who are the people you handled on my property and where are they? And second, who were you supposed to be giving that file to if it wasn't Sharon?"

A rueful grin crossed his face. "First answer, two of the minor grunt workers of the gang I am following, well we are following. And second, I was supposed to give the file to you, Trish. I sent a photo to my partner, and she confirmed you are the one she intended to get the information to."

Trish turned to lock eyes with Sharon, the same question in both their eyes. Why would Trish be the one to get the file?

"Because you are the one seen the most here and the last time the information was shared, it was ignored," Clayton clarified, looking at Sharon.

"Ok, we can talk through that, but where are the morons who were lurking around my property again? Where are they being held?" Trish asked, not sure what she was expecting, but it definitely was not what Clayton told her.

Clayton shrugged and simply said, "They are next door waiting for me."

Chapter 20

"You are going to have to explain that, Clay," Trish said, crossing her arms.

Clayton chuckled. "It seems we have a lot to discuss, huh?"

The three of them were settled around Trish's table, with a tray of tea that Sharon insisted on and some crackers with cheese. Trish would rather have her drink of choice, but there seemed to be a lot of information they needed to unload, and Sharon insisted she needed a clear head. Of course, Trish just rolled her eyes.

"Let's start with Farmer Joe," Trish suggested, still sitting back in her chair, waiting for her ex to explain why the two trespassers were brought from her yard to her neighbor's. "First, how do you even know him and why is he helping you?"

"Well, like I said I didn't know anyone lived here. I met the guy one day out plowing. I asked him who lived here and he just shrugged. For a nice little fee, he agreed to keep some of his rows unplowed until the beginning of December to provide cover for me." He acted as if none of this information was a big deal or in any way important.

Trish wanted to yell and scream. She felt like he was being difficult on purpose. She wanted just simple straight forward answers. But it seemed as if Clayton was either oblivious or just didn't care. Her patience was wearing thin, and she knew it wouldn't take long for her to either blow or Sharon to react and step in for her.

She let out a dramatic sigh and waited for Sharon to get the hint. It would be best if she stepped in before Trish lost her marbles on her ex.

Sharon looked over and raised her eyebrow at Trish. It didn't help Trish's irritation, as if this whole conversation wasn't a big deal to anyone but her.

Finally, Sharon simply nodded and looked back at Clayton. "Clayton, can you clarify the relationship between you and the farmer next door?" she asked quietly.

Clayton turned to her, a little surprised. "Oh, I just met him. We really don't have a relationship. Since me and my partner have been watching this place for an opportunity to get inside and acquire the information we need, I just went to talk with him one day while he was out working." He paused and then added, "Nice guy."

Trish let out a frustrated groan. "Clay, this is like pulling teeth. Spill what you know and what is going on next door to my house. Like now would be great."

"Trish, dear, calm down," Sharon admonished. "We have a lot of information to get through, and you need to work on your patience."

"No, Sharon, I really don't," Trish snapped back. "All this is going on around me and with all the surveillance we have in place, I didn't know this vital piece of information?"

Sharon was quiet for a moment and then added thoughtfully, "Clayton, how many prisoners do you have over there?"

The question caught Trish off guard, but as she thought about it, many of the trespassers had disappeared through the cornfields. That would make sense now that she knew Clayton was "collecting" them. It also now made sense why the fields were still only partially plowed, even though it annoyed her. Her thoughts drifted to the others. She suddenly remembered the gunshot she'd heard before and the person being carried away.

She looked at Clayton with the question in her eyes. "What happened to the person who was shot on my property?" She unfolded her arms and leaned forward.

Maybe there was a lot more information she could get from him besides her sister's involvement with Johnny. She would need to know about these so-called prisoners if she was going to figure out who was after her. Maybe focusing on this will keep her head straight and off Clayton and her sister. With new resolve, she leaned forward, resting her elbows on the table, her chin in her hands.

Clayton let out a sigh. "I can't tell you everything about those people yet. I have to go through the proper channels and then I can share everything I know. For right now all I can say is that no one else should be crossing through here."

Trish looked over at Sharon who met her eyes. She wanted to press harder, but something in Sharon's look told her to wait. Maybe she knew something, Trish thought. Either way, she wasn't known for being patient or understanding. She wanted information. She was smart enough to know, however, when Sharon knew something and when to follow her lead. So, she bit her tongue for now.

"Clayton, what can you tell us about those people?" Sharion asked slowly.

"Not a lot," he said with another annoying shrug of his shoulder, making Trish groan again.

She pushed away from the table and stood. "Ok, I'm done here." She moved into the kitchen and started up her coffee pot. The tea just wasn't going to cut it. She briefly considered sending them both home and just going to bed or digging up her own information. But she knew Sharon wanted to tap into what Clayton knew so she resisted—for now.

Sharon followed into the other room and stood next to Trish at the counter. "I know this is frustrating, Trish," she began. "But we need to be careful. I don't know what he is hesitating about, but we have to give him time to figure out that we aren't a threat to him."

Trish scoffed at her friend. "Do you realize how much I *want* to be a threat to him right now?"

With a chuckle, Sharon put her hand on Trish's shoulder. "I actually do. I think I can read your mind pretty accurately. But we need to tread lightly. Just for a little bit. I need to find out what he knows. Now is my chance to figure out why he believed one of my trusted colleagues was working on the other side."

"I actually forgot about that," Trish admitted. She could wait for her friend to get more information and then kick Clayton out of her life again. She didn't feel like he had really given them much in the hour or two that he had been there so far anyway.

Once she got her pot of steaming coffee, Trish filled her cup and brought the decanter with her to the living room. She would rely on her drink to keep quiet and listen. She'd then follow Sharon's lead and stay focused on that, as if it were any other case they were working on. Trish took a long drink of her coffee and leaned back in her seat.

Clayton looked between the two women and raised his eyebrows. "I really need you two to tell me what you are doing with files on these people." His voice sounded all business-like and Trish resisted a scowl.

She was about to retort when Sharon stepped in. "Clayton, it seems we both have information to share. But we cannot share blindly. If the information you have is not able to be shared with us then I think we are done here."

Trish smirked at her friend. Sharon's voice was calm and quiet, but the underlying message was clear and non-negotiable. She hoped Clayton would take the bait. This was a tactic Sharon used a lot with those not in "the business." Trish also knew that if he didn't start helping, she would walk away, and they would figure out what they needed together anyway, even if it did take a little longer.

There was a long pause at the table. Sharon was the most patient person Trish knew, and she gave her the lead on this. But her patience did have a limit. Trish was ready to kick them both out when Clayton finally let out a long sigh and tapped the table with his knuckles.

"Fine. But nothing I say leaves this room," he said sternly, looking at both women seriously.

Sharon nodded and waved her hand. Trish just smiled at him, her mischievous one, not the sweet innocent one. She wasn't sure he knew the difference but didn't really care at the moment. She really wanted to give him a little teasing but thought better of it for now. They needed information and he still seemed to be in the dark about what she and Sharon did. They would keep it that way for as long as they could. The less he suspected the more he would give up—hopefully.

Trish grinned to herself thinking about their "naïve old ladies" charade. Clayton suspected something, but he obviously didn't know the extent to which Trish was involved and how much her skills played into the whole situation.

Clayton cleared his throat and leaned forward, tenting his fingertips. "I honestly don't know how much to tell you. But since this is your neighbor, Trish, I think you deserve to know a little bit anyway," he began. "Joseph Johnson has had that farm for almost fifty years. His family has lived there for almost a century."

A snort interrupted his story and Trish covered her mouth, trying to keep her giggle inside. Clayton looked at her with raised eyebrows and Trish just waved him off.

Sharon seemed to pick up on what she was thinking, but Clayton just stared at them and shook his head in confusion. "What is so funny? I'm trying to tell you something important and you two are laughing like schoolgirls."

"Sorry," Trish choked out. She waved her hand around, trying to be serious, but Sharon's small laugh didn't help her compose herself.

"Oh Trish, dear," Sharon said, gaining control of herself. "You really do know people."

Clayton looked between them and sighed. "What am I missing?"

Trish grinned. "I called him Farmer Joe, not having any idea who he was. And it turns out he actually is 'Farmer Joe.' Just a little funny," she said with another chuckle.

Shaking his head again, but not hiding his smile, Clayton said softly, "At least you haven't lost your sense of humor."

"Oh Clayton, if I didn't have my sense of humor I would have never made it through this last decade," Trish said. She meant it to be a snide comment, but she found herself meaning it. She suddenly realized that with Sharon by her side, she had been able to maintain a fairly sane mental capacity. She looked over to see her friend staring at her. She couldn't help but wonder where she would be if she hadn't met the woman across from her.

Sharon smiled. "I know exactly where you would be," Sharon said quietly. "And whether you believe it or not, Trish dear, God had a pretty big part in our meeting. Neither one of us would be here if we hadn't met."

Not being a very religious person, Trish didn't pay attention to faith or gods of any sort. She didn't believe any of that would have an influence in her life since she was so brutally destroyed not-so-long ago. What kind of god would do that to anyone? But as she looked at her friend, she wondered if Sharon was right.

She waved her off though, a thought for another day, she decided. "Whatever. Back to my neighbor Farmer Joe. Continue, Clay. What are you both up to?"

Clayton nodded. "My partner had approached him after I had made first contact about working with us. He had been working the minimum on the farm to keep a roof over his head. He doesn't have family and no one to pass the farm on to. So, my partner made him an offer to buy the farm at a good price if we could rent out his buildings, no questions asked, until he retired."

Sharon looked thoughtful and she asked, "So are you running some sort of drug business or prisoner base over there?"

Trish thought about what he had said earlier about the two people he took out on her property. She looked from Sharon to Clayton. "What exactly is going on over there?"

"Well, it is a kind of base for us. Since I have been helping government agencies over the years with some of their cases, we needed an off the grid place to 'interrogate' suspects." He shrugged and added, "Turns out Joe is a former military police officer and has some skills of his own."

Sharon chuckled from her spot across from Trish drawing Trish's eyes to her friend.

She shrugged. "I love former MP's. we share the same, shall we say, 'values'?" Sharon said with a glint in her eye.

Trish just shook her head and grinned. She knew what that meant. Clayton watched the two women like he was watching a high stakes tennis match. Trish noticed the confusion and interest at the same time in his expression. It almost made her smile. The pure curiosity was a look she hadn't seen in a long time. She shook her head to clear her memories. She needed to stay focused.

"Back to my neighbor..." Trish said, waving her hand in Clayton's direction when he caught her looking at him. She hardened her emotions again and turned away, looking for support from her friend.

"Yes, please elaborate about your accomplice," Sharon said, clearing her throat. "It would also be great if we could meet your partner as well." The two women shared a look and then turned back to Clayton.

Clayton looked away and then let out a fake cough. "Well, first things first. Joseph welcomed the extra cash and was more than happy to ignore us. We converted one of his old sheds and he agreed to turn a blind eye. We didn't do anything illegal, really. But it served our purposes." He shrugged and then grinned at Sharon.

"But I supposed it helped your people out a bit, huh?" he added. "Now that I know who you work for though, we may have to limit our knowledge sharing." His voice dropped a bit as his eyes did the same.

Trish looked at Sharon and then back to Clayton. "What the hell does that mean?"

"I think I understand," Sharon said quietly. She looked at Trish and smiled lightly. "Luke wants me to stay away from this for now as well, so I will step out and let you and Clayton take over from here. He has information and you have some as well. Together you should be able to solve all the mysteries here."

Trish tried to ignore the little twinkle in her friend's eye. She could guess what else Sharon might be referring to and decided to just move on from her suggestive tone.

"I think you might be right, Miss Sharon. And I know I can protect Trish if needed," he said, glancing over at Trish.

Trish scoffed. "I can take care of myself. But why, Sharon?"

"Because she doesn't believe me," Clayton said before Sharon could respond. He turned to Sharon and nodded. "But I will provide definitive evidence soon. Be careful Miss Sharon. You are my wife's friend, so that makes you my concern as well."

Trish looked at him with her eyebrow raised. "Wife? Have you been time traveling and forgot everything related to our marriage?" she asked, scorn laced in every word.

Clayton just smiled. "If I could travel back in time, I would in a heartbeat and fix whatever I broke. Then I would make you see the truth."

"You're infuriating, old man," Trish said and moved back to her kitchen. Sharon followed but didn't say anything.

Trish finally turned and leaned her back against the edge of the sink. She crossed her arms over her body and glared at her friend.

"Why are you doing this? I thought we were in this together," she complained.

Sharon lightly touched her shoulder and gave her that annoying sympathetic look Trish hated so much.

"Trish, hon, I need you to trust Clayton. He's the one who gave us the info on the dirty agent a while back, but we didn't believe him. Now with everything going on with Luke, I need to find out what else Clayton has so I know who to trust too. If I stick around, he may not share it with me." She released a small sigh, and Trish knew she was right.

She nodded. "Ok, I get it. But please don't make this into a little matchmaking game of yours, please," Trish said, suppressing the groan.

"What are you talking about, Trish?" Sharon said, putting her hand on her chest with feigned hurt.

Trish pushed her friend and turned to fill her mug again. Sharon just laughed.

"Are we good?" Sharon asked.

Trish just nodded. As much as she didn't want to be alone with Clayton, she knew Sharon needed her and she wouldn't disappoint her. It was an opportunity for Trish to finally pay her back for everything over the years.

Sharon gave Trish a quick hug and then disappeared through the door. She stepped back in to give Trish a smile and thank you and then went into the darkened night. Trish sighed and moved back to her living room, half hoping her ex would have disappeared as well.

"Not so lucky," she grumbled as she walked back into the room, seeing him reviewing files on her table.

He looked up when she walked over to the table and sat down across from him. He had moved to Sharon's spot and Trish was relieved she wouldn't have to sit next to him. Being close to him still affected her and without Shaon's buffer, she worried about what tale he would tell her, and she would believe it because her heart betrayed her brain.

"My neighbor," Trish said simply. "Clay, tell me what's going on in your world, so I don't disappoint my friend."

Clayton just nodded. "Ok. But then I need you to tell me two things. First, what have you been doing for the past 12 years? And second, I need you to explain what's behind the chicken house."

Trish looked up and stared at him. "How do you know about that?" She felt her face drain of color. No one knew about that place, and she had even managed to keep it hidden from Sharon.

"I stumbled on it yesterday when I was trying to scan for any traps or secret hideouts. The people we have been watching around here were looking for something and I was trying to figure out what it was." He studied her face for a long time. "Trish, I need you to let me in. I want to be able to help you."

She cursed at her freshly filled mug and wished she had waited just a little longer to fill it. She couldn't face him right now about that. She was still processing how he found it. She thought it was well hidden back in the dark depths of the dilapidated chicken house. How was she going to explain this without giving out too much information? How much did he already see?

"Trish?" Clayton's soft voice broke into her thoughts. "It's ok. I will wait until you're ready. But I truly believe I can help and if we work together all the questions will be answered. I can promise you that."

Letting out a sigh, Trish just nodded. For Sharon, she would do what she needed to. She knew Sharon had taken chances for her in the past and she needed to return the favor. Besides whoever this agent was, Trish didn't care. But the truth would be valuable to everyone involved. She silently hoped it wasn't Luke, even though she was highly suspicious of his behavior recently. That might crush her stronger than steel friend.

She looked up to meet his concerned eyes, giving him a slight nod of her head. "For Sharon, not you," she quietly vowed.

Clayton let out the slightest of sighs but gave her a nod in return. "I'll take any win I can get, Trish."

"Ok, start with Farmer Joe. Like seriously, what the heck is going on around me and why am I the last to know?" Her irritation started to come through and she just didn't have it in her to fight it anymore.

A chuckle escaped Clayton, but he quickly coughed to cover it up. "Trish, you need to understand. I think everyone thought this was some sort of information station and there was tons and tons of stored intelligence. My partner figured you were a caretaker of sorts and were here now and then to check on things and then you disappeared. We never put together that someone lived here or who you were."

Trish thought for a moment and then nodded slowly. "I guess I could see that, but why would someone think anything other than this was someone's home?"

"I guess because there was never a vehicle outside. All the lights seemed to be on timers and there wasn't much movement around the property," Clayton said with a shrug. "Plus the incredible amount of surveillance was insane for someone to live here—at least someone who wasn't a paranoid mess." He looked up and met Trish's cold eyes.

If you only knew, she thought with annoyance. Then a thought occurred to her. "How did you get around my cameras anyway?"

Clayton cleared his throat again. "Uh, I'm not sure I can tell you that."

"What the hell does that mean? Tell me how you got around my system, Clay. Now!" Trish was quickly losing her patience and was ready to bail out on the whole thing. She could find her own answers, especially now that her sister is back in town.

"Ok, Ok," Clayton said, putting his hands out in front of him. "Sorry. I just don't know who I can tell stuff to and who I can't." He paused and then met her eyes and quietly admitted, "We got our hands on some new tech, and it is supposed to make us invisible to certain systems. It must have worked on yours I guess."

Trish stood and moved to her desk. Instead of answering him, she started it up and lifted her screens from behind. Once everything was in place, she pulled up the footage of Clayton's faceless person wandering around her property.

He had since come to stand behind her. "This is amazing," he whispered.

Trish spun around. "Amazing? Yeah I have been tormented trying to figure out who was lurking around my property, and you sit here in awe. Congratulations, Clay. Your 'new tech' worked great." She kept the sarcasm and anger in her voice, knowing full well she wasn't afraid of anyone who had been there, but she needed to put Clayton in his place. After all she was a single older person living alone.

"Trish, I'm so sorry," he said, genuinely worried. "I never meant it like that. We just weren't sure how it worked in the real world. That's all. I'm sorry I scared you. If I had known…" His voice trailed off.

Waving her hand at him, she turned back to her screen. "Well lucky for me I am *typically* a great shot," she said with pride, but also acknowledging her missed shot at him.

Clayton snorted. "You are an amazing shot actually. Anyone else would have had a shoulder full of lead. But I am sorry Trish. I mean it."

It was her turn to wave him off. "Whatever. Well, you have seen some of what my system can do. But I am not hiding any top-secret intel. This is my house. So, what is it you are looking for?"

Clayton pulled a chair over from the table and sat next to her. "Looking at the files on your table, you clearly have some skills, maybe as much as Sharon does. But I am not sure you have what I am looking for."

"What are you looking for, Clay? Just spit it out," she said, her frustration rising again. The man could push her buttons so easily.

When he didn't answer, she pulled up the enhanced video of his footage to show they got around his "amazing tech." She spun around again and smirked at him.

"I may not have what you are looking for. But I just might," she said with a wave of the screen behind her. "So can we stop talking and start show and tell?" Trish asked impatiently.

Clayton was staring at the screen showing his full face, albeit slightly blurred which is why she hadn't identified him before, where it had previously not existed. He finally shook his head and looked at her.

"Do you need more proof of what I am capable of? Or can we move forward?" Trish asked, folding her arms over her chest.

He let out a sigh of defeat and smiled. "Ok. Let's talk about my suspects and go from there. Sharon had the same people we had, so now I just need to check in with my partner about this new stuff." He waved his hand toward her screen.

"Or how about you and I figure this out and keep any extras out?" Trish suggested a little too quickly.

Clayton raised his eyebrow at her but nodded. "Ok. If that is what will keep you here with me, I'll agree to almost anything."

Trish rolled her eyes and pushed away from her desk. She moved back to the table and laid out all the papers from the files she and Sharon had been working on. When she had finished, she looked up to see Clayton's face filled with something else she hadn't seen in a long time. Admiration and pride. She shook it off and turned back to her pile.

Clayton took his own pile from a bag and lined everything up side by side with Trish's. She watched in shock as she realized he was right. Everything lined up. But they had something Clayton didn't. Oscar's location. She wanted to pat herself on the back. She looked through everything else and saw that he also didn't have the location of the metal shed up in Federalsburg.

"You guys have been busy," Clayton acknowledged. He lifted the photos she had from her deep dive into Johnny's movements.

Maybe this wouldn't be a waste of time after all, she thought as she looked through his pile. She saw some more information they hadn't gotten yet, specifically Johnny's communications while in prison, except Patsy's visits. In fact, there was no information about Patsy at all. She furrowed her brow and sifted through the rest of his documents.

"Nothing," she muttered.

"Nothing what?" Clayton asked, looking over everything as if he had missed something.

Trish just shook her head. "Doesn't matter. Moving on, we have just started to put some things together. Sharon said you had already put things together, so what do you have on Johnny and Billy?"

Clayton looked over his papers and pulled out two. "I don't have anything on a Billy, but I have something on Simon." He handed Trish the papers.

Trish studied the documents and finally looked up, surprised by what she had read. "So, Johnny and Simon are rivals?"

"Yep," Clayton said. "Everything seemed to point to them being partners, but nothing I could find added up. Simon has been trying to undermine Johnny ever since he was arrested."

She studied, looked at the information he pointed to in her hand and glanced at him confused. "How is Oscar connected?"

Clayton sighed. "The wild card. I have been looking for Oscar for almost five years. The guy is like a ghost of sorts. He comes and goes and then reappears somewhere else. But I have reason to believe he is in with the feds somehow." He paused and lowered his voice. "I have believed for years that his partner is a dirty agent."

Trish gasped. "So he is connected. I knew it." She slammed her fist on the table, proud she had figured it out.

"Wait, Trish," Clayton said with hesitancy. "I said connected. I don't think he is an agent. I just think he's the face and the other guy is controlling from the outside, keeping Oscar out of trouble."

"Ah, gotcha," Trish said, nodding. "So, who is he working for?" She sifted through the photos of the people Clayton had to see if she could find a different face.

Clayton sighed. "I can't say right now. But soon, ok?"

Trish shook her head. "No. If we are going to do this, I want everything you know. Otherwise, I take my toys away, and you leave." She crossed her arms and stared at him.

If he still cared so much about her like he said, she would be able to convince him with just a few words. But if he was acting, she knew she would see right through it. Sharon had taught her well, and she wouldn't be fooled by him again.

She waited patiently while he fought with himself, making her smile.

"Fine," he relented. "But what we discuss stays here, Trish. I mean it. Not even Sharon can know. At least not yet."

Trish felt like a little girl who just got her way, but unlike Sharon, she resisted the schoolgirl's enthusiasm.

"Great. So, who is Oscar's partner?" she asked.

"Short answer? Simon," he said simply.

Trish raised her brow at him. "Short answer? What does that mean?"

Clayton chuckled. "Just hold on. I will tell you everything, but I need more before I give you that name. That will cause a ton of backlash as soon as it comes out and I need to be prepared with my own evidence and hand deliver him to Sharon, out of respect for her and her sacrifice to our country's safety."

Trish stared at him, trying to decide if he was playing her, but the sincerity in his eyes made her catch her breath. "Ok," she simply whispered. It had been a long time since she had made direct eye contact with her ex-husband, and she wasn't prepared for it.

"Let's start easy," Clayton said with a raised eyebrow. "What have you been up to?" He waved his arm around as he spun in his chair.

"Not much," Trish said nonchalantly as she followed his hand surveying the room. She laughed to herself as she thought about the last time they had any kind of decent conversation. So much has changed since then. She was more mature and definitely not as gullible as she was back then. She looked over to catch Clayton's eyes and shrugged.

"I finally figured out that no one was going to do squat about my Anyah, so I did what I had to do to get the skills to get my own answers," she said pointedly. "No one believed it wasn't an accident besides me. I was done trying to get someone else to do their damn job and decided to do it myself."

Clayton nodded and dropped his eyes. "I'm sorry I didn't believe you when you needed me to," his voice was full of regret and sadness. "But I do now, and I think I can help you with those answers. These guys are the keys." He tapped the pile of folders on the table. "I am still trying to figure out how they fit in and why they wanted you and our little girl gone."

Trish resisted the scoff at the tip of her tongue, knowing pretty well why. *Save that for another day*, she thought. "Right now it's about getting these lowlifes off the earth. Then we can figure the rest out," she suggested.

"That works for me," he agreed.

Chapter 21

They spent the next several hours working through their pasts. Trish laughed at Clayton's reaction to her last decade or so of work and training. He was impressed, he said, and Trish could tell he was sincere. Between the two of them and their skills, she knew they would be able to get answers. She kept her sister's name out of it for the moment, but she knew it was only a matter of time before she would have to bring that up.

Clayton had been attentive, and not once did he stray from their conversation or give her any inkling that he didn't believe something she and Sharon had found. He just took it all in and nodded.

It turned out he had been following Oscar for a long time but could never get close enough for a clear photo or look to make his own sketch. He seemed to be close to discovering the shed Trish and Sharon had traveled to, so they seemed to be complimenting each other's work well.

As Trish was about to suggest they take a break and reconvene in the morning, or afternoon since it was well past three in the morning, her system lit up, every screen was flashing with multiple trespassers.

Trish shook her head and sighed. Maybe this was the opportunity to take one of them out. She grabbed her trusty old friend and a pocket full of ammunition and headed for her front door. She could shoot from her porch without anyone knowing she was even there until it was too late.

A hand on her arm made her pause. For a second she forgot Clayton was there.

"What are you doing?" he asked quietly as his eyes moved between hers and the screens now behind her.

"I'm tired of these idiots playing on my lawn. Time to give them a wake-up call." She shrugged as if it were no big deal, but his grip on her arm tightened.

Clayton shook his head. "Just wait for a minute. There are three that I can see. Let's see what they do," he suggested.

Trish looked behind her at the screens and let out a small sigh. He was right, which irritated her. She was being impulsive, but thinking about Anyah, she felt that anger rise up again.

"Fine, but I am not taking orders from you, just so we are clear," she warned as she sat down in front of her laptop.

She tapped on the different views and turned on the recording on the others. She would watch and see what they did but if they made any effort to get inside she wouldn't hesitate. On that thought, she loaded her rifle and then moved to get her shotgun ready. She wouldn't be unprepared this time, she thought with a scowl.

A light laugh next to her made her pause and glare at Clayton. "What?"

He just shook his head. "You really should get something more reliable and easier to shoot, Trish," he said pointing at her large weapons.

Trish scoffed. "Yeah right. Just watch and learn." Her challenge was clear, and he just put his hands up in surrender.

"Ok, but I got your back, if you need me. Just like I always have," he said with emotion he coughed away.

Trish just shook her head and turned back to the cameras. The three had since split up but hadn't made any more progress toward the house. She squinted trying to figure out what they were doing. Her screens were lighting up and shifting as they moved around the property. One of them moved past her statue of Mary and subsequently tripped on one of the gnomes, thankfully not her favorite. She was now glad she moved it. The little guy was lying flat on his face and the idiot who tripped it was sitting on the ground holding his foot like a preschooler. She smiled but held in her laugh. She'd save that for when she met him face to face.

Now would be a good opportunity to get her hands on one, she thought. She glanced over at Clayton who shook his head at her, somehow knowing what she was thinking. She hated that he could still read her. Trish simply raised her eyebrows at him and crossed her arms.

"What did I say, Clay? You are not my boss. And this is a perfect time to grab him," she said with frustration.

"We don't need him," Clayton said. "We need…this guy." He pointed at the screen and Trish saw one person moving around her yard with precision.

He had managed to avoid all of her statues, and they couldn't get a clear picture of him with her devices. He seemed to know where they all were and either he was considerate or simply more skilled and nimbler than the others.

Trish just nodded and watched the person move around her property. "What are they looking for?" she asked more to herself than him.

"My guess? He's got the same intel I did and wants to find out what's here. He probably thinks those are traps, like land mines. He has managed to avoid every single one." He pointed at a different screen and grinned. "That guy is useless to us."

Trish watched as the injured guy got up and limped away, disappearing down her road somewhere. "Where is he going though? Should we follow?"

Clayton shook his head. "No, I think he's just running off. Was probably a decoy for this guy. Where did the third one go?"

"Right here," Trish said as she pointed to the screen where her newest camera was hidden in the tree. She watched as he seemed to sense something and stopped moving, looking around. Her eyes moved from him to the other intruder.

Out of nowhere a loud scream was heard and Trish watched as the person turned and took off in the same direction as the one who tripped. She snorted as she watched, making Clayton look at her.

"What was that?" he asked.

Trush shrugged. "Probably a coyote getting dinner. Who knows. But this guy sure knows how to pick his backup." She laughed. She relaxed slightly as she watched the third guy shake his head. He didn't stop his inspection of the property though. She knew one guy against the two of them wouldn't be a problem. Still, she kept her hand tightly gripping her rifle. It had been a long time since she shot it. Thinking about that, she reminded herself to give it a good cleaning and go to the gun club again. It was never good to be unprepared, especially lately.

When the last guy started toward the back of the house, Trish stood and moved closer to the door. Clayton didn't stop her this time. It was still dark outside and even though she knew she could track anything through the woods, it would be a little harder in the dark. She would need a little help if she was to push him back there. This would be her chance to get some answers.

"Trish, what are you doing?" Clayton asked, a bit of anxiety in his voice as he watched her.

She looked over. "If I can push him into the woods, he'll get disoriented. Then it will be easier to catch him and see what information I can get out of him. I'm tired of my yard being the neighbor kids' playground." She scowled at him.

"Ok, but let me help. I'll go out the front and push from that side. How about that?" he asked.

Trish just nodded. She knew she could do this on her own, but if he wanted to be helpful, she would take the backup. This was too important to lose the chance, and without Sharon she knew an extra hand may be needed.

She looked at her screen to see that the person had moved closer to her garage now. She watched as the screen changed to the new cameras she and Sharon had put up, the one that helped her catch Clayton she thought with a smile. Her eyes shifted to where Clayton was now moving toward the kitchen.

Turning her attention back to the backyard, she watched as he moved to the garage door and tried to open it. She just shook her head.

"What the hell!" a loud voice yelled from the front of her house.

Trish laughed as she realized Clayton had made it to the porch. She had forgotten about her dolls and just assumed he knew about them. Even though they weren't visible from outside, she thought he would have seen them with his super senses or something.

He poked his head back inside the room and frowned at her. "Ok, you are gonna have to explain that later." He let out an exaggerated shiver and disappeared again. She laughed again as she turned back to find the intruder again. She noticed the figure had stopped and was staring toward the front of the house.

She wished she had a way of communicating with Clayton because now all she could do was watch silently. It surprised her that she was actually concerned about his safety alone outside but she couldn't do anything but wait and hope for the best. She wasn't prepared for that feeling of helplessness. She shook her head to focus on the issue at hand.

With her enhanced system, she watched as Clayton's figure moved along her house and then disappeared behind the garage without alerting the intruder, who was back to checking out her garage. Trish watched, as Clayton reappeared behind the man and struck him once without him even realizing Clayton was there. The man dropped and Clayton easily lifted him and brought him to Trish's back door.

"Should we bring him inside or do you want me to bring him next door?" Clayton asked as she met him at her screen door. His voice dropped as he asked, "Or we could bring him to your secret lair."

Trish gasped. "What?" She wanted to smack his wiggling eyebrows off his smug face.

Clayton grinned. "I told you I found it. What should we do with him?" He nodded his head in the direction of the figure slumped over his shoulder.

She had thought he was just messing with her, but now as she looked at the limp figure on his shoulder, she didn't hesitate. She wanted answers and this is what she had been preparing for wasn't it?

"Ok, let me find my key and passcode." She rushed back inside and lifted her secret box again and grabbed the key. A tiny slip of paper was stuck to it and after verifying she had it, Trish slipped out the front door to meet Clayton by the chicken house at the edge of her property. She made sure her doors were all locked before she left because she just wasn't sure if anyone else was still lurking around.

Clayton was standing outside an almost invisible door at the back of the structure. She glanced at Clayton quickly before unlocking the door with the key. Once that opened, she had to use a passcode and her fingerprint to open a second door. Before she swung that door open, she turned to look at the man behind her.

"This is not something I want anyone to know about, ok?" She warned. She really didn't want Clayton there but given the situation she didn't have much choice. He wasn't likely to give up the unconscious man on his shoulder without a fight.

Clayton simply nodded. Trish wondered if he had managed to get inside the room before. Even if he did, he wouldn't have known about the other things that were well hidden. But she knew this would be a turning point. Her suspicions were out there, clear as day. What would Clayton do when he saw it all?

She shook her head and opened the second door to reveal a room set up like a darkroom for film development. There were multiple strings crisscrossing the room with a dim red hue covering everything. Hung on the strings were photos of things Trish had printed from some of her video searches over the years. She had limited photos of Patsy, but there were many of Anyah. She had edited the photos of the injuries when Anyah was in the hospital. She kept them as a reminder of what she was fighting for, why she did all the training. It was all for her little girl and justice. It kept her focused.

She sighed as she felt the energy in the room. It was where she went when she felt at a loss. She would just sit there and feel Anyah's presence. It helped revitalize her and refocus on what was important.

Trish heard a thud behind her, and she turned, remembering who was in there with her. She glanced at the still unconscious man behind her and wrinkled her brow. He looked familiar. Clayton was walking around, looking at the photos she had. She inwardly cringed when he came to the photos of Patsy and her various "interests", mostly those she used for drug money. She watched her ex carefully as realization dawned on him who the photos were.

"Patsy?" he asked, almost like he didn't believe what he saw.

He reached out and touched one gently as if it might break. Trish followed his hand and saw it was a photo of Anyah before she was killed. Trish felt the tears behind her eyes trying to push their way out. It was one of her favorite photos of her daughter. She was swinging on the old swing set at her parents' house. It was the summer before she started kindergarten, one of the last they had at her old house. The smile on the little girl's face was priceless and the joy just radiated off her.

A sound came from Clayton that sounded almost like a sob he was trying to control. She reached out and rested her hand on his shoulder. She knew what he was feeling and even with Patsy's involvement, Anyah was his little girl too.

Clayton reached up and grabbed onto her hand and squeezed it. He turned to face her and she noticed the tears on his cheeks. She reached her other hand up and wiped them away.

"I know, Clay. It's hard to see," she explained. "But it keeps me grounded and focused. The joy, the light she put into the world was magical and never should have been taken away."

Clayton cleared his throat and nodded. "I will help you, Trish. I want to see the people behind bars for what they did to her, to us."

Trish blurted out, "Even if it involves Patsy?"

She immediately regretted her words. This wasn't some sort of vendetta against him. This was for Anyah.

"You think Patsy is behind this?" Clayton asked incredulously. "Your sister?" he looked confused as he turned his attention back to her photos.

Trish stayed silent. There was a lot to unpack, and she wasn't in the mood just yet.

As if that mysterious higher power heard her plea, the man on the floor stirred and groaned, bringing both pairs of eyes back to him. Trish moved to a small bookshelf on the far wall and looked back at Clayton. She motioned with her head, and he seemed to understand because he picked up their prisoner and carried him to her.

With a sigh at revealing all of her secrets, Trish pulled out three different books and the wall gave way to a small, dark room. It felt as if it were in a cellar, but they hadn't gone down any stairs. Trish had bricked the entire room inside the old building as a way to keep anyone and anything out. It was the only part of the place that had concrete floors. She pulled the string attached to a single light bulb on the ceiling. She motioned with her hand for Clayton to put the man in a chair in the middle of the room.

After he had secured the man there, Clayton stood straight and looked around. His gaze landed on Trish, and he grinned.

"I think you left out something, Trish hon," he said with appreciation.

Trish waved him off. "It's not what you think," she explained. "I just have some of dad's old tools here and was planning to use it as a way to scare some information out of people—if the opportunity arose that is." She flipped a switch on the wall and the top part of the opposite wall flipped over, revealing multiple old tools hanging neatly on a pegboard.

Clayton laughed and moved to check out her supplies. "I can work with this," he said with a grin. He picked up a rusty old hammer with a pointed end and flipped in his hand, just as the other person in the room regained consciousness and gasped behind them.

Chapter 22

The dark brown eyes of the stranger were wide and held more fear than Trish had been prepared for. She had assumed the man was one of the professionals looking for an opportunity to take her out. His reaction was more like a scared little kid.

Clayton was spinning a new toy in his hand. Trish was convinced it was just for show as she watched him pretend to fumble it around in his hands. He dropped an old piece that looked like a mini pickaxe on the ground right in front of their prisoner and it made a horrifying sound on the concrete making the man jump off his chair in fear. Clayton laughed and said "oops" and picked it up again.

"So, I'm gonna ask you again," Clayton said, pulling up a box to sit on in front of the man. "Why are you lurking around the property and who are you working for?"

Trish thought the man was about to pee himself as he struggled to get a word out. He had never fought his restraints either since he'd regained consciousness. She was completely confused by the intruder and his behavior.

"I...I...don't...kn...ow," he stumbled.

Clayton winked at Trish as he grabbed an old rusted out hammer and tapped the man's knee. "Think *real* hard, kiddo," he said suggestively, not hiding his wicked grin. "I really need to find your boss. And I'm pretty sure you want your knees to still work, yeah?"

The stranger nodded emphatically. "I...never met... him. B-b-but I have...a...n-n-numb-b-ber." He nodded his head in the direction of his breast pocket. Trish had just noticed he had a dress shirt on. A weird outfit to go trespassing in at three in the morning.

She reached out and touched Clayton's arm bringing his attention to her. His eyes held the question he couldn't ask out loud.

Trish motioned for him to move to the side. Once they were away from the intruder, she looked around Clayton. "Something doesn't add up, Clay." She motioned with her hand at the man still tied to the chair.

"I know," he whispered. "He's not a danger to us from what I can tell but he was sent by someone. If not he would have said something about just getting lost or something stupid like that. Don't worry, I got this." He winked at her again and grinned.

Trish just shook her head and gave him a shrug. She would sit by and see what the guy said doubtful if it would be anything useful.

Clayton moved away and pulled a cell phone out of the guy's pocket. "Hm, what's your password man? I can't get in. Oh, wait, smile for me." He let out a bark of a laugh and held the phone to the man's face to see if facial recognition worked.

When the phone lit up on the home screen, Clayton chuckled and showed the screen to Trish who just smiled and shook her head. This man reminded her of the playful dad he was with their little girl so long ago. But this man had an evil and sinister tone as he "played" with this kid.

"Ok, what am I looking for?" he asked as he scrolled through the phone.

"Um…'pay day'…I…I think," the man stuttered.

Clayton moved the phone from his face and stared at the man. "You think?" he sneered. "You don't even know what name you saved it under? Not very smart now is it?" He clicked his tongue at the man and shook his head as if he were disappointed.

"What's your name?" Trish suddenly asked him. It occurred to her that they never asked his name. She watched him struggle to answer the simple question. She took a good look at him and realized he was really young. He looked like he was about nineteen years old and into something way over his head. He didn't look like the professional Clayton seemed to think he was. His skin was dark and the dimness of the room made him look even darker. She was tempted to ask him if he needed to use the bathroom the more she studied him.

The man looked at her and then at Clayton. "Uh Cobra, ma'am."

Trish winced. "Oh, *do not* call me that. I am not old enough for that."

"S-s-sorry," he stuttered, dropping his eyes.

"*Cobra?*" Clayton said with a chuckle. "Seriously? You mean like the snake, right? Some badass name so you sound big and tough, yeah?" He bent over and laughed heartily. "R-r-really?" He was struggling to breathe, but Trish also knew he was making fun of the kid.

Trish couldn't hide the smile on her own face. This kid must be trying to get himself into a gang or something she thought. There was no way Clayton was going to let him go easily, especially after what she had learned about his previous prisoners as the Executioner.

Clayton regained his composure and sat back down, flipping the hammer in his hand, close to the kid's knee to create just a little bit of anxiety for him. "So, Cobra, what is it you are doing? Is this some sort of college rush thing? Or are you trying to pledge for something darker, like, oh, I don't know, a drug ring?"

Trish looked over at him and raised her eyebrow. *He must have found something on the phone*, she thought.

Cobra looked up at Clayton and seemed to stiffen slightly. Clayton leaned back and tossed the hammer in the air, catching it by the handle.

"You gonna spill or am I gonna beat it out of you, kid?" he asked darkly.

Trish was confused but decided to stay silent. Cobra seemed to do the same. She noticed his demeanor had changed suddenly though. He somehow gained some confidence, but she wasn't sure where that came from. She leaned against the wall of toys, as Clayton had referred to them. She wished she had one of her guns with her as she watched the entire scene before her shift.

Slowly a sinister grin appeared on Cobra's face. "You can't hurt me old man," he said, no longer stuttering or stumbling over his words.

Clayton laughed. "You think you're tough just because you have someone backing you, kid? Go ahead be cocky. It kind of suits you actually. Cocky kid who thinks he's untouchable simply because he has a big dog feeding him scraps." He laughed again, making Trish look at the kid again.

Who was Clayton talking about? She wanted to get him outside so she could figure that out.

"Tell you what, little man," Clayton continued. "I'm gonna let you go so you can deliver a message to your boss. You let him know that his time is running out. And don't ever show your face here again or I won't be so lenient."

Cobra smirked at Clayton, making Trish feel a chill. "Tell you what, instead old man," Cobra said with an air of superiority. "I'll let my boss know and then we'll be back with reinforcements. Whatever is inside that house is ours and we will get in. You can count on that."

"Oooh big talk from a teenager who is still tied up and completely unable to move," Clayton jeered. "How about this, little man? I'll give you five minutes to get yourself out of your restraints and if you do, I will shiver in my boots at your threat. But if you don't and I have to untie your weak ass, then you stay away from the property. It's really in your best interests to stay away anyway, but I know you do have free will to be stupid and all that."

He seemed so confident until Clayton reminded him of his current situation. Trish chuckled in her corner as he tried to find a way out. Clayton just stood in front of the kid and watched the time tick away. After five minutes he shrugged and handed the phone to Trish.

"Do you think you can mirror this?" he whispered.

She grinned. "Absolutely." She took the phone and Clayton turned back to his prisoner.

He gave him some mock sympathy and sighed deeply. "I guess I have to let you out now since you couldn't get out yourself."

Trish drowned out the conversation as she used the time Clayton was distracting the kid to use the bench behind her to plug it into an outlet. She had an encrypted system out there that could network back to her main computer in the house. Once the download was complete, she turned to Clayton with a nod.

She hid the phone behind her, since the kid never saw the handoff. Clayton shook his head as if he were sad for the prisoner and then struck his head knocking him out again. He untied him from the chair and slung him over his shoulder.

"I don't want him to know this place is on your property," Clayton explained. "I know who he is working for because he's a stupid and arrogant kid. Now that we have his phone copied, we can sift through it for some more information. We need to get ahead of this." Then he added, "'Cobra' my ass," under his breath as they moved out of the building, Trish locking everything down tightly as it was before.

Clayton told her to go back inside the house, and he would drive the kid down the road where he could wake up on his own. He also had her wipe the phone completely of their prints so his boss couldn't trace anything back to them.

While she waited for Clayton to return, Trish sorted through the files and contacts on the kid's phone, copying everything to her own files and re-encrypting them. She sent a quick text to Sharon letting her know they found something, using their secret code so no one else would know what they were talking about.

If she found a lot of good intel, she would text a message saying something like she picked up burritos. If it was a small bit, she would get cookies. Simple messages letting her partner know she was making progress, since they couldn't communicate directly at the time. She didn't expect a response since it was almost dawn, but her phone lit up with an alert almost as soon as she put it down.

Trish picked it up and saw a thumbs up emoji followed by a message confirming what Trish already knew. Sharon was doing her own work behind the scenes. Her response was a simple, "great! I got the chips and salsa, along with dessert."

But Trish knew that meant that she was making significant progress on her end, staying offline so Luke couldn't track her.

"Hm, a full Mexican meal," she said out loud thoughtfully.

Her screens lit up letting her know someone was on her property. She looked around at her camera views, assuming it was Clayton making his way back there. After confirming, she went back to her files and started to open and sort them.

Clayton came in through the back door and she turned and raised her brow at him. "Why didn't you come in the front?" she asked. "It's closer."

He gave her a glare and shook his head. "What are you thinking with all those dolls up front like that?" He gave a fake shiver. "Creepy. What is wrong with you? You never used to be so scary and weird."

Trish tossed her pen at him, which he grabbed midair and smirked. She huffed and turned back to her computer.

"You'd be surprised what betrayal and loss will do to someone," she muttered under her breath.

She heard him sigh and then move behind her. He must have heard her, she thought, not that she cared if he had.

"Trish, we need to talk about this," Clayton said quietly as she heard him sit.

She spun in her chair and shook her finger at him. "I am not talking about anything in the past. I'm just trying to figure out who shot my little girl and put them away forever. The only reason you are here is because Sharon thinks you are some kind of weird superhero," she scoffed and turned back around. "Let's just get through this and we can go our separate ways again," Trish added, trying to keep the emotion out of her voice. *Damn this man,* she thought.

She felt her chair spin back to face him, and she crossed her arms.

"I am not going to let you run away from me again, Trish," he said, caging her in the chair with his arms. He leaned closely to her ear and whispered, "When we catch the ones responsible for Anyah's death, I will prove to you that I never betrayed you. I promise, Trish."

Looking up, she was struck by the sincerity in his eyes. He wasn't just trying to get out of a lie. He was going to make her believe it or somehow prove his innocence. Either way, she doubted he would be able to do that. Besides, she knew he'd already moved on, so why would he bother with her after so long anyway. Even if he could prove nothing happened between him and her sister, what difference would it make? Deciding he probably just wanted to clear his conscience, she turned away from him.

"Let's get back to work," she said, not wanting to continue with the conversation.

Clayton sighed again behind her, and she rolled her shoulders out. She needed to move on from this.

"Ok, so I got some contacts from the kid's phone and have saved them in an encrypted file here," she explained as she opened two new windows on her screen. "This one looks familiar, but I can't place his name."

Trish pointed to her screen as she pulled up a photo of a man she didn't know by the name on the screen.

Clayton was silent for a moment before he groaned. "Not who I thought would be the first one we'd find but not surprised."

Trish turned and looked at him. "Explain."

"Ok, but it's going to get complicated fast," he said with his eyebrows lifted. "Do you need to take notes for Sharon?"

"Pfft, whatever," she scoffed. "Just explain."

Clayton shrugged and began. "Well, this guy here is the one I have been trying to tie to illegal activities for years. He's an agent but he's dirty. I have him linked to multiple crime organizations, but he always manages to escape. It looks like he can make this look like a legit undercover operation as well."

Trish frowned. Was this the guy Sharon told her the Executioner had warned them about that no one believed? She needed to hear more, since she was an independent party, she could do more digging and see if they could build a case or exonerate him.

"Ok, start from the beginning," she said, as she glanced at the clock. "On second thought, let's get some sleep first and I'll contact Sharon for a complete Mexican breakfast in the morning." She grinned to herself, knowing Clayton wouldn't get the joke.

He just wrinkled his brow and nodded. "Ok, do you want me to come back in the afternoon, or would it be ok if I stayed here?" He looked around and noticed her living space was pretty empty of furniture.

Trish shrugged. "I don't care what you do, but don't stay because you think I'm some vulnerable old woman. There's a bed in that room there." She pointed to a door across the room from where they were.

Clayton's "ok" was barely audible and Trish could feel his eyes on her. She stretched, hearing her bones crack in all the expected places. She moved into the kitchen to rinse her mug and make sure everything was turned off. She flipped the light switch and then moved back to the living room. She hadn't expected anyone behind her and when she turned, she crashed into Clayton.

He grabbed a hold of her arms preventing her from falling, and she didn't miss the smirk that crossed his face. Trish pushed him off and moved through the door.

"Be careful, mister," she warned over her shoulder. "I'm a pretty good shot if you try anything inappropriate."

She heard him laugh as she moved to the stairs and paused. "There should be blankets in there. I haven't had a house guest in a few months, but I'm sure it will be fine."

"It will be," Clayton said softly. "Thanks, Trisha. And I will not give up on you."

His words were quiet, but she heard them. She ignored the flutter she felt in her chest and moved to her own room upstairs. She dropped her phone on the bed and then went into the bathroom. As she got herself ready for bed, she wondered for a very brief second if she had gotten anything wrong all those years ago. She shook her head hard, not allowing herself to have any kind of hope. She knew what she heard and what she saw back then. There was no mistake. And even if there was, how would he possibly explain his way out of it?

Trish tried not to think about anything except the case at hand. She didn't want to think about Clayton being this close to her. It was a toss-up about why it bothered her though, and that wasn't something she would entertain. Focusing on what she could control was a much better use of her brain power and time.

It was light out when she finally fell asleep, but she didn't sleep for long. The loud screech from her phone woke her up. She sat up with a start, looking around. She grinned when she remembered who that sound belonged to.

She quickly dialed the number back and her grin grew as Sharon answered.

"Good morning dear," Sharon said with a soft voice. "How was your night?"

There was definitely innuendo in her tone, but Trish just ignored it. "Pretty eventful actually," she said. "did you get my text last night?"

"I sure did. Mexican tonight?" Sharon asked with a soft chuckle.

Trish grinned. "For sure. What time? I might need to add some rice and beans to that order but will let you know in a while."

She knew there would be more information unveiled as soon as she and Clayton got to work again. She suddenly remembered he was just downstairs, closer to her than she had allowed him in a very long time.

"Sounds wonderful to me. Call me later and let me know what time," Sharon said with her usual sing-song voice.

Trish just nodded and refocused her attention to her house. She listened for any kind of noise but didn't hear anything. She wondered if he had changed his mind and left after she went to bed. It wouldn't have surprised her since he did have a pregnant partner to attend to.

She threw her covers off and looked at her phone. She was surprised to see that it was just past nine. She hadn't slept long but felt pretty rested. With the day ahead, she knew she would have to stay this energized. Maybe they could put this all to bed soon.

As she made her way downstairs a few minutes later, she looked around the darkened living room. For the first time since she moved in, she thought maybe she should get some furniture. It wasn't much of a living room without a couch or chairs. She never had a need before. She wondered why she suddenly felt like making a change here.

The thought evaporated as she heard the door to the small bedroom open. It was rarely used, but she kept a bed and night table in it. The last time it was used was for Sharon's friend during the summer. Her eyes caught Clayton's as he rubbed his hand over his nappy hair. He had always kept it cut neatly, shaved sides with a nice fade on top. She noticed it was shorter than she remembered, like a military cut. She decided it suited him well and found her eyes wandering slightly as she admired how fit he was.

Clayton cleared his throat, drawing her eyes to his and she rolled them as soon as she saw his smirk.

"Whatever, pervert," she said with a swing of her arm. "Want coffee?" She jumped down the last two steps and walked past him into the kitchen.

"Don't you drink anything else?" he asked, following her. "You know you do drink an unhealthy amount of caffeine, Trish."

"Nope. Heard it before, still don't care," she called over her shoulder.

Clayton just chuckled behind her. "Not surprised," he commented.

She ignored him and made quick use of her little coffee maker. She took down two mugs and then took out the sugar she knew he would want in his. She stood in front of the device impatiently waiting for her black goodness to drip out.

As they settled in at her desk again, Trish tried to focus on the situation. "The way I see it, we have four people to find. First, Reece. The trust fund baby who seems to wander in the shadows barking out orders and then only reappears on camera when the deed is being done. Second is Simon, third is Oscar."

Clayton looked at the photos on her screen and nodded along. "Wait, who is the fourth?" he asked, turning toward her.

Trish hesitated. She wasn't sure she was ready to spill anything about Patsy, especially since Clayton had somehow left her off all his own intel. She opted not to and waved her hand. "Oh the fourth is Billy, but we have found him. I wonder if he is conscious yet." She bit her lip, hoping she was convincing enough.

Before he could answer, she changed the subject. "And you are going to come clean about who the people are that have been trespassing on my property."

Clayton nodded and said, "Yes, I will tell you all that, but none of them seem to be dangerous. From what we have been able to gather from them is that they are low level grunts working for Simon or Johnny, or both. Everyone wants whatever information you have hidden here, Trish."

Trish sat back in her chair and sighed. "I have no idea where that information even came from. I don't talk to people and the only ones who know who I am or where I live are Sharon and Luke."

Clayton was quiet for a second and then asked, "Do you have a photo of Luke?"

"I think so. Why?" she asked, as she typed a few things on her keyboard.

Clayton was silent until she pulled up a photo she had from a while ago. It was Sharon, Luke, and two other people she didn't know.

"Well, that's a problem," he said with a sigh.

Chapter 23

"So, you're telling me that this guy is the one you are trying to establish as a traitor?" Trish asked incredulously. "How is that possible?"

Clayton shrugged. "I'm not completely positive, but I would definitely bet on it. The photo isn't great, and his profile is a little distorted."

"Well, no wonder Sharon doesn't believe you. She has known this guy for ages I think," Trish groaned. She wasn't sure what she was going to do. She had her suspicions about Luke for a while, but she was hoping for Sharon's sake it wasn't true.

"Trish we will have to keep this from Sharon as long as we can," Clayton warned. "I need to be able to make a case stick. I need time to do that."

Trish sighed. "I guess so. I am worried about Sharon though when she finds out." Maybe she would just play dumb and let the pieces fall wherever Clayton let them. "Ok, focusing back on these others. I'll let you handle your thing," she said waving at her screen with the photo still on it, "and I'll work on tracking down anything new from Reece."

"Wait," Clayton said, leaning over her shoulder. He pressed a few buttons, and a new file popped up on her screen.

Trish looked over with a confused expression. "What is this?"

Clayton smiled. "You wanted to know where Reece has been. There is our tracker." He straightened and moved away from her.

She didn't miss the smug expression on his face. But she also glumly realized Sharon was right and they did need each other on this, or at least they could complement each other's work. Trish realized she was going to have to hold in a good amount of sarcasm for the case. Sharon would be so proud of her, she thought. But that didn't mean she would have to act as if he were her savior either. His smugness would disappear when she revealed her sister's involvement. *Sweet justice*, she thought.

Trish studied the route in front of her of Reece's movements. It did in fact look as they suspected. He would reappear shortly before and a long time after something happened, including the attack on Billy. After a few minutes, she pushed back from the desk and looked at Clayton.

"So, what do you know about Johnny and Billy?" she asked. She and Sharon hadn't been able to make a concrete connection between them yet.

Clayton furrowed his brow. "I don't know of any connection. Billy is connected to Simon though. It is rumored that he turned himself in to become an informant to the feds against Simon and his attempt to poach some of Johnny's and Del Rios' business. Why do you think they are connected?"

Trish studied his face. *How could he not know?* she wondered. Her expression must have shown her confusion because Clayton leaned toward her and met her eyes when she looked up.

"Trish, what aren't you telling me?" he asked gently. "How do you think Billy and Johnny are connected?"

Letting out a sigh, she pulled up the footage of Patsy and Johnny at the prison. She bit her lip waiting for him to react, but he gave nothing away as he watched the video. His frown deepened as he watched, maybe this was the first time he'd seen Patsy so ill.

"So, you think Patsy had something to do with Billy being attacked?" he asked, leaning back in his chair. His voice was the same as it had been and Trish struggled to find some kind of emotion but couldn't.

Pushing it aside, Trish shrugged. "According to this, Johnny asked her to finish some job involving him. But Luke said Billy was attacked before Patsy left the prison or at least wouldn't have had time to do anything. They tried to tell us the video was prerecorded, but my analysis shows it was accurate for time. It was not recorded before we recorded it. Which didn't add up."

Clayton nodded as he processed the information. Suddenly he looked up. "Trish, you had photos of Patsy all over your room in the chicken house. What else are you keeping from me? Why are you tracking her?"

Trish stared at him. She had hoped he didn't see that before since he hadn't said anything, but what was she supposed to say now? Tell him his beloved was responsible for their daughter's death?

Clayton leaned forward and hesitantly took her hand in his. "Please Trish tell me what you know."

This time she didn't pull back but looked in his eyes. All she could do was nod. She took in a deep breath of air and looked down at their joined hands. She slowly pulled hers from his and then looked up again.

"Yes, I will tell you but first know that this is from years of studying and tracking people. I am not saying this out of spite or anger anymore. It is fact." She looked for any change in his demeanor, but when he simply nodded, she continued.

"I know Patsy is involved in Anyah's death, Clay," she said with a trembling voice. She hated how vulnerable she sounded, but it was also the first time she had ever said the words out loud. Even so, she was still annoyed with herself.

Clayton just looked at her for a long time. Finally, he nodded slowly and took her hand back in his. "Trish, please show me what you know. I may be able to help. I have some leads as well."

She was surprised at what she heard, maybe even shocked. His expression only held sympathy and understanding, neither of which she expected to see. What was she missing?

Feeling numb, she only nodded and stood to lead him back outside. She was about to let him into her private room for the second time. This time, though, he would be seeing everything she had. She wasn't sure how she felt about it, but at the very least she may get some new information. She didn't have anything to lose at this point, unless he destroyed everything she had. She pushed that thought aside and moved toward the door, feeling his presence behind her the entire way.

While they walked, Trish thought about the case. If Billy was working with Simon, was that why Johnny targeted him? Had he been working both sides to give Simon insider info on Johnny's operations? Something about that whole situation didn't sit right with her. She tried to remind herself to ask Clayton about it later. Maybe Sharon too. They must be missing something.

They arrived at the door to her room too quickly. She was abruptly brought back to the present as she turned to look at Clayton for the first time since she told him her suspicions. She was surprised to see curiosity and concern, not anger or judgement. She didn't know what to do with that and just turned back to unlock the door.

Once inside, the night before came flooding back. The door between the two rooms was still open, showing the room just as they had left it. The chair where their intruder had sat and sneered at them, trying to be strong and scary sat where they left it. The random tools Clayton had used to threaten the kid sat on the small shelf. The reminder made her chuckle. He never touched the kid, but he had still managed to instill enough fear to make him wet himself.

Trish felt Clayton's hand on her shoulder, and she turned. His eyes weren't on her though, they were laser focused on the board she had at the nearest wall. She sighed as she moved closer to it and turned on a different light, shutting off the red hue and directly illuminating the board. She pressed a button and the wall closed, leaving only her darkroom space visible. This was what she called her working space.

The board really was her entire eight-foot by twelve-foot wall. Every inch was covered with photos and newspaper clippings, pins and string. In the center was the last school picture Anyah took. She sat with her hair neatly braided, pink and white barrettes at the ends. Her smile was sweet and innocent and every time Trish saw it she would sigh and remember the little girl who was just as sweet as her smile.

She watched as Clayton moved closer and lifted a shaking finger to trace her face. Trish knew this would evoke emotions in him just as it always did when she walked in. She also knew that he never wanted to lose his daughter. He missed her as much as Trish did.

"Clay," she said softly.

He turned and looked at her, a tear rolling down his cheek. He quickly wiped it and cleared his throat. "Tell me what you know, Trish. I want to help."

Trish sighed. "Even if it means putting someone you care about away for a very long time?" she whispered.

Clayton grabbed hold of both of her arms and stared at her. "I only ever cared about you and Anyah, Trish. Please believe that for once. I don't care who else has to go to jail, or hell for that matter. I just want justice for our little girl. For *us*."

This time his voice was laced with anger, and she could see where his vengeance could come in handy, even if he tried to convince her again of something she knew to be a lie. If it got answers for her baby, she would take it for now. There was an annoying tiny part of her that was hoping he could somehow prove nothing ever went on with him and Patsy, but she knew that wasn't possible.

Brushing that thought aside, she turned back toward the board. "Ok, so I have tracked as much as I could from the time of the…incident to now," she explained.

She pointed out various things on the board and Clayton listened intently without asking a single question. She spent a good hour or two explaining her tracking and what each pin represented, the string connecting each person she had traced back to either Patsy or Johnny's accomplice from years ago, when she and Sharon met.

When she finished, Clayton was sitting on the chair he had moved in front of the wall of information. His chin was resting in his hand, his legs crossed. He looked like Rodin's statue of *The Thinker Man*, clothed though, as he stared.

Trish stepped back and watched as only his eyes moved. She almost laughed at the sight but stifled it. The longer it took him to speak, the more nervous she got. When he finally turned to face her, she saw something new in his eyes. Determination maybe? She tipped her head to the side and watched him struggle to speak.

Finally, he dropped his head and sighed. "I have one question, Trish," he said quietly. He looked up and met her eyes. "You suspected Patsy all along. Why?"

"Seriously?" she asked incredulously. "That's the question you want the answer to?" She waved her hand, gesturing toward the wall and looked back at him. She crossed her arms over her body, prepared to defend her actions against her sister.

Clayton stood and moved to stand in front of her. He gently uncrossed her arms and smiled gently. "I am not going to defend anyone here, except maybe you. So please, tell me what you know and why you started there."

Trish sighed. Did she really have to relive this moment in her life again, as if he didn't know? It irritated her and she wanted to just leave. But finally getting justice for Anyah kept her stuck like glue on her spot.

"Fine," she relented. "Since you have the memory of a houseplant, that night I came home from work, you and Patsy were in the kitchen. She was again doing her thing and at first I didn't think anything of it. But you said something like you would never leave your baby girl." She shrugged off the pain and added, "three days later Anyah was gone. I figured she took away the one thing keeping you connected to me. Motive."

She didn't dare look up at his face. She couldn't go through the lying again so she stared at her hands folded in front of her.

After what seemed like hours, Clayton moved and knelt in front of her. When she dared to look him in the eye, she saw humor. Confused and angry, she pushed him away.

"This isn't a joke, Clay. And I'm tired of your lies. Just move on and help me find her and put this whole thing to rest. I'm tired." She tried but failed to keep the pain out of her voice. *Damn him*, she thought, her emotions once again betraying her well-fortified heart.

Clayton moved toward her again and took her face in his palms, forcing her to look at him. "Trisha baby, you have always been my only 'baby girl.' I was talking about you, not Anyah," he whispered. "My little girl, *our* little girl was my baby, but only you were my girl."

Trish stared at him. Could she have really misunderstood this whole time? All these years of feeling betrayed by him and her sister were all an illusion in her own head? *No way*, she chided herself. She shook her head and moved out of his grasp.

"Uh uh," she said weakly. "I know what I heard and there is no way I heard wrong or misunderstood. What about the overtime you were supposedly working?"

Clayton sighed and dropped his hands to his side. "I can show you my pay stubs because yes, I even kept those. I will prove it to you, Trish. You are the only one for me, forever."

Trish narrowed her eyes. "What about your 'partner'," she asked, making air quotes. "Your *pregnant* partner who is mysteriously missing from all this."

Clayton snorted. "You mean Billie?" He let out a bark of a laugh. "She's my partner and has been helping me get a ton of information on this situation and all this. Nothing there, Trish. But you can keep trying if it will make you feel better." He moved again toward her and didn't let her pull away. "You are it for me. I love you Trish. And I will do whatever I need to do to prove it."

Trish didn't pull away this time and allowed him to pull her into him for a tight hug. She resisted the sigh that wanted to be released. She wouldn't give him that satisfaction. She almost admitted to herself that it felt good to be held by him again. But she needed to go back over everything she thought she knew and get Sharon to help her. She couldn't help the sick feeling that hit her stomach as she thought that she could have gotten this all wrong and lost all these years with him. Or was she being fooled again?

She gently pushed him away as something suddenly occurred to her. "Did you say Billie?"

Clayton nodded. "Why?"

"What if Johnny was talking about her instead of him?" she asked slowly.

Clayton stared at her. "Why?" he asked again.

Trish sighed. "This would be easier inside. But when Patsy and Johnny met, they talked about Patsy finishing a job regarding Billy. We assumed it was Billy-boy, who you say is working for Simon not Johnny. But if your Billie is trying to get dirt on Johnny and the Del Rios, is it possible he was talking about her?"

"Interesting theory," he said, thoughtfully. "Let me ask her. I know she was working on some assignment that involved Johnny awhile back but had to pull out because of her pregnancy and some complications."

Trish thought back to her video from the visit and suddenly recalled the question Patsy asked. "She asked about the baby," she said absently. What if the baby wasn't Patsy's but Billie's? Which would mean that Billie was possibly pregnant with Johnny's baby?

"What?" Clayton asked.

Trish looked at him. "What kind of relationship did Johnny and Billie have?" she asked.

Clayton shrugged. "I'm not sure. I only know she was doing some undercover stuff for her previous agency, and it involved the Del Rios. She's been off the assignment for a couple of months. Once they were brought down, she pulled back and has been working behind the computer ever since."

"Would it make sense that he thought she betrayed him, if they had a close relationship?" Trish asked carefully.

Clayton slowly nodded. "She's in danger, Trish. If Johnny ordered a hit on her, she could be in danger."

He stood and moved toward the door. He looked back at Trish and the wall. "We will come back to this." His eyes caught hers and he smiled lightly. "And this misunderstanding between us."

Trish could only nod and follow him out, locking up behind her. The sun had risen high in the sky, and she squinted at the brightness. Her thoughts were all over the place as she thought about what the past few hours have uncovered. She pulled out her phone and texted Sharon, asking if she could pick up their Mexican on the way over. She added that an appetizer of some sort was also in order. Heck she could add an entire additional meal with what was just revealed. They were going to need her on this, and Luke would have to just suck it up, she thought.

They settled in front of her computer again and Trish played the video from Patsy and Johnny's visit. Clayton sat and stared at the screen and pulled out his phone to send a text. When his phone lit up with a response, he nodded and set it back down.

"Ok, she is safe for now. The agency has her in a secure location," he said, turning away from the screen. "Is Sharon coming?"

"Already here," she called from the kitchen.

Trish grinned. Life felt right again. Sharon wandered in with a bunch of brown paper bags. Trish lifted her brow and Sharon smiled sweetly back.

"What?" she asked. She dropped the bags Trish now realized were empty and added, "I needed to get food right?"

Trish laughed and shook her head. "I am actually hungry though. Mexican sounded good."

Sharon waved her hand and pointed to the kitchen. "I know, there's your favorites in there. Catch me up. What are we looking at?"

Trish moved into the kitchen and Clayton followed. Sharon huffed and reluctantly followed them as well.

"I need food first," Trish said, smiling sweetly over her shoulder at her friend, earning her a glare.

They filled paper plates and then settled at the table again.

Trish spoke first. "Sharon, I think we were wrong. Well, only slightly. We were looking for the wrong Billy."

That got Sharon's attention. "Ok, explain."

They proceeded to tell Sharon what they were now suspecting, and she was quiet for the entire conversation, nodding occasionally. She had a thoughtful look on her face that Trish knew meant she was spinning everything in her head.

Finally, she looked over at Trish and sat back in her chair. "So, what does this have to do with Patsy?"

"I'm not sure, honestly," Trish admitted. "She definitely has something going on with Johnny, but how does she know about Billie?"

Clayton sighed. "That's what we are unclear about. I know what she was doing a few months ago, which would match up timelines. But other than that, I don't have specifics."

"Do you think her baby could be Johnny's?" Sharon asked.

After thinking for a while, Clayton shrugged. "I'm not positive. I know she isn't in a long-term relationship, but I can't be positive it's his either. She's only twenty-five, and a bit of a free spirit."

Trish and Sharon locked eyes and Trish sighed. "We don't know yet how everything is connected. But it seems like Clayton's Billie is connected to some agency like you are, Sharon."

"Not my Billie, Trish." Clayton clarified. "My partner for this case maybe but nothing more than that."

Trish waved her hand. "Whatever. Anyway, I think we need to figure out what Patsy and Johnny have to do with each other and how Billie fits into this."

"And how Billy with a 'y' fits into it as well," Sharon added. "This is getting messy."

The group was silent for a few minutes before Trish looked over at Sharon. "You know when you first pulled me into this, you said there was a connection to Anyah. What was it?" she asked. They had been so wrapped up in what Patsy was doing, she was distracted from the real topic at hand.

Sharon shrugged. "I knew you suspected your sister, and I had a feeling she would be connected to someone who knew more. I guess I was wrong, or at least we are heading in a different direction."

"Wait, you knew I suspected her?" Trish asked, stunned.

Sharon grinned and patted her arm. "Of course I did, dear."

Clayton laughed from across the table. Trish just glared at him.

"So where do we go from here?" Sharon asked, looking at Clayton. "Since it is your partner's safety we are concerned about right now. I want to know what you suspect so we can start there."

Clayton nodded. "Ok. We were looking into what Simon had been up to. He seems to have partnered with Reece recently and they are trying to cause friction between the different leads while still trying to keep Del Rios' business running. Our eyes have been on Reece and Oscar." He looked over at Sharon and then looked away quickly.

Trish knew that was about his suspicions around Luke. But she chose to stay quiet.

Sharon nodded. "Ok. Let's dig into Oscar then."

"No, there's not much there," Clayton said quickly. "We are better off focusing on Simon and his operation. Johnny and his group are pretty much dead in the water, especially when it gets out about Johnny spilling secrets while in prison."

Trish looked at him in surprise. "What are you talking about?"

"You don't know?" Clayton asked. "Johnny is trying to make a deal from within the walls of the prison to try to get himself out with some sort of immunity. That may be why he has been more brazen with his attempts to get at Billie. I need to find out what she knows and why he wants her gone."

Trish and Sharon locked gazes. "So, he's not really all that bright, huh?" Trish said with a chuckle.

"There's still the question about why Luke thought the video was prerecorded," Sharon pointed out.

Clayton cleared his throat and excused himself to try to get more information out of Billie.

Sharon looked at Trish once he was out of the room and raised her eyebrow. "What's that about?"

"No clue," Trish simply stated. "So, we don't think Johnny is planning a big prison break anymore?"

"I doubt it. The guards have been pretty straight forward about what they are doing, according to Luke. I'm still not clear about the video though. If one of the prison guards wasn't in on it, then that means it was Luke." Sharon sat back and had a thoughtful look on her face.

Trish kept quiet because she knew Clayton was trying to build a case and it would be in everyone's best interest if he could complete that. If he proved Luke was dirty, Sharon would have to come to terms with that. But they would cross that bridge when it was necessary.

Their conversation was interrupted by her screens lighting up and an alert sounding on her phone. She looked up and moved to her desk to mess with the views. Maybe Clayton had stepped outside.

But he came running back into the room and pulled out a small handgun from his ankle. He glanced at Trish and then Sharon and said, "We have company. Four total. You guys head out back, and I'll drive them your way."

He disappeared just as quickly as he had appeared, and Trish and Sharon jumped up. As Trish headed out the back door, she heard three gunshots and saw two men run toward her garage.

She smirked. "Idiots."

Without waiting for anyone else, she took off into the woods behind them.

Chapter 24

Trish heard several shots ring out behind her. She assumed it was Clayton and his two new friends. She took a quick look behind her and saw that Sharon wasn't next to her. She shrugged it off and followed the one who had disappeared behind her garage. The two had split up and Trish figured Sharon was chasing the other one.

A brief moment of fear went through her at the thought of something happening to Clayton, but she brushed it aside as she approached her garage. She had moved to the side just as she had when Clayton was there. She hoped the person would think she was coming from the side closest to the house for a faster confrontation.

She rounded the corner and lifted her weapon. She double checked the safety and then settled it against her shoulder. A wicked grin crossed her face. She was absolutely sure she would enjoy this encounter.

Just as she was about to reveal herself to the trespasser, a shot rang out to her left. She glanced over because it sounded close. A grinning Clayton met her eyes.

Trish returned his smile with a nod of thanks and turned back to her target. She lifted her gun and snuck a glance around the corner. The man's shoulder was leaning against the wall of the garage, facing away from her. Even the gunshot from Clayton hadn't made him move.

She ducked back and felt the cool steel against her shoulder again. With a deep breath, she moved out of her spot and aimed the weapon at the intruder, only to find the space empty. She resisted a groan and listened carefully, just like granddad had taught her. She finally heard the distinct rustling of the forest undergrowth beyond her garage.

Grinning again, Trish moved with stealth-like care as she quickly moved to the edge of the woods. She looked behind her to see Clayton tying someone up. She still didn't know where Sharon had disappeared but knew she could handle herself just fine. She turned her attention back to the forest in front of her. Her eyes and ears were laser focused on the darkened space in front of her.

She knew what she had to do and was aware this was going to be a challenge to track. As far as she could tell, the target had not been injured so there wouldn't be a blood trail. She would have to rely on her silent steps and lead the person to believe they had escaped. *Piece of cake*, she thought darkly.

Her first step into the woods gave her the confidence she needed to press forward. It had been a while since she tracked an animal in the woods. But muscle memory kicked in and she didn't have to think for long. Instincts took over as she moved deeper into the dimly lit area. The thick canopy of trees gave her complete coverage not letting much get through, rain or sunshine. Trish wasn't sure if it was a protected woodland, but it had remained mostly untouched as far as she could tell.

Trish gave it all little thought as she moved. She stopped periodically and listened to the sounds around her. She slowly moved through the trees, stepping over logs, being careful not to trip on any of the covered branches that had fallen over time. The floor of the woods was layered with so much foliage from endless shedding of leaves each fall and storms that shook other leaves and branches off the trees. Trish felt the softness under her feet as she slowly made her way toward the sounds of her trespasser.

After a few yards, Trish stopped. The woods were silent again and she crouched down. She scanned the area around her and then closed her eyes. She listened intently for anything that sounded outside of nature. Once she was able to again find the gentle swishing of the undergrowth, she opened her eyes and looked in that direction. She squinted and finally saw movement.

Grinning, she stayed low to the ground and moved silently over the soft ground again. But within minutes she lost the trail again. Trish let out a huff of frustration. She knew she should be better than this. She sat on a nearby log and looked around her. She had traveled far enough into the woods now that she couldn't see her house anymore. That didn't matter though. She knew which direction her house was, and which direction led to her neighbor and which way went further into the woods. She looked in all directions and then closed her eyes again.

When she opened them she noticed the sun had ducked behind some clouds. With a small chuckle, she knew she had the advantage, if she could figure out where he went. She could easily navigate the woods without the sun, but it took a highly trained person to do that. Since she now knew the highly trained professional who had gotten around her cameras was Clayton, she could assume this idiot wasn't well trained.

She looked around her and saw a tiny something waving in the light breeze. Trish leaned over and picked a small piece of fabric off a thorny shrub.

"Perfect," she mumbled. She looked up and tried to see if she could find another speck. Sure enough there was a second piece stuck to a low hanging branch just above her head. He must have gotten tangled in the foliage somehow.

Trish picked off the pieces and then started to slowly work her way through the woods, finding more pieces. They were very small and if she wasn't an avid hunter, she wouldn't have seen them. A few more yards from where she found her first piece, a long string was waving at her in the light breeze. Attached to it was a larger piece of fleece. All the pieces were black and fairly thin. It could have been a hoodie, but seemed thin for fleece.

She furrowed her brow. She didn't recall if the person was wearing a hoodie, but then again she didn't really look hard to see what they were wearing. She shrugged it off and continued to move forward. Glancing around, she noticed the woods seemed to get even darker as she moved deeper. There was a slight chill in the air now that the sun was hidden.

Shaking her head of the unimportant things, she refocused on her task. Looking at the pieces she had gathered, she nodded and then stuffed them in her pocket. Flipping her rifle over her shoulder, she moved forward again. Her eyes were laser focused in front of her, scanning for any additional pieces of fabric or clues that she was on the right track.

A sound from behind her made her stop moving and duck low. Slowly she turned and saw Clayton making his way toward her. Confused, she just watched as he got closer. He crouched down next to her and whispered in her ear.

"I think he is headed toward Joe's. I have one of my guys waiting at the edge of the field to make sure. We can keep moving this way and possibly move him into the protected lands and completely disorient him." His eyes stayed focused on something in the distance.

Trish looked up and then around and realized she was in fact on the way to her neighbor's farm. She turned back to Clayton and nodded. Then she pointed to her left.

"We should go this way. I think he may have shifted directions. I found these but it has been a little while since I found another." She pulled the pieces out of her pocket and handed them to her ex.

Clayton hummed as he looked at each piece, like it held the answer to some mystery.

Trish looked around. "Where's Sharon?" she asked.

"She's heading to Joe's with the other three. Trish, this is pretty thin. He could have cut himself on this branch, given how much this appears to be shredded." He held up the last piece she had found.

Trish took it and examined it for any trace of blood. It looked clean, but that didn't mean anything. She got up and looked near where she found it and moved a little bit ahead. Sure enough, she found a couple of leaves from a low-lying branch with traces of red stuff. Looking over at Clayton, she grinned.

"Gotcha," she said, snapping her fingers. She pocketed the fabric and turned to face Clayton. "Which way are you going?"

Clayton gave her a confused look. "I'm following you, Trish. I'm not leaving your side. We don't know what this guy is doing or looking for. With your life in danger, I won't be going anywhere."

The reality of what he had told her earlier started to sink in. For the first time she wondered if she was actually the one being hunted and not the other way around. Maybe this person's plan was to get her in the woods to disorient her and then attack. The feeling in the pit of her stomach wasn't fear, however. It was determination. If this was in fact the one who had killed her little girl, he was definitely underestimating her.

Her thoughts again drifted back to when her Anyah was shot. If she had her head on a swivel, watching for danger like her grandfather had taught her, he never would have escaped. She would have gotten off a much deadlier shot. But this time she was better prepared, and he wouldn't get away clean.

Trish nodded at Clayton. Having another set of eyes—and additional gun—could be helpful. She rarely asked for help, but this was a time she knew she just might be over her own head.

"Let's do this then," she said calmly. "But know this Clay. I am a damn good shot, and I am not accepting your help because I don't think I can handle it. I just want to make sure we catch this bastard."

Clayton laughed softly. "That's my girl."

In spite of herself, Trish smiled back. For the first time in a really long time, she didn't hate this man next to her. She wasn't sure what that meant but she would unpack that later. They had a bad guy to catch.

They moved through the woods side by side, as if they had always done this type of thing together. Clayton covered the left while Trish covered the right. They were able to move forward pretty quickly, Trish scanning the branches for traces of blood. It had been a while before she motioned for Clayton to stop. She thought she saw something in her periphery.

Without making a sound, Clayton dropped down next to her. Trish peered through the branches and leaves and watched a figure in the distance. She wasn't positive it was the one they were searching for, but they needed more information. The blood trail had since dried up and hopefully this was where things came to an end.

The person looked injured or just slow. *Maybe they were disoriented*, she thought. They watched for a few minutes. They seemed to be turning around in different directions but not moving. Trish furrowed her brow, watching the person. She figured it would be a good opportunity to surprise them and take them out before they were comfortable or got their bearings.

All Trish could think about was the possibility that this person was responsible for her daughter's shooting. The more she watched, the more convinced she became. She studied the profile and movements. When the "accident" happened, Trish was focused on Anyah, but she was also watching the idiot run away. She had time to look their way, but her gun wasn't ready or she would've gotten a better shot off. All she remembered was the person's slight limp.

Maybe she had hit him after all, she thought. She wondered if she was responsible for the limp or if he always had it. Either way it was one of the few characteristics she knew about the killer.

The figure in front of her finally moved in one direction, and she stared trying to discern if there was a limp. It was difficult to verify, but she noticed they were walking away from her and Clayton. Narrowing her eyes, she pushed herself up slightly to see over the brush they were hiding behind. As soon as she saw the person's shoulder drop on one side, she felt a kind of adrenaline rush in her body. It had to be him.

Trish glanced over at Clayton and nodded, hoping he understood. She wanted to go after the single figure in the distance. It was her chance to get some answers. She wasn't thinking about training, all she thought about was justice. Her mind wasn't even on the trespassing anymore. She was convinced this one was responsible for the loss of Anyah. Her vision became single focused.

A hand gripped her arm just as she was about to move forward. Trish glanced back and Clayton shook his head.

She pulled her hand away sharply and scowled at him. But something held her back. Considering it for a second, she wondered if she was letting her emotions guide her. Either way, she wasn't going to give Clayton the satisfaction of holding her back.

Trish sat down, hidden by the shrubbery around them. "Clay, that's him. I'm going after him," she whisper-yelled at him. She started to push herself up again, but Clayton held her arm tightly.

"No, Trish. I don't think he's alone. Just wait a second." His voice was firm and gentle at the same time.

She settled back down on her heels and stared at Clayton. She was struggling to find the words to retort back when he grinned and pointed back at where the man was standing. But now a group had gathered, with the first man in the middle seemingly talking animatedly waving his arms around.

Trish glanced over and raised her eyebrows, and her ex just grinned wider and shrugged. She didn't know how he knew there would be more, but they didn't have the opportunity to ask as one of the group stood tall and shot his gun in the air to quiet the group. They couldn't hear what was being said, but they seemed to be in a state of confusion and panic as she watched with interest. *What was this group up to?* she wondered.

A light tap on her arm brought her attention back to Clayton. He pointed his finger in another direction and Trish leaned forward to look through some branches near her face. She slowly pushed them aside and saw a building, or rather a barely standing shack in the distance. It looked like an old hunting structure that could collapse at any moment. She wondered if that was where they had been hiding out.

Clayton tapped her arm again to get her attention. He smiled at her when she turned again. She furrowed her brow. *What was he smiling like an idiot about?* she asked herself with annoyance. She wanted to glare at him, but a rustling not far from them prevented her from speaking. She turned toward the noise and as she did an array of gunfire broke out.

Instinctively, Trish ducked and checked her own weapon. She knew she could take down any of them from where she was, but she had to make sure the old girl was ready before she made her position known.

As she moved to join the fun, Clayton cleared his throat. Angrily she turned again to face him only this time she fully faced him and glared.

"No, Clay," she whisper-yelled at him. "I'm getting this done today. Anyah deserves this."

But as she pushed off the ground, he again grabbed her arm pulling her back down.

"Trish, just sit still and watch," he said back calmly.

She turned again to see what was going on in front of her as it became eerily silent. No movement was seen, and the gunfire had stopped. "What is happening?" she asked out loud.

She felt Clayton move up next to her and she glanced over. He put his arm around her shoulders and lightly gripped her chin in his hand, turning her face away from his. Trish turned and saw about four men being handcuffed and led away by another group of men in all black.

"You know, you take all the fun out of my life, Clay," she said with a pout. She was disappointed because she wanted a shot at Limpy. She grinned to herself at the nickname—one she was proud to have given him.

Clayton snorted and helped her stand up. "Don't worry. This is just temporary. You will still get your shot. I promise."

Trish stood and brushed off her jeans. "I better. I had a perfect shot, Clay. Perfect." She mumbled and grumbled the entire walk back to her house.

Once she reached the back door, she turned and put her hands on her hips. "Clayton, who were those people?"

Clayton sighed and motioned with his hand to go inside. She rolled her eyes at him and turned back to go into her house. She moved through, checking to make sure no one had entered while they were chasing bad guys. Satisfied, she found herself in her kitchen, drawn by the smell of a new pot of coffee warming. She was surprised to see Sharon standing by the sink, looking outside.

"Where did you disappear to?" she asked her friend, who turned at her voice.

Sharon looked distracted. "Trish, this is so confusing, and I think we need to all sit down and get to the bottom of it. Is Clayton back?"

Clayton appeared in the doorway. "Yep, I'm here. Grab your drinks and I'll explain what I can." He disappeared then, and Trish stared at the doors swinging after him.

The pair left in the kitchen exchanged grins at the same time making them both chuckle.

"Alrighty then, let me get some black gold and we can head back in," Trish said moving past Sharon.

They filled their mugs and then headed back into the living room area and settled at the table with Clayton sitting opposite them against the wall.

"Spill it," Trish said simply as she leaned back and folded her arms over her chest.

Sharon nodded. "My understanding has always been that you work alone. Who are all these people we keep encountering?" she asked.

Clayton chuckled and shook his head lightly. "Ok, so here's what I know," he began. He turned to Trish first. "The guys in the woods are not mine. I found their little hut a week or so ago. I figured they were some government agency and knew that if they were there at the time today, the guys we were chasing would be caught by their group."

Trish nodded her understanding. "Ok, so I guess that makes sense. I'm still floored by all the people who have been gathering around my place for so long. What are they looking for?" she asked the room but turned to face Sharon.

It was Clayton's voice though that cut into her silent communication with Sharon. "I told you. My intel said this was some sort of information hub. I am sure others have received the same information."

Trish just shook her head. "I have no idea why though. But ok, let's go with that. What kind of information would be stored here?"

"Maybe some of what we have been researching has been leaked somehow and has been traced back to this IP address, making people think there's some sort of dead server being revived out here or something," Sharon suggested.

"That's possible. I guess we usually use your house to do the bulk of our research," Trish said thoughtfully.

"Add in all your surveillance equipment and it makes sense," Clayton added.

Trish waved her hand. "Ok, but again, what are people looking for here that has multiple agencies and people not so up and up looking for it. What kind of information and who might it be related to?"

"I might be able to help with that," Clayton said, drawing the attention to him. He pulled up Trish's laptop and opened it. He typed a few things on it and then turned the screen.

The entire screen was lit up with two faces. Trish recognized them as Johnny and Simon. She wrinkled her brow and looked at her ex-husband.

"Ok, why these two?" she asked.

Clayton took in a deep breath of air and slowly let it out again. "What I have been tracking for the last few months are these two. I thought they were connected but it turns out they are not, which I have already said. I believe every other agency still believes they are connected and working together, which actually plays to my advantage," he said with a grin.

"I found out that Simon had a falling out with Johnny after Johnny was taken into custody," he continued. "I have been feeding false information to both camps to see what each would do with it."

Sharon laughed. "Brilliant actually. So what have you found out so far?"

Trish noticed Clayton had gradually been letting his guard down around Sharon and she was relieved. She knew she was going to need her friend as they pulled this mystery apart.

"Well, I have been able to separate Johnny and Simon definitively. They actually have nothing to do with each other. I think the feds were hoping to use Johnny's information to bring a final end to the Del Rios country-wide, but he really isn't that smart." Clayton chuckled as he seemed to think about his information.

Trish watched between her friend and ex. It was fascinating to her how much they seemed to think alike. She decided to sit back and listen to how this whole thing was going to play out. She knew they were thinking on a different level than she was. She couldn't deny the fascination and admiration she felt as she watched Clayton. They seemed to have inadvertently gone in similar directions after their daughter's death. It struck Trish that neither of them had ever dreamed of doing what they did now, all because of the loss of one little girl.

She found herself looking at her ex-husband differently. Maybe she had gotten it all wrong all those years ago. Maybe Clayton had suffered like she had, alone and confused. She couldn't help but question if she really did misunderstand the words so long ago.

A sudden ring brought her attention back to the present and the table vibrating under her hand.

"Luke, what's up?" Sharon asked, glancing around the table. She nodded her head and made a few hums of agreement.

Trish and Clayton locked gazes, and he raised his eyebrows at her. She tipped her head to the side, and he nodded toward the kitchen. Trish just nodded and followed him, picking up their mugs on the way. She hadn't even noticed hers was empty. She briefly thought maybe everyone was right and she did have a problem with her coffee addiction.

Once inside the small room, Clayton took the cups from her hands and stood in front of her.

"Trish are you sure you can trust Sharon?" he asked, concern laced in his eyes.

Trish snorted. "Are you kidding me right now? Given what I know and what I don't, I trust her more than you right now." She crossed her arms over her chest and raised her chin with an air of defiance.

Clayton nodded. "Ok, that's fair I guess. I am just worried that you are going to get caught up in something dangerous and I will lose you too."

His concern touched Trish, and she gave him a gentle smile. She touched his arm softly and nodded. "Clay, I am much more dangerous and the opposite of helpless than you can ever imagine. I will be fine."

She hated that she felt a tiny spark of hope at his words, but she also knew she would be fine. She was about to say more when Sharon appeared at the entrance, holding one of the swinging doors in her hand.

"Trish, I need to go meet Luke. Are you going to be alright without me? Can you catch me up later?" she looked between Trish and Clayton, who just nodded.

Sharon nodded back and disappeared through the front door. Trish turned to Clayton.

"I am worried about her though when you prove her fellow agent isn't who she thinks he is," she admitted.

Clayton just hummed a response, and they moved back into the other room to go over more details. She sat across from Clayton and looked over the massive number of papers covering the table.

Trish scanned them and suddenly something stuck out. A photo of a woman in a large hat covering most of her face, long black braids hung below it down her back. She picked it up and studied it. The woman had on dark sunglasses shielding most of her face, but the smirk was unmistakable.

With a gasp, Trish turned the photo to Clayton. "What is going on, Clayton. And don't even think about lying to me."

Chapter 25

Clayton sighed at the photos and papers now completely covering the table in front of the pair. He shook his head and looked up at Trish.

"I don't know how I missed this," he groaned. "I have been over these files so many times and never thought that could be Patsy." He ran his hands through his short hair and folded his hands behind his head.

Trish matched his confused expression. "Could I have been wrong about everything?" she asked quietly, staring at the unmistakable look on her sister's face. Being as close as they were growing up, there were facial expressions that were unique to Patsy and Trish would know them anywhere.

But how could this be the same person as the one in her video with Johnny? That person was clearly an addict. All the signs were there.

"This has to be someone who just looks like her. That has to be it," she said with new conviction. She picked up the photo and looked at it for a long time, trying to convince herself of this new idea. "I can't be wrong about everything."

Clayton looked at her and then took the photo from her hands. He studied it for a long time and sighed again.

"I'm sorry Trish, but I think you are right. This has to be Patsy, but we have to figure out how or why she has two distinct personalities going on right now." His voice was laced with frustration.

Trish leaned back and smirked at him. "You don't like being in the dark about anything do you?" she observed, making him look sharply at her.

His face softened slightly, and he grinned. "I live for this stuff, and I depend on knowing everything I possibly can. I don't like *not* knowing something. That is one hundred percent true." He sat back in his chair and crossed his arms over his chest.

Laughing, Trish waved her hand. "Knowing everything takes the fun out of solving the grand mystery. But I do want to figure out what happened here." She picked up the photo they agreed was Patsy. "I am more annoyed that I am wrong about this or *might* be wrong I guess." She flung the photo back onto the table and watched as it spun and landed on the top of the pile.

Trish felt something stir inside her as she stared at a photo that looked just like her sister and yet didn't at the same time. Was it possible her sister had actually cleaned herself up? After all this time and heartache, was it possible?

They had spent the last hour or so sorting Clayton's photos to try to figure out who the woman in the photo was. She was always shrouded in some sort of huge hat and extra big sunglasses. Her hair was long and hung way past the brim of the hat. Clayton had many photos of her, but few were of her directly. Typically, she was in the background or off to the side of what or who he was photographing. He suggested that was why she was never on his radar as important. She blended perfectly with the background.

"I am going to give Billie a call," Clayton finally said. "Maybe she knows why these photos include this person, not making any assumptions that it is actually Patsy yet." He raised his eyebrows at Trish.

She knew they couldn't afford to make any assumptions, not with all the people converging on her home. They couldn't afford to waste any time either. So, she just nodded and got up to make some more coffee.

It had been a long time since she had heard from Sharon, and she stared out her window thinking about what Luke could have pulled her away for. She briefly wondered if she should be worried about her friend with a potential traitor, but decided Sharon had plenty of training and life experience and she would be fine. They had bigger things to worry about here.

A loud laugh broke through her thoughts from the other room, and she turned to head in that direction after filling her and Clayton's mugs with steaming hot liquid.

Trish set the cups down and met Clayton's eyes. He had a huge grin on his face, and she raised her brow at him. He shook his head and focused on his call. He said a few words of agreement and then hung up his call.

"You aren't going to believe this," he started as his grin grew again. "Billie—"

Trish's phone screeched out a text, making Clayton jump. "What the hell, Trish?"

She laughed and opened her texting app. "I hate these things and the alerts I choose are just a little reinforcement of those feelings."

The text was from Sharon, and she was asking Trish to call as soon as she could. "Something about Patsy," she mumbled out loud and then looked up to meet Clayton's now worried eyes.

"What does she need?" he asked quietly.

"I don't know. She wants us to meet her somewhere, by accident, on purpose kind of thing," she explained.

When Clayton gave her a confused look, she just waved him off. "Just follow along. It has to look like a chance meeting."

He nodded and followed her as she exited through the back door. She led him to the garage and went through her normal routine. A chuckle from behind her drew her attention to him.

"What?" she asked.

Clayton shook his head. "No wonder no one thinks anyone lives here," he said with a grin.

There wasn't enough room for him to get into her vehicle inside the small building, so she backed it out and he got in while she closed and locked the garage.

Trish looked around. "Where is your vehicle?" she asked. She hadn't even noticed that when he showed up the day before he didn't drive.

"I walked from next door," he explained. "Easier to hide my own vehicle when I'm trying to survey something."

She nodded and slowly moved out of her driveway, checking her little friends as she went. Everything seemed to be in order, and she slowly moved onto the quiet road. Nothing seemed out of the ordinary as she moved toward town.

Sharon had asked her to meet at a place they usually didn't meet at to throw off any suspicion. Trish wondered if her friend knew about Clayton's investigation into Luke and that's why she was asking to meet. Or maybe she had made her own discovery.

Trish drove her car in silence. Passing by her neighbor, who was once again out plowing or pretending to, she tried to see anything unusual on his property. She was disappointed that she didn't, but Clayton seemed to read her because a light chuckle came from next to her.

She looked over and scowled at his smug expression.

"You'll never see what's hidden there, Trish," he said with a grin. "But if you behave I might bring you on a field trip."

Trish scoffed and focused back on the road. "Did you bring the photos for Sharon to look at?" she asked, referring to the ones she had discovered in his stacks.

"Yeah. I'm still not positive it is Patsy, but I won't stop you from figuring that out." Clayton turned away from her to focus outside his window, and Trish couldn't help the question that snuck back into her heart.

He swears there was nothing there, but then why is he turning away and not pursuing the answers with her? Shaking it off, she gripped the steering wheel tightly and tried to think about what Sharon might know.

The drive was relatively short, and Trish pulled up to a small building. It had fish and various types of seafood painted on the walls. She didn't usually go out for seafood. It wasn't a favorite of hers since the passing of her parents, but once in a while it sparked her interest. She knew Clayton loved it though and since he spent most of his adult life working in a kitchen that served solely chicken products, she knew he would enjoy the meal. For a brief moment, she wondered if she was trying to please him but shook that off and parked her car.

She looked around and didn't see Sharon's puny little car, so she turned off her ignition and they moved inside before she showed up. They didn't want to walk in together just in case Luke was watching. She felt Clayton's hand on her back as they made their way through the door. She figured they looked like a real couple to anyone else, which was good for their purpose. She wouldn't overthink it.

They were settled at a table and looking at their menus when Sharon came in. Trish resisted looking her way even though she knew the moment her friend walked in. Sharon the agent walked through the door and moved quickly to the table at the opposite end of the restaurant. Trish watched out of the corner of her eye as she made a production of looking at the menu and trying to decide what to order.

After a few minutes, Trish noticed that Gary, Sharon's husband, had appeared and was sitting across from her. Trish turned back to Clayton and gave him a small nod. Their table was situated near the restrooms, making it easy for Sharon to happen to pass by. All Trish needed to do now was wait.

Their food had just arrived, so she focused on her plate. She had opted for clam chowder because no one made it better than Maryland chefs. She would get some crab cakes to go, Sharon's favorite food, if she was still hungry. They reheated easily and made a quick and easy snack.

Trish was about halfway through her chowder when Sharon walked by. She made a little bit of bumping into their table and nearly spilled Clayton's drink in his lap. He made a production of pushing away from the table and brushing off his shirt.

"Hey, it's just water, calm down," Trish admonished. She looked up and winked at Sharon. In her best surprised voice, she exclaimed, "Why Sharon, what a surprise! What are you doing here?"

Sharon gave her the same shocked expression and Trish stood to give her a friendly hug. Anyone watching would think they were old friends and hadn't seen each other in a long time.

"It is so good to see you, dear," Sharon said with a smile. "Gary and I were having a date night but now he's tired and just wants to get it to go." She rolled her eyes dramatically as she waved her hand.

Trish laughed. "Well, it is so good to see you. Why don't you sit for a while? We just got started. They can deliver your food here. Tell Gary to come over." She looked in the direction of Sharon's table.

Sharon glanced around and shrugged. "Sure. It will be a few minutes. So how are things?"

They settled into a quiet conversation after Trish made a big deal of introducing Clayton and Sharon. Sharon sat next to Trish and set down her purse with a paper sticking out of it, Gary soon joined sitting next to Clayton.

"What's that?" Trish asked, as the paper slipped from Sharon's purse.

Sharon looked down and sighed. "Just some work." She lifted it to the table and subtly opened the folded papers. She slid it to Trish and Clayton leaned forward.

"I have found something that isn't adding up. Luke wanted me to meet someone for him, but I wasn't going to do it alone. I was actually hoping Clayton would back me up." She looked over at him briefly and after he nodded almost imperceptibly, she continued. "I am a little bit suspicious of Luke right now. He really has been secretive and not being at all forthright with his information. I am afraid he is setting me up for something."

Trish hummed and pulled the papers closer. There was a photo of a building that looked abandoned, and she could tell it was located down by the river and draw bridge. She was trying to figure out which building it was, but Clayton jumped in.

"Sharon, you can't go down there alone," he warned quietly. "I know what kind of stuff happens there and you are definitely being set up. Or used as bait." His voiced dropped further when he said the last sentence making both women stare at him.

"Bait? For what?" Trish asked.

Sharon's hand rested on her friend's arm, and she shook her head, silencing her.

"I am afraid Luke is up to something. If I am caught, he can claim plausible deniability," she said quietly.

Trish looked between her friend and ex. What was Luke up to? she wondered.

"He could be trying to see who is after him and if you are caught, he would know who or what he was up against," Clayton mused to himself. "I need to make a call." He abruptly stood and left the table.

Trish and Sharon just watched him go. Their gazes connected and Trish sighed. Maybe now was the time to tell Sharon what Clayton told her. But then she promised she would let him work his case.

"What do you think he knows?" Sharon asked suddenly.

All Trish could do was shrug. "I'm not sure."

They sat in silence for a few minutes. Sharon's food order arrived, and she looked around for Clayton. "I don't know if I should go or stay," she mumbled more to herself than Trish.

"I'll go wait for you in the car, Sharon dear," Gary said. He gave Trish a wave and moved out of the restaurant.

As Sharon was about to follow her husband, Clayton reappeared in his stealth-like way. He seemed to appear out of nowhere and without warning. Both women jumped as he slid into the booth.

"Ok," he started, oblivious to their reactions. "I have to tell you both something and then we have to move to the next step. This situation is getting complicated, and I need us to be on the same page." His eyes shifted from Trish to Sharon and back.

Trish looked over at Sharon and shrugged. "I mean what choice do we have?"

Sharon readily agreed.

"Ok, but not here. I don't trust anyone right now and your place is the most secure from what I have seen," Clayton said to Trish.

"So, Sharon, why don't you drop off Gary and then come on over for some coffee and cake? I just bought a new Smith Island cake this morning." Trish grinned at her lie.

Sharon chuckled, understanding right away that Trish never had sweets like that around. "Ok, that sounds wonderful. I'll be there in a little while. Thanks, hon." She waved and then disappeared through the door.

Trish furrowed her brow as she turned back to Clayton. "What do you have, Clay? I'm really worried about her and even if she was a top agent, nothing prepares you for the type of betrayal her friend is going to do to her."

Clayton's eyes clouded over. He seemed to catch her subtle jab at the betrayal she felt from him. He just shook his head though and ignored the comment.

"I am going to tell you some of this on the way home because I am not ready to tell Sharon yet," he said simply.

They paid their bill and made their way out of the restaurant. Trish settled behind the wheel and started the engine. But she didn't put it in gear just yet. She turned to face Clayton.

"I think you better start talking Clay," she said calmly. "I need some information before we talk to Sharon. I need to know about your partner and what is going on."

Clayton just nodded. "Ok. What do you want to know." He folded his hands in his lap and stared at them.

Trish sighed. She really didn't know what she wanted to know, she just knew there was something going on and Clayton seemed to have the answers.

After a few moments of silence, Clayton looked at her. "You want to know what I talked to Billie about, right? And about our evidence on Sharon's colleague." He seemed to already know, and Trish had to admit she felt relief knowing she didn't need to ask outright.

When she nodded, he sighed. Finally, he nodded. "Ok. I have some making up to do anyway, so let me explain a few things. But you have to believe me when I tell you that a lot of this I just found out tonight."

Trish scrunched her eyebrows. How did he not know until tonight? Could she believe that was true, considering how much faith Sharon had in the man? She decided she ultimately had to trust this information. She reassured herself she didn't need to trust everything he says, but for the sake of her friend, and possibly Anyah's killer she would have to trust him a little.

"Ok, but I am limiting my trust to the issue and cases at hand. Nothing more," she said sternly, waiting for him to agree.

He seemed hesitant but ultimately agreed. "Fine, but we need to drive away from here. I do not know if we or Sharon were followed."

Satisfied, Trish nodded and put the car in gear. She slowly moved out of her spot and onto the main road leading back to her place. She wouldn't let him off the hook for long though. When he didn't say anything, she glanced at him. She cleared her throat and brought his attention back to her.

He gave her a small smile and sighed again. "Ok. I will tell you what I know, but you have to trust me." In the dim light, Trish could see his eyebrow raised and she just simply gave him a hum of agreement.

"So, I asked Billie tonight if she knew anything about Johnny new girlfriend. Turns out she does." He paused and looked out his window. He slowly turned back and added, "she knows who Patsy is."

Trish let out a strained chuckle. *Of course she did*, she thought darkly. Why wouldn't she know who Patsy is? She was well known in the drug world.

Before her thoughts could spiral into oblivion, Clayton grabbed her hand and squeezed. "But it's not what you think."

That got her attention, and she gently pulled her hand away and placed it on the steering wheel. When she didn't answer, Clayton continued.

"This is where you need to trust me and Billie," he said. She could feel his gaze locked on her, but she stared straight ahead. "Trish, please look at me so you know how serious I am." His pleading voice somehow drew her eyes in his direction.

She quickly looked back at the road ahead of her and waited for him to continue.

"I guess that is all I can ask for. I do usually work alone, as Sharon mentioned before. But when Billie approached me to help her take down the Del Rios for good, I knew it was the opportunity of a lifetime, and I couldn't turn it down.

"Billie approached me with a plan. She had someone who could go inside and twist Johnny all up. And better yet she had a revenge plan of her own. See, Johnny caused her miscarriage years ago. She had gotten caught in some crossfire and was trying to get clean when she was struck in her abdomen, causing her baby to die.'

Clayton paused to look at Trish, but even feeling his gaze, she remained unmoved. So far nothing was helpful to her.

"Trish, that person was Patsy." He paused again, but still she remained unemotional.

On the inside though, Trish wanted to scream at him. She wanted to laugh at the absurdity of the suggestion her sister somehow changed to the good side. Trish had just seen her on video visiting Johnny and she looked higher than ever. There was no doubt that her sister was high during that visit. But Trish just continued to stare straight ahead of her. She told him she would trust him and that meant letting him finish.

When she didn't answer, Clayton continued. "Trish, Billie said she came across Patsy in one of her assignments and she somehow felt a pull to her. She wanted to help and took her in. I guess Patsy has been staying with Billie for a while. I suppose it makes sense how she was able to keep her hidden. I rarely meet Billie in person." His voice faded as he seemed to come to an understanding within himself.

Trish just continued to nod and stare straight ahead. She wasn't sure what to make of the new information. Her brain didn't seem to process it. She turned into her driveway a few silent minutes later. She went through her routine of putting the vehicle away without much thought. As she rounded the trunk and pulled down her garage door, she nearly ran right into Clayton.

"Hey," he said calmly, gripping her shoulders. "Trish, we have to talk about this."

Trish shook her head. "No. I am not buying this. Patsy had our little girl killed and I will not believe some person I have never met before. I don't trust blindly anymore, Clay. Not anymore." She shrugged off his hands and moved around him to the door. She heard him sigh behind her, but she didn't care. She continued to her door, glancing around her yard to make sure nothing was out of the ordinary.

She heard the door close behind her, which meant Clayton didn't follow her inside. She shrugged it off and went into her kitchen. She needed coffee, maybe something stronger, but she wasn't an alcohol drinker. As soon as her mug was filled, she turned and moved through her swinging doors to the living room just as Clayton and Sharon walked in from the opposite direction.

They both had serious expressions and Trish raised her eyebrows. "Why are we looking so serious?" she asked, moving to the table. Clayton glanced at Sharon and gave her a slight nod to move forward. He stayed where he was and just looked at the floor.

Sharon followed and settled next to her. "Trish, we have reason to believe that Simon is responsible for Anyah's death."

That caught Trish's attention, and she shook her head. "No, Patsy is responsible. I know she is." She looked back at Clayton who looked away.

"Well, what we think is that a misunderstanding is what took Anyah from you, Trish," Sharon said quietly, lightly gripping her hand.

She looked sharply at Clayton and pulled her hand from Sharon's. "Did he put you up to this?" she asked angrily. She stood from the table and moved to face him. "Are you still trying to defend her? Some cockamamie story about how she's on the good side now and all that crap. No way. You can both just leave. I am not going to allow anyone to mock Anyah's death with this b.s."

Clayton stood straight and took both of Trish's hands in his much larger ones. He squeezed them to steady her and Trish couldn't do anything but hold her place and stare daggers at him.

"Trish, stop this. I didn't even come up with this information. Sharon did. Everything that is happening now is connected to you and Anyah. I promise, I am on your side." His voice was pleading as she stared in her eyes. "I promise," he whispered.

Chapter 26

Staring at her screen, Trish tried to focus on what was unfolding in front of her. The revelations of the last few hours, maybe even days, have been unsettling. She found herself questioning everything she believed to have happened, all her judgments potentially based on complete misunderstandings. She couldn't believe that was the truth though. She couldn't have been that wrong in what she heard and saw, could she?

"Trish, I need eyes," Sharon's voice rang out, bringing Trish's attention back to her screen.

She stretched her fingers out and leaned forward to see what Sharon was asking about. She looked from screen to screen trying to figure out what to warn her friend of. Trish had already hacked into the nearby camera feeds to get the best views she could. Unfortunately, everything was from outside. Sharon and Clayton had suggested they try to stay outside the structure as much as they could for that reason. They could easily be ambushed otherwise. That made Trish a little uncomfortable.

"Ok, I got one vehicle parked at the far end of the building, furthest from you," Trish said, getting down to business. "Nothing else anywhere on the property."

"Copy that," the speaker chirped.

Trish continued her search around the property. She noticed Clayton had disappeared before she even had everything set up. She wasn't surprised since Sharon had made a big deal about how "invisible" he could become. Trish had laughed because she had broken through his mask of invisibility with her own system. No one else would likely have that tech like Sharon did so he should be the Invisible Man for the purpose of this assignment.

After she felt like everything else was visible and secure, Trish turned back to the screen where Sharon was standing and waiting just out of her line of sight.

The plan the trio had come up with was that Sharon was going to act as if Luke was assigned somewhere else and she was appointed in his place. Trish still wasn't sure what was going on with Luke, but she and Clayton were speculating that he knew his cover was about to be blown, or he was just being careful, and wanted to keep a little distance in case this meeting was a set up for catching him.

Sharon still didn't believe he was a part of whatever was going on and Trish was fine keeping it that way for now. It allowed Clayton to build whatever case he needed to. They had kept their conversation confidential from Sharon just in case Clayton was wrong, but he was sure what he knew was true.

Trish watched as her friend started to pace back and forth.

"I wonder if the person was tipped off that Luke wasn't coming," she mused into her microphone.

She saw Sharon shake her head and smile at a nearby camera. "Nah. You just need to have patience, Trish dear. These things take time. Whoever is meeting Luke here is probably checking to see who I am and if I am connected to Luke at all. Not a problem, yet." Sharon's reassurance didn't really work for Trish though.

She thought for a change she knew more about the situation than Sharon did, which made her very nervous about Sharon's safety. Trish shook her head of those thoughts and tried to find Clayton while she watched for any incoming movements. A barely visible movement brought her attention to the corner of one of her screens and she enlarged the view to see if it was Clayton. As she squinted, the image disappeared, and the space was completely dark again.

Trish sighed. She didn't see him move; he just disappeared. "I guess he is good," she mumbled. She didn't like things that she couldn't control, and Clayton was one of them.

Voices in her ear drew her attention back to Sharon. She started her recording and looked at Sharon standing with two men. One she knew was Luke's partner and the second was their superior. She furrowed her brow wondering what was happening.

"Miss Sharon, what are you doing here?" Luke's partner asked, looking around.

Sharon's head mirrored his as she looked around as well. "I was asked to be here. What are you doing here, Cliff?"

The supervisor stepped in and placed a hand on Luke's partner, whom Trish now knew was Cliff. He gave the younger man a look and a slight shake of his head. He turned his attention back to Sharon and sighed.

"Sharon, we were hoping to talk to Luke privately. It seems he has been up to something not exactly…legal and outside of our agency's values," the supervisor said, speaking carefully to keep some information between the two of them.

Sharon tipped her head slightly to the side and smiled. Trish knew that look well. It was her "no nonsense, agent mode" and she wouldn't be taken advantage of. She also wouldn't be giving away more than she gets back in this interaction either.

"Well, that sounds a little mysterious, Mister McMichaels. I'm sorry, I just find it hard to believe Luke is up to something. Could you please tell me what you are looking for? Of course, all I want to do is help where I can." Sharon's voice was like an old southern lady's with a hint of concern. Trish knew better though. Sharon was fishing for information and using her age and gender to her advantage. Sharon clucked her tongue and added, "I hate dirty agents, you know?" She shook her head as if in disgust.

The two men visibly relaxed. "I thought you would be more loyal to him, Miss Sharon," Cliff said.

Sharon waved her hand. "My job has always been for justice. If he's up to something, I will help if I can."

Trish chuckled from her seat. Even if she also suspected Luke was up to no good, Sharon didn't share that. Yet she was so convincing, Trish knew the other two would buy it.

And they did. Both men nodded and unfolded their arms. Trish nodded in approval. Body language told her they were relaxed and open to Sharon's help.

She turned up her microphone to catch anything extra they might share and then sat back and listened.

"So, Miss Sharon, have you seen Luke with anything recently that you couldn't identify?" Cliff asked her.

Sharon put her finger to her lips as if she were thinking and then shook her head. "I don't think so, but I guess I wouldn't know what exactly you are talking about either." She gave a slight chuckle making the men nod.

McMichael stepped forward and leaned a little closer to her. "We have reason to believe he took a medallion that when it is connected to a magnetic piece a litany of information becomes available to the one who holds it."

"It is a list of all of the agency's safe houses and who is being guarded at each one," Cliff volunteered quickly. "If it gets into the wrong hands, we could be looking at a major hit to our PR and witness protection program."

McMichael glanced at Cliff and added, "not to mention a huge loss of life and potential witnesses to many significant cases."

Sharon nodded and looked between the men. "So… this is an important piece. What does it look like?"

Cliff spoke first. "It is a black circle, but we have reason to believe he had broken it into multiple pieces to make it easier to hide."

Trish froze. The pieces that she found and George gave her immediately came to mind. She pushed away from her desk, her chair rolling as she did. She stood and looked around her space. Where did she put them? She thought back to when Clayton was there and she showed him the pieces.

"Clayton has the third piece," she muttered. Her eyes landed on the box on her desk, and she moved to pick it up. Unlocking it, the two pieces fell out. The one she found on her property and the other from George. As she studied them, she wondered if Luke had ever been on her property. But she couldn't think of a single time he had been. So that meant that either it wasn't him or someone he was working with dropped it while trespassing on her land.

Trish glanced up at her screens and wondered for a second where Clayton was. She couldn't help the nagging in her heart that maybe he was up to something too. After all, he had the third piece. But if he was, wouldn't he have taken her two to complete the medallion? Why would he be there still trying to get Luke convicted of something?

Pushing that thought aside, she watched again as Sharon and the two men talked, discussing how to get Luke into custody without alerting him and having him disappear.

Trish's phone alerted her to a text and since she knew only two people knew her number and one was in her sights, clearly without her phone, she opened her app.

Something's not right, Trish. Keep recording but watch for anything on your property. I have a bad feeling.

Clayton's text caught her off guard. What did he suspect? Didn't everything they said so far match up? She looked around her small space and even with the setting sun, it was still bright enough to see every corner of her main floor, minus the kitchen. But she was confident enough in her decorating skills that she would hear someone come through her porch.

She opened up her camera feeds on her phone to check her property. She had everything set up to alert her even with the recording set up for Sharon and Clayton. It should switch to a different view of her property if someone tripped a camera. But with the issues she's had recently, she wasn't taking anything for granted. She jumped between her cameras to make sure nothing was amiss. Not finding anything, Trish just shook her head and focused on the warehouse again.

Sharon was still talking to the two colleagues and Clayton was still out of sight. She tried to listen to what they were saying when she heard a subtle thump on the side of her house. It was definitely something hitting the outside wall of the house. She switched her camera view to see what was on that side of the house and carrying her phone with her moved to grab her shotgun.

"No one is going to get the jump on me again," she mumbled as she grabbed a few shells and loaded the gun. She watched the camera feed and loaded the gun without looking. She continued to talk to herself as she moved on automatic.

Once her baby was ready and loaded, Trish stared at her feed from outside. Nothing had moved since she heard the sound against her house. It confused her. She figured it could have been a branch falling or something, but Clayton sending that message seconds before she heard it, she knew better.

The screen door behind Trish made the slightest sound and she turned quickly, moving toward her stairs to get out of sight. She stood firm on the third step waiting for the intruder to show up. For a split second she hoped this wasn't a distraction for her friend to be a target but pushed it aside as she heard the faintest of footsteps move into her laundry room.

This time she would aim a little tighter to the frame, so the person doesn't escape like Clayton did with just a few scratches. She raised her weapon to her shoulder and waited.

"Put the gun down, Miss Trish," an oddly familiar voice said.

Trish didn't lower her trusty friend until a large figure entered her space. "What are you doing here?" she asked, still not lowering her gun but pulling her eyes away from her firing stance.

George chuckled. "I'm here to help. I'm afraid things are not what they seem, honey." His voice was quiet and held something she couldn't identify.

Trish slowly lowered her weapon and tipped her head to the side. There were so many players in the picture at the moment that she really wasn't sure who was trustworthy and who wasn't. Clayton's warning was playing in her mind though and for some reason she trusted him more than George at the moment. Part of her wanted to argue why that was true, but the other part just wanted to get answers.

"What's going on, George?" she asked finally, putting her gun down at her side, but in a way that would be easy to move into a shooting position quickly.

George grinned at her. "Come, sit. We have a lot to talk about." He motioned toward the table, sitting first.

Trish was glad their papers were all put away and hidden, not on purpose but she was more focused on recording than papers. She shrugged slightly, not letting go of her gun and moved to sit across from him. She noticed he sat closest to the wall, leaving her to sit where she could easily escape if needed.

She relaxed a little knowing he put himself in the more restricted position. It would definitely take him longer to come after her if she fled.

Her phone screeched at her from across the room, drawing her eyes that way. She quickly turned back to George and narrowed her eyes.

"What are you up to, George?" Trish asked suspiciously.

George put his hands in the air and smiled. "Just go check that, dear," he said simply. As if he didn't have a care in the world, he locked his fingers together behind his head, leaning back in his chair.

She just shook her head and moved to quickly grab her phone and check the latest message.

Hey I need you to zoom in on Cliff's face for me and send me the photo, Clayton's text read.

Trish glanced back at George who hadn't moved. She felt caught between two things and wasn't sure which one to trust. Her ears were suddenly drawn to the screen in front of her where Sharon and Cliff were having an animated conversation. She sat down and waited for a clear picture to come up of Cliff's face. Once she had a good full-frontal view of his features, she snapped a photo with her phone camera and sent it to Clayton.

The only response she got back was a thumbs up emoji. *Annoying*, she thought.

Trish turned back to George, still sitting in her chair. "You wanna tell me what's going on?" she asked or rather demanded.

George chuckled at her again and stretched his large hands over the table. "Your husband is quite the genius, you know that?"

Trish raised her brow at him. "What are you talking about?"

She knew that George, Luke, and Sharon had all worked together at different times. She also knew that Sharon trusted George as much if not more than Luke. Given her latest suspicions around Luke, Trish was a bit concerned about trusting anything George said as well. But something about the man always made her feel at ease.

"He has been able to figure out so many things that the agency couldn't. And now he is about to blow the entire organization up, figuratively of course," he said with a smirk.

"I just don't know what that means," she admitted. "I know who he is looking into, but I don't know how that is a good thing for you and Sharon."

George gave her a confused look and then shook his head. "I think you may have misunderstood. What Clayton has found is irrefutable and will actually make us a safer organization. We have been chasing our tails for years trying to figure out how he found what he did. Well, today it all comes together. And I can't wait to see him finally pay."

His eyes drifted to the screen on her desk with the stilled image of Cliff. His eyes seemed to cloud over for a second and then he regained his composure. "Why is the screen frozen there?" he asked, pointing to it.

Trish looked behind her and shrugged. "Nothing. So tell me why Clayton is such a 'genius'. As far as I can tell this didn't take rocket science to figure out." She crossed her arms over her chest and glared at George. She genuinely liked the man, but she needed him to spell out what was going on. She wasn't going to give him anything extra.

"Tell me, Miss Trish. Do you still have the piece I gave you?" Georges asked, leaning forward on the table.

Trish furrowed her brow. As far as he knew she only had the one piece he gave her. Why was he looking for it now? Was he up to something or maybe was in on this treason too?

She didn't get the chance to ask. Her phone suddenly rang out and she turned to answer it. Pressing the answer button, Trish turned back to face George.

"We got it, Trish," Clayton's voice said over the line. "I finally have it. Save that photo and then pull up the one of Simon. I am on my way back. Is everything ok there?"

"Yeah, all good here," she said slowly. "Clay, what did you find that has you all excited?" She double-checked her volume, not wanting it to be loud enough for George to hear.

"I have to tell you when I get there," he said hurriedly. "I have to get Sharon and we'll be on the way."

The line clicked and she stared at the man across from her. George smirked again.

"I'm guessing you are a little confused, yes?" he stated.

"I guess a little," she admitted, still not wanting to admit anything.

George leaned back in his chair again and sighed. "Then maybe it is best to wait. Do you have the pieces, Trish?"

This time he said plural pieces. She cocked her head to the side. "Pieces?" she asked.

George's grin widened. "Yes, dear. I know you have two. I believe Clayton has the third. And I believe the plate is—" he reached into his shirt pocket and pulled out a flat piece and set it on the table.

Trish looked up at him sharply. "You have it? But Luke…"

George's face lit up with humor and he laughed loudly. "Luke? No he doesn't have anything of importance. This was never in his possession. It was a trap."

Trish unconsciously backed her chair up and hit the desk, stopping her from going any further. "A…a…trap?"

"Yes ma'am. We needed Simon to believe it was a magical device to get control of his records," George said, pushing from the table.

The shotgun Trish never let out of reach was quickly in her grasp again as George made his way to her. Before she could stand though, he was towering over her. He pressed a few buttons and the image on the screen disappeared and a new one popped up of Simon. Trish turned toward her screen and looked at the photo. He looked vaguely familiar, but she couldn't place him.

"Look very carefully at the eyes, Miss Trish," George said quietly, spinning her chair to fully face the computer. "See anyone you know?"

Trish squinted at the screen. She focused on the eyes, but her mind was distracted about George's closeness to her. She wasn't sure if she was in danger but what mattered to her was how she would get out of the situation if needed. The man was aware of the gun in her hands but didn't seem bothered. She pushed slightly away from the desk and George surprisingly backed up letting her create that space.

She wasn't sure what to make of that. *Was he a threat to her or not*, she wondered. She gripped the barrel of her shotgun and pushed further away, standing to face George.

"Why are you in my home, George?" she demanded. No one would get the upper hand on her, she reminded herself.

George seemed a little taken aback by her and put his hands up in front of his chest. "I am not the enemy here, Trish honey. I am simply here as a protective body to make sure the pieces of evidence you have are kept safe," he explained.

She almost believed him. He had been so helpful and friendly in the past. But what if he had given her that piece of plastic as a way to keep it safe and out of Sharon's hands or the agency's? What if it was all an elaborate plan to bring down the whole organization. Her eyes drifted to the screen where Simon's smug face was posted. She wondered what he had to do with this and how George was now connected too.

"I promise, deary," George said calmly. "I am not the bad guy here. We can just wait until Clayton gets back. All will be explained."

Trish watched him carefully. She didn't know what to believe but he wasn't trying to do anything to her, so she decided to let it go and wait for her ex-husband. She suddenly realized that George had called him her husband, and she didn't correct him. Was there something subconsciously there, she wondered.

After a few minutes of silence, George waved toward the kitchen. "I could make some coffee?" he said more as a question than a statement.

Trish just nodded absently and stared at her screen. Who was this guy and why did he look so familiar? she wondered. She wasn't even sure how long she stared at the face in front of her. She didn't think he looked familiar before so why now?

She turned as George came through the swinging kitchen doors. She narrowed her eyes seeing he was carrying only one mug of coffee. She lifted her eyes to meet his and tipped her head to the side. Maybe it was her love of crime stories, but she couldn't help but be suspicious.

"I hope you know I will not drink that," she said defiantly. She lifted her shotgun and set it across her lap.

George chuckled. "I need you, Miss Trish. Now why would I poison you or something?"

"How would I know? All I know is no one makes a single cup of coffee," she said with suspicion.

"I don't drink the stuff. Keeps me up at night," George said with a shrug.

Her screen suddenly lit up with a camera alert and she looked to see Sharon's obnoxious little car drive onto her property. It didn't take long for Sharon and Clayton to come through the back door.

Clayton looked at George and gave him a nod. Before she could say anything, he took the mug and downed the entire cup. He gave it back to George and then pulled a seat over to sit next to Trish.

Suddenly he grabbed his head and moaned. "What was in that?" he asked. Clayton clutched his chest and then fell to the floor.

George laughed heartily and Trish just stared at the pair, not sure what to do. She looked over at Sharon, whose eyes were locked on her computer screen.

"So you figured it out too?" she asked, looking at Trish.

Chapter 27

"Sharon, what is going on?" Trish asked, as she moved to kneel next to Clayton. She rolled him to his back and felt to see if he was breathing. Relief washed over her as she realized he was, but that didn't mean he wasn't in danger. "Sharon!" she nearly yelled at her friend. What had George put in the coffee?

Sharon looked over and grinned. "Oh Trish dear, he's fine. He's just playing." She turned back to the computer and she and George talked in quiet voices between them.

"Trish, come look at this," George said, ignoring the man lying on the floor. "Do you see the eyes?"

She wasn't sure what to do as panic started to build again. Should she call the ambulance? Did George actually poison her drink?

George stepped toward her and Trish instinctively took a step back. "Trish, he's really fine. He's messing with you." He looked down at the man on the ground and gave him a shake with his foot. "You're scaring your wife."

Clayton didn't move. Trish squatted down next to him, and he suddenly reached up and grabbed her wrists, pulling her down on top of him. His face lit up with a mischievous grin.

"So, you're worried about me?" he asked, his grin widening. "I knew you still loved me."

Trish pushed off of him and gave his side a kick, holding back just enough to not hurt him. "What is wrong with you?" She wished she had kicked a little harder as he rolled to his side and jumped to his feet, laughing loudly. His ninja-like movements caught her off guard and she almost fell into him again.

With a groan, she pushed away from him. "Stop, Clay. This is no time to mess around. I thought…nevermind." She huffed and turned toward everyone else. "Can someone please tell me what is going on?"

George moved a little closer to Sharon, who was sitting at the desk. He pointed to the photos on the screen of Simon and Cliff. "See anything familiar?"

Squinting, Trish focused on the eyes, since they all had been focused on that. She didn't see anything at first, but then it clicked. Not only were the blue eyes the same shade but they had the same flecks of brown and hazel in them.

She looked up at Sharon who smiled. "See it now?" she asked.

Trish nodded. "But what does that mean? Simon and Cliff are related?"

"Nope, they are the same person," Clayton said enthusiastically as he came up alongside Trish. He put his arm around her waist and pointed to the side-by-side photos. "It appears that the 'Mission Impossible' mask tech is a real thing."

The confusion on Trish's face must have shown because George chuckled. "You know, the 'Mission Impossible' movies where Ethan Hunt changes his identity using elaborate masks?"

Trish just shook her head and looked between the three. George and Clayton laughed while Sharon just rolled her eyes at them.

"Ok, let's explain what we found. It turns out that Cliff has been trying to set up Luke for a while now to take the fall for Cliff's activities. Luke caught on to it and let me know. I pulled in McMichaels, so we had backup. It was easy enough to convince Cliff that McMichael suspected Luke as well. He took the bait, and we ran with it," Sharon explained.

Trish shook her head. "So…Luke is not the one Clay is trying to convict?"

"Nope, was Cliff all along," Clayton said from beside her.

Trish turned. "But I showed you the photo of Luke and you said it was him." She leaned over Sharon and pulled up the photo she had shown Clayton before.

Clayton shook his head. "No, I was looking at this guy, the one behind Luke I am assuming. It's a profile view, but I was pretty sure it was him. I guess we never really clarified which man we were talking about," he said with a shrug and smile. Trish just nodded in silence at the turn of events.

George's deep laugh chimed in. "The guy is so vain that he really thought no one was on to him. I mean he did do a pretty decent job of covering his tracks. It did take our secret weapon here a long time to gather what he needed for conviction." He gave Clayton a light shove.

"Ha ha," Clayton said as he moved toward the door. "Now I gotta go see what other intel I can get from my little buddies next door." He waved and disappeared out the door. After a second, he peeked back in and called, "By the way, great cup of joe, George. Just the way my lovely likes it." He gave Trish a wink and then ducked out again.

Shaking her head, Trish just grinned. What was she doing? she wondered. Was she really just giving in and trusting this man who allegedly broke her heart so long ago? What was happening to her?

Trish moved quickly toward her doors to the kitchen. "I'm going to get some more coffee." She was relieved when no one followed her. She needed a minute to gather her thoughts about what was happening in her heart. She couldn't even focus on the case in front of them.

She leaned against the counter looking out into her yard. The sun was setting and the shadows cast over the yard were calm and serene, the opposite of her heart. She couldn't help but wonder if what Clayton had been saying was true. Did she literally sabotage her entire marriage and family over a misunderstanding? Could this all actually be her fault for running instead of listening? The loss and grief of Anyah could have influenced that reaction, but even so she was struggling to come to terms with everything.

"It's crazy, isn't it?" Sharon's voice startled her as she turned to face her friend.

Trish just nodded.

"It's ok, Trish dear," Sharon said comfortingly. "This is a lot. Even I didn't see all this coming," she admitted with a sigh.

Reaching out, Trish put her hand on her friend's shoulder. "I bet you are relieved this isn't Luke's doing. For what it's worth, I am too."

Sharon's eyes widened and she grabbed hold of Trish's hand before she could let go. "It means a lot that you care that much, Trish. I know you aren't an emotional person, but it means a lot to hear you say that."

Trish just nodded and dropped her hand. She filled her mug with coffee and moved back into the living room where George had settled at the computer.

"So, what's next?" she asked. "And how does all this play into Johnny? Clay said that Johnny and Simon weren't actually working together like we thought."

"Now, we set the trap for Cliff," George said with an evil grin. He rubbed his hands together like he had some grand scheme.

Sharon gave his shoulder a light slap. "You know we won't be a part of that. We are technically retired now, George," she pointed out. He turned back to Trish. "And yes, it turns out that Johnny and Simon are completely separate. It actually seems as if Johnny was being played in more ways that you can count." She laughed lightly. "He's not gonna like what he learns in the next few days."

Trish pulled two chairs over and sat down next to George while Sharon sat on the opposite side. "So no big prison break?"

"Nope, not even close," Sharon said, her eyes held something Trish couldn't quite read. "Turns out one of the prison guards was gathering intel for Simon, aka Cliff. He was stringing Johnny along with some immunity exchange for information, but there were no plans for such a move on our part. Cliff showed up to give Johnny the idea he was getting some deal. So Johnny didn't have any idea Simon and Cliff were the same person."

"So do we know who Oscar and all those lowlifes were working for?" Trish asked.

George nodded. "Some of that we are still working on. But it seems everything is connected to Simon's operation. He did a good job of making law enforcement and us believe he was working with Johnny so that he could escape unscathed while Johnny took the fall."

Trish nodded, absorbing the new information. She suddenly remembered what Clayton had said about Billie and Patsy.

"Sharon, Clayton thinks that Billie, with an 'ie', and Patsy might be working together on something," she said, slowly.

As if she weren't surprised at all, Sharon nodded. "Yep. Already working on that." She pushed George out of the way so she could get to the keyboard. She pulled up a file that she printed off for Trish. As it printed, Sharon turned to look at her friend. "This is going to be hard to read, hon, so I am going to print it so you can read and digest it as you need to. I am here to help in any way I can as well."

Trish took the papers from Sharon and set them aside. "I have enough to worry about right now. This isn't on my list."

She knew it would contain information she didn't want to think about at the moment. She wanted to get through this case and figure out what happened to her daughter and then try to move on with life, if that was possible. She had spent so much time trying to find answers that she actually wasn't sure if she would be able to just stop wondering or looking for more explanation.

Sharon seemed to sense what Trish was thinking and simply nodded. "Ok, so what we need to do from here is to start connecting these people to Simon's operation. We still have to figure out why Oscar never showed up on any reports," she said glancing over at George.

"That's easy," George said. "Oscar's records were wiped by Cliff. He has been Cliff's, aka Simon's, muscle for a long time according to this report." He flipped open a file folder and showed Sharon.

"That would explain his cockiness, as if he really was untouchable," Trish mused.

Sharon nodded. "Yep, everything has been redacted, and nothing comes up under his photo or his name. Smart actually," she admitted. "Keeps him from getting picked up and talking, since no one can identify him."

George started flipping through the photos that Sharon and Trish had been working on. "All of these are just extensions of Oscar it looks like."

Trish snickered. "Even Reece? And what about Billy, with a 'y'?"

"Well Billy had been trying to play both sides. When Johnny told Patsy about a 'Billy', Cliff assumed it was with a 'y' but I think Clayton is right and Johnny meant Billie with an 'ie.' Cliff had already taken Billy out, so he tried to get Luke to believe that the video was tampered with," Sharon explained. "That would put the blame on Patsy and Johnny, keeping him clean again."

"Reece was just trying to find his footing in the new organization. We believe he was supposed to take Billy out to show his loyalty. The fact that Billy is still alive could be a problem though," George added with a grim look.

Sharon agreed. "Yeah, we need to make sure we have protection on him until he regains consciousness."

Trish stomach made a sudden angry growl and the trio looked around and laughed. "I guess dinner would be good," George said. "I could eat."

They decided that George would go pick up dinner and the other two would focus on wrapping some things up. Trish suspected her friend wanted to try to coax some emotions out of her about Patsy, but Trish was still trying to figure out the ones related to Clayton. Her sister wouldn't be spending any more unsolicited time in her head than Trish wanted.

Once it was just the two of them, Sharon turned to face Trish. "Has Clayton talked to you at all about back then?"

"Back then?" Trish asked, resisting a sneer. "Like that was some time way back in the past that is insignificant now. Sharon, come on."

Sharon waved her hand. "Sorry. I didn't mean it like that. I just want to know what he has said before I say anything else."

Trish narrowed her eyes. "Just say it, Sharon. You know how I hate beating around the bush. Just say it."

"Fine," she said, with a long sigh. "I don't think anything happened between Clayton and Patsy, Trish. I think it was all a misunderstanding."

She wanted to be mad, she wanted to have a tantrum, but Trish was already struggling with this same realization, or possibility anyway. Clayton had been saying it for years and only since she gave him more than three minutes to interact was she starting to doubt herself as well. She had to keep the steel around her heart as long as she could, but she already knew it was fracturing and chipping.

She didn't know how to respond to her friend, who was staring at her with so much concern it made Trish uncomfortable. She knew she needed to speak, but she didn't know what to say. How could she say anything? If she agreed, she would be that same weak young woman a decade ago. If she stayed strong and defied Sharon's words, she would potentially be lying to both of them.

"I need more," she finally struggled to get out. "I am not dealing with this right now, Sharon. There is too much to do."

Sharon stared at her for a long time and finally relented. "Ok, but please keep an open mind on this."

Trish just nodded, grateful for her friend's understanding and not pushing.

An alert sounded on her phone and then her screens started to bounce all over the place. The pair looked at each other and moved in opposite directions to grab their weapon of choice. Trish glanced at the screen and saw four figures in black moving through her yard with precision. She didn't take the time to notice their movements except that they weren't avoiding any cameras.

She made eye contact with Sharon, who nodded in response. Then they moved with just as much practice as the intruders. It wouldn't be the first time someone had trespassed on her property with a negative ending for the other guy.

Suddenly, Trish stopped moving. "Wait," she whispered. "Look." She pointed at one of the screens and saw Clayton move swiftly through the remaining rows of corn and take out two of the people. The other two had escaped to the back and Trish could hear the shots being fired from behind at Clayton in the front. She got an idea.

"Help me," she said hurriedly. She pushed the table to the side and threw the rug back. Pulling up the hidden panels, she grinned at Sharon. "Cover this up completely. I'm going to get at them from the other side."

Sharon laughed. "I always wondered why you had this shelter here. But I should never question anything with you, hon." She shook her head as Trish ducked down below the floor. She heard Sharon moving things above her as she made her way further down and reached to flip the switch, turning on the lights for her shelter.

She didn't build it. There was a small cellar when she moved in, and she thought it would be a perfect hideaway if she ever needed it. So, she dug it out and made it almost like an apartment. There were enough supplies to last a week at least with small appliances that didn't need electricity if she needed to be hidden for a while. They had used the space last summer when Sharon's old friend needed their help.

After that incident, she thought it might be a good idea to dig out a second exit from the space just in case. So she had begun that work creating a tunnel to get her a little away from the house. She had built the exit to come out a few yards into the woods. She hadn't gotten to use it yet, so to say she was a little excited would be an understatement.

As she moved through her new construction, she wondered who would be still after her. A part of the case she had forgotten about was Clayton's warning that someone was after her. He said she and Anyah were both targets. *But why?* she wondered.

Trish neared her exit point and listened carefully for any sounds. She heard faint gunfire, which suggested she was a good distance from the action. "Perfect," she mumbled.

She pushed gently at the door. It would be a little weighted due to the undergrowth of the forestry. She had made sure to make it look as natural as possible. She pushed a little harder and listened as the floor above her began to give way.

The gunfire had stopped, but she heard rustling that didn't sound like an animal. She held her position until she heard the movement sound more distant than before. Trish lifted the door a little more and looked with her eyes to see if anything or anyone was nearby.

Not seeing anything, she pushed the door completely open and pulled up her trusty shotgun. She closed it immediately behind her and covered it again until it was hidden. She turned in all directions to assess where she was and who was nearby. Not seeing anything, she began to move to her left, away from her house. Sharon would have moved the people to the back of the house, but with Clayton there, they may be trapped between the sides of the house and the cornfield. Either way it wouldn't end well for them.

Trish grinned. This time no one was standing in her way. She hoped whatever deity out there was with her today, bringing her daughter's killer right to her. She was still mad she didn't get a shot off last time she saw him, but that wouldn't happen this time. Clayton wouldn't stop her this time.

She moved through the woods to the cornfield. Looking through the branches at the edge of the field, she didn't see anyone moving. Picking up her gun, she moved a little faster through the brush and finally found a clear space between branches and cornstalks. She noticed that the farmer hadn't cut the side of the field either. She wondered if that was also Clayton's doing.

Movement to her right made Trish stop moving and looked around. She ducked down and watched. She wished she was wearing something a little darker, but with nightfall coming, she would still be pretty hard to see.

The flash of someone moving quickly made her duck further into the brush. She took the opportunity to remove the safety and position her weapon on her shoulder. He wouldn't hear any of her movements while he was making so much of his own noise, she thought.

As she expected, he didn't stop but looked disoriented. He suddenly changed directions and was headed toward her. She immediately noticed the limp and took no time hesitating. Trish watched as he fell to the ground. She knew she didn't hit him with a fatal shot, which was exactly what she wanted. She needed information. Pleased with her work, she stood and began walking toward her catch. Her trusty gun on her shoulder but easily moved for a second shot if needed.

She heard the groaning before she reached him. When she finally saw the man rolling on the ground, she smirked. "Howdy," she said with a grin. "Goin' somewhere?"

The man barely acknowledged her as he continued to roll back and forth. Before she could do anything about him, Clayton appeared and noticed the two. He laughed and reached down to pick up the victim.

"Kid, you done pissed off the wrong girl, you know that?" he taunted the man.

Before Clayton could take him away, Trish pointed her gun at his chest. "Who are you?" she asked.

The man looked at her and grimaced. "Name's Big John," he said with a small bit of bravado. If he wasn't in pain, Trish had no doubt he would be acting tough like the one they caught the other night.

"What's with the stupid names?" she muttered.

"Who sent you and why?" Clayton asked, in a tone Trish hadn't heard before. She looked over and noticed Clayton's face contorted in an anger she had never seen before.

What's that about? she wondered.

Big John looked between the two but landed on Trish. "You aren't gonna last long, even with that little gun, sweetheart."

Apparently that wasn't what Clayton wanted to hear because he hit the guy in the head with the butt of his own gun. The man dropped to the ground again.

"Clay!" Trish shouted. "What's your problem?"

He turned to Trish and grabbed her arms. "Trish, he's here to kill you. I need to get him over to Joe's so we can figure this out. I need you safe. I couldn't protect our baby, but I'll be damned if I don't protect you."

Clayton hoisted the man over his shoulder as if he weighed nothing and turned away from Trish. She noticed as he was lifted that she had hit the man right where she wanted. Middle thigh. Enough to cause max pain, but not enough to sever the femoral artery and let him bleed out before they got what they needed. She was proud of the shot and patted herself on the back, making her way back to her house.

She realized as she walked that she knew without a doubt that this was the man who had fired the shot that took Anyah from her because of his threat to her just then. So, what Clayton said was true. He was after them both all those years ago. She wasn't sure how to feel about it at the moment.

When she finally reached the back door, she looked around. Nothing looked out of place, and she wondered if anyone else was lurking around. She was honestly getting tired of it. Even her "Prepare to Meet Thy God" sign wasn't working anymore. Maybe she needed to expand her baby dolls into the yard, hang a few from the trees or something.

She opened the door and heard voices in her living room. Sharon and George were setting up food on the table as if nothing happened. They both looked up and grinned.

"Come get some food, Trish," Sharon said. "We—"

She was interrupted by her phone ringing. She held up her finger and pressed her answer button. She didn't say much aside from an occasional hum of agreement. When she hung up, Trish had no idea who called or what it was about.

Sharon looked at George and nodded then turned to Trish. "We should make plates to go. We need to get to the hospital as soon as we can."

Trish gave her a questioning look matching George's.

Sharon looked between them and sighed. "Billy's awake."

Chapter 28

Trish sat in the waiting area for the ICU patients' families. They were told to limit guests as the patient had not been awake from his coma for long. They didn't want to overwhelm him again and possibly cause setbacks for his recovery.

Since she had no reason to interview Billy and would just be an extra body, she opted to stay out of the room and let the professionals do their work. She paged aimlessly through magazines, not seeing anything of interest. She finally set down the last one and sighed. Trish was the only one in the small room lined with chairs and side tables. The magazine selection wasn't huge, but she figured if people were spending days here, they would have something else to entertain themselves.

There was a small TV hung in the corner that was playing a game show channel and was barely audible. They had put a small fridge in the room with some bottles of water, and a water bubbler was next to it with cone shaped paper cups. The chairs weren't the most comfortable, but she had sat in worse. She shifted in her seat and picked up her phone.

The door at the other end of the room opened and a man dressed in scrubs slowly entered the room. He looked around and saw her. His back straightened and he moved toward her with confusion in his eyes. He wore a surgical mask, and all Trish could see were his eyes. She narrowed her own, watching what he was going to do. Maybe he thought she was a grieving family member.

Trish tipped her head slightly to the side as the man slowly approached her. She focused on his eyes, which were a shade of blue. As he got closer, she saw something familiar in them. Where had she seen them before? she wondered.

When he was about five feet from her he stopped. Confusion clouded his eyes, and she suddenly remembered where she saw them before. She had never been face-to-face with this man before. What could he want with her? She waited, trying to mask any discomfort, to see what he wanted.

He dropped to his knees in front of her and grabbed her hand. "Patsy? I have been looking everywhere for you! Where have you been?"

Trish's surprise was missed by the man in front of her as he bowed his head, nearly resting on her crossed knees. It had been a long time since she had been mistaken for her sister, and her thoughts started spinning. How did he know her sister? She was contemplating the answer when the door burst open and Sharon and George came walking in.

The man in front of her jumped to his feet and looked between the door and Trish. His expression changed immediately to anger, and he pointed a finger at her.

"Did you set me up?" he screamed at her. The calm and sad man shifted personalities faster than Jekyll and Hyde. The personality shift was remarkable and Trish suddenly realized how someone could pull off two completely separate identities for so long.

Trish held her hands in the air and shook her head slowly. "No, I didn't." She tried not to say too much because she didn't know what name her sister knew him by. "I swear, I don't know anything about this."

Cliff looked back at the older couple at the door. "What are you two doing here?" he sneered. "Think you got something? Ha. Forget it. I'm clean and you won't find anything!"

He grabbed a hold of Trish's hand and tried to pull her up with him. When she refused, he dropped her hand and faced her. "What? You still think you are better than me? I'll let you in on a little secret, my dear." He stooped down so he was eye level with her again. "I came to finish off Billy, but it looks like I'm getting a two for one deal today."

Trish immediately regretted not standing earlier. Now she was trapped. She didn't dare look away, but she hoped Sharon and George were well prepared for this kind of situation. She kept her focus on staying calm and not showing any kind of emotion. Besides she had to find out what this man and her sister had been up to.

Cliff leaned in close to her ear and she could smell the stale stench of cigarettes and beer on his breath. She resisted the urge to gag.

"I should have done the job myself, you traitorous bitch. I should never have hired someone to do what I needed done. You wouldn't be here breathing if I had," he whispered with a dark chuckle. He pushed up and reached behind him. "This time, I won't miss. You and that bastard kid deserve this after what you did to me."

He stood and pointed a pistol at her face. Trish smirked. "Ah, I get it now," she said, crossing her arms, realization setting in. The anger she felt pushed down, because she knew she would get her chance. This man thought she was Patsy. Could this all be a tragedy of mistaken identity? Was it possible he believed Patsy cheated on him and Anyah was hers?

Trish pushed up off the chair and walked toward the crazed man. She hoped he was drunk enough that she could mess with him a little and maybe give Sharon and George time to assemble a team. "You were bested by a woman. How sad for you. Big, strong, tough guy being beat by a lowly weak woman. Ha. You really are a joke, Cliff." She shook her head.

His face twisted with confusion and shock. "How dare you insult me again! I won't back down, no matter what you try to do or say. I am not letting you get away with making a fool out of me!" He raised the gun again and Trish heard shuffling behind her.

She looked around Cliff's massive size and saw Sharon with a grin on her face. Behind her was a group of about 6 other officers. Trish faced him again and smirked.

"Um, you might want to rethink your vengeance," she said smugly, pointing at the door.

Cliff slowly turned and made eye contact with the group at the door. He tried to reach around and grab a hold of Trish for protection as a hostage, but she saw that coming a mile away and ducked, stepping aside before he could grab her. He stumbled and dropped the gun in his attempt to catch himself.

Trish quickly picked it up and looked at it. She groaned. "Why not have a real gun instead of this little plaything?" she taunted. "My gun is definitely bigger than yours. No wonder you got cheated on." She shrugged her shoulders and added, "your gun's too little."

She put the safety in place and tossed it to George who easily caught it and chuckled as she walked past them. Trish sat on a bench in the hall outside the room. The chaos that ensued after she left wasn't even close to what she was feeling in her heart.

Did she really misunderstand all of this? Anyah wasn't killed to get her out of the way for Patsy, she was killed because Patsy's boyfriend thought she had an affair and a kid with someone else. How did she get it so wrong?

Someone sitting next to her made Trish raise her eyes. Clayton's hand gripped hers tightly. And he gave her a sad smile.

"I think we have all the pieces now," he said quietly.

Trish just nodded, her body felt numb. She felt Clayton lift her from the bench and pull her into a tight hug.

"It's going to be ok, Trish. We are going to figure all this out. For Anyah's sake. I promise," he said soothingly.

* * * * *

The group met at Sharon's house not far from the hospital. Trish had been sitting on her friend's deck, staring out at the pool's calm water for a long time, letting the professionals figure out their case. Her thoughts weren't any clearer as she sat there.

Sharon came out of the house and sat next to her. "I think we have everything," she said quietly. "How are you holding up?"

Trish looked over. "I don't know what to think right now. How do I even come to terms with this? I had this all wrong for so many years. I blamed Clayton. I disowned my own sister. How can I be ok?" Trish sighed. "I don't even know how to atone for this? It's my fault. All of it." She sat back in her chair and stared straight ahead.

Sharon sighed. "I don't think you were completely wrong here, Trish. The information you had might have been wrong, but you did what you thought was right with what you had. You are not at fault as much as you think. We all make mistakes."

"Yeah, maybe, but this is a bit bigger than 'oh I'm sorry, I thought you took my sandwich, but it turns out I actually ate it. Sorry' kind of thing, Sharon," Trish scoffed.

Her friend chuckled. "I know, I get it. But the only way to see if it can be fixed is if you try. Take the first step." Sharon patted her leg and stood.

Trish watched her move into the house and was surprised to see Clayton standing there. She turned away, not sure how she was going to start this conversation, and a little more embarrassed than she wanted to admit. That was not a feeling she was familiar with.

"For what it's worth, Trish baby, I don't blame you," Clayton said softly, settled next to her. "I always wondered why you wanted to leave me so badly, but I never blamed you for anything."

Trish sighed. "There's no way to make up for what I did." She stood to walk away but Clayton stopped her.

"Please don't run away again," he pleaded. "I really don't want to lose you again."

"Clay, I don't deserve to have a second chance. I messed this up beyond repair." She turned again, but this time he took her hand.

"Ok, let me rephrase that. I am not *letting* you go again," he said more emphatically. "I am not going to go another minute without my wife by my side. And I will do whatever it takes to get you back and make you see that I forgive all this, not that it needs forgiving. I have my own part to play in all this too. I should have fought harder. I should have made you tell me what I did. Anything. Everything. I could have done more too."

Trish let out a self-deprecating laugh. "Right. So did you cheat on me with my sister?" She crossed her arms and faced him again.

Clayton looked her straight in the eye and said, "Absolutely not. I would never betray our vows."

"See?" Trish said, waving her hand. "You didn't do anything. There is nothing here that you are responsible for."

Seeing he was caught, Clayton chuckled. "Ok, fine you win." He paused for a minute and then grinned. "So how about this? We start over. We get to know each other again, maybe become partners in crime fighting. It could be fun. Like the new 'Incredibles' fighting crime side by side. With your tech skills and my fighting, we could be unstoppable."

He made a superman sort of pose and Trish laughed in spite of everything going on. She had to admit she did want to try to make up for the past, and having Clayton by her side would be worth a shot.

"Ok, Clay," she finally conceded. "Starting over."

Clayton pulled her into a tight hug. He whispered in her ear, "Thank you, baby girl. I couldn't ask for anything else right now."

Sharon's voice broke up the reunion. "So, you guys wanna come in here and get the details? We still have a few things to get done, but that won't require you two." She disappeared behind the large glass door and Trish and Clayton followed.

Once they had settled at the table, Luke looked over at Clayton and gave him a nod. "Thank you for all your intel on Cliff. This has been a long time coming and who knows how deep his betrayal has reached. All we know right now is that the ones around this table are trustworthy and the rest we will tease out."

Clayton nodded. "If you need anything else, let me know. I have my ways of getting information." He winked at Sharon who chuckled in response.

"I think the dozen or so men you captured on Miss Trish's property are enough for now. They are full of information. I don't know how you got them to talk, but they are pretty scared and willing to do just about anything to get immunity or a less than maximum security prison stay," Luke said laughing.

George chimed in, "Yeah well when you don't have the government breathing down your neck you can do a lot more, uh, persuasion shall we say." His deep laugh made the rest of the table nod and laugh as well.

Trish looked around and saw Luke, McMichaels, Sharon, George, and two others she didn't know. The group seemed to know exactly who she and Clayton were and didn't seem to hold any suspicion, which she was grateful for. She was also glad she could now step out of this and figure out what her next life steps would be. She still had to figure out what else her sister was up to and if it was even possible to have a relationship with her. She decided a long time ago that she wouldn't as long as Patsy was still using.

"Oh, Trish dear, one more thing before we all adjourn for today," Sharon said. She slid a file across the table over to Trish.

Gingerly picking it up, Trish opened the file. The photos made her catch her breath. The photos of her parents car crash. Her heart started to harden as she thought about that incident. She tried to remind herself that she was wrong before, maybe she was wrong about this too. She looked up at Sharon who had a sympathetic look in her eyes and shook her head.

"Patsy was not involved, Trish," she said quietly. "It was another way Cliff, as Simon, had tried to control her. He had suspected she left him for whoever was the father of her child, and he orchestrated the car accident to get her to comply again. Apparently it worked since she disappeared again right after that."

Sharon paused and then added, "Look at who the investigator was."

Trish flipped through to the police report. Signed on the line at the end of the investigation was Cliff's signature. The only reason she knew it was his was because it was printed underneath the scribble. She knew it was a setup accident from the beginning and now she had proof. But again, it eliminated Patsy as culpable or responsible.

She tossed it back on the table. As the older sister, she failed to protect or even believe her. She didn't even give Patsy a chance to explain or if she had, she didn't listen. What kind of sister was she?

"Hey," Clayton said beside her. "Stop beating yourself up. The path was laid out long before any of these things happened, Trish. No one would have believe Patsy wasn't responsible. But relationships can always be saved and mended. Baby steps and you will get there. And I'll be right beside you the whole way."

Trish sighed. "I don't deserve that," she said, barely audible. She thought about all the horrible things she had said about her sister over the years. Maybe not out loud, but definitely in her head. The things she had to atone for were turning out to be much more than her sister, who had unknowingly shouldered the blame for years.

"Everyone deserves a second chance, Trish dear," Sharon said from across the table. "My purpose in showing you this wasn't to add more to your feelings of guilt, but to show just how deeply Cliff cared about Patsy, albeit a little bit obsessively."

George hummed his agreement. "And we now know that he was Simon when they were together, so he has been working this for a long time. Ironically, if it wasn't for Patsy, we might not have gotten as much as we have. And if he had approached Patsy instead of you, we may not have anyone to talk to right now."

Trish looked up. "What does that mean?"

Luke laughed. "Your composure in the situation earlier is what gave us the time to pull together the team we needed to get him into custody without any incident. You saved us a lot of time and effort, Miss Trish."

"No one else would stand in front of a loaded gun and taunt someone," Sharon agreed with laughter in her own voice. "Only you, hon, only you."

Trish smiled. "Never been afraid of a gun in my life and knowing he was responsible for my Anyah's death, I wasn't going to give up my own chance at justice. I just wish I could take him hunting in my woods sometime," she said with a dark look in her eyes.

The group around the table laughed. "If only," Clayton said with a chuckle.

"I just have one more thing to take care of," Luke said as he stood. "Billy is being released soon, and I am going to stand guard to make sure there are no more surprises. We got a significant amount of intel from him about what Simon has been up to the last decade and a half. But I need someone there to record and verify. I'll catch up with the rest of you later on."

The two men Trish didn't know stood with him and the trio left Sharon's, leaving only Clayton, Sharon, George and Trish.

"So, the pieces you all talked about before?" Trish began. "The medallion and plate. Are they really what you say they are?"

Sharon nodded. "Yep. Cliff had managed to get a hold of the plans for the device but couldn't get his hands on the device itself. His cronies had one and were looking for additional ones, which is why they were circling your property. Everyone thought it was an intelligence hub for some reason and thought the pieces would be there."

"That's why I found the one on my property?" Trish stated, making the connection. "But how did George get one? And Clayton." She looked around the table at the others.

"I had always had one. I gave you mine so they would be well protected just in case someone came looking for it from me. I knew with your security measures being nearly impenetrable, they would be safe there," George explained.

Clayton chuckled. "*Nearly* impenetrable," he teased. "Seems to me I was able to get through—twice I might add."

Trish slapped his shoulder. "Yeah? And look what that got you," she said pointing at the shoulder she had hit.

"Ow! Don't remind me. You're brutal with that old thing," he said, acting as if he were still hurt. He leaned close and whispered, "You're poppop would be so proud, baby girl."

She swung to smack him again, but he grabbed her hand and waved his finger at her. "Hey, I was giving you a compliment. Learn to take it, ok?" he winked and moved a little so he was out of her reach.

Trish just scoffed and crossed her arms in front of her. Looking back at Sharona and George, she asked, "So what else are you going to throw at me tonight?"

The other two looked at each other and laughed. "I think we covered everything," George said.

"All that's left is finding your sister," Sharon said gently.

Trish sighed. "Nothing will bring back my parents or my little girl. That man has created so much pain in this one family. I can't imagine how much he has inflicted on countless others for so many years," she mused more to herself than anyone.

"You got that right," Clayton said. "But all we can do is this. Let's move forward as best we can and not let his destruction win."

Trish just nodded. There was nothing else she could do either. She had searched for these answers for over a decade and now she had them. They might not be the answers she thought she knew, but they were the facts. She would have to find a way to come to terms with not only being wrong, but how to atone for her own part in destroying her family. Because now she had her own sins to account and apologize for. That might just be the hardest part of finding out the truth.

Chapter 29

When Clayton said he knew where to find Patsy, Trish had just gone along with him, not thinking it would lead to a confrontation with her long-lost sister in less than twenty-four hours. She figured she would have a few days to try to find the words to apologize for not trusting her, for not believing her, and for being the worst big sister on the face of the planet.

They sat in his truck outside a house that looked like it had seen better days. The blue siding was covered in green from the humidity of the Shore weather. Some of the windows had shutters while most did not. The tiny porch was uncovered and had a single chair sitting beside the door. Two steps led up to it with a wrought iron railing on each side. One of the steps looked like it was about to crumble.

Trish had to admit it reminded her of her own house, minus the fun porch with all her babies. She chuckled at the memory, in spite of everything going on in her heart.

Clayton sat beside her, holding her hand tightly in his large and rough one. "You can do this, Trish. And I'm right here."

Trish nodded. "I know. I can do anything. I just don't even know where to start if I'm honest. I mean I blamed her for so much over the years. How do you even begin to say sorry?"

"You just start," he said simply. "Just start."

Trish sighed and opened the door. Clayton came around to her side and stood next to her. He held out his hand for her and she looked at him before taking it. She couldn't believe the change in her world in just a few days. Everything she thought she knew was upside down and backwards. But he was right. The only way to move forward was a little bit at a time.

She looked again at the house in front of her. Clayton had contacted Billie, and she gave him this address. Neither was sure if this was where Billie lived or where Patsy lived. Clayton had called Billie to explain what they had all found. Billie revealed that they were working with Luke as well and would finally be able to live free of threat from Johnny. Even if he ever got out of prison, she and her baby would be protected.

Clayton had found out that she would be testifying against Johnny in his upcoming trial. Given the new evidence and threats, prosecutors were going to retry to possibly get a stiffer sentence for him. After she provided additional testimony, Billie would be entering a witness protection program to keep her and her baby safe.

She didn't explicitly say that Johnny was her baby's father, but the way she spoke about Johnny and the case, Clayton was pretty confident he was.

Billie didn't say much about her involvement with Patsy, only that she was instrumental in Billie getting the evidence she needed to keep Johnny away longer. Trish knew that already from her video of their visit. It was clear he had ordered a hit of some kind on Billie and that alone would be hard to fight in court.

Trish looked again at Clayton, who was looking at her. "I guess there's just one thing left to do, huh?" she said, tipping her head toward the small structure.

Clayton didn't get a chance to answer because the front door of the small house opened, and Patsy stood at the threshold looking at them. She hesitated only a moment before she jumped off the step and ran to Trish. She stopped in front of her sister and Trish couldn't help but see the pain in her sister's eyes. But she noticed they were clear, no sign of use, only sadness and maybe a little fear.

"Trish?" Patsy said slowly. "Is it really you?" She grabbed a hold of her sister's hands and squeezed.

Trish tried to smile, but she knew that pain and fear was because of her. She caused this in her sister; she'd hurt her sister in the worst possible way.

Suddenly Patsy pulled Trish into the tightest hug she had ever felt. She was stunned and didn't know how to react. Her arms hung limply by her sides as Patsy clung to her.

Trish felt her sister's body begin to shake and she knew Patsy was sobbing. "I missed you so much. I'm so sorry for everything, Trish. Please forgive me," she said, repeating over and over how sorry she was.

Trish pulled away and studied her sister's tear-streaked face. "What are you talking about? I'm the one who should be apologizing, not you. I got it all wrong, Patsy," Trish insisted quietly.

Patsy just shook her head. "No. I deserved all the blame. If I hadn't tried so hard to be different and independent, I never would have gotten myself involved in all that and none of this bad stuff would have happened." Her hands were holding Trish's sweatshirt so tightly that Trish could see her knuckles turning almost white.

Gently moving Patsy's fingers, Trish held her sister's hands. "I should have done more, Patsy. But we can move forward now." She paused and said the words she never thought she would say, "I want my sister back."

* * * * *

Trish and Patsy sat at Patsy's small kitchen table looking at old photos of when they were kids. Trish marveled at how much things had changed and what they had both gone through to get to where they were. Her guilt over the last few years was waning slightly, but she knew her sister's insistence that it was her fault alone wouldn't help her guilt but would instead increase it. She needed to find a way to atone for her own part in their relationship.

Patsy had insisted as part of her program for sobriety and Billie's help that she had to take responsibility for her behaviors even if she was using at the time. She couldn't hide behind her addiction as an excuse. Trish understood that but also was very aware that if she had fought harder instead of writing her sister off as a lost cause, they both could have had very different outcomes.

Clayton had left hours ago, and Trish welcomed the time with just her sister. They never had a chance to grieve the loss of their parents. Trish had saved the old photo albums when she cleared out their house after the accident and secretly had hoped to sit right where she was again with Patsy. She had given up that hope a long time ago, but she felt like she finally was getting a second chance.

The time with Patsy went deep into the night. Before she knew it, the clock on her sister's microwave read three in the morning. She stretched her hands above her head and yawned.

"Maybe we should get some sleep," she suggested.

Patsy looked exhausted but didn't seem to want to end their reunion. She reluctantly shrugged. "I guess. But will you be here when I wake up?"

Trish looked at her with confusion. "What do you mean?"

Rubbing her hands together, Patsy stared at the table. "I'm afraid, if you leave, I won't see you again." Her voice was quiet, and Trish just stared at her.

"Are you kidding?" Trish asked. "No way am I going to disappear, Patsy. I really am glad we can reconnect, and I still have some making up to do to you. I promise I will be here as long as you let me. You are my baby sister."

The vulnerability in her sister's voice and behavior struck Trish. She could feel Patsy's fears of rejection and loss ran deep. She had a lot of work to do to help repair her sister's confidence it seemed.

Patsy jumped up from her chair and knelt by Trish's side. "I always have wanted you beside me. I never wanted to hurt you. I'm so sorry my problems got my niece hurt. I will never forgive myself for that."

Trish took her sister's hands into her own and squeezed. "It was not your fault some crazy person had some sick fascination with you that caused him to do the unthinkable. That was *not* your fault Patsy. I don't blame you for that anymore."

The sisters hugged and Trish started toward the door. It wasn't until she opened it that she remembered Clayton had driven earlier that day. She had forgotten after he brought back the albums he had left for the night.

Patsy nearly jumped up and down as she suggested, "Sleepover?" in a giddy voice.

Trish couldn't do anything but laugh. Her sister missed out on so much while she was stuck in her addiction. This could be a good first step in rebuilding all that she had lost; all that they both lost during the last two and a half decades.

Chapter 30

Clayton and Trish stood by the edge of the water, watching the waves crash against the sandy beach. It was mesmerizing and soothing at the same time. It was an unusually warm November day, and Trish only wore a light jacket. She felt the breeze in her freshly twisted hair, without the gray strands for the first time in years. Closing her eyes, she listened to the gulls chatter and waves roll.

She felt Clayton take her hand and she opened her eyes to look at him. He held up the photo they had of Anyah right before she entered first grade. Her smile was contagious and her laugh so full of joy it made anyone around her smile.

"She loved this place," Trish said simply.

Clayton nodded. "She did."

They settled on a blanket near the edge of the water. Trish removed her shoes to let the waves slowly reach her toes, the water still warm from the summer despite it being almost Thanksgiving. They had packed a small lunch and planned to spend the day in Anyah's favorite place. Trish had decided it was the perfect place for a new beginning and to start to repair the brokenness of their family.

Clayton and Trish had never grieved her loss much like Trish and Patsy were robbed of grieving the loss of their parents. The night she spent with her sister was healing for Trish and together they laid out their path to recovery together. Trish hoped she and Clayton could do the same.

The sun dipped behind a cloud and Trish looked up at the near perfect sky. It couldn't get any better than this, she decided.

Sharon and George had wrapped up their case and Cliff was being held in federal custody with no chance of getting out. Patsy had begun to break out of her solace and was meeting with former friends, trying to make amends. Trish stood by her through it all, helping her to make the connections and then staying for the meetings to be sure Patsy was taken care of.

Trish marveled at Patsy's strength. Not only did she risk her life to get justice for the friend she found in Billie, but she also stood up in court and testified on Billie's behalf and her own in Cliff/Simon's first hearing. Trish sat in the courtroom listening to her sister's harrowing life outside of her family's protection, adding to her own guilt of discounting their connection. She wondered if she could have protected her sister from any of these horrific things had she stayed available to Patsy.

Clayton continued to reassure Trish she couldn't have known any of this and continued to stand beside her. Trish felt lucky to have them both back in her life and she would be forever grateful that the truth came out, giving her family the chance to heal.

It would take time and probably a lot of it, but Trish was confident her little family would be close to whole again. Without Anyah, it would never be complete, but they could all be connected again.

Trish looked up at Clayton and smiled. "Thank you for being there for me even when I didn't deserve it."

"Oh Trish, you will always be worth it to me. I told you, it has always been and always will be just you," Clayton said with a grin.

A loud yell from behind made them turn to see a group of people heading down the beach. Trish laughed as she watched the group make their way to her and Clayton.

"We couldn't let you exclude the rest of the family now could we?" Sharon asked with a chuckle.

Trish watched as Sharon, her husband Gary, George, and Patsy all spread out blankets and drop baskets in the middle. A family picnic to be sure, she thought. Just like her parents did when she and Patsy were young. Only this time, family was much bigger than just blood. This family all began with the union of Clayton and Trish, named Anyah.

Other works by this author

Bellbrook Springs Series
A Journey of the Heart
A Journey of the Mind
A Journey of the Soul
A Journey for Justice—coming soon
A Journey for Peace—in the works

The Sense of Belonging Series
Shared Blood, Book 1
Bonded Blood, Book 2

Following me:
Instagram at brendabenningauthor
TikTok @brendabenningauthor
Website: brendabenning.com

www.ingramcontent.com/pod-product-compliance
Lightning Source LLC
Chambersburg PA
CBHW021137161125
35483CB00001B/2